Coronation Talkies

Susan Kurosawa is based in Sydney where she
is a senior editor with *The Australian* newspaper.
She has lived and worked in England, Japan
and Australia and has spent her life travelling.
After almost thirty visits, she admits to
an obsession with India.

Susan is the author of seven non-fiction books;
this is her first novel. She lives in a bayside
village on the Central Coast of New South Wales
with the actor and biographer
Graeme Blundell.

Coronation Talkies *is an engrossing and touchingly*
funny read . . . Characters and places are vividly created
and her eye for detail is impeccable . . . I honestly have
not enjoyed a novel this much for some time.
AUSTRALIAN BOOKSELLER & PUBLISHER

When it rains, it rains on all alike.

HINDU PROVERB

SUSAN KUROSAWA

Coronation Talkies

VIKING
an imprint of
PENGUIN BOOKS

VIKING

Published by the Penguin Group
Penguin Group (Australia)
250 Camberwell Road, Camberwell, Victoria 3124, Australia
(a division of Pearson Australia Group Pty Ltd)
Penguin Group (USA) Inc.
375 Hudson Street, New York, New York 10014, USA
Penguin Books (Canada)
10 Alcorn Avenue, Toronto, Ontario, Canada M4V 3B2
(a division of Pearson Penguin Canada Inc.)
Penguin Books Ltd
80 Strand, London WC2R 0RL, England
Penguin Ireland
25 St Stephen's Green, Dublin 2, Ireland
(a division of Penguin Books Ltd)
Penguin Books India Pvt Ltd
11, Community Centre, Panchsheel Park, New Delhi –110 017, India
Penguin Group (NZ)
cnr Airborne and Rosedale Roads, Albany, Auckland 1310, New Zealand
(a division of Pearson New Zealand Ltd)
Penguin Books (South Africa) (Pty) Ltd
24 Sturdee Avenue, Rosebank, Johannesburg 2196, South Africa

Penguin Books Ltd, Registered Offices: 80 Strand, London WC2R 0RL, England

First published by Penguin Group (Australia), a division of Pearson Australia Group Pty Ltd, 2004

1 3 5 7 9 10 8 6 4 2

Cover and text design by Nikki Townsend © Penguin Group (Australia)
Cover photograph, styling and digital imaging by Samantha Everton
Cover photography location courtesy Back Bar, Windsor
Map illustrated by Bettina Gutheridge
Typeset in 13.5 pt Perpetua by Post Pre-press Group, Brisbane, Queensland
Printed and bound in Australia by McPherson's Printing Group, Maryborough, Victoria

National Library of Australia
Cataloguing-in-Publication data:

Kurosawa, Susan.
Coronation talkies: a novel of 1930s India.

ISBN 0 670 04279 X.

1. Kodaikanal (India) – Social life and customs – 20th century – Fiction.

823

This project has been assisted by the Commonwealth Government through the Australia Council,
its arts funding and advisory body.

Australian Government | Australia Council for the Arts

www.penguin.com.au

For Graeme, as ever

This book was substantially written in Room 304 of
The Imperial Hotel, Delhi, and in the hill station
of Shimla, Himachal Pradesh, at Chapslee, home of
Kanwar Ratanjit (Reggie) Singh of Kapurthala.

With special thanks to Kirsten Abbott, Andrea Black,
Shanker Dhar, Aruna Dhir, Julie Gibbs, Justin Kurosawa,
Ping Lam, Christine McCabe, Jill Mullins, Anil Oraw,
Gusain Ram, Sujata Raman, Anne Rogan, Reggie Singh
and Lyn Tranter. Bless you, Subash, for endless cups of
tea and cheese toast during Shimla snows.

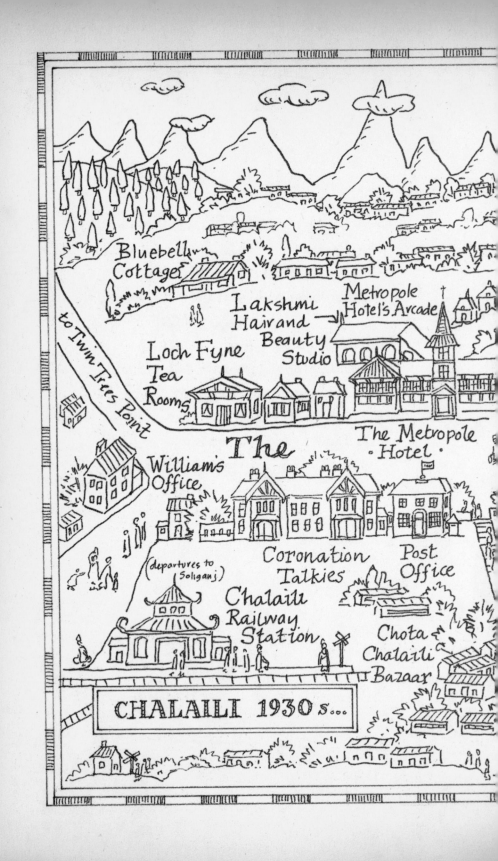

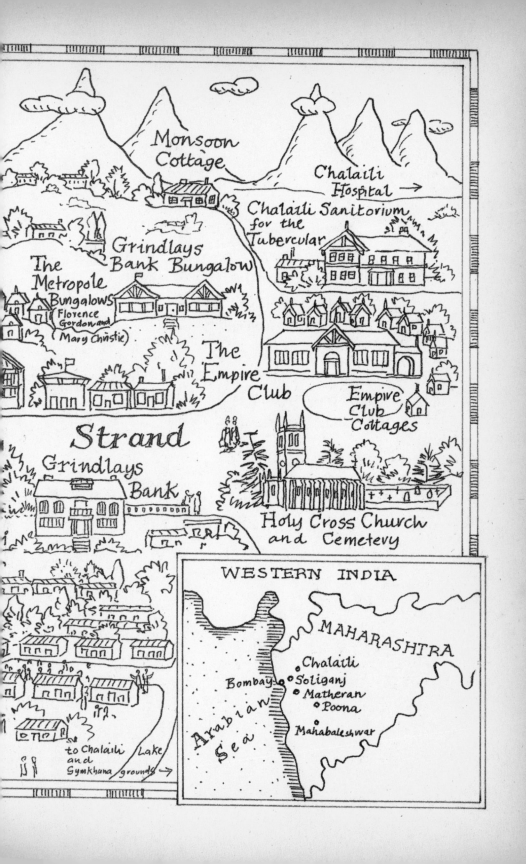

A NOTE FROM THE AUTHOR

The hill station of Shimla, as it is now known,
was called Simla in the 1930s and is
referred to as such in this book.

Chalaili is a mythical place, a composite of hill
stations I have visited in Himachal Pradesh
and the Western Ghats of India

Prologue

'I want to do it because I want to do it. Women must
try to do things as men have tried. When they fail,
their failure must be a challenge to others.'
LAST FLIGHT BY AMELIA EARHART, 1937

Mrs Banerjee wound the film on to the spool of the bulky grey projector and shifted her ample rump on a three-legged stool. The wooden seat practically disappeared from view and her stomach lay low and round in her lap. She smiled to herself, surveying its squashy plenitude.

The snappy-smooth film snaked and curled beneath her bejewelled fingers, like long and tensile straps of licorice. 'All the time I think of food,' she giggled. She was alone in the projection- ist's booth of her Coronation Talkies picture theatre in the Indian hill station of Chalaili. Her servants, Anil and Vinod, were sta- tioned in the little box-office in the foyer, its windows curved in a perfect crescent, the counter adorned with a gay pot of scarlet

1

geraniums. The two men were seated side by side and uniformed in bright yellow silk shirts. When viewed in dim light from the front doorway, yawning and engaging in idle chat, they resembled a pair of gasping fish in a tropical aquarium.

Mrs Banerjee knew they would be arguing over who got to dispense the change and tear the tickets from the wheel-sized roll and whose turn it was to wave about the usher's torch, usually anywhere but at the correct seat.

She had given Mr K. K. Rao, her projectionist, the evening off. He said he had a must-keep engagement. Mrs Banerjee suspected his absence could have something to do with his puffy hair, which had recently made an alarming transition from grey fleck to a fascinatingly deep blue-black. He was a furtive fellow these days, thought Mrs Banerjee, always regarding her in the eyebrow-arched manner of someone privy to embarrassing secrets. Although she found the very idea ridiculous, she wondered if he had designs upon her widowed mother, who was not perhaps without her attractions, if one liked to be bossed about and insulted in a colourful manner.

It was a Monday and Mrs Banerjee knew there would not be a big crowd at Coronation Talkies. Those who turned up would have come to sleep in the toasty warmth of the centre seats or canoodle in the back row, all silk-swish fumblings and the occasional exhalation of breath, like a kettle just off the boil.

The imperious rule of the Raj in India was doomed to end within a decade but, for now, Chalaili sat comfortably as an outpost of fading empire high in the Western Ghats. There was a cluster of Indian Civil Service officers stationed year round, numbers swelling early in the summer season when the perspiring British higher-ups and their braying wives escaped the dust-worried plains of summer

2

for the cool heights. Each July they would move on to more desirable hill stations as Chalaili was southwest-facing and inconveniently exposed to the furious onset of the annual monsoon. There were those who claimed Chalaili was the wettest place in India, but even that title, one of rather undesirable status, was not certain, it being a neck-and-neck race for rainfall supremacy with a more talked-about town in the forested foothills of the Himalaya.

Chalaili's mouldiness thoroughly annoyed Mrs Banerjee. She considered herself a progress-making businesswoman and would have chosen a more reliable hill station to open a talking picture theatre if only she hadn't trusted her dolt of a Bombay lawyer to purchase the property on her behalf. Mrs Banerjee sighed and hauled herself up to look through the booth's window slit. She saw Campbell and Patricia Nightingale taking up their positions in a centre row, even though each month her servants would show them to their lesser complimentary seats, further to the front. As soon as Anil or Vinod withdrew, they moved. This odd little shuffle happened as if by clockwork every fourth Monday.

The furtive nap-takers and the young lovers would drift in when the lights went down, around the foyer, sneaking through the side door, scuttling like anxious ghosts past the velvet curtains. Finally Mrs Banerjee had the spool threaded and she waited for her mother to come charging in, quarrelsome servant in her wake. A majestic liner attended by a tugboat.

The image of her mother as a stately ship amused Mrs Banerjee and she popped a caramel in her mouth. It had been caught in the recesses of her cardigan pocket and was slightly furry. She looked again at the film on its big spool and imagined the dense aniseed taste of licorice. 'Such dreadful cravings,' she laughed. Mrs Banerjee often talked to herself, sometimes at unsettling volume.

It was a habit she put down to a lonely childhood governed by her permanently distracted parents.

She heard the creak of a seat, the protesting whine of old wood, and the whoosh made by the cracked leather upholstery as it was pressed into place. Mrs Banerjee peered down to confirm it was her mother, started the projector and, gathering the folds of her imposing purple sari around her calves, made her way carefully, very carefully, down the booth's ladder-like steps, then along the corridor, through the curtains with their royal crest, the heavy material caught with the old odours of tobacco and a hint of lavender.

'*It Happened One Night*,' whispered Mrs Banerjee to her mother, settling beside her and nudging her elbow in a girlish aside. 'Clark and Claudette, my favourites.' Mrs Banerjee's mother knew her overwrought daughter always cried at films, even the most preposterous of comedies. She took out a white Irish linen handkerchief monogrammed with a cursive L, the upper and lower loops voluptuously rounded. 'Such foreign workmanship,' sighed Mrs Banerjee as her mother passed it to her, shaking loose its pressed pleats so the L gave a dainty leap.

'L is such an elegant initial,' sighed Mrs Banerjee, running her finger along the stitching. 'Is the handkerchief yours?'

'Of course it's mine,' her mother retorted. 'My name is Leela, you foolish girl . . .'

'Lydia starts with an L, too, Mother. I just thought perhaps Lydia Rushmore had lost it . . .'

'You accuse your own parent of thievery? Is there no end to your wickedness?'

Mrs Banerjee's mother wrapped her light woollen shawl tightly around her shoulders and cocked her head at an uppity angle.

'Mother . . . Mummy, please, I meant to say that Lydia must have given it to you before she left Chalaili, it being foreign-made and all . . .'

'Maybe . . .' conceded the older woman, yawning extravagantly. It took her less than a minute to fall asleep.

As Clark Gable hung the Wall of Jericho curtain in his shared accommodation with the runaway Claudette Colbert, Mrs Banerjee let out a scream so loud that three rows from the back, caught in a still-innocent tangle of unfurling shawls and popping buttons, two visitors to Chalaili, Anita Mehta and Sonny Raman, shot to their feet and hurried in opposite directions. It took some time for Sonny to realise he was wearing Anita's hyacinth-blue pashmina wrap. The Nightingales stayed put, sharing a box of assorted chocolates. They were quite used to Mrs Banerjee's startling outbursts.

'Come, come, Mother,' Mrs Banerjee squealed, holding both arms of her seat as if attempting to prevent the contraption becoming airborne. 'It's time.'

Chapter One

WEST GAMBLE, SURREY
MARCH, 1937

THE FINCHLEY EXAMINER, PUBLIC NOTICES
St Martin's Anglican Church, Parish of West Gamble,
7th of March, 2 p.m. The wedding of Mr William Ellis
Rushmore of Chalaili, the Bombay Presidency, India, and
Miss Lydia Elizabeth Burnett of The Oaks, West Gamble.
Rector: The Reverend Percival Sidgwick.

*I*t was a bright Saturday, the thin winter sun casting a buttery sheen over the village of West Gamble. Lydia Burnett dressed carefully for her wedding but with no undue extravagance, assisted in the light-filled upstairs front bedroom of her family home by her married sister, Evelyn, who did not approve of the likes of silk stockings and permanent waves, having primly sacrificed such luxuries for the sanctity of wifedom and motherhood.

'Is the flower too much, do you think?' asked Lydia as she surveyed her dove-grey jersey dress, belted firmly to accentuate her slender waist. Above her left breast burst a floral outcrop in the same pliant fabric. The weight of the flower gave it a droop and the two sisters stared at this bunchiness in the full-length mirror. Both were silent. Lydia fidgeted with the cloth petals. Behind the sisters, a breeze lifted the white lace curtains at the bedroom window and their reflections shimmered against the sun-latticed backdrop. Evelyn imagined, for an instant, the ghost of their recently departed mother peeping through the lace, her lips pressed in sour-lemon disapproval.

'If Mummy were here, she'd say it was too much,' said Evelyn. 'Let's take it off. Stand very still and I'll snip the stitches.'

Lydia did not protest. She understood Evelyn's permanent air of disappointment. As the elder daughter, Evelyn seemed destined to carry the load of their mother's bitterness. Elizabeth Burnett had 'married down', as she was fond of saying to anyone with the inclination to listen. Their father, Dennis, had retired early from his position at the local post office and soon removed himself from the realm of his wife's influence, preferring to potter in his garden shed and stay far too long each evening at The White Horse Inn.

Lydia had been the one despatched to the high-street pub to bring him home. Her mother, so strict and class-obsessed in other matters, used to think nothing of sending off the young girl alone in the early evening, to knock on the window of The White Horse Inn to attract her father's attention and summon him with a wave. Dennis Burnett referred to the pub as The Old Nag and made jokes with Lydia as they ambled to The Oaks that his wife would feel right at home there, too. It was some years before Lydia understood the message behind his joke, by then repeated hundreds of times by Daddy but never failing to be followed by a beery chuckle.

Evelyn bent towards the offending flower, scissors in hand, and Lydia looked at the top of her sister's head. Her brown wavy hair was scribbled with grey. A couple of pure white strands had sprung free from Evelyn's careful brushing and were standing steely and strong, like pig bristles. Lydia laughed at the thought, her meagre bosoms shook and she felt the steel point jab lightly at her brassiere.

'Damnation,' muttered Evelyn. 'Now, look what you've done. I've cut a hole.'

The sisters looked in the mirror. The flower had not come away cleanly. A patch of white cotton could be seen through the dove-grey jersey.

'I wonder if William will be disappointed by my underwear.'

Lydia had not really given the matter of undressing in front of her new husband much thought. 'Maybe he'll expect lace . . . and satin . . .'

'Oh, for heaven's sake, Lydia. Next you'll be wanting me to pull down Mummy's lace curtains and run you up a pair of knick-ers! The least you can do is to stop wriggling while I put this flower back somehow. I'll try a small safety pin.'

Lydia longed for a drink. A straight gin. The pleasurable burn in her throat. The softening of her limbs. The gayness to her giggle.

When Evelyn had finished fiddling, they stood side by side and surveyed their reflections. In their early thirties — Eve-lyn older by a year — neither was a great beauty, but there was a neatness and freshness about the Burnett sisters that was instantly appealing. They were above average height, straight-backed and bony-shouldered. Dependable looking. Their hair was thick and lustrous, both had light-hazel eyes that were almost feline in their unusual slant and occasional tawny flashes. Lydia smiled, the broadening of her rather thin lips bringing her face to life. She was prettier than Evelyn but easily flustered. She lacked her sister's wifely confidence.

'I can't believe I'm getting married!' Lydia brought her hands together as if she were about to clap with joy. Or pray she would get it right: the wedding, the sex, the mysterious place called India.

Evelyn did not smile. She couldn't believe, either, that her sister had found a husband, let alone one who was about to whisk her so far away. She couldn't tell if her slight headache was caused by anxiety about the wedding or a fear that Lydia had unexpectedly pulled off an almighty coup. Either way, Evelyn was about to be left behind.

☙

Lydia Burnett wed William Rushmore in the little village church of St Martin's in the parish of West Gamble with a bobbing flower above her left breast that fell off midway through the service, landing at her feet like a dead-headed rose. Her father, Dennis, stood up and moved forward from his seat in the front pew, shirking off the grasp of Evelyn who, he had privately decided, was in danger of becoming as much of a shrew as his recently buried wife.

He picked up the bunch of material and looked at it oddly, surprised at its lack of texture and smell. 'For you, Princess Liddie Diddie,' he whispered to Lydia, down on one knee, like a knave.

'Thank you, Daddy,' she said, wondering if her heart was about to burst with happiness. It would be the last exclusive exchange between father and daughter, for Dennis Burnett was to die later that year. Evelyn would become mistress of The Oaks, her husband eventually self-exiled to the garden shed where his father-in-law had sat, too, in front of a small radiator, reading every last inch of the papers and lingering over the corsetry ads.

Evelyn would relish the role of lady of the house, never noticing, as her mother had so keenly, that the residents of West Gamble laughed about the mock-grandeur of The Oaks. Behind her back, they referred to it as Acorn Cottage. My sister Lydia, Evelyn would tell all and sundry, even stiff-lipped pensioners in post-office queues, is married to a military man in India. Evelyn had inherited Elizabeth Burnett's insouciant regard for detail. William Rushmore actually was a meteorological officer attached to the Indian Forestry Service whose specific duty lay in the charting of the annual monsoon. His colleagues referred to him, with a snigger, as Rain Wallah.

Lydia and William Rushmore left for India the evening of the modest village wedding. They were waved off from West Gamble station amid excited cries and shouts. Evelyn's young daughter, Anne, ran along the platform with a small posy and tossed it at her Aunty as she leaned out of the carriage window. Lydia caught the unravelling flowers and waved a handful of stems to and fro, like a victory flag. Her new life, she thought, would be so wildly removed from cloistered West Gamble that she had begun to feel rushes of blood to the head. She alone had been chosen to transcend the curse of ordinariness.

Lydia was smiling broadly as she and William reached St Pancras Station to board the boat train to Tilbury, where they would embark the *Viceroy of India* bound for fantastically faraway Bombay. If only the Old Nag could see me now, Lydia chuckled. She would be kicking herself.

Chapter Two

BOMBAY

MARCH, 1937

'No spitting. No consumption of alcoholic substances.
No mingling of the First Class sexes.'
BY ORDER OF THE COMMISSIONER, INDIAN RAILWAYS.

At Bombay's Victoria Terminus, Mrs Rajat Banerjee was boarding the First Class Ladies Coupé of the Soliganj Limited Express. Aside from the need to heft aboard her majestic rump, she was loaded with a large black handbag and a string-secured cardboard box full of fruit, vegetable samosa and cheese sandwiches prepared by the kitchen of the hotel where she had been residing for the past two weeks in a top-category room. Mrs Banerjee was not one to put her discerning digestive system in the hands of common food peddlers.

Courtesy of the quick thinking and agile hands of her servant girl, Aruna, she escaped being wedged in the doorway by mere inches. From behind, with legs spread for better balance, Aruna pushed and twisted her mistress like a gigantic spinning top and sent her rotating sideways through the entrance. Mrs Baner-jee's revolutions were slow and heavy and Aruna was able to leap aboard in time to steady her before she fell.

'Good, good,' trilled Mrs Banerjee, as Aruna returned to the platform to instruct the red-turbaned porter to load a fur-ther assembly of boxes and cases, none of which her employer had any intention of entrusting to the unimaginable perils of the baggage car.

The train was already moving as the sari-swathed madam and her girl installed themselves upon facing leather-covered bench seats in one of the private compartments. Mrs Banerjee hummed as she fidgeted with her endless upper draperies and wiped her glowing brow. There was a foreign lady ensconced by the window. She put down her book, looked over her tortoiseshell-rimmed reading spectacles and regarded the intrusion of flying silk shawls and gaily tied bundles with the same horror as one might if a cir-cus suddenly appeared in the front parlour.

'This carriage is reserved,' she said, in a loudly transmitting English voice. She was a sharp-featured woman with annoyed eyes, her face as frontal as a rodent's. She was dressed entirely in dowdy brown, from lace-up shoes to an unflattering beret adorned with a defeated peacock feather. Her implication was firm: this seat-ing was exclusively intended for Europeans. Mrs Banerjee and her small attendant clearly were natives.

'My dear lady, we have the appropriate tickets for Soliganj with onward seats for Chalaili,' smiled Mrs Banerjee as she re-adjusted the debutante pinkness of her glitter-edged Benares silk sari and patted the fine displays of gold bangles on both arms. 'No need for any fuss-muss . . .'

The Englishwoman winced at the interloper's playful use of

12

the imperial mother tongue. Really, these middle-class Indians with their garish jewels and flowery phrases were behaving more and more as if they owned the bally place.

'I am Mrs Rajat Banerjee and this is Miss Aruna . . .'

The mistress and the servant looked at each other. Mrs Banerjee had no idea of Aruna's family name and, in turn, Aruna was astonished to be riding aboard the First Class Ladies Coupé instead of in the fetid realms of Third Class, where she knew the foreign lady's servant would be installed. Until a month ago, she had been in the employ of Mrs Banerjee's mother, a woman not given to the exuberances of her daughter.

'Miss Aruna Chowpatty,' said Mrs Banerjee, plucking from the air the name of the beach suburb of Bombay where her family home had just been sold, owing to the untimely death of her father. She patted the seat opposite and indicated the terrified Aruna should sit. Aruna hoicked the last bundle she was holding upon the seat and squatted on the floor.

Mrs Banerjee indicated to Aruna by way of raised eyebrows and an emphatic jerk of her head that the girl should get up and so she did, carefully removing her worn rubber chappals and climbing upon the seat, where she continued to squat with bare, dirt-crusted feet, in peril of flying off with every chug of the locomotive.

The Englishwoman gave Mrs Banerjee and Miss Chowpatty a final withering look and turned towards the window, indicating by the rigidity of her shoulder that she had no interest in fraternising with natives, gold-trimmed saris or not.

⁙

Aruna dropped off to sleep, seemingly unperturbed by the forward-and-backward rocking motion that gave her the appearance

13

of a bouncing toy on a weighted base. Mrs Banerjee closed her eyes but she couldn't doze even a little. Her head was full of swirling images, collisions of colour and two words that played over and over like a mantra. Coronation Talkies, Coronation Talkies, she said to herself, the repeated words forming a rhythm hastened by the chug-a-chug of the train.

She had not seen the theatre that would bear this grand name but her Bombay lawyer, who had purchased it on her behalf, had furnished diagrams and descriptions. It stood on the main street of Chalaili, known as The Strand, a name that sounded wonderfully solid and British to Mrs Banerjee, as if it must have been engineered with special attention to accommodate the finest shops and banks. One of her first missions must be to have stationery printed and in her mind she devised the exact wording.

Mrs Rajat Banerjee, Proprietress,
Coronation Talkies, The Strand,
Chalaili, India.

She toyed with using her given name, Premila, but that sounded too independent and husbandless, especially for something as important as official correspondence. The notepaper would be creamy, with the thickness of parchment, budget providing. The embossing, she decided, must be a stylish royal blue, the type style to flow in the most cursive of copperplate. Perhaps she would have a small crown designed to place above the name and address. She opened her eyes and looked out the carriage window. The train was still slicing through the muddled outskirts of Bombay to the main line railhead at Soliganj, where she would change to the narrow-gauge steam train up to Chalaili. She was looking forward to the steep ascent. The air in the hills, her lawyer had assured her, was as crisp as English cracker biscuits.

Mrs Banerjee knew little about Chalaili but it was enough reassurance for her that it was a British hill station, a recuperative bolt-hole for soldiers and civilians plagued by myriad subcontinental malaises. The high altitude, the cool climate, the forest walks and splendid gallops conspired to provide a perfect *cordon sanitaire* for those unable to cope with the heat and disease-riddled air of the plains. But most of all, it was far enough from Bombay for her to make a new start. Aside from that always-wailing mother of hers, resettled in a modern apartment block with partial sea views, there was much that Mrs Banerjee wished to leave behind.

Chapter Three

AT SEA
MARCH, 1937

THE VICEROY OF INDIA GRAPEVINE

Captain James Cunningham and his officers are most
pleased to welcome all passengers on board, in particular
four newlywed couples bound for Bombay: Mr and Mrs
Ernest Hill, Mr and Mrs Dickie Rimmington, Mr and
Mrs William Rushmore, Captain and Mrs David Strange.
We wish all of you a safe and enjoyable passage.

At the age of thirty-two, Lydia may have resigned herself to spinsterhood but she had read sufficient romance
literature to be aware of the possibilities of lust and abandon. Living at The Oaks, marooned amid its clenched silences, time had
moved with glacial majesty and she would often sit in the front
parlour, on an old lounge covered in faded chintz, and wonder
about the secret physical lives of her parents and of Evelyn and
her husband, Thomas Moss. She could imagine no naked com-
munion between Mummy and Daddy. Perhaps he manoeuvred his

penis into her on the odd occasion, somehow wrenching away her sturdy cotton unmentionables and pinning her to the bed, clamping his hand over her mouth to shut out whatever whinings were sure to issue forth.

'Penis, penis,' Lydia said to herself, savouring the word. She realised she had never heard it said out loud. Such a noun was not on the English syllabus at St Martin's primary school, where she taught grade three boys and girls.

'Pardon, Lydia?' enquired William, who was sitting in the teak steamer chair next to her. She lay aside her book, *Murder in the Mews: Four Perplexing Cases for Poirot* by Agatha Christie. Lydia was devoted to the locked-door mysteries of Agatha Christie. She frequently felt as if her life consisted of wandering through a maze of shut doors, unsuccessfully trying each handle, hoping someone would turn a key on the other side.

Lydia and William were on the promenade deck of the *Viceroy of India* and in the unlikely event that anyone had asked, Lydia would have confidently replied they had had sex four times. Twice on their first night together, as snug as sardines in a single berth. And then every third night as William swung over the top bunk, lowered his long legs to the floor and hopped aboard Lydia, plunging deeply. Lydia noted each of these urgent drillings in her journal, with a school-mistressy mark out of ten and a small asterisk. She made her assessments based on the time taken by William to reach his groaning crescendo. Each time, it seemed to take a little longer. Meanwhile, Lydia received no pleasure worth recording, save for a slight internal ache as if she had been kicked.

Mrs William Rushmore. She murmured the complete title to herself. The name Lydia, her identity, had been neatly excised.

Was she half of a whole, she wondered, or a nameless appendage, something useful on a daily basis, like a handbag or a teapot.

'Lydia?'

'Oh, it was nothing, dear.' She smiled as William stood to wander off on his morning constitutional, striding around the deck, always against the wind, his hair swept back. Later his face would be lightly crusted with salt and she would long to lick it off, running her tongue over his cheeks and nose, teasing the sea-smelling grains from his lips, exploring his mouth. But she dared not. Last night she had lain awake, wondering if he would swing down from his top perch and take her. There was no sign of movement so Lydia got out of bed and groped for the small metal ladder that led to the upper berth. William had no need of the apparatus but her legs were short. The ladder wasn't properly attached and after beginning her ascent, it broke free and she fell to the floor amid an almighty clatter.

'For Christ's sake, Lydia, what are you doing?' he said after snapping on his bedside reading light and surveying the tangle. She looked up at his tanned face, his hair pillow-tousled and slightly flecked with grey, his eyes an extraordinary blue. The blue of cornflowers on a high-sky summer's day. He was almost as classically handsome as any hero she had imagined in the robust romances she borrowed from West Gamble Public Library. He looked at her but made no move. And then he laughed, his teeth strong and white but slightly crossed and protruding in the front so at certain angles he looked like an amiable hare.

He jumped down, lifted her up and placed her back between her messy bed covers. 'Come on, old girl, back to sleep.'

Lydia did not sleep that night. She still could not believe that this debonair man had materialised in her life as if via a puff of smoke. He was back in Britain to visit his only relatives, an aunt and uncle. His parents had died in a train crash when he was a boy. Lydia wanted to talk to him about his mother and father but even a hesitant mention of the subject made William's face harden.

John Rushmore, his father's brother, was the history teacher at the high school attached to the little primary annexe where she taught. 'My nephew, William, is looking for a wife,' John had told her. 'Not a silly young thing but a mature woman, someone sensible, who will fit into life in India.'

John had invited Lydia to afternoon tea at his house in Finchley, a few miles north of West Gamble. William was occupying the double bedroom at the front of the small Tudor cottage while John and his wife, Sylvia, appeared to be split between two singles at the back. Sylvia told her guest about the sleeping arrangements, although Lydia wondered why it mattered. Her hostess clinked the Royal Doulton tea service in a quiet kind of rage. Lydia took this to mean that Sylvia thought the sooner William found a bride and her life resumed its comfortable double-mattressed status quo, the better.

It was John who talked up Lydia's achievements to William, embellishing what little he knew of the demure teacher, referring to unsubstantiated prowess in cooking, needlework, gardening and dancing. Lydia's cup trembled in its saucer as she blushed and gave Sylvia panicked looks. John spoke of Lydia with such admiration it made her uncomfortable. He looks at me in too personal a manner, she thought. Lydia realised the buttoned-up Sylvia thought so, too. John's wife was not the least bit happy about the circumstances of Lydia's so-called social visit.

'Dancing is good,' William commented. 'There is a lot of dancing in Chalaili. I have a servant for the rest.'

Lydia felt like a piece of mutton being appraised by a committee of carnivores. Aside from John's covert looks, chiefly at her stockinged legs, the three of them spoke as if she were not in the room. 'In India, marriages are arranged by the respective families,' William was saying to his aunt and uncle. 'Horoscopes are consulted, birth charts are drawn up to make sure everything is auspicious for the union. Sometimes the young couple has no more than a glimpse of each other's faces before the deal is made and the wedding date set . . .'

'Do such marriages work out?' Lydia interrupted.

William looked directly at her with those summer-sky eyes. 'More usually than not. Often the parties involved are no more than seven or eight years of age.'

John and Sylvia set down their cups in a crescendo of wobbling bone china. William laughed. 'But that's just when the deal is made between their families. They wed much later.'

Lydia tried to imagine what it would be like to be betrothed at an age of dolls and hopscotch, tea parties with teddy bears and skipping ropes. When she was seven, she considered boys to be about as desirable as a dose of measles.

'I am thirty-two,' she remarked to no one in particular, swirling the dregs of her tea over a posy of violets at the bottom of her cup. And a virgin, she said to herself, smiling at what she imagined the reaction would be if she dared utter such a statement.

'She will do quite nicely. I must be back in India in a month,' William told the Rushmores later that evening, kissing his aunt on the forehead before he went to bed. His lips, thought Sylvia, are still as soft and moist as an autumn dew. Just like his father's.

Chapter Four

CHALAILI
MARCH, 1937

Mrs Banerjee and Miss Chowpatty stood on Chalaili Station, boxes and bundles piled around their feet. The peacock-feathered passenger had sat in another carriage, amid a great flouncing of skirts, when they had all changed trains at Soliganj. She was stomping off towards the platform exit, followed by a young servant girl, without a backward glance.

Mrs Banerjee looked up at the hills. And up and up. She had

expected pleasant and rounded picnicking hills of the Jane Austen pastoral variety. The landscape of Chalaili was perpendicular, like the Swiss Alps. She had seen alpine pictures during geography lessons at St Sophia's Convent for Young Ladies in Bombay. There had been cows perched at awkward angles and blond children in unfortunate felt hats.

Even the path leading up from the station was on an alarming incline. She could see the retreating Englishwoman climbing slowly, using a wooden handrail to haul herself along. Mrs Banerjee feared this was the sort of discouraging topography that called for walking sticks, smelling salts and sedan chairs.

Two porters sat on their haunches surveying Mrs Banerjee's cumbersome bundles. They looked very glum and completely disinclined to do any portering.

Aruna was surprised at her employer's stillness. Surely it would take more than a hill to render her speechless. But Mrs Banerjee was thinking not so much of the short-term problem of tackling the incline into town but whether she had made a ghastly mistake. Her first impressions of Chalaili smacked of smallness, sleepiness and no doubt a sorry lack of followers of talking pictures.

Little Chalaili Station had segregated men's and ladies' waiting rooms, Mrs Banerjee noted, and a pagoda-roofed office in what she took to be the Burmese style. The stationmaster approached and looked Mrs Banerjee and her servant up and down.

'Good morning,' he offered.

He was clearly Anglo-Indian, thought Mrs Banerjee. Grey eyes, dark hair, long nose on an otherwise flattish face. Anglo-Indians always made it their business to be involved with railways and the flashier the architecture the better, or so her mother had once told her.

'Is it?' countered Mrs Banerjee. 'I am not sure that it is good at all. May I ask a few questions?'

The man nodded, perplexed.

'Is this the main Chalaili station?'

'It is the only station, Madam. Small but efficient, if I might say so, with a special pagoda roof and two arrivals and departures daily.'

'I see. What is the population of Chalaili?'

'Just a few hundred at this time of year but more expected during the very hot weeks in advance of the monsoon. Madam, you are very inquisitive. May I know if you are a newspaper reporter?'

Mrs Banerjee sat down with a thump on one of the sturdiest bundles. Aruna rushed behind to support her back.

'If you must know, I am a top Bombay businesswoman who has come to invest in this . . . this place. I have purchased The Elphinstone Theatre. I presume you know of it?'

'Of course, everyone knows of everything here. It is on The Strand.'

'Yes, The Strand. May I have directions, please?'

'The Strand is the main street . . . the only street, really. It starts over there.'

The stationmaster pointed towards the hill up which the Englishwoman was still climbing, now a dot, her peacock feather a faint ripple against the sky, a tiny pin-point servant in her wake.

Mrs Banerjee took a gulp of mountain air lest she faint clear away.

☙

An hour later, rescued by The Metropole Hotel car and suitably uniformed driver and installed in the dining room with a large pot of tea, Mrs Banerjee felt much invigorated. She was reading a copy of *The Soliganj Weekly Observer* she had found discarded on the next table. She had already surmised Chalaili was not important enough to warrant its own journal, even a weekly bulletin such as this, printed on inferior paper.

'Gary Cooper should have won!' she announced to Anjali Gupta, who had already introduced herself as the wife of the hotelier. She had come to sit at Mrs Banerjee's table and inform her the room she had reserved was ready but there was no need to hurry.

'Won what?'

'Here, here.' Mrs Banerjee stabbed at the newspaper. 'The Best Actor Award. Gary Cooper was nominated, you see, and I had every confidence he would win. I plan to show *Mr Deeds Goes to Town* at my new talking picture theatre. What do you think?'

'I am not familiar with talking pictures. That is why it is so exciting that you are here, Mrs Banerjee, to bring the world of talkies to Chalaili.'

Mrs Banerjee smiled graciously.

'Now, if your servant is ready also . . . that is, once she has assisted you to unpack, she can move into the staff quarters behind the hotel, near the garage.'

Aruna understood the key words servant and garage and pouted with displeasure. She had enjoyed the novelty of a first-class rail passage and had been hoping Mrs Banerjee was sufficiently unconventional to let a servant share her hotel room.

Mrs Banerjee stayed seated, pouring another cup of tea.

'The stationmaster informed me there are just a few hundred people in Chalaili. Is that correct?'

'Yes, Mrs Banerjee, that sounds about right . . . although he hasn't included the residents of the bazaar.'

'The Indians?'

'Mrs Banerjee, we are all Indians, are we not?'

'Yes, yes, I meant the lower classes . . .'

'Well, there are several thousand people in Chota Chalaili bazaar, I would say, plus the residents of surrounding plantations. There is tea and coffee grown around here but not as successfully as elsewhere in the Western Ghats.'

'Why is that?'

'The rain, of course. Chalaili is famous . . . or infamous, I should say, for its rain. And for its hills.'

'Hills? Mountains more likely. Now, if you don't mind, I will go and lie down.'

'Follow me,' said Anjali Gupta, leading Mrs Banerjee into the foyer.

Mrs Banerjee looked up. Of course her room would jolly well be on the first floor, at the top of a steep staircase.

She patted Anjali Gupta on the shoulder and with a weary smile thanked her for the tea. Aruna got into position at the rear of Mrs Banerjee, ready to push.

Chapter Five

BOMBAY
MARCH, 1937

THE BOMBAY ADVOCATE

The Governor of India Act, which comes into force next
month, will see sweeping changes to the way our country
is governed. It must be acknowledged that British power
is in retreat.

From the second Lydia stepped on to the docks at Bombay,
she felt nauseous. It wasn't just the extraordinary smells
of India but the noise and heat, the clamour and push of people.
On the way from the bottom of the gangplank to an ancient taxi,
a distance of a few hundred yards, she found herself the victim of a
horrible commotion, lost her hat, twisted her ankle and was spun
around like a dervish as she collided with a beggar woman with
a baby at her breast. The woman had one eye. The empty socket
was festooned with flies feasting on what appeared to be congealed
milk.

William propelled Lydia to the taxi, guiding her firmly

26

under the elbow as if she were a petty criminal being rushed into court. He helped her into the back seat and slammed the door. In the front, William spoke with the driver in a sing-song chant she couldn't understand. He banged the dashboard and raised his voice and Lydia presumed he was arguing about the price. She felt as though she was about to vomit and wound down her window. The beggar woman had followed her to the car and stood there, framed and absolutely still, like a terrifying gargoyle. Lydia made choking noises to indicate she was about to be sick but the woman did not move.

Suddenly Lydia retched, expelling a porridgy cascade that landed on the baby. The infant turned its face towards Lydia but continued to pull on the woman's distended nipple. Her breasts were as shrivelled as spent balloons. Lydia knew there could be little milk in them. Then she saw with horror that the woman was removing her nipple and pushing the vomit into the baby's mouth.

Lydia screamed and threw her purse, hoping the woman would catch it and run away. It fell open as it arced towards the beggar and wads of English pounds fluttered in confetti clouds. Lydia wound up the window, curled herself on the back seat and sobbed. She heard William get out, there was shouting and what sounded like a thwack of his furled umbrella. He returned and the taxi lurched off into a surging current of traffic.

The noise was amazing to Lydia's Surrey-attuned ears, even with her window firmly shut. Horns beeped, jingle-jangle music blared, the car see-sawed in and out of wheel-swallowing ruts. There were urgent bicycle bells and screeching brakes and smells that surpassed all outrage. At one stage the taxi must have pulled alongside a peanut vendor as the odour of roasting nuts temporarily swamped the stink of rubbish and excrement. All the while, William shouted at the driver as if barking military commands.

'Look, Lydia, a camel,' she heard her husband say but she couldn't open her eyes and, turning sideways and hugging herself, pressed her head against the gritty towelling cloth of the taxi seat-cover. She refused to look up even when the car stopped and she heard William shouting again, his voice only just discernible above an unimaginable cacophony.

Lydia peeped through her pressed hands as William carried her in his arms amid an ocean of bobbing heads. She felt as if she had landed in hell itself, a sweaty-hot and sewer-smelling vastness occupied by snorting camels, coolies with enormous carts piled high with sacks and the occasional over-dressed English dowager being push-pulled in a rickshaw. The size and majesty of the women afforded them the appearance of recumbent elephants.

She found it impossible to believe she was at a railway station. The cathedral-like building was high-ceilinged and pigeon-nested but the birds were not the only permanent dwellers. Families were living in makeshift shelters, ingenious contraptions of cloth and hessian, cardboard and wooden crates. Women were cooking on little fires and children were asleep in compact bundles around embellished pillars as if resting in an over-decorated nursery.

Dogs with toast-rack ribs slithered in and out of the crowds, eyes haunted with hunger. Beggars pulled at Lydia's cotton dress and William muttered at them in what she imagined was Hindustani. She knew she would have to learn some basic conversation but, for the moment, William's growling utterances sounded like unsolved anagrams. Just ahead she could see her suitcase on a porter's head, perfectly balanced, his turban acting as a cushioned base. Unengaged porters were charging about on the hunt for business. From Lydia's vantage point, their red headgear made them look like an exotic species of randomly planted tulips.

At last William popped Lydia down and steadied her with a hand on her shoulder. She saw they were beside a steam train on a long rubbish-strewn platform and the porter was opening a carriage door. She realised she had lost a shoe.

William hastened his wife aboard the First Class Ladies Coupé of the Soliganj Limited Express. Lydia clung to his arm but he told her gentlemen weren't permitted on this part of the train. A conductor appeared and delivered her to her seat. As she slumped into it, she realised her purse had been placed back in her handbag, smeared in lumpy yellow. The conductor hovered, smiling and doffing his braided cap. Lydia managed a thin smile in return but still he stood. Reaching into her purse, she handed him a British note. He looked at it in wonder, turned it over, held it up to the window, flicked his thumb and forefinger against it and, finally, folded it over and over and pushed it into the side of his shoe, performing a little stomping dance until he felt sure the note was secured.

Lydia squeezed shut her eyes and wondered what she had done in letting her husband bring her to such a perfectly ridiculous country.

❧

William arranged himself in the First Class Gentlemen's Compartment and shook open that morning's edition of *The Bombay Advocate*. He was concerned about Lydia but knew the worst thing he could do would be to namby-pamby her through the period of acclimatisation. He had been sick, too, the first time he arrived in India, his refined English stomach unused to the smell of raw sewage, the sight of rats the size of guinea pigs gnawing at gunny sacks of grain on the Bombay wharves.

William settled into his newspaper. He imagined his bride would be well looked after in the ladies coupé. There were several other memsahibs aboard, back from England after home leave, about to reunite with their civil service husbands who had remained in India to attend to the hundreds of thousands of minor machinations that went into the daily running of the Empire. They would be kind to Lydia, he decided, with the misplaced male notion that women with the power of hard-earned experience feel it their duty to help the hapless newcomer.

The clickety-clack calm of the train soon started to send him to sleep. Lydia will be making friends already, he decided. She wasn't that young or beautiful that she'd get up the noses of the Raj dowagers.

๑))

Lydia knew she must look as weepingly unattractive as a crumpled rag.

'Nightingale,' said the woman seated opposite.

They were alone in the carriage and the top bunks had been pulled down, set with pillows, starched sheets and folded blankets, suggesting a long and leisurely journey. Somehow, her suitcase had got up on the opposite bunk and was perched precariously above the woman's head. With its decoupage of labels from the *Viceroy of India*, the case looked like a parcel that had survived an intricate journey. Lydia felt completely disconnected from it.

'Nightingale,' repeated Lydia's fellow passenger.

'Where?'

Lydia looked through the window and saw no nightingales.

She saw nothing, in fact, but rows of dun-coloured shacks and the odd tree with a canopy of broad paddle-shaped leaves. The hazy landscape looked as exhausted as she felt.

The plump woman had piercing eyes the colour of a blue-green sea and looked to Lydia to be about forty. She inspected Lydia up and down, taking in the missing shoe, the yellow stains on the front of her dress. A home-tailored dress, she noted, but still, it was a pity about the tear above the left breast.

'No, I meant that's my name, dear. I am Patricia Nightingale,' she announced, stretching her words like an eisteddfod contestant.

Lydia's eyes widened. 'I am Lydia Rushmore.' Copying the other woman's style of speaking, she enunciated every syllable.

The Nightingale woman didn't appear to notice Lydia's exaggerated speech. 'What rank?' she continued, as Lydia smoothed down her dress and attempted to sit up straight on the cracked brown leather seat, which felt as if it had been constructed without recourse to springs or padding.

'Rank . . .' Lydia was bewildered by the older woman's curiosity.

'Your husband!'

'Oh, he's civil service,' Lydia murmured, wondering if that also entailed a rank. She knew so little about William, he could well have some fancy title for what he did with his weather warnings. Commander of Clouds, or suchlike.

'Mine, too. So, what is it? Teaching? Administration? Railways?'

'Forestry service, I believe. Actually, weather . . .'

Patricia Nightingale's questions came in a rapid-fire series of volleys, as if she were serving at a game of tennis. Lydia's returns were slow and awkward. Given the brevity of her relationship

31

with William, she found it hard to satisfy the Nightingale woman's nosiness.

'How long does the journey take?' Lydia asked, anxious to halt the interrogation.

'About two hours to the railhead at Soliganj and passengers going on to Chalaili must change to the narrow-gauge train for a further journey of more than an hour. But such things are never certain in India, as you will discover.'

Lydia sighed. She wondered how she would find the energy to change trains and, given her one-shoed state, there was the unwelcome prospect of bribing the conductor to carry her.

Eventually, Patricia Nightingale took pity on Lydia and helped her up to the bunk above her seat, where she fell straight asleep, as if she had not rested her body for months.

'It was like lifting a scarecrow,' she would tell her cronies the next night as they played their customary Thursday gin rummy.

Patricia Nightingale and her husband, Campbell, a government housing administrator, were stationed at Soliganj, a large military cantonment of solid slate-roofed bungalows set on wide unpaved streets. It was also a workshop town for the maintenance of the region's rail network and was overrun with Indian Railways employees of all classes and a great number of Eurasians. It must be the dustiest, sootiest place in existence, Patricia Nightingale often thought, and she envied the Chalaili crowd with their pine trees and forest walks and absence of shunting trains.

With uncharacteristic punctuality, Campbell Nightingale was at Soliganj Station to meet his wife and he hurried her off before she could engineer an introduction to William Rushmore, whose name she had not at first recognised but had now slotted into context. She had heard something about him from her husband. There had been a scandal concerning this man they called Rain Wallah and the wife of the visiting British Resident of Kashmir. Patricia Nightingale had been marooned at home with a fearful migraine the night it had all come out at The Empire Club in Chalaili. Her husband had been irritatingly economical with details, claiming it was all a storm in a teacup, although she had heard from others he had actually been an eyewitness to proceedings.

Patricia Nightingale wished she knew what had really happened. She would tell her circle that the bedraggled Lydia looked as if she had been fished out of a river, and finding the catch not totally unappealing, William Rushmore had decided to keep her.

☙

Lydia refused to open her eyes at Soliganj Station until William had guided her to the narrow-gauge steam train. She sat beside him, blinking, on a slippery rexine-covered bench in a little carriage no bigger than her father's garden shed at The Oaks. The train had been moving for less than ten minutes when William announced he was getting off for a stroll.

'Are you mad . . . we are moving . . .'

But he was gone. Out the door, clicking it behind him.

The train climbed so slowly that passengers could alight and amble alongside, conducting conversations through windows. Vendors of fruit and oil-glistening snacks clung limpet-like to the sides of the carriages, baskets balanced at alarming angles.

William suddenly appeared by Lydia's window with a bunch of dog violets and pushed the flowers through. She tried to smile graciously but knew she looked completely wild and William's actions were forced, as if he'd just read a book of etiquette on what a gentleman should do if his wife is discomposed. Lydia couldn't even begin to grasp the absurdity of a train that moved like a tortoise and passengers who chose to walk and boys with baskets of fruit and nuts who lay on the roof on their stomachs and hung over the side regarding her upside down, their eyes as dark and tight and buried as currants.

'The engine is by the famous North British Company of Glasgow,' William told her gravely as he continued to stroll alongside. As the train was coiling like a sluggish snake, she could look out the window and see the tank-style locomotive ahead. 'The gauge is two feet six inches and the speed is approximately seven miles per hour,' William continued. 'The journey will take about seventy minutes, although it is less than thirty minutes by road. Some of the chaps at The Empire Club call the train The Corkscrew.'

At this disclosure, Lydia burst into hysterical giggling.

'I will let you rest, dear,' he said, avoiding eye contact with his dishevelled bride. He hoped she would not turn out to be mentally unbalanced.

The air became cooler as they climbed into the hills and wind-charged clouds went racing across the sky. As the track became too steep to walk comfortably, William reboarded and promptly fell asleep. When the train terminated at Chalaili, Lydia woke, too, and there was William on his knees, looking under the bench seat and asking rather crossly what she had done with her shoe, as if she had somehow contrived to deliberately misplace it.

She closed her eyes and tears rolled down her cheeks. William lifted her in his arms and backed out of the ridiculous little carriage and on to the platform. Lydia complained she was terribly thirsty and he said he would purchase her an orange from a vendor on the railway platform. This required him to put her down, and she stood with one foot hooked behind the other calf, leaning against her husband's side. William checked several pieces of fruit, piled high in a wicker basket, before selecting one with completely unbroken skin. The vendor wiped the glossy fruit with a rag, a spurt of loud haggling followed and Lydia closed her eyes. How was she to eat an orange with no knife to cut it?

When Lydia said she was thirsty, she meant she wanted a cup of tea. English tea. Bone china cups and saucers. Cricket greens and bumblebees, robin redbreasts and hollyhocks. Lydia was murmuring but William couldn't quite discern her whisperings.

Please don't let me be homesick. Don't let me be like Mother. Don't let me be too disappointed with life.

Lydia decided not to open her eyes again until she was safely installed in bed at Bluebell Cottage, William's government bungalow.

Two days later, Lydia felt strong enough to get up. She had fallen with a fever and had been barely conscious of William's comings and goings. As she propped herself up on her elbows, she noticed a small brass bell by the bed. How sweet, she thought. Lydia smoothed her hair and adjusted her bedjacket so that it was loosely tied at the front, sweeping across her nightdress. She planned to raise her arm and pat her forehead when William appeared, allowing him a glimpse of her silk-encased breasts.

She tinkled the bell and heard movement outside the room. The door was slightly ajar and as it began to push toward her, she arranged her pose, lowered her eyes and whispered, 'There you are, my darling.'

'Tea, Memsahib?'

A man stood in the doorway wearing loose white pyjamas, the long top reaching to his knees. In one hand he held a polishing rag, in the other a battered tin of Brasso. Lydia pulled up the covers and sank beneath with just her fingers gripping the edge, like a child hiding from a doctor advancing with a needle. She saw with horror that the man had set aside his cleaning utensils and was taking a chamber pot from under her bed, its contents shielded by a bright blue cloth.

'Who are you?' Lydia demanded.

'I am houseboy,' he said. Even in the shadowy dullness of the room, Lydia could tell he was no boy. He was of average height, slim and very dark-skinned. She guessed he was about her own age.

'No, your real name,' she insisted, trying not to look at the pot, which he was clenching in both hands and holding slightly away from his body, like a sacred offering.

'It is Anil,' said the man, after an awkward hesitation.

'I am Lydia.'

'Yes, Memsahib.'

'No, it's Lydia. L-y-d-i-a. Now, you say it.'

'Cannot.'

'But . . .'

'Tea coming, Memsahib.'

He turned and walked out, gently closing the door. Lydia shrugged, made a back rest with the pillows and stretched her arms. The bedroom was small, with a polished timber floor and white painted ceiling, also made of wood.

'A wooden ceiling . . . that's odd,' she said aloud, looking up at the planks.

The room was modestly furnished, with one tall window leading to a side veranda. Aside from the double bed, there was a chest of drawers in one corner near the window and a small bookshelf. Lydia could see that the books were disordered and speckled with mouldy stains.

The largest piece of furniture was a carved wardrobe, disastrously heavy for the size of the room. On either side of the bed were tables with a single drawer, cane legs and glass top, each holding a small lamp with a shade in deep-green fringed silk. She noticed her suitcase on top of the monstrous wardrobe, presumably empty.

Lydia wondered if the houseboy had unpacked it, his hands exploring her underwear and folded jumpers and blouses. She presumed her clothes were now apportioned between the wardrobe and the chest, mingled with William's.

The thought made her feel warm and happy as Anil knocked lightly and pushed open the door. He brought her tea on the smallest wooden tray she'd ever seen. It was painted with extravagantly costumed warriors riding elephants on a background of postbox red. The pale blue cup and saucer were what her mother would have dismissed as utility china. The tea was milky and slightly frothed with a fragrance Lydia would later discover was cardamom.

She sipped it and the sweetness almost made her gag.

'You want separate tea?' asked the servant, watching her intently.

'Pardon?'

'Tray tea . . . separate milk and sugar?'

'Yes,' said Lydia reaching for a glass of water on the bedside table so she could wash down the sugary muck.

Then she changed her mind. 'I mean no. No thank you.'

'Yes, no?'

'No!'

Anil bowed his way out of the room and she heard his sandals

37

flapping down what sounded to be a long hallway. His fingernails, she had noticed, were filthy and the sleeves of his long white cotton top imprinted with yellow stains that she took to be vestiges of those devilishly hot spices William told her she would encounter in Indian cooking.

In her head, she was already writing a letter home to Evelyn. 'Bluebell Cottage,' she would begin, 'is sorely in need of a woman's touch . . .'

Chapter Six

CHALAILI
MARCH, 1937

THE SOLIGANJ WEEKLY OBSERVER

Ladies are advised that Mrs Hugh O'Brien, Proprietress of Lakshmi Hair and Beauty Studio, The Metropole
Hotel Arcade, Chalaili, has in stock Fair Lady Skin Whit-
ening Cream, as manufactured by C. Mohammad and
Co of Calcutta. Mrs O'Brien has informed *The Soliganj
Weekly Observer* that 'British ladies will find it invaluable
to restore fairness to hands darkened by the effects of the
native sun'.

On the glass front door of Lakshmi Hair and Beauty Studio
in The Metropole Hotel Arcade was painted an image
of the goddess who gave the salon its name. Consort of Vishnu,
Lakshmi sprang forth, according to Hindu mythology, from the
ocean, holding a lotus.

The manageress of Lakshmi Hair and Beauty Studio, Veronica
O'Brien, was a pretty Irishwoman, widowed when her husband,

Hugh, was killed in a rail accident on a journey from Bombay to Calcutta, across the dusty Indian dreadfulness. An obstruction on the tracks. A derailment. The appearance of dacoits. The singling out of white passengers. Robbery and revenge against the *having* British.

The O'Briens had been stationed at Soliganj. He did something high up in the railways and they'd lived in a very comfortable bungalow in a good part of town. The streets of Soliganj were an exercise in symmetry, with a declining order of grandeur from the residence of the Commissioner-in-Chief of the Railways outwards. The O'Briens had been inner circle. Not inner-inner circle, but close to the heart of power nonetheless.

Anjali Gupta was acquainting Mrs Banerjee of all such pertinent facts concerning the prominent citizens of Soliganj and Chalaili. The hotelier's wife was enjoying her role as interpreter of social histories, although the term 'dusty Indian dreadfulness' was not one of her own. It had emerged from the pursed lips of Dorothy Creswell-Smythe as she butted into the conversation of the two Indian women as they chatted across The Metropole's front desk. Dorothy Creswell-Smythe was a widow, too. But a widow of an entirely different class, having been left behind by the distinguished Surveyor General of India, Richard Creswell-Smythe. She had retired to one of four well-appointed cottages in the grounds of The Empire Club, of which her husband had been a life member. The thought of returning to England terrified her. She knew no one would take the slightest bit of notice of a sixty-year-old husbandless woman there, even with the impeccable credentials of her widowhood.

'So now poor Veronica O'Brien is a businesswoman. A small businesswoman, that is,' continued Dorothy Creswell-Smythe.

'I am a businesswoman, too. A large businesswoman.'

Mrs Banerjee laughed merrily at her own joke and Anjali Gupta joined in, relishing the unaccustomed intimacy that her new friend looped around each situation, like a rope-curling cattle rustler from one of her talking cowboy pictures. Dorothy Creswell-Smythe managed a polite smile and bustled along the tiled arcade towards Mary Christie's little shop, on the hunt for the latest magazines from her damp green homeland.

Mrs Banerjee wasted no time in securing an appointment at the Lakshmi Hair and Beauty Studio, knowing that its perfumed environs would be a simmering pot of gossip and information. Her mother, Leela Dhir, was a great habitué of Bombay's top beauty salons and even her late importer-exporter husband, Shyam Dhir, had been frequently astonished at the snippets she was able to extract from her fellow dome-drying ladies.

Only the top salons, naturally, were good enough for Leela Dhir. The Queen's Necklace was a particular favourite. It had recently been visited by Lady Linlithgow, wife of the Viceroy. The Vicereine had been sequestered from the other ladies by lacquered screens and draped towels but Leela Dhir had spied her tan leather laced shoes and the hem of a box-pleated skirt and after a few retellings to wide-eyed acquaintances, she felt justified in dressing the encounter with more detail, hinting that she had all but knelt at the Vicereine's feet and adjusted her shoelaces, advising her on the advantages of a double knot.

Oh yes, Leela Dhir always used to bring home juicy morsels of salon chatter, duly plumped up. Freshly uncorked snatches of hearsay and intrigue to be sprinkled across the frosty silences of the Dhir family dinner table.

Premila Dhir reading at the table. Infernal talking-picture

41

magazines, full of smouldering eyes and puckered lips and cattle-
men in curiously tight trousers.

Shyam Dhir staring into space to a land beyond importing
and exporting. Wretched tea, coffee, jute, wheat. His wife had
no interest in such lowly and unwearable commodities, even if
they did support the Dhir family and keep her in glamorous hair
appointments.

Leela Dhir running an index finger around the polished silver
of her traditional water tumbler. Slowly, absently. A hand raised
in the air as if in epiphany. A smash of descending gold bangles.

'Sujata told me such an interesting thing today. It has come
to me just now. I simply cannot believe she let it fall from her
lips.'

A tinkle of the little brass bell for the houseboy.

'How much longer must we wait for our soup? Are you all
asleep out there, you scallywags? Go, go.'

'You were saying, Leela dearest?'

'Ah, yes, that's right. Sujata. You have heard me speak of her?'

'Isn't she married to that Patel fellow, the Gujarati cloth
exporter?'

'The very one, Shyam. Well, as I was saying, she was very
indiscreet today, boasting about her husband being on the verge
of setting up a new business arrangement with some foreign
place . . .'

'What foreign place?'

'Oh, dear, let me see. Geography never was my strong
point.'

The mock-fluster, the eyes rolled to the ceiling, the encour-
aging words from her husband, his white-white smile that could
split her heart in half.

42

'Japan. Yes, that's it. Japan. I wrote down the company name. It's on a slip of paper. I hid it down my sari blouse . . . that Sujata is so easily distracted. Later, Shyam, I will show it to you in our bedroom. When we are alone . . .'

'We are alone, Leela. Only our beloved Premila is here . . .'

The chair pushed back from the table. The graceful wave of a bangled arm. 'Come, come, Shyam . . .'

❧

So Mrs Banerjee knew all about the indiscretions of beauty salons, how secrets seeped out in the steam from the electric dryers, mingled with the fug of perming solutions and reassembled their atoms to emerge sensationally distorted and engorged.

When Anjali Gupta introduced Mrs Banerjee to Veronica O'Brien, the Irishwoman instantly warmed to Chalaili's newest arrival. The entertaining colours of Mrs Banerjee's saris and her loud laughter seemed to fill the petite salon. If viewed from on high, perhaps from a particularly fine congregation of cumulus clouds, Lakshmi Hair and Beauty Studio would have appeared as a joyous pink confection, the shapes of women moving in languid rhythm, the tantalising drift of jasmine and full-blown rose, sweet voices carrying into the fragrant air as gaily as those of schoolgirls.

Face. Hair. Hands. Feet. These were the acceptable denominators to be shared by the British and Indian women in Chalaili. Safe territory. Female business. At Lakshmi Hair and Beauty Studio, white and brown mixed freely. Even black, mused Mrs Banerjee, if you counted some of the memsahibs' servants, Tamil girls with skin the purplish colour of aubergines who squatted outside on the floor of the arcade, leaping up to fill orders for pots of tea from The Metropole Hotel's dining room.

43

Dark skin was always a sign of low breeding according to Mrs Banerjee's mother, an indicator one worked outdoors in fields or toiled in sooty kitchens and had no time to engage in lady-like pursuits, such as afternoon naps and applications of Fair Lady complexion cream. Mrs Banerjee was very pleased she hadn't been born a servant as ever since early childhood she had been of a wealthy build, not ideal for squatting and sudden errands.

The few Indian women in Chalaili who could afford the services of Lakshmi Hair and Beauty Studio had husbands in minor civil service roles and while they may not have mixed easily at The Empire Club on the few occasions when invitations were extended, they held dominion over the little pink salon, explaining beauty secrets to the memsahibs, swishing their long hair as black as bombazine, as shiny as satin. Red bindis painted on to foreheads, mehendi tattoos of creepers and flowers applied to hands and fore-arms, as discussed in intricate detail when Anjali Gupta's niece arrived on her honeymoon: three nights in The Metropole Hotel's second-best category of suite, the premier lodgings always on reserve for the possibility of higher-up guests.

Veronica O'Brien was delighted at the increase in custom and the sheer gaiety Mrs Banerjee's arrival had brought. Even her serving girl, Aruna, who answered to the most unlikely name of Miss Chowpatty, was deployed as unexpected labour. Whenever the girl stood still, hovering for her employer's next command, Mrs Banerjee would trill at her to sweep Lakshmi Hair and Beauty Studio's floor or otherwise occupy her disgracefully under-utilised hands. The orders were sung. Miss Chowpatty performed ululating dances as she swept and dusted and puzzled the clientele with her non-sequiturs, copied from her mistress's talking-picture vocabulary.

Monkey-face palooka.

Bamboozle.

Cheek to cheek.

Spick and span.

Span and spick.

News of Mrs Banerjee's talking picture theatre spread from Lakshmi Hair and Beauty Studio like a scent, carried on the breeze and curling around corners. Details were distorted. Claims madly exaggerated. Clark Gable and Claudette Colbert would attend the opening. The Governor of Bombay was to cut a gold silk ribbon to announce Coronation Talkies officially launched. The hitherto unsighted Mr Banerjee was a millionaire businessman poised to invest money into Chalaili, to elevate its status to upper-upper class. Talking pictures would be filmed there . . . in the woods and atop the sky-scraping ridges. Romance pictures. Dark dramas. Pictures about rain. Perhaps such pictures would be a curiosity for people living in dry places. The inhabitants of Chalaili certainly hoped Mrs Banerjee did not intend to show too many talking pictures about rain. There was far too much of it about already.

On the door of Lakshmi Hair and Beauty Studio, firmly shut against the world of men, the goddess's serene face floated amid lotus flowers. Held aloft in both hands was a bud, its petals clasped as if in prayer.

Mrs Banerjee booked thrice-weekly appointments, with a small discount from Veronica O'Brien for such a show of regularity. And every time she pushed open the glass door, the proprietress of Coronation Talkies thought how very much the doe-eyed Lakshmi looked like Claudette Colbert.

Chapter Seven

CHALAILI
MARCH, 1937

'Beware the influence of a vertical sun.'
INDIAN FORESTRY SERVICE HANDBOOK FOR FIELD OFFICERS, 1902

When it was 100 degrees in Calcutta and Bombay, Lydia dutifully read one morning when William had already disappeared to his office, it was an average of 74 degrees at elevated hill stations. The British colonial government in India decamped in summer from Calcutta to Simla, the 'Queen of Hill Stations' as she was proudly known, with her high society and backdrop of snow-doilied Himalayan mountains.

There were close to eighty hill stations, large and small, at the height of the Raj, in the late-nineteenth century. Their altitudes ranged from just over 2500 feet to more than 8000 feet. Lydia had already read all this on board the ship as William did his incessant deck pacing and cloud watching. He had presented her with a reading pack of books, all by waffling colonel types and the odd doughty dowager who Lydia just knew would be a loud champion of sensible shoes and botanical walks. Simla, Darjeeling, Ooty, Mussorie, Naini Tal, Dalhousie . . . Lydia had practised the names over and over but nowhere had there been a mention of Chalaili.

Lydia continued to read of blackbirds and ferny dells, cuckoos and mossy paths, woodpeckers and hedges of heliotrope that exploded with flowers after rain. A certain Mr Horace Black, she learned, had nurtured a heliotrope 12 feet high and 30 feet in circumference and a verbena attaining the height of 19 feet, with the branches of a tree. This was in the Nilgiri hills, she read, a name meaning blue, and she closed her eyes and imagined a high misty place of greens and blues populated by enormous plants, like a sort of mighty conservatory in which people lived and went about their business, pushing their way through leaves as if they were curtains and breathing the clear scent of pine.

She had also fossicked in the library aboard the *Viceroy of India* and found a little volume on the *Botany of India* by a Lady Bertha Montgomery, published in 1933. The index revealed what Lydia had been looking for: Chalaili, pages 121 and 130.

The mentions were brief but Lydia had copied Lady Bertha's observations into her journal. The first revealed that Chalaili was established by the British in 1858 as a minor sanatorium after a similar experiment at Cherrapunji, in the Assam Group of Hill Stations, had failed in 1834. Chalaili was listed in the Bombay Group of Hill Stations along with neighbours bearing such mellifluous names as Poona and Amboli. The land had been acquired from the local Raja of the time, who apparently confessed to an inconvenient fear of heights and a thorough dislike of climbing.

Chalaili, she had read, boasted 'woody eminences' and its

47

cool climate served 'to relieve the summer ills of the heat-wasted British civil servants of the Bombay Presidency'. By the summer of 1900, there were at least 200 officers on sick leave 'besides visitors and those in residence'. Lady Montgomery deemed it impossible to calculate the number of 'native hill people'.

It fell out of fashion as a summer retreat in the early twentieth century when the accumulated impact of the annual monsoon weakened the main ridge and houses began to subside. Lady Montgomery dubbed Chalaili 'as troublesome as a thundercloud' but further advised that due to its relative proximity to Bombay, the 'very minor' hill station continued to be of interest to 'followers of mountain scenery' due to its good air, cleansing rainfall, natural springs of sweet water and unusually tropical flora.

But the rain, advised Lady Montgomery, lest the reader should imagine a well-mannered sprinkle, was 'Indian rain'. With no punctuation, perhaps to imitate a torrent, she rattled off her thoughts: 'ghastly thundering hissing hindering oozing morbiferous malodorous miasmic slimy sickening rain.'

The next mention was less judgemental. 'The matching jamun trees at Twin Trees Point, a well-regarded scenic lookout in Chalaili, blew away in the record monsoonal downpours of 1932. The local population continues to call this elevated vantage point by that descriptive name, although it is entirely bare.' Lydia had laughed out loud at the fate of Twin Trees Point. That night she would dream of her mother aboard a flying jamun tree, its smooth, slender trunk like a giant broomstick. Not that she knew exactly what a jamun tree was but she imagined it to be tall and strong, a worthy mountain species. She had consulted the glossary at the back of Lady Montgomery's volume and written down its Latin name, *Eugenia Jambolana*, laughing as she did so.

48

'It's not so much the name of a tree as a writer's nom de plume,' Lydia had whispered to no one in particular, certainly not the ship's snooty librarian at her too-neat polished desk. Lydia had wished she possessed the courage to approach the stern woman. 'I say,' she longed to announce, 'I don't suppose you have a copy of *The Scandal of the Missing Trees* by Eugenia Jambolana?'

Lady Montgomery wrote in such a prissy tone that Lydia, for all her naivety about her new home, wondered if the titled author had so much as placed a well-shod foot in Chalaili. She closed her eyes and remembered what William had told her aboard the *Viceroy of India*, as she snoozed off below him in her narrow bunk.

He had spun fantastical stories of a hill station hovering in the clouds. She had seen dreamy outlines of wild strawberry and raspberry bushes, of glow-worms that inhabited hedges and flashed like torches, of tropical flowers that shot to the heavens like botanical fireworks and mushrooms sprouting to the size of a child's parasol. She had been told by William of the immense darkness of the evenings as if the air was solid, like a substance to be pinched or punched. If Lady Montgomery really had been privy to the effects of the pre-monsoonal weeks in Chalaili, she would have experienced humidity so thick she may have been tempted to take a knife and cut an outline of her approximate shape, slit it and walk through.

❧

If Lady Montgomery had been sparse in her description of Chalaili, it was because the hill station was most definitely out of fashion. When the narrow-gauge railway from Soliganj opened in 1907, Bombay's higher-ups had flocked to its dramatic heights, enjoying the ozone-rich air and orange sunsets, the mare's-tail skies of early summer, the splendid bridle paths. At an elevation of 4380 feet, Chalaili was a minor player in the realms of sanatoria and only just above the official malaria line. The undisputed leader was Simla, far to the north, scene of flower fetes and gymkhanas and dramatics at the Gaiety Theatre, where military chaps frequently acted the women's parts, roundly refusing to shave their moustaches.

Lydia sat on Bluebell Cottage's veranda in a wicker chair topped with a lavender-and-white gingham cushion, a pretty farewell present hand-sewn by Evelyn, who must have imagined her sister transplanted to a polite little country cottage, serving cream teas in a springy green garden. She adjusted her reading glasses and continued to consult her small educational library, determined that William would not be embarrassed by her lack of knowledge about India.

Chalaili, she read, had a certain fame that from its many lookouts on an unsullied day one could see down the Konkan Plains to the coast and even the glittering Arabian Sea on a particularly clear day. Lydia had been for several walks up and down Chalaili's attenuated ridges and the presence of such telescopic views appeared an extravagant claim. The panorama points were perched abruptly, tormented by winds and unpopular with all but the hardiest of British residents. But Lydia would soon discover William was a regular figure at barren Twin Trees Point, even on days when the grey sky was as shiny as a sixpence and the hills were slick with yellowish waterfalls, like cascades of stained lace.

Chapter Eight

CHALAILI
MARCH, 1937

THE SOLIGANJ WEEKLY OBSERVER

Local tea merchant Mr P. K. Kumar has announced that
supplies of First Flush Darjeeling Tea are now available
at his emporium on Railway Road, Soliganj, adjacent to
Soliganj Station. 'First Flush leaves are full of flavour,' Mr
P. K. Kumar told *The Soliganj Weekly Observer*, 'and preparing a pot of tea in the English manner requires less than
one full rounded teaspoon measure. When steeped, the
leaves are brownish-green in colour.'

At The Metropole Hotel on The Strand, Mrs Banerjee
was also reading. She had taken to her bed with a head
cold. Aruna was curled up asleep on the floor and did not
respond to her mistress, no matter how shrill the command.
Mrs Banerjee envied the girl's uncomplicated repose. Her
own sleep was interrupted by vivid dreams, sometimes starring the dashing screen star Clark Gable but, more often, the

51

disappointing Rajat Banerjee with his silly epicene nose and girlishly waved hair.

Mrs Banerjee threw an empty cardboard box of chocolates at Aruna. She calculated, correctly, that it would land on the floor, just by her head. The girl jumped up and crept off to bring fresh tea. Mrs Banerjee decided she would have to invest in a sturdy brass bell like the one her mother had always kept by her bed at the Chowpatty Beach family home. Her father, however, never responded to the urgent rings. 'Send a servant,' he would always tell his daughter, as a tinny symphony racketed from the marital boudoir. 'Another storm in a teacup, you mark my words.'

Mrs Banerjee wished she had done more reading about Chalaili before agreeing to purchase, on a grand whim, the theatre she was intending forthwith to transform into Coronation Talkies. She hadn't been well enough to see inside the building yet, although its peeling bulk loomed on the opposite side of The Strand. Aruna arrived with hot tea and Mrs Banerjee tried to concentrate on her book.

'The clammy little hill station stands 172 miles south-west from Bombay in the Western Ghats, a chain of rugged mountains stretching for 1000 miles down the west coast to India's southernmost tip.' The description made Mrs Banerjee feel feverish. How was she supposed to create a moving picture theatre worthy of the highest society when some nincompoop writer could airily toss in a word like clammy and think nothing of the consequences for a modern businesswoman such as herself.

'The ocean-facing cliffs of the ghats bear the full fury of the summer monsoon, like gigantic retaining walls fending off waves. The lashing rains form moated islands, hardy residents move ghost-like in grey or battle-green sou'westers and umbrella sellers work around the clock assembling new shelters of double the average size from bony wreckages.'

'Lashing rains, wrecked umbrellas!' moaned Mrs Banerjee. She took a stout mouthful of tea and glared at the next page.

'Chalaili's attractions for over-heated Bombayites are its flourishing forests, glades of tiger-striped light, its high meadows dense with wildflowers, the record-sized rhododendrons and the mountainous quiet of the evenings, unbroken by the troublesome noises of Indian villages. The visitors from the coast have well and truly scuttled back to the plains before the affronted purple skies of the encroaching monsoon make their entrance, waiting to disgorge the first drops of rainwater that make craters in the dusty ground and hang from leaves like giant globes of mercury.'

'Affronted! I'll tell you who is affronted!'

Mrs Banerjee shouted so loudly that Aruna leapt up and lunged at what she presumed was Mrs Banerjee's empty cup. She succeeded in spilling a puddle of First Flush Darjeeling tea over the pages of the leather-bound book and was taken aback when her employer shook mightily with laughter and hurled it at the wall.

Chapter Nine

CHALAILI
APRIL, 1937

'Beware the prospect of imminent precipitation.'
INDIAN FORESTRY SERVICE HANDBOOK FOR FIELD OFFICERS, 1902

*D*espite scepticism (Lydia Rushmore) and fury (Mrs Banerjee) at the sardonic commentary of guidebook writers of the era, both newcomers were forced to acknowledge Chalaili's meagre size. The town conformed to the essential colonial hill station blueprint. Its main thoroughfare was a promenade known as The Strand where, in its late-nineteenth century heyday, tourists thronged in season, checking out each other's clothes and consorts, walking up and down for as long as it took to be thoroughly noticed. It had once been a preserve for pedestrians but by the 1930s, traffic was allowed, although cars in Chalaili were few and the sight of a vehicle crawling along attracted so much attention that driver and passengers were likely to find curious faces glued to the windows during their slow passage.

At the eastern flank of The Strand stood the Holy Cross

Church, a Victorian Gothic edifice with an alarmingly over-stocked cemetery, some graves grandly topped with sorrowing angels on plinths from the much-vaunted marble-dressing firm, Paul and Paul of Simla. Most of the markers revealed deaths from typhoid, cholera, malaria and dysentery but the occasional misadventure was recorded, such as hornet stings and sunstroke. Those women who had died of homesickness and loneliness did not have such afflictions officially noted but had been merely despatched to rest in the arms of God, or in the case of widows, to be reunited with their beloved spouses.

When Mrs Banerjee took an inspection tour of the grave-yard, she decided that such promised reunions might not have pleased all the deceased ladies. She was a young woman but a keen observer of the matter of marriage. Her father's recently chiselled tombstone, for example, did not suggest any future rendezvous with his wife. Shyam Dhir was not a Christian but Mrs Banerjee's mother, Leela Dhir, had organised a society burial with full party catering and a substantial donation to the bemused Reverend Gill-ingham-Gregory of St Mark's Church, Bombay.

'Shyam was a cosmopolite,' Leela Dhir had assured the puzzled guests, who had not forgotten her devotion to a certain fertility goddess at the local Hindu temple during her negotiations with top Bombay families to secure a prominent marital union for her difficult daughter.

Mrs Banerjee knew her mother's overblown arrangements for her father's funeral were compensation for her daughter's disastrous wedding day.

Above the church on a bosky knoll stood Chalaili's social epicentre, The Empire Club, a solid white stucco bungalow with an imposing porte-cochere, affixed like a snub nose and supported by four ionic columns. Its broad red-tiled terrace offered hill and valley vistas.

The Empire Club's timber-walled interiors were hung with the trophy heads of elk and spiral-horned Himalayan goats. The black-painted timber flooring of the front hallway had as its centrepiece a leopard-skin rug, its intact head the bearer of topaz-coloured eyes that, although of course only glass, had a habit of appearing to follow the comings and goings of club members. On garden-party nights in summer, the trees were hung with pink-and-green Chinese paper lanterns with tassels that danced in the breeze.

Indians were permitted membership of The Empire Club, after glacial scrutiny by the elected committee, but women were not, although they were welcome on the arms of their menfolk at any time and were designated Tuesday afternoons for such ladylike pursuits as knitting bees to clothe Bombay orphans and the ritual taking of tea.

The Chalaili Sanatorium for the Tubercular stood behind The Empire Club with two wings of rooms for convalescents from the plains. Four British doctors and a team of Eurasian and Indian nurses cared not exclusively for the tuberculars but soldiers of shattered constitutions, malaria recoverers and those diminished by dysentery, cholera and typhoid. Some of the chaps suffered from undiagnosed debility. Boredom, perhaps, or drinking. Mrs Banerjee's enquiries confirmed that there were no female patients. Obviously British women were just supposed to get on with things, like their Indian sisters, she fumed to herself.

Mrs Banerjee also discovered it was not unknown for the single men among them to be repatriated to Soliganj or beyond with a nursely wife on their arm to minister to their future needs.

Anjali Gupta told her such mixed unions were frowned upon by Chalaili's in-charge memsahibs, possibly because they suspected their husbands could also be easily seduced by the flashing dark eyes of young women who never complained of homesickness.

The sanatorium adjoined Chalaili Hospital, where residents were treated for the usual ailments, although rabies patients were despatched with haste to the Pasteur Institute of India at Kasauli in the foothills of the Himalaya or to its sister establishment at Coonoor in the Nilgiri Hills. There had once been talk of such an institute being founded in Chalaili, but that was before the rains came and came and came and washed away the town's fortunes.

There was no British school for there were very few eligible children. The handful whose fathers were Chalaili-posted braved the narrow-gauge train down to Soliganj or were despatched by daily taxi to the cantonment classes or, in a few rare cases, were taught at home by imported governesses.

On the northern side of The Strand stood the rather gloomy Loch Fyne Tea Rooms run by the eccentric Misses Craig, but the most imposing building was its neighbour, The Metropole Hotel. Above its arched entranceway was hung a painted wooden sign, only slightly peeling: FOR THOSE WHO VALUE THEIR REPOSE. Underneath in minuscule lettering was a further enticement, added when Chalaili's reputation as a holiday redoubt began to collapse: FREE LODGINGS FOR SERVANTS AND INDEPENDENT MOTOR VEHICLES.

The genial hotel owner Ram Gupta had his Empire Club membership application pending in the club secretary's locked top drawer. The secretary knew they would have to let Gupta in eventually as, aside from any question of racial discrimination, his hotel had an excellent arcade with the Lakshmi Hair and Beauty

Studio much favoured by the wives of club members and an odd little shop run by the widow of a decorated army captain, Mary Christie, who sold such desirables as Viceroy Filters, Peak Freen's biscuits, imported caramels, cold cream, hosiery, hat pins and pearl buttons. There was talk of under-the-counter merchandise, too, although that was strictly the preserve of the ladies and appeared to consist of substances no more intimate than specially engineered undergarments.

Directly across The Strand from The Metropole Hotel stood the disused Elphinstone Theatre, awaiting Mrs Banerjee's transformation to Coronation Talkies. The theatre had once been the venue for recitals, amateur plays and the occasional lecture by a visiting expert in such peculiar disciplines as bee keeping and steam trains. Mrs Banerjee had discovered from Anjali Gupta that the theatre had been one of the first buildings in Chalaili, named The Elphinstone at its inception in the 1850s, in honour of the then Governor of the Bombay Presidency. But it had quickly become known as The Elephant. Now it stood boarded up with a troop of langur monkeys usually in residence on its front steps, legs crossed, heads cocked, who could not have looked more like an assembly of old men on a park bench if they'd been wearing overcoats and caps.

Next door was the grey brick post office with a flagpole protruding from its roof. The flagpole was an unusually tall affair, visible from most points around Chalaili and in use not as a bearer of the Union Jack but for a red flag to be raised when the overseas mail was in. Its pillar box, in matching red, with a little show of allegiance, was topped with a white-and-gold coronet.

Below The Strand, clinging to the hillside in an avalanche of timber and tin, was Chota, or Lesser, Chalaili, home to the bazaar and what the British casually referred to as native housing. If the timid Lydia or the high-heeled Mrs Banerjee had ventured down the slippery hill, they would have seen that the accommodation was mostly mud and thatch with a few grander buildings constructed from porous stone and swaddled with kulum grass to protect from the abrasive monsoonal rain. Like the British bungalows above, these poor residences were pinned at precarious angles, their access paths a sharp zig-zaggery carved into the hillside.

The bazaar proper was a more level affair spread along in rows, a bustling market of stalls and strolling vendors. There were rough divisions between the grain merchants, the purveyors of fruit and vegetables, the butchers, the spice traders and the little shops piled with hardware, bolts of cloth, readymade wearings and utensils. But to an outsider it was one big raggle-taggle affair, jostling and noisy and full of punchy smells. Honey was a speciality of the hills, made from local scented flowers, and from late February to May, strawberries were in season, stacked in glistening red mounds, as enticing as jewels. One section of the bazaar was reserved for flowers and the vendors all spoke enough English to parlay with the memsahibs when they tarried with their servants, negotiating best prices for armfuls of molten-gold marigolds, bunches of fiery salvia and divinely plump double nasturtiums.

The smell of the bazaar was of spice and smoke and sizzling mutton and its cacophony of noise rose up the hill, across The Strand and into the ears of the Britishers above. On the terrace of The Empire Club, enjoying a bracing gin and tonic on a warm evening, members would be assaulted by the odours of spice-basted chicken and complicated curries drifting on the breeze.

William called them 'red smells' and the chaps would chuckle grimly at his standing joke as they prepared to join their wives indoors and dine on the gravy-drenched grey roasts and overdone vegetables of imperial cuisine, as interpreted by the bored Indian cooks in the club kitchen.

Chalaili was not an exciting place but it was pretty and sociable and lacked the awful snobbery of the more important hill stations. Many of its British residents had simply been marooned there. Some were retired and lacked the stamina or inclination to return home to England, though when they spoke of that great green land, their eyes glistened with nostalgia. A few, like William, were properly employed, but their positions were antiquated.

On the two serried ridges above The Strand stood the government bungalows. These were half timbered cottages, mostly white and black in mock-Tudor style, with red corrugated-iron roofs and verandas on three sides. Some residences were as bare as building blocks, others prettied-up with roses and hollyhocks and daisies and hanging baskets, depending on the emotional health of the owners. The more cared-for bungalows sported battalions of potplants, mostly pelargoniums, petunias, candytuft and geraniums in terracotta tubs. Bluebell Cottage was located along the lower ridge, a saving of five minutes of concerted climbing as the road did not continue to the upper level.

The residences were angled at such steepness that climbing required heroic gulps of air and strained calf muscles. The few taxis in Chalaili did good business but usually for journeys of no more than five near-vertical minutes.

At the western end of The Strand, looming above the railway station, stood the principal government building, a once-grand two-storey Victorian affair clad in creepers. It was still imposing

60

from a distance, although more minute inspection revealed lep-
rous paintwork and creeping damp.

❧

William's office lay within the government building's dank cat-
acombs, his being the only one occupied on the mouldy upper
floor. Lydia, whom William had failed to introduce to anyone, soon
heard sniggering about her husband in queues at the post office.
It was whispered that the tall blue-eyed man known as Rain Wallah loved his blessed monsoon reporting so much he would work
at his desk under an umbrella while the water seeped through the
ceiling.

William had been posted at Chalaili for five years and had
dutifully carried out his monsoon warnings, climate studies and
every three months he travelled to Bombay to present his reports
to his overseer, George Windsor, a barrel-shaped whiskery fellow who had once toured all over India lecturing on the monsoon
and astonishing audiences with his wind machine, a cantanker-
ous contraption that he would fire up on stage. Its grand finale,
as it happened, was at Chalaili's Elphinstone Theatre, where the
machine had gone strangely amok, and instead of emitting polite
gusts of air, it produced a blast that sent ladies' hats flying and,
unfortunately, the hairpiece of the visiting Governor of Bombay, in
Chalaili under sufferance for the wedding of his sister to the pastor
of the Holy Cross Church.

George Windsor had taken to drink after that unfortunate episode. He cancelled all further travelling engagements and
always looked forward to William Rushmore's visits to Bombay
as an excuse for an entire afternoon and evening at his club. William surmised his reports went largely unread but he didn't mind

too much. He liked his superior and for hours they talked of wind and water and the vagaries of clouds, the problems inherent in the rapid changes of precipitation over space and time and atmospheric circulation patterns — all topics that William had long ago realised were not of immediate interest to just anyone.

William knew he was jokingly referred to by his colleagues as Rain Wallah but he relished his role of Chalaili's chief (and only) meteorological officer. His duties included the measuring of rainfall and wind, the monitoring of the passage of the annual monsoon, the siphoning of information to Bombay via an intricate system of telex and post and the occasional scratchy, crackling telephone call in times of crisis.

Above his desk was pinned a hand-painted sign that his forestry service colleagues, the Jungle Wallahs as they were known in their superiors' circles, had long ago drawn up for him as a birthday gift. He loved its tone and orotund language. Each of the warnings was preceded by a crude drawing of a tree, like a stick figure with several pairs of outstretched arms.

BEWARE THE PROSPECT OF PERIODICAL
INUNDATIONS

BEWARE THE AQUEOUS BURDEN OF
THE MONSOON

BEWARE THE CONTINUED ACTION OF
VIOLENT WINDS

BEWARE THE RAVAGES OF INSECTS
AND VERMIN

BEWARE THE DESTRUCTIVE EFFECT OF
SPONTANEOUS VEGETATION

BEWARE THE POTENTIAL PERILS OF
A MACKEREL SKY

William showed the sign to Lydia during her one tentative visit to his office but she had simply smiled dreamily and repeated 'aqueous burden' over and over in a way he found astonishingly salacious. He had moved close behind her as she looked through his office window and lightly kissed her neck. She didn't react so he pressed himself against her and murmured, 'Beware the prospect of imminent precipitation . . . imminent precipitation.'

Instead of a romantic response, she had spun around and hooted with laughter.

'That's the most amusing thing you've ever said to me, William,' she chortled, her feline eyes twinkling merrily. And with that, she had straightened her pink poplin sun frock and disappeared with a skip into the corridor.

'Women,' said William, with a shrug, and returned to his messy desk. He was quite relieved, though – he had to admit – that Lydia didn't seem all that interested in sex. He found the whole business too emotional and time-consuming and had learned to live without it.

While the majority of Indian Civil Service officials at Chalaili went through the motions of their desk-bound jobs, William was what he liked to think of as a field man. His idea of absolute enchantment was to camp overnight in the forests around Chalaili with a complicated rigmarole of equipment that enabled him to measure temperatures, frosts and precipitation. He would record his findings with utmost meticulousness in a small notebook that he kept buttoned in the top left-hand pocket of his khaki shirt. It was closer to him, he would frankly admit, than any human.

Chalaili suited William. His days had pattern and purpose, he was possessed of an almost brazen wellness. William knew the days of the British in India were numbered and change was inevitable but, for now, life was about as pleasant as a chap could want.

Chapter Ten

CHALAILI
APRIL, 1937

'Native servants are to be kept in their place
at all times. They will neither obey nor respect their
memsahib mistress if she attempts to befriend them.'
ETIQUETTE AND MANNERS FOR THE COLONIAL MEMSAHIB
BY HENRIETTA WEATHERBY, 1895

Lydia's first few weeks in Chalaili passed in a whirl-wind of novelty. She'd never had her own home before. When her mother had died, Evelyn and her husband and children had moved back to The Oaks from their rented rooms above a bank in the West Gamble high street to help Lydia look after Daddy and had settled in almost overnight. Lydia was not really consulted about the new arrangements and it was never discussed that the house could eventually be sold and Lydia's share used to buy herself a cottage. In her early thirties, she had already been labelled as the family spinster, expected to inhabit, with a minimum of fuss, the room she'd slept in since childhood, and contribute a percentage of her teaching wages to the running of The Oaks.

She loved Bluebell Cottage, its petite size and vertiginous views, and relished the cool cement, polished timber and silk-woven scatter rugs underfoot. It was all so foreign and exotic compared to the prickliness of carpets. The name, too, was perfect. 'It was bestowed by some pathetically homesick exile,' William told her. When he spoke of expatriates, his upper lip would curl, repelled by the notion of nostalgia for the polite order of England.

'There aren't any bluebells, really,' she said to William and he looked at her with eyebrows raised, as one might observe a silly child. The garden was deep and fecund, thick with glossy plants. It was surprisingly tropical, Lydia thought, for such hilly altitude. William tried to explain to her the micro-climate of Chalaili and how the monsoonal rains nurtured the trees and shrubs. 'You will like the taste of summer mango,' he told Lydia with one of his skew-toothed grins.

'Mango, mango,' she laughed, savouring the word's succulence.

Lydia took morning walks along the ridge, past the single row of stone and half-timbered bungalows with pitched tin roofs, pillared verandas and neat fences, like mirror reflections of Bluebell Cottage. Lydia already knew, thanks to the generic hill-station tutorials of Lady Montgomery, that beyond their genteel facades they would be beset with skittering mosquito-eating lizards and unconquerable dampness.

The memsahibs obviously had instructed their gardeners to recreate stiff English cottage gardens. Honeysuckle and jasmine vines trailed their sweet way up and around the tight mesh of metal fences. Lydia thought wooden pickets would have been so much prettier but perhaps the cold sturdy barriers had to do with that windy monsoon business. There were potted fuchsias, dahlias and cosmos. Hollyhocks, foxgloves, daisies, violets, anemones, dog roses and bushes of springy lavender stood to attention in varying stages of abundance. When the rains come they will probably collapse, she thought. The idea of their demise appealed to her. The over-gardened rows reminded her of Mother's flowerbeds at The Oaks, so stitched and regimented.

Lydia never saw the occupants of the dozen cottages but she was aware of the slight movement of curtains and the occasional shadow drifting behind a bamboo matting pulled down from the eaves of a veranda and tied with knotted rope to a hook on the cement floor. William told her there were bank employees and their families resident in a few. The postmaster Harold Gilbert was at the end, pickled in whiskey and entertaining native dancing girls while his wife was on indefinite leave in England, according to William, who made the pronouncement with a grim smile. Other houses were used by Soliganj railway folk who came up to Chalaili on weekends and during the worst of what William told Lydia was referred to as The Hot, the insufferable weeks before the monsoon.

Lydia decided to leave the unruly garden at Bluebell Cottage exactly as it was. She liked its waywardness, the suggestion of secrets deep in the glossy rhododendrons and climbing yellow roses, spider lilies, allamanda and hibiscus. The bungalow was situated at the far end of the row, half hidden by wild strawberry bushes and with uncleared forest beyond and she could see why William had chosen to keep the vegetation in its natural state. The garden acted as a spongy green buffer between the over-civilised residences and the tall pines and Himalayan cedars of the steep mountains. William was pleased Lydia was not going to turn into a rose botherer, as he had once heard a chap at the club refer to his wife.

The cool veranda of Bluebell Cottage ran around three sides and was covered with a deep roof that sloped to an overhang, like the shady brim of a hat. The floor was simple cement, painted red and occasionally blistered so that grey patches showed through. Above the front door, Anil hung basil leaves and marigold blossoms to bring protection and good fortune. It was a Hindu tradition, Anil advised her, although he also mentioned he had taken convent classes and could recite the Lord's Prayer. Lydia suspected that the servant's notion of religion could be a bit like William's beloved weather patterns, changing at whim and with enviable contingency.

The bamboo mattings at Bluebell Cottage had been stiffly rolled underneath the rim of the veranda and looked to Lydia as if they had not been shaken free for a long time. The servants at the neighbouring cottages let theirs up and down according to the heat of the day. On one side of the veranda, facing the next bungalow, a deep purple bougainvillaea vine had woven itself around the stone pillars and had begun to rampage towards the roof. When a breeze blew, the petals would shimmy and Lydia saw that soon it would form a living curtain. It seemed unutterably exotic to her to have a permeable barrier through which she could spy quite nicely at the comings and goings of her so-far frosty neighbours.

Lydia soon set up a routine of early-morning tea, taken on the veranda's top step. She sat to one side, out of Anil's way, as he swept the stray leaves that blew in from the bushy garden. She wore a soft pink dressing-gown, wound tightly around her slim frame and caught with a matching pink tasselled cord. Her thick hair, usually so thoroughly brushed in front of a gilt-framed mirror in her small bedroom at The Oaks, she left tousled so it formed dancing waves. The unaccustomed humidity turned the ruffs of hair near her ears and temples into kiss-curls and she liked her converted appearance. She felt less structured in India, more girlish and carefree, although she was aware there was no audience to witness and remark upon her transition.

Her regular breakfast companion was a langur monkey, a small male, unaccustomedly alone, who delighted in snatching the starched white napkin from Lydia's tray and dancing about with it held around his waist in the fashion of a tropical sarong. Anil would chase him with a broom while his mistress squealed with delight and flocks of lime-green parakeets swirled into the instant camouflage of trees.

Even at Lydia's veranda tea hour, just after dawn, William was preparing to cycle into town to his office. She had no desire to see his place of work again. She had barely been able to fit beside him in that jumbled cavern of triplicate forms and carbon papers and a miniature merry-go-round of rubber stamps he would twirl until he found the one with the appropriate message. She coloured slightly when she thought how he had pressed his engorged penis against her by the office window and she had been so embarrassed she quickly turned the moment into a joke.

Lydia was puzzled by all this monsoon business of William's. The prospect of Lady Montgomery's hissing hindering oozing and messy etceteras seemed out of kilter with the cool, crisp climate of their mountain outpost.

William tried to encourage his wife to go into town more often, to have her hair done or browse around the bazaar. 'The house needs ornaments,' he had said to her on several occasions, presuming she would be anxious to fill the rooms with Indian arte-facts and carpets from the Chota Chalaili bazaar. The other British wives in Chalaili would often be seen fossicking through the wares at street stalls, a retinue of servants in tow to carry home, high on their heads, in a triumphant processional, the booty of the mem-sahibs. The women haggled furiously, shouting the few words of Hindustani they had deigned to learn. How little they paid and how the stall holders had shrunk under their expert bargaining would be all the talk of their card-playing soirees at The Empire Club.

Lydia had little interest in shopping, even though upon arrival at Bluebell Cottage she had thought everything to be slightly shabby. Under her instruction, Anil moved around some furniture and she threw some bolts of embroidered textiles she found in a cupboard over the backs of the front parlour's matching lounges. Anil told her the material had been intended for cush-ions. Sahib purchased it from a trader who had been selling door to door, spreading his wares on bungalow verandas for the inspec-tion of the madams along the ridge. William had haggled for an hour and then put away the textiles, advising Anil that one day he would get cushions made.

'It was a waste of time and money, Mem.'

'Call me Lydia,' she said, looking Anil square in the eye. She must have told him a dozen times not to use the grandiose mem-sahib term.

'Yes, Mem,' he muttered, staring at the ground.

'Well . . .' she continued, holding the length of material against the light. It was in furious shades of red and orange, aflicker with gold thread and beautifully thick. 'Maybe not such a waste after all. My father has a saying, Anil, that he always uses when things take an unexpected turn of events.'

'Holy damnation?' suggested Anil. It was William's favourite.

'Not quite,' she smiled. 'He says "galloping galoshes".'

Then Lydia threw back her head and laughed, her hair tossing. Anil laughed, too, even more loudly, though he had no idea what galoshes were. A type of horse, perhaps. He didn't want to spoil the moment by asking for an explanation.

As the pair continued redecorating the bungalow, Lydia decided to have Anil turn around the double bed she shared with William so it faced the side veranda, allowing her to enjoy the purple shimmy of the draped bougainvillaea when she woke from her afternoon nap.

'I like the fact you have turned the bed,' William complimented her that evening, as if she had accomplished a feat of great importance.

Conversations with William were often like an exchange of postcards. Short, polite, totally unenlightening and usually arriving at inopportune moments.

Chapter Eleven

CHALAILI
APRIL, 1937

THE SOLIGANJ WEEKLY OBSERVER

Mrs Rajat Banerjee, formerly of Bombay, is in residence
at The Metropole Hotel, Chalaili, overseeing the res-
toration of The Elphinstone Theatre. Mrs Banerjee is
converting the disused theatre into a talking picture cinema. She told *The Soliganj Weekly Observer* that modern
residents of India, of all races and classes, have embraced
the talking picture phenomenon and she looked forward
to screening all the latest productions.

*M*rs Banerjee would have killed that no-good lawyer
of hers if she could have got her hands on him. She
had recovered from her assorted acclimatisation ills and was ready
to propel herself into the ambitious Coronation Talkies project.

The key he had given her to The Elphinstone Theatre opened
the door right enough but what she found inside made her heave
with horror. She had hoped for a marble staircase and wall-to-

wall posters of MGM masterpieces but the theatre was a tangle of dust and cobwebs and her appearance set off a scurry and scuttle of who knew what dastardly creatures. The electric lighting didn't work so she sent Aruna running off down The Strand in search of candles and matches.

The two women stood in a little circle of wobbly candle-light, their eyes wide and lips trembling. They advanced together, gingerly taking steps and praying their feet wouldn't fall on something soft or furry. When Mrs Banerjee's eyes adjusted to the gloom, she held the candle aloft and swept it as searchingly as a lighthouse beacon until she found the stage. Sure enough, her worst expectations were confirmed. There was no sign of a picture screen, just a wooden stage leading to a black-as-Hell-itself chasm and, at either side, a set of steps rising from moth-ravaged carpets.

'Talking picture theatre, my jolly bottom,' she shouted, holding tight to Aruna's hand. As usual, the servant barely grasped what her employer was talking about. The convent-educated Mrs Banerjee spoke English peppered with occasional Hindustani words and phrases and the overall effect was a mumble jumble that Aruna did her best to interpret. She started sobbing so Aruna thought she had better cry as well, although she thought her employer was over-reacting as surely a few dozen workers with mops and buckets could get the place looking spick and span.

Aruna knew that phrase spick and span inside out and, frequently, back to front, as it had been the favourite of Mrs Banerjee's mother, before the house at Chowpatty Beach had been sold and Leela Dhir had been informed by her take-charge daughter that she would be assigned just one retainer at her new apartment. The fashionably modern lodgings definitely would have no space for extra servants and their bothersome bundles and job-seeking acquaintances of distant uncles turning up as surely as waves on the beach or, as Leela Dhir was wont to put it, never-seen relatives at wedding feasts.

Aruna looked at Mrs Banerjee's damp eyes and drooped shoulders and felt her sadness, too. The woman was so good to her, always trilling her thanks and rarely snapping a command. She'd heard from the now-unemployed servants in the once-grand Dhir household that even as a child Premila had spent all her spare time in the kitchen, including in her games the children of the cook and the gardener and the driver and dispensing hugs all round. That is until her parents dragged away their daughter and lectured her on the need to keep menials in their place and that place was not in the middle of her hopscotch or skipping.

Aruna gave Mrs Banerjee's hand a tentative squeeze and she responded with a wan smile. Then they walked out of The Elphinstone Theatre arm in arm and Mrs Banerjee squared her shoulders and took such a hearty breath that she almost toppled Aruna sideways.

Chapter Twelve

CHALAILI
APRIL, 1937

'The cup anemometer has a vertical axis and three cups
that capture the wind. Normally, the anemometer is
fitted with a wind vane to detect the wind direction.
Instead of cups, anemometers may be fitted with
propellers, although this is not common.'
INDIAN FORESTRY SERVICE HANDBOOK FOR FIELD OFFICERS, 1902

William was beginning to feel stifled by Lydia's presence. He had been happily resigned to a bachelor
existence until what he could only bear to think of as The Incident
had occurred. There were plenty of single chaps in the Indian Civil
Service, so many in fact that the annual invasion of unattached
women had been known since the 1800s as The Fishing Fleet. They
would arrive in Bombay at the start of The Season, every October, disgorged from the ocean liners like scavenging insects. With
their letters of introduction to third cousins and casual friends of
friends, they referred to themselves as debutantes but William

knew they were husband hunters. There had been a defeated pack of them ready to board the ship, along with the carpets and cloth and tea and rolls of sisal, when he and Lydia had docked at Bombay. He'd told her that those who sailed back to England unwanted were known as Returned Empties. She had laughed long and loud at the term, tossing her honey-brown hair so it fell in bouncy waves.

But William had managed to remain defiantly unhooked, a situation he defended as being due to the remoteness of the succession of small cantonments and hill stations to which he was posted. He found women to be curious creatures, far too demanding in trivial matters and over-needy of affection. He was seven when his parents were killed and he had been brought up by his aunt and uncle, but mostly his aunt, who had suffocated him with constant attention and made it difficult for him to invite friends to the house, especially female friends.

Aunt Sylvia had once told him a gentleman never looks lower than a lady's chin, an inhibiting piece of information that still made him feel confused in front of the opposite sex, as if he were left over from the Edwardian era. One of the Indian Forestry Service chaps, Nigel McDonald, had been brought up by his grandparents and on an overnight bivouac around a convivial fire William had told him about Aunt Sylvia's pearls of advice, guessing that Nigel would understand. He did, instantly, and the two single men watched the orange flare of the fire and sipped neat whiskey until their heads softened and into a clear cold Indian mountain night they sang the bawdiest songs they could imagine.

Aunt Sylvia would find all sorts of excuses why William should spend his evenings and weekends with her. In the end, it was too difficult to rebel. He could stand almost anything except

76

women's tears and pleadings and the tense silences that filled the house. His uncle was kind but remote and he, too, caved in when Sylvia demanded that things be done a certain way.

It was not Lydia's fault that he felt so disconnected. She was not to know that he had been given a month's grace by his superiors to find a wife and bring her back to Chalaili. William had made it clear to his aunt and uncle that he was in something of a hurry but they didn't appear to suspect any unusual motive. Aunt Sylvia didn't even dissolve into her usual tear-filled theatrics but seemed possessed, instead, of a chilling calm. As it turned out, he had been lucky to have found someone so outwardly suitable who seemed to expect little in the way of expensive gifts or ambitious promises.

William looked through the grimy window of his musty office. He wondered, with a wry smile, if it had been cleaned since his arrival in 1932. That year, Chalaili had been heralded as the wettest place in India. The monsoon had been particularly fierce, waves of water pounding houses like white caps on a reef. An astonishing seventy-five feet of rainfall had been recorded. The following year, the wet title had been wrested back by its rightful owner, Cherrapunji in the north-east, but the damage had been done. The chaps at The Empire Club joked about Chalaili being an official backwater, and they were right.

The medical and military goons were to blame. Useless was the only word for them, in William's opinion. When Chalaili had been chosen as the possible site for a sanatorium, the government medical superintendents had come up with reams of research on the 'exact medical topography' of the Chalaili Hills, and all of it was destined to be inadequate. While they were busy examining physiology ('circulation, secretion, digestion, respiration, loco-motion . . .' William could quote entire slabs of the pompous documents on the workings of invalids), the surveyors were over-loading the in-trays of Calcutta bureaucrats with their findings on elevation, vegetation and climate.

'Climate,' William muttered. From what he could deduct, not once did anyone consult an Indian Forestry Service mete-orological officer about the peculiar nature of the humidity and precipitation of the Chalaili Hills. In the monsoon season, the hill station was completely awash, rains rushed down its paved roads and mud tracks, uprooting trees, pushing over the fragile huts of the natives clinging to the forested lower slopes. William's usual forest walks gave way to slides down mud-shiny defiles that plunged through copses slippery with decomposed vegetation.

The tennis courts at The Empire Club became covered with slime and when the sun shot forth in sharp, near-electrified bursts between downpours, the clay surface would steam. In the final few days before the gigantic rains erupted from fleshy skies, clouds hung low like hundreds of headaches. Faint British memsahibs would instruct their servants to bring ice packs in convoys as they sat on verandas shaded by wet mattings. No sooner had the small blocks of ice, wrapped in layers of cotton, begun to melt and slip down their foreheads then another would appear and the house-boys would move with expert speed, like baton changers in a relay. He'd even seen otherwise prim ladies sitting in the lounge of The Empire Club with cold water bottles on their heads, held in place by ribbons as if they were garden party hats. Droopy clothing hung in damp almirahs, books became spotty with mildew and their spines collapsed to pulp.

When the rains finally came, life was conducted indoors, the stormy downpours battering windows, keeping families impris-oned in musty rooms where fungus formed on shoes and clothing and weak lungs breathed the air as if inhaling grey-green mould. When the sun broke through, steam from the ground fizzed about one's ankles and the light was so intensely clear one's eyes became telescopes, trained to infinity.

So the hill station sat like a rain-quarantined satellite in the annual wet season, an escalating discharge from the mists and electrical storms of early May through the monsoon months from June to August to the calm of early September. William had mentioned the word monsoon to his new wife one evening as they promenaded arm-in-arm aboard the *Viceroy of India* and she had smiled dreamily, working the word around her mouth, elongating it as if it were something desirably illicit.

It was early May and William was already late in commencing his pre-monsoonal field trips. Although he suspected his carefully recorded calculations and investigations sat in yellowing piles on George Windsor's desk, he took his work seriously. It had been a close shave that he had been allowed to keep his position.

The tale, as he replayed it in his mind, sitting on the corner of his desk overlooking Chalaili Valley, was a sorry one, his punishment in no way worth the small brush with pleasure he had enjoyed with Petal Cameron, the wife of the visiting British Resident of Kashmir.

Petal Cameron was a tall, shapely blonde in her mid-thirties, some twenty years her husband's junior. Despite her vigorously maintained youthfulness and willowy grace, she was no great beauty, William recalled. With something of a jolt, he realised that Lydia was, in fact, more striking, at least when she smiled, with her yellow-flecked eyes and quivering lips. But Petal Cameron, he conceded, did possess that indefinable quality that made it instantly known she was available.

79

Petal Cameron had shown an amazing interest in William's meteorological business, attaching her eyes to his at an early-evening soiree at The Empire Club. Her husband had been pontificating to some junior civil servants at the bar, surrounded by a fug of cigar smoke. William had mentioned to Petal Cameron that the smoke rings were forming the shape of various clouds. 'A perfect cumulus,' he had announced as one of Sir Ambrose Cameron's cigar emissions hung in the air.

'I am so awfully attracted to clouds,' Petal Cameron had declared, with a becoming blush. Remembering the scene, William was amazed that he could have been so flattered.

But he had been easily seduced. 'Cumulonimbus are the thunderhead clouds,' he told her as she drank deeply from her whiskey and soda. 'I like to think of them as a sort of cloud factory,' he continued, 'giving birth to other clouds as their anvils shear off into cirrus and cirrostratus.'

'Where do you keep this cloud factory of yours?' she had giggled, well onto her third drink.

'It is dark at present, of course, so we can't go cloud watching but . . . as a matter of fact I have installed a three-cup anemometer in The Empire Club's garden. You may be interested as well in hearing about my aneroid barometer . . .'

'Lead the way,' purred Petal Cameron, with a wink.

It had been wretched luck that the wife of the visiting British Resident of Kashmir insisted they kneel on the grassy edge of the embankment while he demonstrated the three-cup anemometer. Things deteriorated when she fell forward, landing on her side with her flimsy dress drawn up in the region of her waist. As he hastened to pull her up, their awkward coupling was illuminated by two oil lamps. Sir Ambrose's manservant and one of the waiters

80

from The Empire Club were standing above them, eyes wide with fear. Behind them, hovered several shadowy figures.

The largest of these ill-drawn ghosts, defined by the shrill white of his dress collar and cuffs, could be no other than her husband. The others he recognised as various desk wallahs, including that absolute bore among bores, Campbell Nightingale.

'Hello, Amby,' hiccuped Petal Cameron. 'William was just showing me his, er, adenoids . . .'

Petal Cameron, he would recall next morning in bed, as Anil brought him two aspirins, scalding tea and a quartered orange, was wearing panties that seemed to be engineered from little more than a triangle of pale apricot satin.

Less than twenty-four hours later, William received a hand-written letter from Bombay. The matter had gone over the head of George Windsor to Sir Seymour Strong, the Inspector General of Forests. The note was precisely folded in a creamy envelope and at least Sir Seymour, a bluff chap with whom he enjoyed a good rapport, had the heart to write to him personally, rather then sending an official memo, which despite how many confidential commands might be written upon it, would be read by a chain of inquisitive eyes, from upper-upper deck downwards.

'Rushmore,' the note blared, 'you have thirty days to find a wife or there will be hell to pay.'

Chapter Thirteen

CHALAILI
MAY, 1937

THE SOLIGANJ WEEKLY OBSERVER

The dirigible Hindenburg has exploded 200 feet over its projected landing spot at Lakehurst, New Jersey, USA, killing 13 passengers, 22 air crew and one crewman on the ground. The zeppelin had just crossed the Atlantic Ocean after departing from Frankfurt. The cause of the disaster has not been established but various theories have been expounded. Mr William Rushmore, chief meteorological officer for the Chalaili district, told *The Soliganj Weekly Observer* last night that lightning could have played a part and he would be reading further reports with much interest.

Mrs Banerjee was leaning over the front desk of The Metropole Hotel where she had just converted her daily booking to a one month's extendable lease. There were no telephones in the hotel guest rooms so Anjali Gupta had put through a call to Bombay for the new picture theatre proprietress. Mrs Banerjee seemed very agitated and her too-familiar servant girl was standing almost under her arm, patting her on the bottom.

The call was taking a long time to connect and Mrs Banerjee did not appear pleased to be positioned next to Anjali Gupta's pet bird, a hill mynah with glossy black coat and bright yellow bill and legs that swayed on a little swing in a metal cage on the front desk. It let out a series of sharp creaks and although Mrs Banerjee didn't know it, the bird was an accomplished mimic. Within days it would be shrieking 'Come! Come!' every time Mrs Banerjee approached, although she was perfectly oblivious to its copying and presumed the call was part of its tiresome cawing chorus.

At last the call went through and Anjali Gupta withdrew, but not to such a distance that she couldn't hear Mrs Banerjee's side of the exchange. She appeared to be talking to her lawyer, although the shrieking tone she was using was not of the kind one would expect her to employ to address such a professional. An odd woman, thought Anjali Gupta, yelling at her lawyer on the one hand and, on the other, getting about with her servant as if they were friends of equal breeding. As for those saris of hers, the colours were alarming. Today's was a pistol-packing pink. Pistol-packing was one of Anjali Gupta's newest expressions as she had heard Mrs Banerjee use it on several occasions and it was no doubt quite the term about town in Bombay this season.

Mrs Banerjee was demanding various pieces of equipment to be despatched forthwith to Chalaili or there would be hell itself to pay. Anjali Gupta couldn't quite keep up with the extent of the inventory but a talking projector was mentioned and a full-sized screen and even a brand new motor car, the latest full-luxury ultra-modern model.

'Hill station!' she screamed into the receiver. 'You refer to this place as a HILL station? If you must know, I am on the top of a jing-bang mountain. Yes, that's right, a MOUNTAIN. My latest leather footwear with Jaipur beading is entirely unsuitable. UN-suitable. Got that, you idiot? I DEMAND a full-luxury ultra-modern automobile!'

Just when it seemed Mrs Banerjee's demands had been exhausted, she gripped the telephone receiver with both hands, a cocked elbow landing on Aruna's shoulder. Her voice took on a strange accent, which Anjali Gupta took to be American. 'Got all that, you big tub of mush?' she yelled and then crashed the receiver into its cradle.

During the exertion, Mrs Banerjee's sari skirt had worked its way up, almost to her armpits, as if it were swallowing her whole. She was covered with a light sweat and clearly flustered. The bird stopped swinging and fixed her with barley-sugar eyes. Anjali Gupta asked if she'd like a glass of cool water but Mrs Banerjee shooed away the suggestion with a bangled arm. 'You are very kind, my dear lady, but everything is now sorted and in tip-top shape.'

'Come, come,' she called to Aruna and the pair stomped upstairs to Mrs Banerjee's room. 'Tub of mush, tub of mush,' the servant repeated to herself over and over. It was the sort of expression that could come in handy if she were to oversee the no-doubt lazy coolies who would be needed to get the theatre up to scratch. 'Yes, dear, we can thank Mr Clark Gable for such an excellent and useful expression,' said Mrs Banerjee, instructing the girl to draw the curtains so she could take her well-earned afternoon nap.

Chapter Fourteen

CHALAILI
MAY, 1937

THE SOLIGANJ WEEKLY OBSERVER

King George VI has been crowned at Westminster Abbey, London, as King of England. The former Prince Albert, Duke of York, took the throne on December 12, 1936, upon the abdication of his brother, King Edward VIII. Proprietor of The Metropole Hotel, Chalaili, Mr Ram Gupta, contacted *The Soliganj Weekly Observer* to divulge that the disused Elphinstone Theatre on The Strand, opening its doors as the Coronation Talkies picture theatre later this month, has been so named by proprietress Mrs Rajat Banerjee to celebrate the ascension of King George VI.

'The club?' Lydia queried when William finally mentioned an outing. 'Is it awfully formal?'

She had a limited wardrobe of what she now considered very drab dresses. In her feverish desire to escape West Gamble, Lydia had packed one small suitcase. Her bedroom had been abandoned with the coverlet hastily pulled up on her single bed and books still bulging from a set of wooden shelves, just as she would leave it each weekday morning as she dashed off to teach school. She wondered if Evelyn had already commandeered it as a bedroom for Anne, her elder child. She was probably getting too old to share with Redmond, three years her junior.

Lydia emerged from her reminiscences and realised William had left the front parlour and was standing on the front veranda, lighting a cigarette, cupping his hand around the match. She watched him through the bay window, a solitary figure, as aloof as a statue. 'They only ever erect statues of men who have caused deaths,' her father had once told her, laughing hugely. He'd gone on to say that counted him out from a posthumous appearance as a pigeon roost in West Gamble Park, although Lydia wondered if he had ever contemplated killing Mother. Impaling her with a carving knife, perhaps, during one of their arid couplings.

William is so self-contained. He doesn't need anyone else to feel whole, she thought, shivering. A clock ticked loudly in the room and then struck the hour with a chime. The night was very still and William heard it, turned and came striding in. 'Eight o'clock news,' he said, opening the big cabinet that held the wireless. He turned on the government-run All India Radio and crouched forward in an armchair. Lydia excused herself from the room, although she knew he would barely notice she was gone.

⁘

The next evening, William, dressed in his best dark suit, waited for Lydia on the veranda. The taxi driver was also waiting, sitting on his haunches smoking a beedi at the end of Bluebell Cottage's front path. William could see the red glow of his hand-rolled cigarette, shining like a faint beacon to illuminate their passage. A taxi was parked at the end of the ridge past the neighbouring houses and William hoped Lydia was not wearing tomfool evening shoes. Usually he walked or cycled to the club but the track down into town was rough and sharply angled and he didn't expect Lydia to be able to negotiate it in the dark. Finally, he heard her coming down the corridor, with Anil chattering by her side. As they reached the open front door, she turned sideways and Anil reached up to her breast. He appeared to be stroking it.

'What the hell!' roared William. Anil jumped back as if struck by an electric current. The cloth flower fell from his hand and Lydia turned to face William, her face rubious with rage.

'Why are you shouting?'

She was shouting, too. Anil scurried off. He knew the sahib's temper well and wondered if he would lose his job. It would be a pity after fifteen years and hardly worth it for the very slight frisson of pleasure he'd felt upon investigating the bony mound of Memsahib Lydia's left bosom. Like a half-puffed chappati, he decided morosely.

William saw the flower as Lydia bent to pick it up and immediately regretted his anger. He remembered the scene at their wedding as that strangely silent father of hers had gone down on his knees and rescued the fallen corsage. Her face had shone so radiantly.

'Here, allow me,' William said, his hands trembling. When she leant forward and kissed him deeply, he lost his balance on the front step and stumbled backwards. Her breath carried the taste of gin. 'You are wearing your wedding suit, darling,' she said, striding ahead of him to the waiting driver, who leapt to attention and extinguished his beedi at the sight of the approaching memsahib.

Perhaps it was the little victory over the flower that set the course so awry that evening. Lydia's eyes were glowing as they arrived at The Empire Club, she held William's arm with a proprietorial grip. He told her she would have to sign in as his guest.

'I can't wait to join,' she told him brightly as a servant in immaculate white drill held the club register open and she signed Lydia Rushmore with a cursive flourish, perhaps a little extravagant with the skywards loop on the final letter.

The clerk's eyes widened. It would be a matter of minutes before the news crackled around the club like a runaway forest fire. 'The new memsahib thinks she can be a member, too,' they whispered in the kitchen, at the bar, around the lounge with its pillowy armchairs set in convivial semicircles.

'It's gentlemen only, Lydia,' William told her as they took their drinks from the barman and stood on the terrace before adjourning to the table he had booked for dinner.

'There are women everywhere . . .' she protested, waving her glass towards the clusters of over-dressed females seated in the lounge, the sweetness of their perfume escorted around the room by the gust of a punkah fan.

'Yes, but they are guests of their husbands. It's the rules. The only exception is Tuesday afternoons, when ladies can . . . well, do things ladies do. Then they are allowed in without a male companion.'

'How do you know they are ladies?' Lydia hissed, gulping deeply from her tumbler of gin and tonic. She seemed so reckless that William wondered if they should just go home. He could plead a headache. She was fidgeting with that ridiculous flower on her dress and although he knew nothing of female fashion, he suspected it was not the latest vogue. The garment appeared homemade and, if even he thought so, there would be no escaping the scrutiny of The Crows, as he liked to think of the senior wives of The Empire Club circle.

'Liddie . . .' he began.

'Oh, so I'm Liddie, now?' She smiled at him, coquettishly, and moved closer. He panicked at the thought of her searching tongue attacking him again as it had done less than half an hour earlier on Bluebell Cottage's front steps.

'Wait, I don't feel well,' he said, handing her his glass and striding off in the direction of the gentlemen's lavatory. She watched him hurry towards the door with its motif of a maharaja with a turban. The adjoining door carried a drawing of an almond-eyed beauty, one hand holding a corner of her veil.

William referred to her as Liddie during what she chose to refer to as their intimate relations. It was the only time he used any diminutive of Lydia and how she longed to be called by a name that had different personalities. Katherine, she imagined, would be ideal. She would convert to Kathy when they walked hand-in-hand and Katie in bed or at parties. 'You must meet my wife, Katie. She's a tigress in the cot.'

Her husband was taking his time returning from the room guarded by the comical maharaja so she walked into the lounge and stood by one of the circles of ladies, planning to introduce herself.

'What an interesting dress,' commented a woman garbed all in black with a small peacock feather engineered into her French roll. 'Did you make it yourself?'

'No,' said Lydia, blushing slightly. 'My husband's aunt made it for our wedding.'

'What a quaint idea,' said another of the group, holding a

black-and-gold lorgnette. The magnifying device had the effect of making her right eye swim and advance, then retreat, like a curious goldfish in a bowl. Lydia was mesmerised by the effect.

'Rushmore,' she announced, remembering how her fellow passenger had introduced herself on the Soliganj Limited Express.

'Rushmore!' they repeated in chorus, appraising her from top to toe and simultaneously exchanging sly glances. 'My husband calls me Liddie,' she laughed, knocking back the remains of her drink, cracking a sliver of ice cube with her front teeth.

At that moment William appeared. The peacock-feathered woman beckoned him over and gave him a slender social smile. William hadn't seen Dorothy Creswell-Smythe for several months and he registered how unattractive she really was. She had a face that belonged to the sort of creature one would find under an English hedgerow.

'William, dear, proper introductions if you please!'

Her artificial tone appeared to be mocking them both but William recovered his poise. 'My new wife, Lydia,' he announced and proceeded to reel off the six names of the seated females. One by one they nodded at her, as Lydia repeated their names in a stage whisper.

'Well done!' barked the woman with the lorgnette. 'Dorothy?' Lydia stammered, realising she may have forgotten the running order.

'Charlotte Montague!' she roared. 'That's dear old Dorothy Creswell-Smythe over there.'

She waved a diamond-garnished hand in the direction of the bobbing peacock feather, whose owner had visibly stiffened at the employment of the word old. But then they all burst into raucous laughter and closed in on themselves, a pointed signal that Lydia and William were dismissed.

William caught his wife's elbow with his hand and walked her away from the group, as effortlessly as if steering a rowboat rudder. 'Grey is such a difficult colour,' she heard one of the harpies announce and a ripple of laughter followed. 'It's dove,' Lydia tried to retort over her shoulder but William's hand was gently covering her mouth and no one heard her.

The head waiter positioned them at a table for two near the open glass doors to the terrace and next to a dish-clearing station. 'Nice and cool,' she said, as they were seated, starched napkins snapped open and orders taken. In fact, it was cold and William knew they had been sequestered at the Club's worst table. 'We are in Siberia,' he said to Lydia, but she didn't understand his inference and was already ordering her next drink. They left after bowls of peppery mulligatawny soup and stringy slabs of roast chicken. The Crows had departed their perches and were dining, silently, at tables for two with their husbands, with the exception of the widowed Dorothy Creswell-Smythe, who was still seated in the lounge and snoring like a train.

Only a party of young men, whom Lydia took to be single, were making merry, smoking and joking at the bar and, eventually, whipping one another with rolled-up menus. Lydia fell asleep in the taxi, her head on William's shoulder.

That night they made love with a vigour that startled Lydia. William drove himself into her with uncustomary urgency and Lydia lay beneath him fighting back waves of alcohol-induced nausea. The tall window leading from their bedroom to the side veranda was slightly open, the thin curtains lightly whisked by the evening breeze. She imagined a movement beyond the rustling fabric and fancied she saw the outline of Anil. She reached to click off the bedside light and her heart quickened. 'Call me Liddie,' she moaned, but William had finished and his weight lay upon her, like decades of loneliness.

Chapter Fifteen

CHALAILI
MAY, 1937

THE SOLIGANJ WEEKLY OBSERVER
Mrs Rajat Banerjee has announced a slight delay in the
opening of her Coronation Talkies picture theatre due to
the need for extensive renovations. There have been no
performances at the Elphinstone since Monsieur Pierre
Melvin, the famous French cyclist, held a reverse cycling
demonstration there in 1928 after successfully pedalling
his unicycle backwards around the Bombay Presidency,
with some towing assistance along the narrow-gauge railway line between Soliganj and Chalaili. 'Many prominent
Chalaili residents have helpfully informed me that the
stage collapsed during Monsieur Melvin's presentation
and he suffered light injuries,' commented Mrs Banerjee.

Mrs Banerjee still had much to achieve before Coronation Talkies opened its doors that Friday night.
Her Bombay lawyer had done her bidding and despatched to her

by rail and road the projector, the ready-to-assemble screen and other necessary items on her list, although there was still no sign of the motor car. All in good time, she thought grimly. She wasn't through with him just yet.

Picture Madam, as her staff already referred to her, was a hurricane of activity. Since that first shocking glimpse of the theatre's interior, she had commissioned armies of cleaners to repair broken chairs, scrub the red leather seats, wash and polish the coloured glass globules of the chandeliers, brush the wall-to-wall carpet to within an inch of its life and, where it could not be fully revived, discreetly place patterned Kashmiri rugs. Sweepers were beating stratas of dust from the heavy velvet curtains that hung across the front and side doors leading into the theatre's recesses. She had considered having new curtains made but the originals were patterned with the vice-regal crest and this prevented her from pulling them down. If the memsahibs got wind of such disregard for Empire, who knows what gossip would ensue.

Seamstresses from the Chota Chalaili bazaar were patching mothy holes and tears. 'Invisible mending!' she roared at the women who pedalled furiously on Singer sewing machines, bobbins spinning wildly. The needlework proved expert but the new material was not quite a match for the old. Mrs Banerjee made a mental note to keep the lights dim, in case any of the elegant British women noticed the makeshift nature of the draperies and engaged in snooty remarks.

The night before Coronation Talkies was due to open, sleep eluded Mrs Banerjee. She shifted and turned in the big double bed in her room at The Metropole Hotel. The sign on the front of the picture theatre had been freshly painted the previous afternoon, in a dazzling peacock blue against the ochre walls of the stone building.

She had demanded a neon sign from Bombay but that palooka lawyer of hers had said such things were not easily available and he would be ordering her one if only she would show some patience.

Patience, patience. Only a random inspection of the sign-writer's pencilled sheet at the very last moment had prevented one of the petty disasters that routinely stalked Mrs Banerjee. The stupid fellow had been about to paint Carnation Talkies, having taken his instructions from Aruna. Who would have thought that silly lisp of hers could cause such mischief.

'Carnations, carnations,' she moaned as she heaved herself up on The Metropole Hotel's slightly over-starched sheets and plumped up a hillside of white pillows. She wondered what other disasters lay in wait. The life of Mrs Banerjee, nee Miss Dhir, had not been without its complications and she knew that settling into her new life in Chalaili was unlikely to be free of incident.

❧

Miss Premila Dhir was the daughter of a well-connected Punjabi businessman who had moved his family to Bombay when she was a small child to further his import and export dealings via India's busiest port. Precisely what goods had their comings and goings entrusted to Shyam Dhir, his wife and only child had never quite known. Whatever these mysterious trading items were, however, they had no proper showplace in the Dhir residence. Electrical goods turned up from time to time but the suspicious servants refused to use them so the cardboard boxes were kept deep in the kitchen where they served as stools and small tables. When itinerant vendors or third cousins of the cook or would-be under-gardeners came calling, they would rest upon cartons containing toasters, electric fans and kettles.

But much to the loud and continuing regret of Premila's mother, no British bone-china shepherdesses, wafting lengths of fine French chiffon, glittering glassware or other such boast-worthy foreign falderals found their way into the comfortable Dhir residence near Chowpatty Beach. Premila sometimes fancied her father was dealing in opium or prostitutes or some such illicit wonderment. She had no evidence nor indeed any knowledge of what form black marketeering might take. She simply noticed the jauntiness in her father's step on certain late-for-dinner evenings, when he would pluck a flower from the front garden and present it at the door to her mother who would be forced to unfold her arms to receive it. Premila would stand behind her mother and there would be an exchange of looks between rummed-up father and daughter, an unspoken conspiracy that did not include Mrs Dhir.

They had married late and Leela Dhir was in her thirties when Premila suddenly arrived 'as triumphantly as a monsoon', as her mother was wont to declare, unprompted.

Premila was doted upon by her father, lavished with food and sweet milky drinks by an assortment of ancient servants, several of whom seemed entrusted with no other duty but to bring Missy Baba her chota hazri, or little breakfast, consisting of bed tea (five spoons of sugar, heaped) and a plump sugar banana, neatly peeled, at the pip of seven on school days and to ensure that sweet snacks and a frothy glass of buttermilk would be waiting for her when the rickshaw dropped her off after her expensive convent lessons. A servant would be positioned at the gate, to greet her and take her schoolbooks, lest she tire as she walked along the crescent-shaped driveway of the Dhir residence.

It was a life as soft and unresisting as marshmallow and Premila often spent all weekend in bed, ringing a little bell for the servants to bring jalebis, her favourite whorls of deep-fried batter dipped in syrup, or ladoo sweetmeats or rasmalai in saffron milk. She read British and American novels her father brought home for her and imagined fantasy scenarios in which she was raced off by a handsome hero intent on romancing her in a faraway cave, albeit one furnished in the latest style and with plenty of barfi milk fudge on hand. Her marks at St Sophia Convent for Young Ladies were adequate but she had little ambition, preferring to fill her mind with foreign stories and films and avoid the worthy debates and discussions of her brainbox classmates.

Leela and Shyam Dhir believed a Catholic education was the best available: the nuns were strict, the English tuition superior. They boasted to their friends about the attributes of St Sophia Convent for Young Ladies, sidestepping the topic of their daughter's academic achievements.

Premila had been known as Big Bum since the day she started school. Classmates would imitate her waddle and collapse into giggle-wheezing heaps at their imagined cleverness. She endured all sorts of taunts about her size until the roly-poly Queenie Bhatt enrolled in high school. Premila joined in the chorus of 'Queenie Fat, Queenie Fat' with the loudest voice of all, but she couldn't keep up the taunts. She discovered Queenie crying so violently in the toilet block that she held her hand and promised to be her best friend.

'Bosom chum?' asked Queenie, with a damp smile, and the girls assessed the bounciness of their respective chests and hugged each other with a wild, fierce laughter.

Premila's father deemed university a waste of time and money for his daughter, despite her mother's wailings about the status it would bring to them all. For once he paid little heed to his wife's hysteria about the need for further education, given that the girl was no great beauty and suitors would be thin on the ground, if on the ground at all, and at least if they could make a teacher or a nurse of her, the Dhirs could hold their heads high.

'What have I done to deserve such a double-chinned daughter,' Leela Dhir moaned day and night, to her husband, the servants, the pictures of her ancestors, the paisley-patterned wallpaper in the formal sitting room and the brass-knobbed wooden chest in the hallway that had been acquired on her honeymoon in tranquil lakeside Udaipur, that sweet period before she had had a baby elephant wrenched out of her. Of course, she blamed her husband's family for the mountainous outcome. Neither his mother nor his two sisters were what you would call feathers.

Premila's father used his importing-exporting connections to acquire her a position at Bombay's Galaxy Talkies, working in a stuffy little office at the rear of the theatre. Premila's duties involved answering the telephone and dealing with complaints from the public, of which there were many, as the owners disliked spending money on their operation and the seats frequently collapsed. She took to wearing an old pair of her father's spectacles, even though her young eyesight was excellent, and shoving her copious hair into a bun at the nape of her neck. She felt these alterations gave her an air of wisdom and authority. Premila also spoke only in English at Galaxy Talkies, the language of her Chowpatty Beach home and her convent lessons, even though her Hindustani was perfect, particularly when used in sweet shops.

'It is the language of the starving classes,' was how her mother referred to Hindustani. Leela Dhir gave all instructions to her household servants in English and they had to guess at the meaning of her ringing commands. Premila knew this was so she could moan about their disrespect and general worthlessness.

When complainants found their way to Premila's cupboard-like office at Galaxy Talkies, she pretended she understood not a word they said, squinted at them through her thick glasses and handed out refunds so they would disappear quickly, leaving her to her novels and imported caramels. Even when a disgruntled customer brought a non-complainant, a dead rat the size of a mongoose, to Premila's cubicle, she simply raised her eyebrow and produced a sticky handful of free tickets.

Premila watched every film that played at Galaxy Talkies, some many times over, marvelling at the ease with which celluloid heroes and heroines conducted their lives, almost entirely without interference from their mothers.

Then one evening as the Dhirs were finishing their evening meal in the dining room overlooking the rear garden, Premila's mother clapped her hands and made a cheery announcement. 'It's all arranged!'

Mr Dhir looked into the profound depths of his pudding bowl as if it might contain clues to the creation of the universe. Premila took no notice, presuming her mother was referring to one of her drinks parties, the holding of which always involved complex shopping expeditions, migraines and mock resignations by at least two shouted-at servants.

Mrs Dhir shot her husband a dark look but he remained silent, head bowed. Premila's chair was closest to the window and she looked out at the emerald patch of over-tended lawn and saw the mali standing by a bed of canna lilies, sloshing water from a length of black hose. A flock of golden orioles was gathered in a peepul tree. Peelolo, peelolo, they sang in fluty whistles. A wobbling dewdrop hung from a leaf and the pendant glistened in the fading light, seeming to hold within it the colours and reflections of an entire world.

It was an image that would forever stay with Premila. That perfect moment, the peach-pink sky, the tinny notes of the yellow birds, a peacock mewing in a neighbour's garden, the safety of her parents' home.

'Six suitable marriage partners have been selected. We start on Saturday.'

'Marriage!' Premila spluttered, a spurt of gulab jaman in sugared rose water erupting from her mouth and landing inches short of her mother's clasped hands.

'I am still not sure about this, dearest one. Premila may yet find a love match . . .'

Mrs Dhir turned on her husband, eyes blazing. 'Love match! How is she going to find a love match when she never goes out, just pictures, always pictures, sitting in that Galaxy Talkies den of foreign carryings-on while her hips widen to the size of a bus . . .'

'Sweetest Leela, please, don't talk about our darling girl like that . . .' He tried shooting her one of his handsome Friday-night late-homecoming looks, but to no avail.

'Don't you "Sweetest Leela" me. Where is this love match appearing from, pray tell? Is one of her talking picture cowboy heroes going to gallop along Marine Drive and sweep her up on his horse, although how he'd shift her off the footpath is a mystery to me . . .

'I told you everything is arranged and you have no idea the concessions I have had to make. Everything is flexible, I told the families, weight and height and other such things, all matters are negotiable, just I told them probably no boy under five feet tall.

The wedding pictures would be so awkward, even sitting down Premila would be too unbalanced . . .'

Premila pushed back her chair, preparing to run.

'And, what's more, you can forget all those follow-fashion colours, my girl,' tut-tutted her mother. The sari Premila was wearing was one of her favourites, utterly yellow with matching hair-ribbons, and she flew off in a golden swoosh like an enormous wounded canary, slamming her bedroom door with such ferocity that the pin-up of Clark Gable behind it became dislodged.

Shyam Dhir followed her and tried tapping lightly on the door but Premila had turned up her radio, privately purchased from Galaxy Talkies earnings, extra loud. He decided to go for a walk and let his temper cool, although it was inevitable he would have to sit down again with his wife and listen to what over-complex arrangements she had already made.

Leela Dhir was bored to the marrow with her life and the prospect of a lavish wedding had lifted her spirits so high she felt as if she was about to take flight. Premila's size and laziness and the fact she had inherited the Dhir family hips and her father's shifty-winky eyes only made arranging her nuptials all the more scintillating a challenge. Everything about the wedding would be modern deluxe, no interfering astrologers getting in the way with their best-matching birth charts and auspicious dates. She could not see past the actual wedding, to a lonely existence in the Dhir household without even her uncooperative daughter for company during the long days when her husband was importing and exporting.

The bride-viewing sessions would take place in their amply furnished front room, where Leela Dhir also kept the family's new Kelvinator refrigerator. It had come to her husband as part payment of some awkward deal, but the cook had threatened to resign on the spot if the gaping monster set foot in his kitchen. So Leela Dhir left it right where the delivery wallah had dropped it, plugged it in and spent the day opening and closing the door every few minutes to see if the chicken she had placed inside was getting nice and cold. With so many gusts of warm air it remained at room temperature so, with loud declarations about newfangled rubbish, she left the refrigerator overnight on the maximum setting and the contents turned to a bird-shaped mush of ice.

Eventually she unplugged the infernal thing and displayed it like an electric shrine, always contriving to allay guests in its vicinity, forcing them to make an admiring comment, as only the most prominent households in Bombay were known to be Kelvinator-equipped. If guests showed any sign of opening its door, she would hastily ferry them away, lest they uncover a cargo of walking shoes and wellington boots. It was close to the hallway and the front door and she was ever a practical woman.

Premila's mother treated each bridal viewing like a party, grandly playing the hostess, making sure the parents of the prospective groom and his assorted relatives were perched on velvet-covered chairs she had the servants haul from the dining room. She lined them up along the walls, as if in the vestibule of a doctor's surgery. The carving chair from her dining setting, with its long arms and wooden corona, looked like a mini-throne and it was on this that she insisted the would-be groom sit and be served by Premila, who swayed in and out of the kitchen, bearing platters of finger food. The bun was replaced with blue-black plaits, into which the servants had inserted jasmine flowers looped on a length of green twine. She was forced to wear only royal blue saris as her mother had read in a magazine that royal blue promoted a slimming look and it was a fact that no other colour Leela Dhir knew of did her daughter any favours.

'Very fair-skinned,' the mothers of sons conceded. 'There are sons in those wide hips,' one of their husbands murmured approvingly, giving Premila's rear a longer-than-necessary assessment as it disappeared into the kitchen past the silent Kelvinator, which she desperately wanted to fling open so her mother would be mortally embarrassed. Her father forced himself to smile graciously, as if the various assemblies had been presented with a mounted photograph of his daughter and, after a pause had, as one, agreed it was quite nicely framed.

Premila lied about making the samosa and international savouries herself, as her mother had instructed she must, nodded obligingly at everyone and tried not to yawn too noticeably as the sessions stretched into late-afternoon. None of the boys came close to being handsome. Their defects ranged from weeping acne to a minor limp to double-thick spectacles to a lazy eye that looked everywhere except where it was meant to. One was as fat as herself and she matched him samosa for samosa while his parents shot each other despairing looks, no doubt wondering how they could afford such a ravenous girl as a daughter-in-law. Another boy, tall and thin, refused all food so she waved the platter under his nose and leant forward, hissing in an American accent, 'Hunger strike, eh? How long has this been going on?' It was a line from *It Happened One Night*, presently showing at Galaxy Talkies. She had seen it six or seven times and had key sections of dialogue down pat. Until all this silly marriage business began, she had been toying with the idea of changing her name to Claudette, as she fancied a resemblance to Miss Colbert, at least from the neck up.

She had all but forgotten the lot of these monkey-face pal-ookas until a week after the final bride-viewing afternoon when her mother came running in, 100-per cent-guaranteed-pashmina wrap flying. She held aloft an envelope in the style of a victory flag. 'Finally! The Banerjee family will take her!' she gasped to her husband, as if Premila were a shoddy commodity they'd had the devil's own job trying to shift.

Shyam Dhir was impressed. The Banerjees were a notable Bengali trading family recently relocated to Bombay from Cal-cutta and the would-be groom's father was a competitor of his in import-export circles. Such an alliance between the families could only bring prosperity. He imagined striking extravagant deals with his daughter's father-in-law, pushing them through with jovial persistence.

'Excellent news!' he trumpeted, banging the breakfast table.

'Does he have a name?' asked Premila. Her parents turned to look at her, disappointed that their reverie had been inter-rupted. 'I think Rajat or somesuch,' her mother snapped. 'Details, daughter, always you want details.' Mr and Mrs Dhir took a turn in the garden, arm in arm, while Premila remained at the table, shooing away her servant who tried to bring more tea. Then she watched the old woman shuffle off, both hands holding the silver pot in its knitted cocoon. After her marriage, tradition dictated Premila would take up residence with the Banerjees. The servant's days, she thought grimly, were numbered, too.

Chapter Sixteen

CHALAILI
MAY, 1937

THE SOLIGANJ WEEKLY OBSERVER

This week marks the thirtieth anniversary of the opening of the narrow-gauge railway line from Soliganj main
line terminus to Chalaili. Mr S. Forshaw, President of the
Soliganj Railway Appreciation Society, told *The Soliganj
Weekly Observer* that he hoped to secure the presence of
the Commissioner of Railways, Sir Randolph Cosgrave,
at a ceremony on Soliganj Station and commemorative
ride to Chalaili aboard a carriage fitted with a wet bar and
airconditioning unit.

'Memsahib?' Anil stood in front of Lydia's chair in
the front parlour of Bluebell Cottage. Lydia looked
up from her book. 'The new picture theatre on The Strand is
opening on Friday. May I be allowed to go?'

'I will ask, Anil,' she replied.

Lydia knew William would never agree. Servants didn't

have outings. He condoned his wife's visits to the market with Anil because it was common decorum that she would require a boy to carry her purchases. He didn't want to believe they walked together, chattering away like a pair of chums and that Lydia usually carried the shopping while Anil sauntered along, greeting his stallholder friends and stopping at the chai stand for a milk-sweet glass while Lydia patiently waited. The servants of the Empire Club Crows talked incessantly among themselves about the behaviour of Memsahib Lydia and Anil. She had upset the order of their world and they viewed her with contempt. As for Anil, that fellow led too soft a life and maybe he was party to the memsahib's favours as well, although he assured their servant spies that was not the case, she being too much like a carcass for his taste.

William paced the veranda after dinner that night. His wife was at the back of the cottage with Anil and he could hear their kitchen-sink babble. 'Lydia!' he bellowed and she came, hurrying along the corridor, a cotton dish rag in her hands. 'What do you think you're doing?' He grabbed the cloth and threw it out through the front door and into the garden, where it landed on a rhododendron bush and stuck, like a mob cap. 'This hanging around in the kitchen has to stop. You are not to do any housework. That is why we have a servant!'

'Anil is my friend,' Lydia countered, in a small, tight voice.

'Nonsense, woman! I've told you before that if you persist with this rubbish, we will have to let him go.'

After William left for work the next morning, Anil knelt beside Lydia as she sat on the veranda on her favourite top step overlooking the valley.

It was an unusually cool morning for early summer; the chiffon mists hung like curtains in the valley's cleavage. He ran and fetched a woollen shawl for her, one she'd bought a few days earlier from a Himalayan trader in the bazaar. He handed it to her and she wrapped it around her shoulders. Anil wanted to perform the action but kept himself in check. There was something childlike about Lydia and although he had positioned himself on occasions to afford a surreptitious look at her breasts, he did not find her desirable. Even the night he had hidden on the side veranda when Sahib made love to her was less than exciting. He had expected his penis to rise and harden in his hand, ready for him to fondle its pleasurable firmness until his hand was runny-sticky.

But that region remained inert. He had seen Lydia's face, reflected in the lamplight, and she looked tired and alone. When William's hand strayed down to sample her breast, he did so with the detachment of a cook squeezing a lemon.

He snapped back. Lydia was thanking him and snuggling into the softness of the wrap.

Anil retreated to the garden pump to do the washing. Shockingly, while Anil was alone at Chota Chalaili bazaar one day, Lydia had done the laundry herself, working away in the hut behind the house, taking buckets out to the pump, filling them and soaking and wringing the clothes, then spreading out their cold dark wetness on bushes and fences to dry. Like most residences in Chalaili, Bluebell Cottage had only cold running water. Hot water for baths was prepared by heating pots in the earthen fireplace and transferring it to buckets to be lugged into the bathroom until the big claw-footed tub was full.

The majority of British families in Chalaili had dhobi wallahs who collected the clothes and returned them, spotless and pressed, from the communal laundry ghats by the river. William had never liked this detached system, much preferring the idea of Anil being thoroughly occupied every moment of the day. He also knew that dhobi wallahs were practised gossip gatherers and their trips to and fro the bungalows on Chalaili's ridges were like the passages of courier pigeons.

When Anil returned inside, Lydia was lying down before lunch with a headache, which he attributed to the sinking levels of the gin bottle on the polished teak sideboard. He retreated to his tiny room off the kitchen and dug beneath his mattress. His fingers quickly found the calico pouch, tied with a twist of string, where he stashed his savings. The amount was growing, alluringly, as he was able to add the change from the household shopping. Lydia had no interest in keeping track of domestic finances and handed him money as they entered Chota Chalaili bazaar, pointed to what she wanted, and never expected any to be returned as they began the long uphill walk back to Bluebell Cottage. A paisa here, two there, the money was mounting.

꙳

The opening of Coronation Talkies was the talk of Chalaili. Anil was not entirely sure what a talking picture entailed but he suspected that it would be Mrs Banerjee who did most of the talking. He knew he could not sit with Lydia. Several of his chums at Chota Chalaili bazaar had been involved in The Elphinstone's conversion and had told him that the non-Indians had their special section. Anil knew a side-by-side seating manoeuvre with Lydia would cause Chalaili to hold its collective breath in such a massive inhalation that the hill station could bounce wildly from its moorings, like a lightly tethered balloon.

It would be enough to peep back from the third-class front-front seats and see Lydia in the European section, wearing her wedding dress – the one with the uncooperative flower. He would have to be careful to be early so he didn't end up right under the screen, a position from which one could develop permanent neck strain if there were as many talking-picture ladies in petticoats as his bazaar friends suggested.

Printed notices, with an almost-kissing picture, announcing the opening of Coronation Talkies picture theatre had been circulating around Chalaili all week. Mrs Banerjee had employed some local youths to hand them out. Their instructions had been to visit every shop and house, every little stand in the bazaar, even the makeshift shelters on the town's outskirts where itinerant traders and beggars made their homes.

'Those people in the shacks cannot read, madam,' the oldest of the pamphlet boys had told Mrs Banerjee, who seemed to be in charge of every last thing, in the curious absence of her husband. 'That is beside the point,' she retorted, adjusting her shawl over a fleshy shoulder. 'Pictures they can understand. You give them the papers, you point to the picture of Mr Clark Gable and Miss Claudette Colbert staring into each other's dark-dark eyes and you tell them time and place. Now go, go!'

The boys did as they were bid for a few hours but were soon sidetracked by the appearance of a sugar floss maker in the bazaar. Digging deep into a metal tray beneath his glass-fronted contraption, he spun his hands around and around and like a conjuror with a freshly plucked rabbit, suddenly brandished the feathery substance on a wooden stick. They spent the few paisa Mrs Banerjee had given them in advance in an instant and spent a leisurely afternoon licking and savouring the sticky substance, watching it harden and change colour to a deep rose when they wet it with their spittle. As darkness crept over the bazaar and the stallholders shut up the intricate lockings on their barrows and stands, the boys gathered the pamphlets they had failed to deliver.

Running up and down The Strand, they stuck them hurriedly under doors, disposed of a great wad in the post office's ornamented pillar box and shoved a handful in the outstretched hand of a langur monkey sitting on the front steps of Grindlays Bank. The monkey had been leisurely picking fleas from his partner's shaggy coat and, after inspecting the pamphlet, licked off the sugary remnants from its corners and tried the taste of newsprint, too.

Chapter Seventeen

CHALAILI
MAY, 1937

THE SOLIGANJ WEEKLY OBSERVER
Mrs Rajat Banerjee's Coronation Talkies picture theatre will open on Friday evening next at 7 p.m. sharp. Attendance is by invitation of the proprietress or purchase of tickets by advance reservation or at the door. The premiere presentation will be *It Happened One Night* starring Miss Claudette Colbert and Mr Clark Gable. For further information, contact Mrs Banerjee care of The Metropole Hotel, Chalaili, telephone 240.

*M*rs Banerjee rose early, washed and was the first at breakfast in The Metropole Hotel's high-ceilinged dining room, a battalion of waiters lounging against the wall beside the kitchen door. Guests were so few that several of the serving staff spent their work shift sleeping in a standing position, one leg cocked against the wall for support. They reminded Mrs Banerjee of stick-thin wading birds.

'Big day, today, Madam,' beamed Ram Gupta, wringing his hand obsequiously. She smiled at the manager and requested a pot of Darjeeling, extra strong. 'What time is Mr Banerjee arriving?' he asked, snapping his fingers for tea. Waiters ran in all directions.

'That is not known,' she replied. 'He is arriving from overseas, delays are possible.'

'What is it that Mr Banerjee is doing overseas?' asked Ram Gupta. She gave him one of her most imperious looks. He was a small man, his hair over-oiled, his nose so long and sharp that his glasses kept sliding down, prevented from their ultimate descent by a deep brown-black mole that acted as a boulder on a slope.

'Import-export business.'

Ram Gupta was impressed. He had been deciding whether to give the Banerjee couple his most splendid room, a suite with separate parlour and shuttered porch overlooking all Chalaili. It was reserved for health officials, minor government dignitaries and the occasional guest who might need to be greased up, most particularly kitchen inspectors.

'Madam,' he began, and Mrs Banerjee looked at him over the rim of her tea cup, her pinky finger stuck at a pukka angle, as if she were pointing at something of scenic interest. He noticed the finger was all but smothered by a gold ring, a star ruby the size of a pea protruding above a nest of diamonds. He looked into her eyes, deep and brown and quizzical. What a terrifyingly handsome creature, he thought to himself, pushing the errant glasses up his slippery nose.

'Yes?'

'Madam Banerjee, would you do my humble establishment the very great honour of occupying our Maharani Suite for the remainder of your stay?'

112

She looked at him in surprise. The Metropole Hotel had no Maharani Suite that she knew of. If it had, she would have demanded such superior lodgings from the start.

'Such a suite has only just been named,' murmured Ram Gupta, guessing the reason for her puzzlement. 'Until now it was being known just as Room Three. Such an unworthy title, no?'

'That depends,' she smiled, studying the hotel proprietor's sweaty brow and slightly shaking hands. She realised she was having a romantic effect upon him and it pleased her deeply. 'Show me Room Three, and I will decide. On behalf of my husband, too,' she added, as Ram Gupta bowed, pulled back her chair and gestured the way upstairs.

❧

While Mrs Banerjee was settling herself into the capacious surrounds of the Maharani Suite, the foreman of her building team, Mr Sham Lal, was sitting in the theatre's little goldfish-bowl office, testing the padding of the cashier's stool. He was feeling particularly pleased with himself, having skimped on various orders that Mrs Banerjee had placed and pocketed the difference. She had wanted new tracks installed for the stage curtains. He had suggested that an oiling and tightening was all that should be required but she had been most insistent, raising her voice at him in front of his workmen.

The workers had giggled behind his back at the vision of this large woman bossing him mercilessly, waving her hands and all but thumping him with the large black handbag that accompanied her everywhere. He had tried to help her with it as she stepped over the workman's materials on one of her early visits to the refurbishment site. She had snatched back the bag from his hand as if he were a common bazaar thief about to abscond.

113

So it served Mrs Banerjee right, he mused, that she had been short-changed. The theatre would function well enough for a brief period and by the time the problems materialised, he would be well clear of this laughable outpost, back in his beloved Bombay. Sham Lal heard a rattle of keys and the front door of Coronation Talkies sprung open. Mrs Banerjee stood on the threshold, a beam of sunlight catching her new domed coiffure, with the effect of a golden halo.

'Welcome, Madam,' cried Sham Lal, springing out of the glass cubicle like a flying fish. She sashayed in, wobbling ever so slightly in new blue shoes. 'Your hair! First-class job, I must say.'

'Enough, enough,' she replied, shooing him aside, but she was delighted at the greeting. After moving into the Maharani Suite that morning, she had been escorted like a queen to the Lakshmi Hair and Beauty Studio by Anjali Gupta. Brushing aside various ladies who were waiting in the salon's small anteroom, the hotelier's wife had advanced her to the top of the queue. 'Picture Madam, Picture Madam,' she whispered, like a muted mantra. Mrs Banerjee wondered if all Chalaili referred to her in this way. Anjali Gupta had picked up the title in Chota Chalaili bazaar, where conjecture about Mrs Banerjee was at fever pitch.

One of the women shouldered aside in the bustle was Lydia Rushmore, who smiled at Picture Madam.

'Good luck for tonight,' she said warmly.

Mrs Banerjee was taken aback that such a beautifully spoken Englishwoman should address her so, as if she were an actress about to mount a stage for a gala performance. 'Thank you,' she mumbled, disappearing into Lakshmi Hair and Beauty Studio's inner sanctum as three of the Empire Club Crows burst through the salon's pink-curtained door in a rush of sun parasols and anxious servants attempting to both go before the women to announce their arrival and to follow in their wake in case of snared fabrics and umbrella crises.

☙

Sham Lal was shouting last-minute orders to his labourers. Mrs Banerjee could hear the din beyond the curtains with the vice-regal crests and patchwork effect of velvet repairs. She looked around the theatre, pulled down several seats at random, testing their springs and then letting them fly shut. 'Good, good,' she said to herself. Preparations were almost complete.

The projectionist, Mr K. K. Rao, had arrived that morning and was set up in his tiny booth high at the rear of the theatre. He was a quiet man, recommended by her no-good lawyer in Bombay, who had connections in the film industry. She prayed he really was a projectionist and not some scoundrel her lawyer had despatched to embarrass her.

'Excellent choice,' was Mr K. K. Rao's only comment when she instructed him that *It Happened One Night* would launch the premiere season at Coronation Talkies. He took over the projection room silently and competently and Mrs Banerjee sighed with relief.

From the foyer came an almighty crash and the sound of splintering glass. Sham Lal's voice could be heard roaring above the wailing of a worker who was obviously being boxed about the head. She emerged to see the framed photograph of King George VI on the carpeted floor, its glass shattered. The foreman's face was contorted with rage. 'This is what happens when you employ idiots!' he ranted to Mrs Banerjee, as if she were responsible for the composition of his work force.

115

'Take out the glass and hang it anyway,' she instructed.

'Yes, Madam, right away . . .'

As she began to walk off, Sham Lal spoke again. 'Mr Banerjee is arriving, when?'

'Unfortunately delayed,' Mrs Banerjee replied, swinging the crested curtain behind her with a vigorous swish.

Chapter Eighteen

CHALAILI
MAY, 1937

THE SOLIGANJ WEEKLY OBSERVER

Thought for the Week: 'Truth and non-violence are not cloistered virtues but applicable as much in the forum and the legislatures as in the market place.'

M. K. (Mahatma) Gandhi

Lydia begged William to allow Anil to go with them to the opening night of Coronation Talkies. 'For the last time, Lydia,' William said, trying to keep his voice low and controlled, 'this is not Anil's night off and we have no need to be accompanied by a servant on a social outing.'

Anil was standing in the corridor. He had washed and starched his kurta suit and oiled his hair. He smiled at William and Lydia, a near-blinding flash of white. William saw that Lydia smiled back and then clapped her hands as if Anil's freshly laundered presentation was worthy of applause.

'Please, Lydia,' urged William, pushing her outside and

shooting Anil a punishing look as he closed the door. 'I don't know when you will ever learn,' he admonished as he clicked shut the gate to Bluebell Cottage. 'Servants do not respect their masters unless the right balance is maintained.'

Lydia remained silent but hooked her arm into his as they walked to their taxi waiting at the end of the lower ridge. Unbeknown to William, Mrs Banerjee had asked Veronica O'Brien of the Lakshmi Hair and Beauty Studio to slip Lydia a double invitation to the post-screening drinks party she had arranged at the Maharani Suite of The Metropole Hotel. Lydia knew that Anil could be home from his secret theatre excursion and have their evening cocoa ready well before she and William left the party and arrived back at Bluebell Cottage.

A large crowd had gathered outside Coronation Talkies. The doors were not yet open but dozens of Chalaili residents had arrived early. Mrs Banerjee's printed flyers had promised half-price seats and free refreshments. Taking advice from the young men who had distributed the papers for her, she had hired the services of the sugar floss man from the bazaar. She had no real idea what was involved in the mysterious floss-making nor how long it took him to concoct his confections.

Setting up his mobile apparatus as the doors finally opened, the roly-poly sugar floss man would not be hurried, despite the surge of customers. He twirled and twisted the frothy pinkness and even bowed with a tummy-wobbling flourish as he presented his finished creations. The queue in front of his cart was becoming long and troublesome, with much pushing from behind to hurry things along.

Fearing a riot as the customers shouted and jostled for their free sweets, Mrs Banerjee leapt from her ticket counter and bustled up and down the line. 'Later, later, all you can eat. Come now, or you will miss the show.'

There was a rush through the curtains, several of the more slippery customers evading Sham Lal, whom Mrs Banerjee had redeployed as ticket collector.

Only the English, observed Mrs Banerjee, walked regally past, ignoring the sugar floss vendor, and took up their positions at the back in the bank of Reserved seats, its best linen anti-macassars embroidered with a swooping R. There seemed no question that the simple matter of white skin entitled one to enjoy this special section. It was fully occupied when she noticed that Lydia Rush-more, the nice lady from the Lakshmi Hair and Beauty Studio, was still walking along the aisle, arm in arm with a tall blue-eyed man. Panicked, Mrs Banerjee noticed that Mr and Mrs Ram Gupta had squeezed themselves into two seats on the far side of the back row of the Reserved section. She mimed at them to move, pointing to Lydia Rushmore and the man she presumed was her husband.

She had desisted from erecting the Europeans Only signs one saw at railway stations but the R-insignia chair cloths served the same purpose. She regretted moving the Guptas on. They were kind people and Anjali Gupta's hair was elaborately constructed, as if she had spent the entire afternoon cooking under one of Lakshmi's Paris-model dryers. But Ram Gupta merely smiled and indicated it was of no consequence. They moved off in one smooth move-ment towards the fast-filling front section and the Rushmores were seated. Lydia had not noticed the flurry. Her husband, thought Mrs Banerjee, had seen it all and accepted that was how things should be. She was momentarily annoyed by his patrician aloofness and made a note to correct the slight against the Guptas at her supper soiree.

The lights dimmed, the projectionist started the film with

perfect timing. Mrs Banerjee had seen *It Happened One Night* so many times that she stood against the side wall, nervously playing with her Hyderabadi gold bangles. In the sulphurous glow of the theatre, she saw the uplifted faces, many enhanced with sticky pink moustaches. She noticed Sham Lal and the fat sugar floss fellow had slipped inside, too, drawing the curtains behind them. At the very front of the theatre, in the third-class neck-breaker seats, there were boys sitting piled in threes, rotating every few minutes so each had a turn on top. Mrs Banerjee sighed with frustration. At first she had not intended to introduce a cheap section but she had surmised there weren't enough Britishers and high-up Indian families in Chalaili to make Coronation Talkies profitable. So the bazaar scallywags with their infuriating lap gymnastics had to be let in, even if it was unlikely they had purchased a ticket between them. While Mrs Banerjee was still fuming at the situation, another pack of the scoundrels crept in from the rear exit, which was supposed to be guarded by Aruna.

The boys got to their knees and scuttled past Mrs Banerjee's feet like alley dogs. She managed a few well-aimed kicks at the procession and was about to charge off and have cross words with Aruna when she saw the girl pressed against the wall, an arm's length away from her. Aruna's hands were clasped, her eyes saucer-wide with excitement. Aruna had never seen a talking picture and she was positively glimmering in the dark.

She turned and smiled at Mrs Banerjee. 'Everything hunky dory, Madam.'

'Everything is not hunky . . .' But Mrs Banerjee couldn't bring herself to berate the girl. She heard the strident voice of Leela Dhir hissing in her ear, 'Servants are not to be trusted. Especially the pretty ones, you mark my words . . .'

'Shut up, Mother,' Mrs Banerjee exclaimed, a little too loudly. Several heads turned her way. She stared solidly at the screen and groped for her servant's hand.

'Hunky dory, Miss Chowpatty.' They giggled softly, in unison.

☙

The film was rolling smoothly. The air smelt of expensive foreign perfume, overlaid with Mrs Banerjee's excessive attar of roses. The cheap beedi cigarettes of the bazaar boys shone in the dark like the eyes of foxes. Mrs Banerjee had a momentary concern about fire safety but the bulk of the audience was in the second and first class seats with exits all around. She allowed herself to breathe deeply, squeezing Aruna's hand. The opening of Coronation Talkies was shaping up as a great success. Her social standing in this little hill station, far from the gossip and speculation of Bombay, seemed assured.

Mrs Banerjee should have remembered what her mother had told her on her wedding day. 'Never be complacent, dear girl. Just when you think life is all fizz and bubble, Fate can step in and cast its giant shadow.'

The shadows, in this case, were quick and furry and bearded with pink. The kerfuffle started in the foyer. Sham Lal had not shut and locked the doors to The Strand, as he had been instructed, allowing a troupe of monkeys to cavort through, their noses twitching at the sweet promise of the sugar floss cart. They had jumped aboard the trolley and dug deep into its cavernous entrails, scooping out crusts of sugar. As they jockeyed for position and dived in, tails waving in the air like rodeo ropes, the cart overbalanced and they jumped off, heading not for the open door into The Strand but through the imperial curtains to the darkened bowels of the theatre.

A great scream went up as the first monkey landed in the lap of one of The Crows in the Reserved seats and peered at her with interest, its white ruff framing a black face as perfectly as an Elizabethan collar.

Members of the audience started jumping up. Some suspected the commotion was a fire, others thought the shadowy explosions of fur must be giant rats. Anil, who had been too late even for the triple-decker third-class section, had also sneaked in at the side entrance, unnoticed by Mrs Banerjee or Aruna, and was standing close enough to touch Picture Madam.

He must save Memsahib Lydia from these disease-riddled creatures! He grabbed the chair upon which Sham Lal had been seated and began dancing down the aisles, as he had seen a tiger-tamer do many years before at a travelling circus that had visited his village. There was no question of harming the animals, however, as such creatures were considered incarnations of Hanuman, the Hindu monkey god.

Someone shouted to put through an emergency call to the District Superintendent of Police at Soliganj. It was rumoured he kept an official Monkey Misdemeanour File with a view to ridding Chalaili altogether of the louche pests, sacred monkey gods notwithstanding. There was a general roar of approval at this suggestion and an impromptu round of applause.

Mr K. K. Rao pressed a master switch in his projection booth and turned on the lights. Lydia saw Anil in action and laughed heartily, especially when a frisky female presented him her rump and began shuddering with desire. Luckily for Anil, William was otherwise occupied, assisting the Manager of Grindlays Bank, Edmond Montague, recover his wife, Charlotte, from her undignified sprawl between two rows of Reserved seats. She had dived for cover at the mention of rats but had become unfortunately wedged and dislodged her hat, a wide-brimmed affair of the fete-opening variety that prior to her little accident had been successful in blocking any view of the screen for the unfortunates seated behind.

Although the melee was in peril of getting out of hand, with ladies standing on seats, swaying and screaming, no one had actually left the theatre. Once the threats of fire and rats had been quashed, the appearance of the monkeys had turned the evening into something of a romp. Anil was being cheered wildly as he jousted along the aisle. Mrs Banerjee was shrieking for a microphone as she stood at the centre of the stage in front of the giant pull-down screen (she was determined her lawyer would pay for this sorry lack of fitted wall-to-wall model), an imposing vision in grasshopper-green silk sari and blue shoes of terrifying elevation. As she shook her fist at Sham Lal to get on with it and bring the microphone, her rolls of flesh undulated in waves. Between her choli blouse and the navel-skirting waist of her sari drapes, a generous circumference of bare skin bounced like a life-saver ring. William was transfixed, as were many of the British chaps, whose attentions should have been directed towards pacifying their outraged wives.

While the microphone was being put into place, Mrs Banerjee lost her balance for a precarious moment and grabbed the velvet curtain at the side of the screen to steady herself. At that moment, the rusty old fixtures Sham Lal's workmen supposedly had replaced gave way and Picture Madam collapsed on to the floor of the stage, acres of velvet toppling on her, expelling puffs of ancient dust.

Chapter Nineteen

CHALAILI
MAY, 1937

THE SOLIGANJ WEEKLY OBSERVER

The British journalist and explorer Mrs Rosita Forbes unexpectedly visited Soliganj on Monday evening last when her car broke down during her tour of the Bombay Presidency. Mrs Forbes is researching material for her forthcoming book, tentatively titled *India of the Princes*, and she made contact with the senior staff of *The Soliganj Weekly Observer* to discuss political issues of the day, including the inevitability of Independence. 'There is no longer any possibility of ruling India with a handful of our best men,' she said.

The ill-fated opening of Coronation Talkies was the number one topic in Chalaili for weeks but the hoopla certainly was not bad for business. Mrs Banerjee's lawyer did, in fact, have excellent connections in Bombay and she was able to devise an entertaining agenda of films for the theatre's first month, changing titles every three days and then repeating them some time later, on a carefully calibrated roster. Mr K. K. Rao was proving to be a steady and reliable projectionist, and she had special offers every week, from Ladies Night to Chums are Fun, with the promise of two-for-one tickets. When it came to publicising her assets, Mrs Banerjee was a canny operator. She had no idea the unmarried chaps at The Empire Club referred to those Thursday screenings as Bums are Fun.

After a month installed in the Maharani Suite at The Metropole Hotel, she knew she had to find a house. It did not befit her status to be living at a hotel and with Aruna marooned in the staff quarters somewhere in the building's straggling rear yard, she was unable to summon her at a finger's snap.

Mrs Banerjee liked the slightly crumbling hotel, where the owners treated her with such respect and the servants fawned over her. She was pleased that she had managed to avoid complex questions about Mr Banerjee by alluding to his overseas trips. 'Chalaili is so far away for him,' she told Anjali Gupta one evening as the hotelier's wife massaged her feet with fragrant patchouli oil. 'I will have to live alone for now.'

Mrs Banerjee's Bombay lawyer had failed so far to send her a full-luxury ultra-modern car so Ram Gupta arranged for the hotel's vehicle and driver to take her on a house-searching mission. There were empty bungalows on the two ridges above Chalaili, most of which had been occupied by minor British officials and their wives who had moved on to other postings when the hill station's dampness had become an unavoidable issue. He had the car specially polished and the driver was instructed to put himself at Picture Madam's beck and call for the duration of the afternoon. She was to meet the regional housing administrator, a certain Mr Campbell Nightingale. He would be travelling up from Soliganj to show her several residences.

Mrs Banerjee wondered at the authenticity of any such transaction, being aware that such houses must be government property. She also felt a little confused at the protocol of dealing with an Englishman who would be attempting to secure her business.

'Ah, Picture Madam,' exclaimed a portly middle-aged man who squeezed himself out of a shiny black car as The Metropole Hotel's smaller vehicle drew up alongside. She bristled at the use of such familiarity. It gave whatever dealings would be done, she thought, far too frivolous a tone.

'Mrs Rajat Banerjee,' she announced firmly, extending her gloved hand.

The Englishman quickly shoved a file of papers under his left arm and shook hands heartily.

'Greetings. I am Campbell Nightingale. May I call you Rajat?'

Mrs Banerjee withdrew her hand in surprise. 'Rajat is my husband's name.'

'Ah, yes, of course, silly me. Please, let's walk to the upper ridge. I have a particular residence in mind . . .'

Mr Nightingale set off with Mrs Banerjee tottering in his wake. If she were to live up on the lofty ridge, she realised, she would have to resort to firmer shoes. The bungalow he presented at a distance was not grand, its paintwork exhausted, dead vines, as ragged as lengths of rope, stretched across the timber boards of its exterior. But as they skirted the front corner and crunched along a narrow pebble path, the view hit her like a punch between the eyes.

The position was superb. Chalaili lay below, as textured and rippled as a freshly flung eiderdown. The bungalow felt as high as an eyrie, sitting proud on brick pylons with three broad front steps leading to a terracotta-tiled veranda. Mrs Banerjee liked the tipsy angle of the house and its slight forward lean, as if at any moment it might sail off the precipice. Any airborne passage would be kept in check, she noted, by an old wire fence choked here and there with bursts of peach and white bougainvillea. It stood very close and high to the house as if it had been erected as some kind of precautionary device. 'Monkeys?' she asked, noticing the closeness of trees and being convinced that those furry Chalaili rascals were capable of all manner of thievery and interruption.

'The bungalow has been empty,' Campbell Nightingale was saying, disregarding her question, 'for about five years. Most of the regional departments were moved to Soliganj, you see, so many homes were vacated.'

'But the government still owns it?'

'Yes and no.' The Englishman was inspecting his fingernails for imaginary specks of dust. He coughed lightly and led the way up the trio of steps. He removed a bunch of keys from his pocket and after four flustered attempts found the right one and pushed open the heavy front door.

The house was a classic bungalow with a centre hallway and four sizeable rooms leading off it. The front two were sitting and dining rooms respectively and the two behind would serve as bedrooms. Mrs Banerjee noted, approvingly, that there was a windowseat in the right-hand front room, indicating it had been planned as a reception salon and lounge. Plaster was peeling off the walls in great strips, but she surmised that could be easily repaired. One of the back rooms had a door which led to a cement-floored bathroom in the centre of which sat a cast-iron bathtub with a rolled rim and claw feet. Its enamel was clotted with rust and a vitreous green stain surrounded the plughole.

'The kitchen, Mrs Banerjee,' announced Mr Nightingale, giving a door at the very end of the hallway a light push. She was astonished that he imagined a woman of her class and breeding would ever need set foot in a kitchen but she noticed the puzzled look on his face, so she followed him in, through a small breeze-way. The two of them stared at the bare low-roofed room with its pressed mud walls. The ceiling had caved in over a bench containing two cement recesses, which she took to be washing-up hollows of some sort. There was an earthen cavity in one wall which she imagined to be a fireplace. A screech owl nesting in the wooden beams visible through the rotted plaster ceiling regarded the intruders with startled eyes and hurriedly took flight, its whirring and fluttering echoing around the bleak room. An open door in one corner led to a tiny cubicle where a sunken charpoy was pushed against a far wall. That would be Aruna's room, she thought, but it was essential she did not show any undue pleasure at the suitability of the residence.

'Much work would be required, Mr Nightingale.'

'True, but perhaps Mr Banerjee is well connected in building circles?'

She was shocked that the Englishman should imagine she was married to someone in the lowly business of construction, some kind of glorified hutment wallah. Campbell Nightingale caught the look of displeasure and recovered himself quickly. 'What I meant, Madam, is that The Elphinstone has been so magnificently refurbished to become Coronation Talkies. Such a project could not be accomplished without the very best connections in architecture and engineering.'

That was better. The use of the word engineering restored her status so she gave Mr Nightingale one of her brightest smiles. 'Is it possible to look at your other residences?'

'This is by far the best, both in condition and situation. I am too embarrassed to show you the others. Even now, I didn't realise the kitchen had deteriorated so badly . . .'

'How much?' she asked, lest the Englishman start wringing his hands like a common carpet trader trying to wrangle a sale in Chota Chalaili bazaar.

'The actual rental is something we must discuss,' he answered, not catching her eye. 'And Mr Banerjee . . .'

'Mr Banerjee prefers I make all the household decisions. Now, what is the price, sir?'

She put an emphasis on the honorific that she suspected Mr Nightingale did not deserve. She very much doubted he had the authority to be wandering around Chalaili showing off disused British bungalows and negotiating their extended leases.

'Would you be requiring furniture?'

This was too much for Mrs Banerjee, that this man should think she had arrived in Chalaili like a genie popped from a bottle, with no family heirlooms, sandalwood almirahs, Kashmiri double-knot carpets and finest copper kitchen utensils to her name.

'How much?' she spluttered. If he was going to resort to cheap marketplace tricks, so would she.

He readjusted his papers and named a price far less than she had expected, a ruse that immediately confirmed her suspicions.

Looking towards the expansive sweep of view and squaring his shoulders, Mr Nightingale made a little speech. 'The rent would be paid direct to me, Mrs Banerjee. To save you the inconvenience of despatching money to Soliganj and relying on the imperfections of telegraphic transmissions, I would call every month at a mutually agreeable time and would possibly spend the night in Chalaili with my wife. I have heard much about your Coronation Talkies theatre and my wife, Patricia, is a devotee of the moving picture, and we would be grateful if you could commence a standing reservation for our seats.'

The orotund language amused Mrs Banerjee, who could spot chicanery from miles off. But she didn't much care that the pompous little pen-pusher was probably going to pocket the rent she would pay for the bungalow. It was absurdly cheap and, as he had mentioned, its situation would have to be among Chalaili's finest.

'Standing on seats at Coronation Talkies is not allowed,' she giggled. It took Mr Nightingale a few seconds to understand her joke but, when he did, he shook with laughter, revealing fine white teeth, slightly pointed. 'Like a rat,' she thought.

'Of course you and your wife must be my guest every month.' I will make it a Monday, she thought with satisfaction. In cinema circles, Mondays were always slow nights.

Chapter Twenty

WEST GAMBLE, SURREY
MAY, 1937

THE FINCHLEY EXAMINER

West Gamble Infants School will close on the thirtieth of June. Pupils will be re-enrolled at Finchley and any inconvenience caused by this closure, due to the declining number of pupils, is regretted by the Surrey Education Board.

Evelyn Moss sat on a garden chair in full afternoon sunshine and positioned a cup of tea on a little side table. She wanted both hands free to tear open her sister Lydia's letter in its airmail envelope, the right-hand corner a carnival of colourful postage. Later she would carefully cut off the stamps for her son, Redmond, but for the moment she put the envelope in the pocket of her apron and smoothed out the creases in her sister's two-page letter.

'Dearest Evelyn,' Lydia began, 'I hope this finds you and the family all well and safe. I scarcely know where to start in describing my new life. Everything here is so very different from West Gamble and I would not be surprised if you find my descriptions rather too colourful to believe.

'Our home here is called Bluebell Cottage and it is very satisfactory and the front parlour, in particular, is most comfortable, with a beautiful aspect over the valley and pine trees lined up like rows of soldiers. You would be surprised to see William's garden or I should say our garden, as it is now. As part of his ongoing meteorological experimentations, he has planted many tropical trees and although some have fallen to frost in the winter just past, he has advised me we can expect a profusion of fruit in the summer. I am particularly looking forward to trying a mango, of which there are many varieties in India. We may even have guavas in the garden, which is a pink, fleshy fruit, I am told.

'I visit the bazaar in the village of Chalaili each day as we have no ice-box at Bluebell Cottage and it is necessary to replenish fresh meat, fruit and vegetables. Everything spills out of enormous wicker baskets and the shops are not shops as you would imagine, but makeshift stands with no proper windows or even doors. The butchery, if one could call it by so formal a name, has meat hanging outdoors, including headless goats with their skinned haunches exposed but their poor old tails still attached.

'You would be amazed to see the variations in produce: the tomatoes are orange in colour and the carrots a pinky red. Apples are sugar-sweet and tiny enough to crunch in one or two mouthfuls. Peaches are as pale as pearls and the brussels sprouts are the size of coins and full of flavour. The grapes are unimaginably delicious and range from purple to green with every mottled shade between.

'Rice, lentils and oil are delivered every couple of weeks by a man with a barrow and there are a few shops in Chalaili where I can purchase other household necessities. I am always accompanied to the bazaar by our servant, Anil, who I believe could be around my own age but he will not reply to my questions directly so I have not pressed him on this point. He has been very helpful in explaining to me the various foods sold at the little stalls. He takes with him a whisk of straw and chases away the insects, and even the occasional monkey, of which there are many, before I look and we decide what to buy. As he does all the cooking for us, the purchases really are his concern, unless William has requested a special dish. I believe William would exist solely on a diet of Indian food but, I believe, in deference to my unaccustomed stomach, he often tells Anil that we will eat roast chicken and boiled potatoes, or a simple omelette or cheese macaroni, prepared without spices.

'When the shopping is accomplished, we walk back up the hill, quite slowly because the slope is almost as steep as a ladder. Sometimes I stop at one of the vantage points to rest on a wooden bench and look at the view. The first time I did this, Anil dropped to his knees and began to fan me with his whisk. I told him I was perfectly able to do the fanning myself and he became very sulky, hanging behind as we continued our walk and banging around the pots as he prepared lunch.

133

'William tells me I must remember Anil is a servant, not a friend, and there are certain tasks he must perform for me, as they are part of his duty.

'There has not been an opportunity to meet many of the other English people here but William has taken me to his club and we enjoyed the recent excitement of the opening of a cinema. It is owned by a very successful businesswoman from Bombay and William says that more and more businesses are being run by Indians and the British should prepare themselves for the worst, although I am not quite sure what he means. Sometimes men leave one adrift with so very little else to say, don't you think?

'Anyway, dear Evelyn, please pass on this letter to Daddy and tell him I miss him very much. Hugs to the children and with fondest love to Tom and yourself. Lydia.'

Evelyn reached for her tea. The cup was still hot, Lydia's long-awaited news had taken just a few minutes to read. She had expected a long and lively letter, full of amazing tales of elephants and camels, holy men and rogue tigers and all the glittering totems of a storybook India. Evelyn had imagined her sister transformed by marriage to William into a brighter, more daring person. The very thought of India carried such a gauzy glamour. She had pictured Lydia walking through fields of wildflowers in a mountain outpost that looked like an extreme version of Switzerland, complete with wandering cows. Indians, Evelyn had read somewhere, were very fond of cows.

Evelyn closed her eyes and tried to imagine Lydia and William living up in the clouds but the small unsatisfactory picture she got was like looking through the wrong end of a telescope. Reading between the lines of her sister's short letter, Evelyn decided she was having a grisly time, fascinating new fruit and vegetables aside. She wondered if she should mention to Lydia in her return letter that the school where she had been teaching was closing down. 'Better not,' Evelyn murmured, refolding the letter and placing it back in its envelope.

'Lydia is as lonely as hell,' she would tell her husband that evening, when the children had kissed their parents goodnight and trotted off to bed. She finished her tea just as the side gate was flung open with an animal-like squeal and Redmond and Anne came careering into the garden, schoolbags flying. She wondered if Lydia and William had given any thought to a baby.

Chapter Twenty-one

CHALAILI
MAY, 1937

THE SOLIGANJ WEEKLY OBSERVER

Mr John D. Rockefeller, American multi-millionaire and founder of the Standard Oil Company, died on the twenty-third of May. He was 97 years old. When contacted by *The Soliganj Weekly Observer*, Mr David Oakley, President of the Soliganj Businessmen's League, commented that Mr John D. Rockefeller's philanthropy, especially in the area of education, should serve as a model for all successful businessmen.

William knew he should take Lydia out more often and let her partake of what limited society Chalaili afforded. That insufferable Dorothy Creswell-Smythe was always organising moonlight gymkhanas during which the likes of Harold Gilbert would fall off his damned horse, or holding seances in the library of The Empire Club to summon her dead husband. Whether he was ensconced with angels or down with the devils below, the Creswell-Smythe blighter should stay well put and not encourage her, thought William.

Luckily, Lydia was not particularly sociable and appeared to be enjoying life within the boundaries of Bluebell Cottage, nattering away to Anil as he swept and dusted, supervising the meals. William continued to try and stop her from such fraternisation but she would have none of it.

'You are gone all day,' she said firmly. 'I must be allowed to talk to Anil while you are . . . investigating the weather.'

He had thought her passive and undemanding when they met, but he discovered she was stubborn over little things. The idea of masters and servants had seemed a novelty in her first few days at Bluebell Cottage but now she openly informed William the system appalled her.

Anil told William one Saturday afternoon, as Lydia took her nap, that the memsahib walked beside him when they went out and always insisted on carrying the heavy vegetables. Everyone in Chota Chalaili was whispering and laughing.

William explained to Lydia that evening that Anil must be allowed to do his work or else they would have to let him go.

'Would he go home?'

'Home? This is his home.'

'But where does his family live? You must know where he comes from.'

William looked at his wife in despair. 'His village is hundreds of miles from here, in the south. He goes there once a year and gives his father all the money he has saved, gets roaring drunk for a week and returns to Chalaili.'

'Poor Anil. That doesn't sound like much of a holiday.'

'Servants don't take holidays!' William laughed, gulping

at his peg of whisky and water. 'They are a different race, Lydia, get that through your head.' He pushed back his dining chair and strode to the glass-fronted drinks cabinet.

'My father taught me there is only one race, William, and that is the human race.'

Her husband had his back to her, mixing himself another drink, and her soft-spoken words were lost in a melody of splashing water and clinking ice. But she knew Anil had heard. He appeared through the doorway to clear the table, one broken sandal flapping. He must have been positioned in the hallway during their exchange, thought Lydia. His arrival along the hallway from the kitchen would have been signalled by the slap of leather on wooden boards.

William turned and looked at Lydia's sad face. Anil dropped a knife and hurriedly recovered it on to his tray.

'How much do I pay you?' asked William.

Anil shot him a confused look and then turned to Lydia with appealing eyes.

'Enough,' he mumbled, continuing to stack the tray.

'This month there will be a bonus. Mem thinks you need a holiday.'

'That's not exactly what I said, William . . .'

'Go back to your village for two weeks, not a day more. But find us a girl in town to do the housework while you are gone. Maybe the Guptas at The Metropole Hotel know of someone . . .'

'I will do the housework myself, William,' announced Lydia, leaving the table with a toss of her used serviette on to Anil's tray. She marched out to the veranda, clutching her pack of Craven A cigarettes.

'Oh, Christ,' said William.

'Oh, galloping galoshes,' exclaimed Anil with a huge grin as he returned to the kitchen.

Chapter Twenty-two

CHALAILI
MAY, 1937

THE SOLIGANJ WEEKLY OBSERVER

At 12 noon on the twenty-eighth of May, President of the United States of America Franklin D. Roosevelt pressed a telegraph key in the White House in Washington to officially open the Golden Gate Bridge in the city of San Francisco to vehicular traffic. Some 200 000 pedestrians had been allowed to cross the bridge since the previous day. The Golden Gate, which took four-and-a-half years to construct, is the longest suspension bridge in the world.

Lydia felt suspended in Chalaili, like something caught and undigested.

She had a leaden feeling her life in India was destined to be meted out in meaningless triumphs. She wondered, in fact, where this fantastic place called India actually was. It seemed to her she had parachuted into the hill station, her one miserable suitcase labelled Bluebell Cottage. She had little memory of the Bombay docks or the disorienting train ride and felt as if she were living in the rarefied clouds while India in all its mystery and magic was spread below.

'Sometimes I feel like a seagull and Bluebell Cottage is my nest,' she said. Her verbal postcard to William went undelivered. Lydia tried again.

'I'd like some flying lessons.'

'Ask Anil for anything you need, dear,' he said, looking at his wristwatch. 'Time to switch on the wireless for the eight o'clock news.'

Lydia decided she had to grab Chalaili by the throat and try to make some sense of it. Apart from her visits to the bazaar with Anil, she had only ventured to the Lakshmi Hair and Beauty Studio in The Metropole Hotel Arcade on a few occasions and had her hair done. The time had passed companionably and the pretty owner, Veronica O'Brien, appeared to have access to all the latest products from Europe. She told Lydia that the new Permanent Waving System by Eugene and Emil of London and Paris was very popular and both Dorothy Creswell-Smythe and Charlotte Montague had availed themselves of its merits. That was enough to discourage anyone, Lydia laughed to herself.

She had also dropped into Mary Christie's little shop and purchased a bar of milk chocolate and some lovely writing paper and matching envelopes patterned with peacocks. Mary asked her a few cursory questions about how she was settling in and then turned her attention to a large rose-smelling Indian lady in a thrilling scarlet sari whose arms were festooned with so many bangles they reminded Lydia of the sets of quoits on the games deck of the *Viceroy of India*. Lydia continued to browse and when the fragrant customer loudly purchased a box of imported caramels and turned to leave, Lydia saw her face and realised it was Mrs Banerjee, back in fine form after the unscheduled entertainments of her opening night.

Without consulting William, Lydia had walked down to The Empire Club one Tuesday afternoon, hoping she could muster the courage to infiltrate the tight-knit circle of The Crows. They would have none of it, pointedly turning their backs as she approached. In an auctioning voice, Charlotte Montague was boasting of the exquisite perfume and vigorous climbing prowess of her Gloire de Dijon roses.

'Rose botherers,' quipped Lydia from behind their stockade and wandered off to explore the rest of the club. To her delight she discovered a reading room, amply stocked with shelves of books about India and a sprinkling of the classics. There was a small white-headed woman just on the verge of leaving. She smiled and introduced herself as Miss Heather Craig of the Loch Fyne Tea Rooms on The Strand.

'Oh,' said Lydia, 'I have been meaning to drop by for a cup . . .'

'I wouldn't bother if I were you,' laughed Miss Craig. She spoke with a light Scottish burr, the ends of her sentences in danger of taking flight. 'We hardly ever open.'

She reminded Lydia of certain school teachers at St Martin's Primary School in West Gamble. Energetic, determined women, always in rude health and given to unexpected outbursts.

Miss Craig had small pale-blue eyes and a crinkly smile. She assessed Lydia. She saw loneliness. She smelt it, creeping from Lydia's pores.

'Are you free at three this afternoon?'

Lydia nodded. 'Meet me outside the Post Office and I'll take you on a tour of Chota Chalaili. It's time you got to see what goes on behind the scenes at our little hill station. Fresh air will do you good.'

She bustled off without expecting a reply.

Lydia turned her attentions to the Reading Room. FOR REFERENCE PURPOSES ONLY announced a hand-written sign above the rows of books on India. Damnation, thought Lydia. She had hoped to borrow an armful and retreat to Bluebell Cottage. Instead, she perused the shelves and their various categories: Natural History, Horticulture, Military History, Equestrian Affairs and so on. She ran her finger along the frankly uninviting spines until it landed on *A Guide To Simla: With A Descriptive Account Of The Neighbouring Sanatoria* by W. H. Carey.

Sitting in an easy chair by the window she flipped through its age-dunned pages. The book had been published in 1870 and there was no mention of Chalaili in the copious index. Imagining that Mr Carey's pronouncements on health probably would apply to all Indian hill stations, she read his views on early rising, of which he was an energetic fan. 'Bracing, pure air fans the cheeks of the early riser,' he had written and Lydia looked out the window and imagined William setting off on his bicycle in the mornings.

He never looked happier than when he was off to attend to some kind of weather matter. Lydia was dreading his bivouacs. He had pointed out to her the forestry service's *dak* bungalow on the opposite side of the valley. It stood tiny and alone as if clasped like a brooch to the vast green bodice of the hills. 'I will stay a night or two there soon,' he had said. Seeing her gloomy look, he had patted her on the shoulder and told her she would be able to wave to him from Bluebell Cottage. Lydia knew she could dance naked along the ridge with a monkey on each shoulder and William wouldn't be able to see her from such a distance.

One of the club's servants came into the reading room and turned on a brass lamp near Lydia's chair and asked if she'd like a drink. 'Gin and tonic,' she replied, not giving a toss if information of her daylight drinking winged its way straight to the Crows.

She resumed her reading of Mr Carey's views on healthy bodies and minds. 'Exercise is well entitled in various respects to be considered a common aid to physique . . .'

The drink arrived and Lydia reached for her purse. 'No, Mem, sign chit please.' Lydia signed her name guiltily, wondering if it would appear on William's monthly statement as alcohol or something slightly less incriminating, like an afternoon beverage.

'There is no one in the way,' continued the athletic author, 'you can walk, trot or race as suiteth you best; your blood warms, and your spirits rise with the rapid rush through the air, and you have acquired a blithe vitality that does not desert you for the rest of the day.'

Lydia gulped deeply and happily clinked the ice cubes around her teeth. When the waiter appeared she ordered another G&T . . . a double. Lydia declared to herself that there was something irresistible about the tartness of tonic water, not to mention the courage-giving properties of juniper berries.

She browsed a few more chapters and Mr Carey went on and on and on, pontificating on posture, the ideal ventilation of one's hill-station cottage, the correct space for a sleeping chamber (no less than 1440 cubic feet) and the fact a full-sized male consumes over two hogshead of air every hour, even when sleeping (no mention of the breathing capabilities of the weaker sex).

She finished her drink and sauntered back to the main salon.

Standing by the bar where at least one arc of The Crows' circle could clearly see her, she launched into deep-breathing exercises, flinging wide her arms and bringing them back to her chest. She did this for a few minutes while The Crows stared, rubbernecking for a good view and chortling behind their hands.

'Almost half a hogshead,' she announced and then walked off, leaving the women to fantastic conjectures about the sanity of the new Mrs William Rushmore.

☙

At three sharp, Lydia stood outside the Post Office. She saw two Misses Craig approach and she rubbed her eyes, wondering if her habit of ginning up in the afternoons was affecting her eyesight.

'There you are, my girl,' said the right-hand vision. 'Let me introduce my sister, Margaret.'

The left-hand vision whipped out a hand to be shaken. 'We're identical twins, dear,' she said.

'Peas in a pod!' they trilled in unison.

Lydia burst out laughing and the women joined in her chuckling, two pairs of small pale-blue eyes shining like polished buttons.

They stood either side of Lydia in their duplicate green cotton dresses and commenced the descent to Chota Chalaili. Lydia had never attacked the bazaar from this upright angle. Anil always took her down the slope past The Empire Club, Holy Cross Church and Chalaili Hospital, pausing for a rest by the lookout.

With a Miss Craig at each elbow, Lydia was hoisted along as they zigzagged their way down a stony defile to a set of steps, which if they were any more vertical would be a ladder. The sisters were shaped like hens and at least twice Lydia's age but they seemed amazingly spry. Courtesy of their cupped hands under her elbows, Lydia felt herself drifting downwards as if she were gently parachuting.

When they reached the bottom, Miss Heather (or was it Miss Margaret) stopped at the first stall and began chattering in fluent Hindustani. The man was presiding over an assortment of bulging open-topped sacks, their cargo a range of marvellous colours, textures and smells.

Using a stick he pointed in turn to each sack and Miss Margaret (or was it Miss Heather) rattled off the descriptions to Lydia, who felt like a child being explained complicated problems on a blackboard as a teacher drummed a cane marker.

'Fennel seeds, peppercorns, mustard seeds, black cardamom pods, green cardamom pods, fenugreek seeds, curry leaves, coriander seeds, tamarind pods . . .'

Lydia's head was whirling. She hoped there wouldn't be some kind of test later to make sure she'd been paying attention.

The Misses Craig proceeded to Mr K. Wallia's Pickles and Daily Needs where an enormous array of moist chutneys and pickles were on display in big glass bowls with metal dipping spoons. The Daily Needs section seemed to be comprised of towers of uncooked pappadums, rolls of pink toilet paper, boxes of matches and bottles labelled 'English Spirits'.

'English by name only,' said the right-hand Miss Craig, with a nudge. 'It's homemade but damnably weak.'

As they strolled along, Lydia learned about Bombay Duck ('Not a duck at all, dear, but dried pike, bit on the pongy side'), watched oil-dripping snacks being juggled in and out of blackened cast-iron pots and several times she was almost sent flying by cyclists with flopping dead chickens draped over their handlebars.

Then they turned the suggestion of a corner and stopped in front of an evil-looking canvas-draped shelter.

Before she could protest, the Peas In A Pod had spirited Lydia inside.

And so it was that Lydia Rushmore was introduced to the substance that kept the Misses Craig so merry and bright-eyed and so disinclined to ever actually open the Loch Fyne Tea Rooms and do anything resembling afternoon-tea hostessing.

The three women sat on a saggy charpoy while an enormous man in filthy pyjama-style pants and singlet clattered about. 'He's a bootlegger,' said the right-seated twin as if this was a noble calling and Lydia ought to be impressed to be in his presence.

On a little tin tray, he lined up bottle after opened bottle until the Misses Craig clapped their hands in unison and whispered, 'Yes.'

He produced three small metal cups and poured to their brims.

Lydia took her first sip of distilled coconut palm sap and she could have sworn her head was poised to blow off. Her scalp tingled so fiercely she could feel every last follicle. She gagged and gasped for breath while the Peas In A Pod sat demurely, pinkie fingers outstretched as if they were taking elevenses with the vicar.

'Ha . . . ha . . . what is it?' coughed Lydia.

'Arrack,' they chirped in duet.

The left-seated twin leant against Lydia and giggled. 'You look as if you are having an arrack attack.'

The Misses Craig downed their glasses, a tinkle of coins changed hands and the trio emerged into late-afternoon sunshine. Lydia was sure she was going to be sick.

With one in front and one behind, they push-pulled Lydia

up the slope to The Strand. Her knees were wobbling when she reached flat ground. The twins stood side by side regarding her with eyebrows raised in amusement.

'Same time tomorrow?' asked Miss Margaret (or was it Miss Heather?).

'I . . . I . . . I will have to ask my husband,' whimpered Lydia as she turned and wobbled along The Strand towards the Holy Cross Church. She wondered if any of the gravestones carried postscripts about the deathly effects of native liquor.

Chapter Twenty-three

CHALAILI
MAY, 1937

THE SOLIGANJ WEEKLY OBSERVER

Mrs Rajat Banerjee, proprietress of Coronation Talkies, Chalaili, has contacted *The Soliganj Weekly Observer* to complain about comments published herein by Mr David Oakley, President of the Soliganj Businessmen's League. She referred to Mr Oakley's observation that the late Mr John D. Rockefeller's philanthropy 'should serve as a model for all successful businessmen'. Mrs Banerjee pointed out that there are many successful businesswomen in Soliganj and environs, herself primarily included.

*S*imon Fraser-Gough had been watching Lydia for some weeks. Her Tuesday afternoon ritual rarely varied. She would arrive on foot at The Empire Club and take an abnormally deep breath before ascending the front steps. Her hair would be plastered in kiss curls on her forehead and her skin so aglow there was the impression her body heat could perform cooking feats.

Simon Fraser-Gough smiled to himself at the idea of Lydia Rushmore toasting crumpets at ten paces simply by standing still and radiating.

'A rare talent indeed,' he chuckled aloud as he lounged in a cream-painted wooden chair set to one side of The Empire Club's front garden. It was his usual position on Tuesday afternoons but Lydia had never thrown him so much as a sideways glance.

Like most of the memsahibs in Chalaili, Lydia approached all matters British, The Empire Club included, it being an edifice of colonial power as its name so roundly attested, with head-high resolve, like a standard-bearer for expatriate women of her kind everywhere.

Simon Fraser-Gough was sure that Lydia was a secret tippler. He had all the time he needed to study her as she left The Empire Club, dizzy-stepped and bright-eyed, after her Ladies' Afternoon socialising.

Socialising with books, that is, as a few well-placed coins to The Empire Club staff had revealed she was snubbed by The Crows, who disapproved of her lack of couture tailoring and her semi-wild husband who eschewed hats and stiff collars and the accepted courtesies that lubricated Raj society.

Instead of chatting and cackling, Lydia drank in The Empire Club library.

Doubles.

A dash of lime juice.

Easy on the tonic.

Little ladylike burps smothered by the rustle of pages of illustrated volumes. *The Butterflies of India*. *Botany of the Western Ghats*. *The Linguistic Survey of India (1903–1928)*.

She was perfect for his purposes.

Simon Fraser-Gough had been convalescing at The Chalaili Sanatorium for the Tubercular for six months and was becoming dangerously unstuck. He had been run out of the Indian Army Corps of Clerks in Calcutta for embezzlement. His position of Staff Sergeant had largely been attained due to the influence of his Major-General father and now he was effectively disowned by the senior Fraser-Gough, a man not familiar with forgiveness.

More recently, Simon Fraser-Gough had been in the hill station of Simla, squandering his savings on gambling at the races and trying desperately to conceal his diminishing health.

He was of medium height, sandy haired and possessor of a perpetually sun-tarnished nose that would pass for a sweet potato were it to feature in a line-up of starchy vegetables. The tuberculosis had rendered him hollow cheeked and frail chested, a sunken combination that did little to enhance his appearance. But Simon Fraser-Gough was a flatterer of women and that was his principal attribute and greatest personal liability.

Weak women.

Lonely women.

Unhappy women.

Silly women.

Gin-sloshed women, displaying signs of aforementioned tendencies.

Chalaili had not delivered him the females he sought. In Calcutta, women of his preferred silly-dilly type were very often alone, their husbands frequently out of station on business or, at the least, properly detained by the endless male-dominated rituals of club sports.

But in Chalaili, the chaps did nothing much at all, save for disappearing into banks and government offices for short stretches.

The buggers even went home for lunch.

Lunch! The time of day comfortably close to the siesta hour when a bored memsahib might be already loosening her garments and shaking free her hair in preparation for a nap and, in high summer, applying an ice-cold towel to her pretty forehead and fair neck.

Fair. Had to be fair. Simon Fraser-Gough believed in the purity of the white race, its superiority and right to rule.

The fair widow Veronica O'Brien of the Lakshmi Hair and Beauty Studio had seemed a likely target for his attentions. Widows were always so grateful. Fair game, as he liked to put it. But it was widely rumoured Veronica O'Brien preferred her pleasures to be tar-tinted. That's how the fellows at the bar of The Empire Club had put it, and they all thought it such a shame as she was a comely sort and why should a grubby native have access to the pleasures she denied her own kind.

Simon Fraser-Gough shuddered at the thought of dark hands against white skin and the inevitable procreation of yet more half-caste babies with their caramel complexions and strangely pale eyes. Nothing annoyed him more than the taint of other, lesser blood. Like Florence Gordon, the assistant postmistress, for instance. Oh, he saw the looks she gave him when he called by the post office, the hints she dropped about dances at The Empire Club. He had been tempted, as any man would, by her sensational curves and pouting lips, unfurling like a clam shell. What that opening could be capable of was anybody's guess . . .

But Simon Fraser-Gough saw beyond Florence's siren-silk looks and ready availability. He saw hunger. Hunger for acceptance, for status, for a ticket to an imagined home called England. No, that half-and-half Florence Gordon would not do at all.

∞

Lydia tripped as she made her way down the front steps of The Empire Club, dropping her spiral-bound journal in which she was scribbling observations of hill station life. She was later than usual. It was almost five and Simon Fraser-Gough deduced she had imbibed several more drinks than usual, perhaps deliberately out-staying The Crows who had tarried so long the two taxis that customarily picked them up on Tuesday afternoons had left and then were re-summoned by the club's staff as the women stood on the steps, an awful abundance of dowdiness that even peacock feathers and loud red-and-yellow sun parasols with frilled necks could not remedy.

Finally, they had shot off, barking commands at the drivers.

As Lydia teetered midway down the steps, Simon Fraser-Gough made his move.

'May I assist you?'

The doff of a soft straw hat, an unleashing of springy hair the colour of a beach, the gleam of white and even teeth.

The sweet potato nose.

Gin-giddy Lydia stared at him and waited for the wavy, swimming image to coalesce into a steady whole. Oh dear, the nose was not a consequence of her dizziness after all.

She allowed him to assist her to the bottom step. They stood facing each other. Lydia was the same height as Simon Fraser-Gough, a fact he had not reckoned upon. She looked smaller from a distance, fragile and softer featured.

'You are?'

Her voice was genuinely well-educated, not like most of the Chalaili wives who had elocutionised their tones to sound so strangled it was as if they had clothes pegs on their noses.

'Simon Fraser-Gough.'

He gave a little bow.

'Lydia Burnett . . . no, no, Mrs William Rushmore. Silly me. Hic.'

She giggled.

He winked. Or was it a trick of the late-afternoon light. Lydia was finding it very hard to concentrate on his face without dwelling on the nose, thereby appearing to be investigating its craters.

'I haven't seen you before, Mr Fraser-Gough. Have you just arrived?'

'Chalaili Sanatorium for the Tubercular.' He lowered his head and put a hand on his chest, as if in severe pain.

'Oh dear, I mean, well . . . are you very, very ill?'

'Recovering slowly and feeling all the better for seeing you today. A little ray of English sunshine, if I may say . . .'

He allowed his eyes to mist up at the mention of the word English and looked away from Lydia's concerned face to the Chalaili Hills. He wore such an air of determined concentration that Lydia imagined he was willing the pine-forested slopes to turn into rolling downs studded with golden daffodils.

'I say,' he said, clapping his hands as if the idea had just occurred, 'would you join me for tea tomorrow in my rooms here at our little Hotel des Invalides?'

'Rooms?'

Lydia paled.

Surely one such chamber would be his bedroom.

'Please, Mrs Rushmore, it would be something I could look forward to. It's just that I don't know how long . . .'

He turned and looked into the distance, daffodil-summoning with half-closed eyes.

'Just the two of us?'

'Well, yes, aside from doctors, nurses and other patients, some of whom I would not entertain with a cup and saucer for all the tea in India.'

They shared a laugh. He is quite jolly, Lydia thought, and surely harmless, what with such a dreadful illness and the sort of unsatisfactory face that one rarely, if ever, would expect to find upon a romantic predator. Besides, he would know things about India. Colourful, entertaining things she could jot down in her journal.

'Say, three o'clock?'

She nodded and Simon Fraser-Gough sauntered off across The Empire Club's immaculately pressed grounds.

Lydia usually walked home to Bluebell Cottage, up the punishing hill that led to the two ridges, but she had one of the club doormen order her a taxi. She felt unsettled in the stomach as the vehicle negotiated the curves. Looking out the window at the dark green blur of pine trees, she reassured herself that tuberculosis surely wasn't catching and even though there was really nothing improper about tomorrow's appointment, she had no need to tell William.

She had made a new friend, the first one of her own in Chalaili. An outing with an invalid was not an assignation, after all.

⁂

Simon Fraser-Gough's plan was very nearly foolproof, which was not to say he ever thought himself a fool. His room at The Chalaili Sanatorium for the Tubercular was completely private, opening on to a terrace set with wicker furniture, and that was where refreshments would be served. A small bribe to the kitchen servant would ensure he didn't suddenly appear to remove the tea tray or perform some other damn-fool tidying-up that would provide a cue for Lydia Rushmore to take her leave.

His bed was deliberately unmade, the covers drawn down at an angle, suggesting how very easy it would be to slide inside and while away the dregs of the afternoon beneath an only slightly creaking electric ceiling fan.

Simon Fraser-Gough had thought of wearing his pyjamas and a dressing-gown with racy scarlet and black stripes, but surmised his quarry would be too quickly discouraged by such an overt invitation. He settled for cream linen slacks with a tan leather belt and a burgundy cotton shirt, buttons open low enough to reveal a thatch of gingery chest hair. Perfect.

Lydia was punctual and all in blue. Pastel blue poplin sunfrock with button-down front.

Easy access, thought Simon Fraser-Gough.

Pastel blue sandals with double straps. Legs that looked invitingly bare, although perhaps she was wearing those sheer skin-coloured stockings that could confuse the hell out of a chap.

'Bluebell!' he cried as she stepped on to the terrace.

She blushed and looked over his shoulder.

'Where are the . . . the nurses?'

'Nursing, I should expect. Sit down, my dear Bluebell.'

'That's the name of my . . . our cottage. Did you know that?'

'How could it be called anything else with such a beautiful flower in residence. Now, I believe I promised you some tea.'

Simon Fraser-Gough pressed a buzzer on the wall by the double French doors behind him.

'Our afternoon tea will be here in a few minutes.'

Lydia was still standing, fidgeting with her handbag.

'Please sit down.'

He patted the cushion on the rattan seat beside Lydia and she sat, stiff-backed, still clutching her bag.

'Well, let's get to know each other . . .' he began.

She smiled nervously and finally let go of the bag, carefully arranging it under the swing of her skirt, as if it might contain something she was afraid of misplacing, like a small revolver. Or a silver hip flask, Daddy's initials almost fingered to oblivion.

The tea arrived, borne by a servant who kept his eyes averted as he arranged the cups and saucers, milk jug, sugar bowl and silver teapot on the low glass-topped table between Simon Fraser-Gough and his lady visitor.

'I didn't expect to be alone with you,' whispered Lydia as the servant retreated. 'It's not proper. I am married.'

'Sugar? Milk?'

'Yes, er . . . no, sorry. I have become accustomed to drinking Indian tea. You know they add the milk and sugar while boiling . . .'

'Yes, I do know, Bluebell. I've been in India all my life. Born here, actually.'

'Born in India? I had no idea.'

Deftly ignoring his guest's earlier protestations about the impropriety of their unsupervised meeting, Simon Fraser-Gough settled into his hard-backed wicker chair and began regaling Lydia with stories of his life in India, embroidering and embellishing without restraint.

Lydia was swept away by Simon Fraser-Gough's expansive anecdotes. Tiger shoots, elephant polo, vice-regal balls . . . he spoke colourfully, persuasively, transporting her from Planet Cha-laili to the hot, dusty, vivacious plains. She closed her eyes and drifted off.

'Gin, Bluebell?'

Lydia opened her eyes. The tea things had been cleared to the side of the low glass-topped table. From somewhere near the side of his chair, Simon Fraser-Gough was producing a bottle of gin and two tumblers. No ice, no tonic water or crescents of lemon.

Without waiting for her reply, he poured two generous slugs. The liquid looked oily against the thick glass of the cheap tumblers.

'Memsahibs' ruin.' He chuckled. Lydia smiled. She took the drink from his ginger-freckled hand.

☙

Well into her third gin, Lydia worked off her pastel blue sandals with double straps and wriggled her bare feet on the cement floor. Simon Fraser-Gough looked at her unstockinged toes and grinned.

She was regaling him with stories of her teaching days at West Gamble. He laughed at the name of her home village and she laughed, too, wondering why she had never questioned its ironies.

'So, Bluebell, does anyone take gambles in such a place?'

Lydia looked at him over the rim of her glass. He wasn't quite in focus, which made the sweet potato nose look as if it had been affixed, like a plasticine party costume prop.

'Yes, I did. Marrying William. Coming to India. Not many women in West Gamble would have done that. In fact, Mr Fraser-Gough, I can't think of a single one.'

'Do you love your husband?'

'What an impertinent question.'

Loud clunk as the cheap tumbler was placed on the low glass-topped table.

The mewing cry of a peacock strutting the great sweep of lawns merging The Chalaili Sanatorium for the Tubercular and The Empire Club.

A cool silence.

Finally, 'He doesn't love me.'

'Ah, ha.'

'He needed a wife, you see. For appearances and for . . . for intimate things, but perhaps not really for intimate things. He loves clouds and rain and being alone in the woods. He's a good man . . .'

'Of course. Everyone says so.'

'You know him?'

'No, not really. I've heard his name in connection with Petal . . . I mean to say, flowers and weather matters.'

'He hates flowers, actually. The ones you have to prune and fuss over, that is. He prefers trees and yes, you are right, his name is usually heard in connection with weather matters.'

Lydia reclaimed her glass and drained it. Fourth, fifth, shixth, sheventh gin. She had lost count.

She drifted barefoot to the lavatory adjoining Simon Fraser-Gough's invalid bachelor quarters at The Chalaili Sanatorium for the Tubercular. He added a crushed tablet to her gin and refreshed his own glass with the water he had been drinking from a separate bottle for the past hour.

Just a small tablet. A muscle relaxant. The sort of encourager to make a demure girl from West Gamble take an unprecedented punt.

Chapter Twenty-four

CHALAILI
MAY, 1937

'Beware the effects of alcohol in the harsh
Indian climate, especially in the headache-inducing weeks
prior to the annual monsoon.'
ETIQUETTE AND MANNERS FOR THE COLONIAL MEMSAHIB
BY HENRIETTA WEATHERBY, 1895

As Lydia stumbled from The Chalaili Sanatorium for the Tubercular, over the tweezered lawns and through its stone-arched gateway, she was amused to see a wooden sign with a bright red arrow: Head Doctor.

That's exactly what I need, she thought. Her head was thick and thumping, her throat parched. There had been no sign of Simon Fraser-Gough when she woke. She was lying primly on his single bed, fully dressed, even down to her sandals, which she remembered throwing aside earlier in the afternoon. Her watch read 5 p.m.

She attempted to recall the full events of the afternoon. The feel of smooth cement against her feet. The cool gust of a ceiling fan. The comfort of gin coating her throat. Its juniper berry tang. Heat in her mouth and nostrils.

She lent against the stone archway trying to remember exactly what had happened next. Had he had his way with her? There was no stickiness in her cotton knickers.

A rubber condom, perhaps?

She had never seen a condom but would not the rough force of elastic have irritated her? She felt no sense of internal ache. None of the dullness she experienced after William's penetrations.

I passed out, she reassured herself, and Simon Fraser-Gough lay me gently on the bed while he went off to attend to, er, business, yes, that's it, business. Men were always attending to business, even tubercular chaps, one would have to imagine.

Lydia patted her hair and began to walk into Chalaili. Rather than detour to The Empire Club and call a taxi, she needed the extra thinking time and the invigorating piney air that a stroll would allow.

As she reached the hill road leading to the upper and lower ridges, she encountered Charlotte Montague. The older woman was approaching from the opposite direction, a servant behind her, leading two springer spaniels wearing saddle-shaped cloths on their backs, like a pair of rackety ponies.

Lydia paused and smiled. Charlotte Montague gave her an examining look. Then her eyebrows shot up so far they were in danger of launching into the heavens.

'Is that the latest fashion in Surrey, Mrs Rushmore?'

Lydia looked down at her pastel blue poplin sunfrock, fearing the buttons must be wrongly fastened. There were no buttons. She was wearing it back-to-front.

Ten minutes later, Lydia was sitting in Charlotte Montague's front parlour, correctly buttoned. Her hostess was roaring into the telephone somewhere down the hallway. She was speaking very forcibly in Hindustani and Lydia hoped she wasn't dictating an article about her disarrayed dress to *The Soliganj Weekly Observer*.

'No, can't be that,' said Lydia aloud. 'She would want all the details first.'

A young male servant brought a tea tray topped by an engraved silver pot and poured Lydia a pale Earl Grey into a bone china cup so fine it was almost translucent.

Lydia sipped and relaxed slightly, considering the rich irony of her visit. Charlotte Montague had never deemed the Rushmores worthy of being entertained in her spacious bungalow with wrap-around stone verandas. William had told Lydia it was known as the bank bungalow, the residence of a succession of Grindlays Bank managers, of whom the florid Edmond Montague was the present incumbent. It was quite the finest private house in Chalaili, set aside from the row of cottages on the lower ridge, with gardens leading to a scenic point above the valley.

'I envy your view,' roared Charlotte, unexpectedly. She had finished her loud telephone call and was now seated opposite Lydia. Her voice had such resonance that even a simple statement sounded like a railway platform announcement. There was no evidence of the investigative lorgnette she had favoured the night Lydia was introduced to her at The Empire Club.

'Thank you very much,' Lydia replied, taking full responsibility for the outlook from Bluebell Cottage.

'I know it sounds silly, really, when this bungalow is so big and has such beautiful grounds but you can't see the valley view

162

from the windows and I find that frightfully inconvenient. Do you see what I mean?'

Lydia nodded as she held her teacup. The bungalow certainly was large. Closed doorways lined the long hallway and the front parlour in which they sat was twice the size of the equivalent at Bluebell Cottage. Lydia inhaled furniture and floor polish, the rich fumes of beeswax overlaid with a musty jasmine. Charlotte Montague had incense burning in a small ceramic holder on a patterned dish atop a corner cabinet. Lydia watched the spent curls of perfumed ash drift down the slender stick like grey snowflakes.

Charlotte Montague's fingers were encrusted with diamonds. She was stroking a silent chihuahua that looked to Lydia like a peeled rat. The little dog's chocolate-brown eyes darted everywhere, pausing occasionally to look adoringly at Charlotte Montague. Lydia hadn't noticed the chihuahua when they had first entered the house and she imagined Charlotte Montague keeping it in a box or drawer and retrieving it like a favourite cushion or piece of embroidery when she sat in the front parlour.

Lydia's hostess was dressed in a short-sleeved white blouse of soft lawn and a pretty skirt, full and patterned with leaves and butterflies. It was a young, fresh costume at odds with its wearer's matronly demeanour and wide hips. Lydia guessed she was about fifty-five. Her face and hands were slightly sunburnt and she had a gardener's cracked and soiled fingernails, a fact Lydia liked very much. If she mucked about with flowerbeds, perhaps she wasn't such a prim and proper dragon after all.

'Well?' said Charlotte Montague.

'Yes, quite well, thank you.'

Lydia continued to look around the room, taking in its mixture of heavy Victoriana and lighter cargo of Indian objects, many intricately carved and inset with corners and fastenings of polished brass. A silent cuckoo clock hung at a slightly wrong angle, its double doors not quite closed, as if at any moment a lopsided bird might shoot out with a protesting screech.

The room had a lustre. Glowing surfaces, little mirrors with frames of mother-of-pearl and gleaming onyx, a vermilion-painted cabinet so polished Lydia could see the reflection of her form. Did Charlotte Montague drift alone around this twinkling room, Lydia wondered, catching glimpses of herself at numerous angles, like a passing ghost. She imagined the woman toasting her mirrored self by candlelight, alone with her dreams while Edmond Montague busied himself in a polished study with after-hours business matters, in the way men conspired to do.

'I am not enquiring after your health, Mrs Rushmore.'

'Call me Lydia. Please do.'

'Well then, Lydia, I wouldn't have thought it necessary to explain that we British women have an example to set to . . . to everyone, really. The natives look to us for guidance and expect us to behave impeccably, not just in our personal deportment but our morals.'

'Morals? You don't think . . .'

'It's not altogether relevant what I think but I know what I saw, Mrs, er, Lydia, and what I saw was a woman, an Englishwoman, skipping along in broad daylight with her frock on back to front.'

Charlotte Montague uttered the word front with such vigour the tea things rattled on the wooden traymobile.

Lydia grabbed a handful of her pastel blue poplin sunfrock's full skirt and clenched the yielding fabric into a ball. She feared she was going to cry.

164

'I was visiting a patient at The Chalaili Sanatorium for the Tubercular.'

'A male patient? To the best of my knowledge, there are no female tuberculars.'

'Yes, a male friend. But not even a friend. An acquaintance, actually, who asked me to tea to discuss many things. Elephant balls and . . . no, it was elephant polo . . . and then . . .'

'And then?'

'And then it was so hot, so terribly hot. He wasn't well at all and the doctors took him away.'

'Away?'

'Yes, removed him somewhere and I decided to bathe myself and there was no mirror because when you are tubercular, perhaps it is unwise to be reminded of your unfortunate condition by mirrors. So when I dressed again, I got muddled up.'

'You must be extremely dextrous, Lydia, to button your dress with your hands contorted behind your back.'

'Oh, it's very loose. It just pulls on and off over my head. Shall I show you?'

'I don't think that will be necessary. Your tubercular acquaintance . . . what's his name?'

'Simon Fraser-Gough.'

'Good Lord.' Charlotte Montague spluttered as she swallowed a slice of Madeira cake.

'Do you know him?'

'Know him? He was run out of Simla last summer, I believe. A first-class cad and a blackmailer to boot. I had no idea he was in Chalaili.'

'He hangs around the lawns of The Empire Club.'

'Well, I've never seen him but then I would scarcely

165

recognise him. It's said he's not exactly handsome but very smooth and charming. Drugs young ladies and . . .'

'And what? I don't believe he laid a hand on me.'

Lydia leapt to her feet and walked across to the window with its unsatisfactorily distant view. Charlotte Montague was right: the hills looked like faint bruises on the horizon.

'The doolally story about your frock isn't true, is it?'

Lydia turned and felt herself wilting under Charlotte Montague's obsidian eyes.

'No, but I am sure he didn't have his way with me. I mean to say, I definitely would know if he had.'

'But he undressed you, presumably, and then perhaps photographed you . . .'

'Photographed me?'

'Koi hai!'

Charlotte Montague shouted for a servant and then dispatched the young man who had brought the tea on another errand. Lydia caught the word scrapbook amid Charlotte Montague's cascade of Hindustani.

'Just wait until you see this,' she said, pouring more tea. Lydia noticed Charlotte Montague's heightened colour and realised her hostess was enjoying the scandalous interlude.

The servant arrived with a large soft-covered book and Charlotte Montague reached for a magnifying glass resting on an opened novel on a small brass side-table. Lydia was intrigued to read the title on the face-down book's spine: *Flora's Faraway Fantasies* by Anonymous. She giggled to herself.

'Now, let me see.'

Charlotte Montague flicked page after page. Many of the spreads of press cuttings and pasted invitations to social events were so full the effect was almost of decoupage, the assembled and overlapped life and times of Charlotte Montague, Queen of the Crows, unofficial protector of the honour of expatriate English-women in His Majesty's extended colonies, and devotee of racy fiction.

'Here!' She tapped a finger at a newspaper cutting and turned the scrapbook at an angle so Lydia could see the page. The piece was from *The Simla Argus*, dated six months prior.

'Mr Simon Fraser-Gough, originally of Calcutta, pleaded guilty yesterday morning in the Simla District Court of black-mail in connection with the entrapment of a young lady (name suppressed at the request of her family). His photographic equipment has been seized and confiscated and Mr Fraser-Gough was escorted on to the afternoon train to Kalka. The family in question has not requested compensation.'

There was a photograph, very small and blurred. The women's heads touched as they peered at it.

'I think that's why I remembered his name,' said Charlotte Montague.

Lydia noticed her breath was as ginned as her own. The fumes, she smiled to herself, could almost curl the pages of the scrapbook.

'Why?'

'The nose.'

Lydia leaned further forward.

'It looks like a turnip. You must have noticed it.'

'Yes, I did. A sweet potato, I thought.'

Charlotte Montague broke into high, loud laughter and a dozen tiny brass bells and godly figurines shuddered.

Against the tinkling backdrop, she continued.

'He got away lightly. Dorothy Creswell-Smythe had more details, as she invariably does . . . Anyway, it was an army captain's daughter, apparently. Got her drunk, photographed her in her underwear and then demanded money from her father on threat of circulating the evidence all over Simla.'

'I didn't see a camera.'

'He would hardly have had it set up in the corner. Even someone as . . . as . . . trusting as you would have found that rather irregular.'

Lydia began to cry.

'I just thought he could be my friend.'

Charlotte Montague put her arm around her.

'Look, leave it to me. I have contacts in Chota Chalaili. Good contacts. I might be able to intercept the film. He'd have to send it to the studio in the bazaar to get it developed.' Good, a new project, thought Charlotte Montague. There was nothing she liked better than a project, and the more intrigue the better.

'You would do that for me, Charlotte?'

Lydia straightened up and looked into her deep brown eyes.

'I thought you despised me. I thought you were ringing the . . . the press to tell them about my back-to-front dress.'

'There, there, girl. What a ridiculous notion. I was just cancelling an appointment with my dressmaker. She's an absolute dear but I couldn't have her turning up while you are here and out of sorts as it would be all over Chalaili within the hour. She's making me an interesting skirt and headdress. Dorothy Creswell-Smythe is having a fancy costume party at The Empire Club and we all have to dress as Apaches. Do you know what an Apache is, Lydia?'

'A sort of Indian? Not our kind of Indian, that is . . .'

'A red Indian they call them, and half naked with it. That Creswell-Smythe creature is obsessed with feathers. You are lucky not to be on her invitation list, particularly for her seances. That poor dead husband of hers. She'll never let him rest in peace.'

'I am not on anyone's invitation list.'

'Lucky you, my dear. Still, it's a shame you have just arrived when it's all about to end.'

'What's about to end?'

Lydia's question was lost amid Charlotte Montague's hearty clapping of hands

'You must realise it just takes a while to be accepted in this place. I *was* you once, you know, new to India and out of my depth. Now pull yourself together and Rajiv will order you a taxi home.'

'Taxi! Taxi!' she yelled with another thunderous round of clapping as if the vehicle would appear along the hallway in a beeswax-scented puff.

Chapter Twenty-five

CHALAILI
JUNE, 1937

THE SOLIGANJ WEEKLY OBSERVER

American actress Miss Jean Harlow has died from kidney failure at the age of twenty-six. The actress was variously known as The Platinum Blonde and The Bombshell, the names taken from her two popular movies of 1931 and 1933 respectively. As a tribute to Miss Harlow, the proprietress of Coronation Talkies, Chalaili, Mrs Rajat Banerjee, told *The Soliganj Weekly Observer* it is her intention to screen special sessions of *Saratoga*, the talking picture being made by Miss Harlow at the time of her untimely death, as soon as the studio distributes final prints. 'The picture also stars Mr Clark Gable, who many prominent Soliganj and Chalaili residents will know is a personal favourite of mine.'

Sham Lal couldn't believe Picture Madam had called him back to Chalaili from Bombay. She made the commission to supervise her move and renovate her new residence sound enormously grand, as if she were about to occupy a palace. After the brouhaha at the opening night of Coronation Talkies, his conscience had forced him to install new curtain rails and to generally tighten and reinforce the many beams and patches of aged plaster that he had overlooked. He had nightmares about the ceiling collapsing on top of dozens of theatre-goers, including those terrifying Englishwomen who even if they expired would surely reappear as ghosts, piercing his dreams with their ridiculous umbrellas.

He found himself again on the narrow-gauge train to Chalaili, the carriages looping higher and higher on the slender track until, at times, he felt as if the sky were a protective cloak. This time, he was accompanied by his nephew, Vinod Sharma, who would help him oversee a band of local workmen. The young man's parents had despatched Vinod Sharma after a disgraceful incident. They discovered he had been renting out their small Bombay flat by the quarter hour while they worked at a cousin's nearby restaurant.

His mother had returned one afternoon to change her sandals after a strap broke, only to find the marital bed occupied by a sweating traffic policeman pumping himself into a pretty young girl. In the lounge room, sitting politely like patients at a surgery, two other couples occupied the Sharma family lounge and matching armchairs, awaiting their fifteen-minute allotment. Whenever Anita Sharma repeated the story, she would add, with a dramatic flourish, that the lounge furniture was shop-fresh, its cushioned seats still protected by plastic covers and for that she would forever be grateful as who knows what special cleaning fluids may have been required to shift the germs of such sexed-up animals.

☙

171

The move of Mrs Banerjee into her new rented abode was an undertaking of mammoth proportions. Her furnishings and personal possessions had to be transported from Bombay by train. The belongings were packed by Sham Lal and his men into tin-lined tea-chests, each one numbered with painted slashes. Much of the goods were coming direct from the Dhir family residence, recently sold but still standing conveniently uninhabited. Her father had died several months earlier and her mother had been swiftly transplanted to an apartment, accompanied by one of the ancient cardiganed servants who had looked after the young Premila. She was not happy about being abandoned by her only child, with no one but a short-sighted retainer for company. But Mrs Banerjee was like a juggernaut once aroused and Leela Dhir had known she had little resort.

Her daughter had organised all the legal aspects of the will and division of the spoils while Leela Dhir took to her bed, knowing full well there would be far too much loss of face in her card-playing circles to make an issue of the matter. She had been somewhat estranged from her husband at the time of his premature death, from a heart attack. They were keeping separate bedrooms but she had been expecting an imminent reunion, with the possibility of gold jewellery.

For years she had tolerated the picture-house outings of her husband and daughter, the two of them trotting off every Thursday evening to Galaxy Talkies on Marine Drive. Obsessed with it, she would mutter, but never with much rancour. She liked to have the house clear that night for her card soirees, with half a dozen of her lady friends being dropped off by their drivers amid such flurries of Benares embroidered silk that if they arrived en masse, it was like a waterfall rushing in. If Premila were home, she would often wander through the front room in her pyjamas, always on the tight side around what passed as her waist, and the women would smile and mouth platitudes about such a healthy-looking girl and what a hearty appetite.

Later, at their homes, she could imagine the conversations with their businessmen husbands. 'Poor Leela Dhir is never going to shift that lump of a girl into a good match . . .'

No, it was much better that Premila accompanied her father to Galaxy Talkies and kept out of sight of the card circle.

What Leela Dhir did not realise was that her husband installed the teenage Premila into a very nice seat in the Dress Circle, purchased her an ice-cream and salted peanuts funnelled in a twist of newspaper and then excused himself 'on Daddy's special business'. His daughter learnt to attune her eyes to the darkness and was able to make out, every Thursday evening, her father's form in a seat several rows behind, at the very back of the section. She knew it was Daddy as his face was usually in profile, his moustache a bristly protrusion. He would tilt his handsome head to one side and sometimes, if Premila stared hard enough, she could see his tongue whip out and deposit itself with a hungry urgency into the waiting mouth of Miss Dolly de Souza.

She knew the tongue recipient's name as she had been introduced to her once in the foyer. Premila had seen the film several times before as Daddy was never one to pay attention to programming. She was feeling slightly unwell, so she waited on a velvet-covered bench for the curtains to open and the crowds to meander out. She knew Daddy and his friend would be among the first to have left their seats, such was the weekly pattern.

Mr Dhir saw his daughter waiting and after less than a second's hesitation, he introduced Miss Dolly de Souza, a business colleague he had had the good fortune to bump into after the house lights had come up. 'Such a healthy girl,' said Miss de Souza, with a slow smile. Her teeth were smudged with Ruby Revolver lipstick. Her lips were strangely pouty. They reminded Premila of the opening of a hot water bottle.

Premila knew it was in her interest to keep 'Daddy's little secret' and so she did. Unfortunately, smudges of Ruby Revolver found their way on to his fine shirt collar one Thursday evening. Mrs Dhir kept the shirt aside and conducted various first-hand colour matches at the make-up counters of the Queen's Necklace Beauty Salon. She decided it was not one of her own collection of lipsticks. Although her husband's protestations had been persuasive and Premila insisted Daddy had never left her side, Mrs Dhir withdrew her sexual services and moved into the spare bedroom, already planning what tissue-fine sari she would wear to show off the new gold brooch or pendant she felt was less than a week away.

Her husband did not seek her out during the stirring hours of late evening, however, even when the arrangements for the marriage of Premila to the Banerjee boy were well advanced and there was a need for lengthy discussions concerning guest lists and catering. He complained of chest pains and requested his wife put herself in charge of all necessary planning. When the day of their daughter's wedding dawned, they had not slept as man and wife for months.

Premila's father died of a heart attack a few days after the wedding and when the obligatory period of mourning had passed and the shocking revelations contained in his will came to light, Premila announced that the residence would have to be sold as there were business interests she wished to pursue.

The Dhir family home was in a good district, substantially built with bird-busy gardens, near enough to Chowpatty Beach for a salt tang to be apparent in the air on breezy porch-sitting evenings. Ignoring her mother's pleas, Premila chose an apartment for her on the fourth floor of a new building named Pink Fantasia, with distant views of Bombay harbour. Leela Dhir protested it sounded like an establishment of ill repute but her daughter made much of the fact there was a lift in the building, a cunning contrivance that gave everything about the move a very special status. Her mother was unconvinced and the elderly servant flatly refused to use it, making her excursions to the market for daily supplies annoyingly long businesses as she crept up and down the stairwell, with rest stops on each of the three landings during the return journey.

The apartment was large and modern, with electricity connected in every room and a covered balcony large enough for a comfortable cane chair on which Mrs Dhir could sit to one side, looking out on the neighbourhood like an all-seeing goddess. Occasionally she was tempted to wave, as she had seen King George VI do from the balcony of Buckingham Palace in newsreels on the rare occasions her husband had taken her to Galaxy Talkies.

'My daughter has purchased a picture theatre,' she announced to her card circle on their first visit to her new apartment. There had been a problem with the lift and two late-comers had had to walk up the three flights, daintily raising their sari skirts and gingerly placing their sandal-clad feet in case they came in contact with foreign substances. The pair of ladies had noticed the faint odour of urine in the stairwell, a matter that would make for animated discussion as they shared a car on their way home.

No piece of news that Leela Dhir could impart about her

175

elephant daughter would have surprised her card cronies. 'Galaxy Talkies?' inquired Sujata Patel, hopefully. It would be convenient indeed if the Dhir girl was able to arrange cut-price tickets for the latest foreign films.

'At a very important hill station, many hours from here,' announced her mother, gesturing at the old servant to bring more sugar-varnished sweets and hot tea. 'She will be showing English films only. Many high-up officials are living there.'

'What is the name of the hill station, Leela?' Sujata Patel continued, her lipsticked smile so taut it resembled a bloodied gash.

'Chalaili.'

'Is that so? I had heard that place almost washed away in the monsoon a few years ago. What an interesting choice. Always such a brave and healthy girl, your Premila.'

The women exchanged surreptitious looks as they chewed the store-bought sweets. Leela Dhir's remaining servant was incapable of hand-fashioning such silver-leafed delicacies. Really, such collapsed catering standards and her occupation of an apartment in a building with a temperamental lift could mean a rethink of their weekly card gatherings.

'Full house,' squealed Sujata Patel's closest friend, Bina Verghese, fanning her cards on the table. Sujata Patel gathered her shawl around her shoulders. 'Goodness, I haven't seen Premila since her wedding,' she purred, turning to Leela Dhir and slowly picking a piece of silver leaf caught perilously close to a filling in her right-hand molar. 'How are the Banerjees these days?'

The thunderous look on Leela Dhir's face and the servant's hurried retreat to the kitchen were signals for the group to disperse.

Chapter Twenty-six

CHALAILI
JUNE, 1937

THE SOLIGANJ WEEKLY OBSERVER
The famed aviatrix Amelia Earhart has arrived in Karachi
after completing a long and interrupted flight from Mas-
sawa, Eritrea, on her aerial flight around the world. Miss
Earhart told reporters at Karachi airfield that she planned
to stay a day or two, depending on weather conditions.

Anil waited on Chalaili Station for the afternoon train
to Soliganj and Bombay. The very idea of a holiday was
terrifying. His village was far to the south, and when William despatched him there once a year for what he grandly referred to as
a family reunion, Anil visited for just a day, handing over money to
his drunken father and layabout brothers. The rest of the time he
spent in Bombay, prowling Juhu Beach and visiting the huts of the
willing women who serviced the itinerant hawkers and fishermen.

His mother had died more than twenty years earlier when
Anil was fourteen. His sister, Sunita, older by a year, had to assume

all the family responsibilities of cooking and cleaning, fetching water from the well and walking to market every morning to purchase the simple necessities of their lives. Anil couldn't bear to see his beloved sister mired in such drudgery. His older brothers were drunkards, following in their father's footsteps of sugar cane toddy addiction. There seemed no way to raise money for Sunita to be married off unless Anil left for the city and found employment.

He had worked at a tea stand at the railway station in the nearest town, was paid a pittance each day and given shelter in a corner of the kitchen of the stall-holder's house in return for the endless boiling of pots of heartily sweetened chai for the streams of workers flowing in and out each day. When he had saved enough for a one-way train fare, and a little left over, he headed for Bombay.

Anil had been sleeping under a frangipani tree in a Bombay park when William came across him. Rain Wallah was out on one of his dawn constitutionals looking for butterflies and taking soil samples. He had practically stepped on Anil who was covered in a ragged piece of jute, his pillow a neatly arranged hillock of leaves.

Anil had not seen a Britisher before and despite the fact this man was carrying a net rather then a gun, he was convinced he was about to be arrested. But William had absent-mindedly given him the net to hold while he took out a glass phial from his pocket and filled it with rain-freshened earth. Then William removed a banana from his bag and passed it to Anil, expecting him to hold it while he fished for his water bottle.

Anil was so hungry, he almost demolished the banana, skin and all, in his ravenous haste. He waited expectantly for the Britisher to produce more food from his magical bag.

William just laughed so Anil smiled, too, and indicating he'd like to try William's net, he expertly caught a rare Indian red admiral butterfly that had landed on a frangipani leaf. This time it was William who smiled as he transferred the butterfly to a small wooden box with a mesh front and placed it in his bag. When he stood, William indicated Anil should follow him.

It had been William's intention to order his cook to give the ragamuffin a good breakfast at his government bungalow and then boot him on his way. But as fate would have it, word arrived via the labyrinthine workings of servant networks that the cook's mother was dying and he asked if he could return immediately to his home village.

Anil assured William he could take over the kitchen, even though a speedy lesson on British cooking from the departing cook revealed a horrid mystery of saltings and boilings and stewings.

'That is what is meant by galloping galoshes.' Anil spoke aloud, in his inflected English, as he pressed his face against the window of his third-class carriage aboard the Soliganj Limited Express. His fellow passengers appeared to pay him no attention, but the foreign words caught the attention of a tall moustachioed man opposite him. He silently appraised Anil's quality gaberdine coat and his new leather chappals.

William had been kind and patient with Anil in those early days, wordlessly eating the eggy messes he produced. Then William suggested Anil cook Indian food. And so he produced masala dosa stuffed with onions, potatoes and curry leaves. He presented chapa pulusu, red fish curry flaring with spices. His pakora were filled to bursting with red chilli powder that would occasionally creep up on William and render him speechless. He swept to the table with puffed-up pooris as big and bouncy as the breasts of harem girls.

He knew he could not cook as expertly as Sunita, but he

had watched her often in their mother's cooking alcove, apprenticed to a life of blackened pots and the troublesome appetites of men. As he ground spices in William's kitchen, he would hear his mother's voice and sometimes she materialised in the smoke from the earthen oven, wrapped in a hospital sheet and lightly coughing. 'Turmeric to heal the spirit,' she would murmur. 'Coriander leaves to promote good humour . . . chilli to cheer the heart . . . coconut milk to soothe the soul.'

He always felt she was looking over him as he cooked.

'More cumin, Anil . . . add a little caraway . . . have you thought of fenugreek . . . Flavour the food with memory, my dearest sweetest son.'

Sometimes it was his tears that provided the final seasoning.

Soon he had saved enough money for Sunita's dowry but as he couldn't be away from William's kitchen to spend much time acting as her agent, she was promptly married off to a far-removed cousin, a merchant in Bombay's Crawford Market. With no mother to oversee the intricacies of bride-viewings and compatible horoscopes, the wedding had been so hasty that eyes had been raised about the possibility of pregnancy. Distant Aunties who had materialised at the prospect of a wedding feast prodded Sunita's stomach during the meagre ceremony and reported their findings in loud asides to the Uncles.

'A small bump, anything possible,' was the verdict. But Sunita had not been with child, the merchant's or anyone else's, and Anil had lost contact with her when William was posted to Chalaili. The last time he'd been back to his village there was whispered talk at the chai stand that she had been seen there, alone and roaming.

Anil pressed his face against his carriage window aboard the

Soliganj Limited Express and thought of poor sad-eyed Sunita. Anil hoped the rumour wasn't true. He remembered the husband's corpulent stomach that parted his shirt from his trousers and the way Sunita's mother-in-law's cruel eyes appraised the dowry items, her bony fingers eagerly grasping the English china cups and saucers William had donated.

William is a kind man, thought Anil. He just wants a peaceful life, surrounded by people who perform various needs more or less to his satisfaction and ask, in return, for nothing more than he is willing to give. Mem Lydia will soon find this out, he said to himself, as the train pulled into Bombay's Victoria Terminus.

Chapter Twenty-seven

CHALAILI
JUNE, 1937

'Energetic use of native spices is known to excite
the senses. Instruct servants to serve in moderation
to male dinner guests.'
ETIQUETTE AND MANNERS FOR THE COLONIAL MEMSAHIB
BY HENRIETTA WEATHERBY, 1895

Lydia was beginning to wish she'd agreed to William's suggestion of a housegirl to sweep and clean in Anil's absence. The more conventional households in Chalaili were run along the usual Raj lines of a retinue of servants, each with their assigned task, from gardener and sweeper to housekeeper and cook. William had told her that many single military men had just one manservant, known in the old days as a 'bachelor's familiar'. The expression caused Lydia to shake with laughter, although she knew full well Anil was far more familiar with William than she was.

William, in his cavalier way, wanted none of the gossip-mongering that a brigade of servants would involve so Anil performed all the necessary tasks, which in a bachelor household was no onerous duty. William had a hearty appetite and Anil knew exactly what dishes he liked best. On those days when his Ghost Mother paid the smoky kitchen a visit, the food was particularly delicious.

But William never entertained at Bluebell Cottage, preferring to repay hospitality by hosting a table from time to time at The Empire Club.

Anil had been worried the new memsahib would be a society lady, putting unwelcome demands on his stewing skills. As it was, Bluebell Cottage boasted not even a full dinner service or silver cutlery canteen. The contents were Indian Civil Service issue but Lydia seemed as uninterested in all that as William and gave Anil dazzling smiles as if he were a feted chef even when he dished up something as uninspiring as aloo mattar curry of potatoes and peas (extra-mild; Ghost Mother had arrived in the nick of time to explain memsahib constitutions were as delicate as a baby's). Lydia, he did not realise, had never so much as boiled an egg, and thought anything that came to her plate warm and unmoving was a magical feat.

'We will have to eat at your club, dear,' she told William the day after Anil's departure. The previous evening, still shaky from her recent encounter with Simon Fraser-Gough, she had managed to serve the cold chicken, boiled eggs and tomato salad that Anil had prepared and left on plates under a wet tea-towel in the kitchen, ready for her to carry to the table.

'Nice cold supper, nice cold supper,' she had repeated to herself as she walked down the hallway, the tray wobbling in her hands. She clung to the words as if the gift of food might consolidate her marriage. We will be joined over the tomato wedges,

William and me, mixed with a little vinegar and curls of cut onion. Just the two of us, William, pass the salt, there's a love . . . Erase all memory of Simon Fraser-Gough, dear William. A little lemon juice, perhaps, applied to his image. Sprinkled, smeared, rubbed, vanished. Just the two of us now . . . Smudge a little sugar in my wounds.

'Can't you cook?' he asked. It was not a challenging question, more a casual enquiry one might make to a new acquaintance.

'You didn't indicate it was a requirement,' Lydia replied, a hint of defiance in her voice.

'We'll eat at The Metropole Hotel. When Anil returns and prepares my dress suit, we'll go to The Empire Club again.'

Chapter Twenty-eight

BOMBAY
JUNE 1937

THE SOLIGANJ WEEKLY OBSERVER
The monsoon is very delayed this year and the Ministry of Agriculture has declared drought conditions in many parts of the country. Mr William Rushmore, District Meteorological Officer, Indian Forestry Service, Sub-Branch Weather Warnings, told *The Soliganj Weekly Observer* that the rains could arrive as late as July.

Anil did not realise he was being followed from the station by the hairy-faced stranger who'd been seated in his railway carriage. He had his wages, a wad of folded rupees, in a small purse tucked deep inside the pocket of his overcoat, a cast-off from William and instantly too thick and heavy for the heat of the plains.

A night in Bombay, thought Anil, and then the train south tomorrow. He planned to hand over about half his savings to his no-good family of males and then return to Bombay. He had no thorough idea how to fill two weeks but, for now, his physical needs were pressing. He would visit the shacks of the fisherwomen on Juhu Beach and enjoy instant relief from the lust swelling deep in his groin. Then he would visit a talking picture. The disastrous opening night at Coronation Talkies had not damaged his enthusiasm and he would treat himself to first class rather than being elbowed around in the third-class seats right beneath the screen, trying to breathe amid the collision of cheap cigarette smoke, coconut oil and stale sweat, and ending up with an aching neck for his trouble.

He picked his way over the rocks on the beach and surveyed the huddle of huts with their roofs of pressed kerosene tins, sheets of waterproof material and jute bags stitched together in a rough patchwork. The configuration of huts looked different to his last visit, about six months earlier. He had been hoping to visit a shapely girl from the south who lived in a lopsided shack a little removed from the rest but it appeared to have been torn down to make way for a sturdier dwelling or devastated, probably by an errant wave.

He saw the flash of a sari appear in the second doorway as a length of hessian was pushed aside and he caught the full smell of jasmine. The sari was of cheap cotton, block-printed in bright blue and mango yellow, and the blazing combination of colours stirred within him a powerful nostalgia for his childhood home by the beach. I will eat the best mango in Bombay, he thought, no matter what the cost, after tasting the delights of this woman. He called out and asked a price. A man appeared from the side of the hut and quoted a fee. A bit of haggling followed and Anil handed over the money. The man pulled aside the curtain and waved Anil in.

The woman was lying on a charpoy cot, the folds of her sari

already hoisted up above her waist. Her head was turned away, her hair flowing free so Anil caught just a dim glimpse of her profile. Her short choli blouse was intact and Anil was about to ask her to take it off. She was slim but well-rounded and he imagined her breasts to be deliciously ripe. But then he saw the burn marks along her right arm, extending toward her shoulder and running up from the blouse's low neckline towards her throat. She probably was a victim of a dowry burning, a mother-in-law dissatisfied with the wedding booty having contrived to set the new bride alight, then claim a faulty kerosene stove had caused the unfortunate kitchen incident.

She lay with her face still in profile, legs spread wide, offering him her nakedness. The scene, lit by a small kerosene lamp, was surprisingly artistic, thought Anil, with the meanness of the hut soothed by the flickering light. It was early evening but all sense of time and space was suspended.

He began to undress, neatly folding his clothes in a pile, and then when he was completely naked, he ran his fingers through his hair. He knew from his chatty cohorts in Chota Chalaili that few of them ever undressed with prostitutes, preferring to be in and out, as they put it, with minimum effort. But Anil wondered if the smoothness of his lean body might bring this poor woman some unaccustomed pleasure, that he might take her tenderly as if they were making love, not customer and client locked in a transaction neutered of all emotion.

'Hurry,' she said.

꩜

Hurry, Anil, hurry. The voice of his mother in their hut, its floor of sand and roof of palm leaf. To one side, its beauty mocking the shabbiness of the hut, a tamarind tree with feathery leaves and bulging pods and yellow flowers that shone even at night as Anil looked through the bare window. A little boy dreaming of the pods splitting open and showering money and jewels upon his mother and sister.

Beyond the marooned hut, a supple orchard of mango and guava, jackfruit and coconuts. Hurry and eat your breakfast, you will be late for school. Hurry, Anil, hurry. The voice of his sister as she raced ahead of him through thickets of cardamom and pepper vines, books tied with rough string swinging over her shoulder. Hurry, Anil, hurry. If you can't keep up, we will miss the bus. Flocks of rose-ringed parakeets wheeling overhead, fruit bandits en route to lusciously heavy trees, their screeches a victorious hurrah.

Hurry, Anil, hurry. The sister's voice suddenly older, hoarser and more commanding as they prepared to visit their mother in hospital. Hurry, Anil, hurry. The sister dragging him to the bus stop for the long ride home to their village. Their mother lay dead in the hospital, her bony body covered with a sheet whiter than any sheet he'd ever seen. Anil noticed the ends were badly frayed, wisps of cotton pulling free as if they were trying to escape. Even in death, their mother was denied the best.

Hurry, Anil, hurry. Off the bus now and his sister urging him along, past mud-brick houses painted the blues and greens of the ocean and little tea and toddy stalls on the edge of the straggling market, their kerosene lamps moving in the breeze with a festive gaiety. One of the lamps rocks and throws its jaundiced puddle of light on to a man, drunk and singing, straddling a low stool and on his lap a woman with a face slashed with lipstick. It is their father.

Hurry, Anil, hurry, we must get home. The sister, more and

more anxious, races along the muddy path, sure-footed and swift in the dark; the brother tries to keep up but he slips and his shirt is covered in slime. It is his best shirt, the shirt his sister washed for him to visit the hospital, tucking it into his shorts, patting the collar. We must be smart for mother, Anil.

The sister stops and picks him up. He expects a scolding but she holds him tight, as tight as his mother held him when he was scared of the monsoon's thunder and lightning. She cries and he cries and their hot tears splash together. She uses the hem of her skirt to wipe his eyes and nose. He smells the acrid lemon of cheap coarse soap. Hurry, Anil, hurry, I must prepare father's dinner. Her voice is tired, older.

☙

The woman on the bed began to move. She reached down and spread her vagina apart with her fingers, suggestively raising her hips. She hoisted herself on to one elbow, shaking her hair but not revealing her face. Anil guessed it must be scarred as well.

'Hurry,' she repeated. 'Hurry, hurry.'

Anil stood naked, the small hut swaying, a dreadful sweat beginning to form on his brow and drip into his eyes. He felt his body burning. Two steps back and one to the side, retracing his entry, he bent to pick up his clothes and bag of money. There was nothing there. The hairy hand of the stranger from the train had crept through an opening in the side of the hut, stealthily removing his belongings as he stood in his fevered reverie.

'Who are you?' she shouted, her voice angry now. She pulled down her sari and wriggled up the cot on her bottom until she was squatting on the thin pillow. She was almost invisible, just a shape crouched like a frightened animal.

Anil looked around for something to cover his nakedness. There was nothing in the hovel, just a few cooking implements and a tin trunk with a heavy lock. In desperation, he pulled the length of hessian hanging over the door and wrapped it around his hips.

The woman was turned towards the wall. The dusk light released by the torn curtain made everything more visible in the hut. Her defensive position suggested she expected a beating from this madman. Anil waited for her to shout for her pimp but instead she was quiet and unmoving.

He sat on the side of the cot and put out a hand.

'Hurry, Anil, hurry,' he whispered, his voice so cracked he barely recognised it as his own.

The woman lurched at him from her dark corner and almost succeeded in shoving him off the bed. One of her poor blistered arms clung to him and she kicked him with her bended knees. She was sobbing and flailing, shaking her head from side to side so her stream of hair was constantly flicked across her face.

He managed to hold her still, almost smothering her in his arms. Her head was buried in his chest, her tears so stinging hot he wondered if they would mark his bare skin.

The man he'd paid appeared in the uncovered doorway of the hut and asked what was going on.

'Go away,' Anil shouted, his voice stronger now, heavy with menace. The man turned his back to the entrance of the hut but did not move.

'Who is that man?' Anil lifted her head and stroked the wet strands of hair from her face.

'He owns me,' she said, fresh tears pouring down her face. 'He owns me.'

Anil and the woman sat together. She rocked and cried. He smoothed her hair again and again until his hands were sweet with its jasmine smell.

'I thought you were my sister,' he said, finally, tears streaming down his face.

'I am nobody's sister or daughter or wife,' she sobbed. They spoke the language of their district, the straggling clusters of huts that cuffed the coastline of the Arabian Sea, a name so much more sparkling and romantic than the gritty reality of the shores it washed.

Her fingers held him like a vice. He touched the smooth blisters on her skin, his hands felt the craters of her face, her left eye half closed, the skin as taut as webbing.

'This is the road to the village,' he said, running a forefinger gently-gently across a length of scar. With his thumb delicately brushing a corrugation on her cheek, 'Here is a beautiful grove of mangoes, ripe and ready for us.'

He stopped to gauge her reaction. She was smiling.

'Here is the creek that runs to the Arabian Sea . . .'

The pimp appeared again and Anil saw the glint of a knife. He whispered to her that his money was all gone. She reached under the bed and withdrew a knotted piece of red cotton. In the half dark, Anil saw the folds of notes. She must have been saving for years. She told Anil to pay the man. Anil couldn't make out the denomination of the paper she handed him but this woman knew. She lived in the dark.

'I will stay the night,' Anil said rather grandly, shoving the money at the man. He had temporarily forgotten he was wearing a swathe of hessian sack, stiffened like a board by the salt of the sea.

☙

In another hut in a different part of Bombay, Sunita lay asleep on a battered charpoy, her thin cotton sari unwound and haphazardly bundled around her shoulders and arms. She was dreaming of her brother, Anil. They were running together through plantation fields where butterflies darted in the air like scraps of shiny silk and parrots circled and swooped in an aerial ballet. They were swinging their school books and laughing. She hoisted Anil on to her shoulders and he shook plump red-orange mangoes from a tree and they peeled the thin skin and gorged themselves on the satiny pulp until their faces were slippery and flecked with gold. And then they flapped their arms and they flew into the sky, side by side, and the mango juice dripped into the sun-warmed air and formed globules of yellow rain and they saw the rain fall on their hut far below and their mother looked up and smiled at them with the face of a beautiful princess.

And then Sunita sat up on her thin bed and shivered, her small body wracked with fever. She coughed and coughed, her chest rattling, her shoulders trembling. The other two women in the hut moaned and turned away from her. It was nearly morning and they needed that last hour of rest before they were herded up by the beggar chief who controlled their territory. The fact Sunita was suffering from pneumonia had raised her stakes. She could cough and shiver at her railway station position and passers-by would toss her coins, knowing her pathetic days were numbered with such a hacking fever

'Anil, Anil,' she murmured, as if by mentioning his name she could summon him. Her small-time big-talking market merchant husband had died in a traffic accident and her mother-in-law wasted not a second in throwing out Sunita, ranting about age-old curses and village whores and poor dowries. She had scrounged enough money from a kindly neighbour for her train fare home and walked across the fields where the butterflies and birds continued their bold performances as if the audience below were a schoolgirl with plaits and swinging books and not a thin, wretched woman, old and used up before her time.

Sunita reached the family hut and saw her father and two brothers lying on their charpoys, dragged outside in the afternoon sun. They snored, their arms dangling to the ground where half-spilt cups of toddy were encrusted with ants and flies. She crept closer and one of her brothers stirred and raised his head. In his drunken haze, he didn't recognise Sunita. 'Go away, you old crone!' he spat.

She stood still, allowing herself to take in the scene, to imagine the future that awaited her if she stayed to cook and clean for these men. And then she backed away, as a jewel-bright butterfly danced about her head.

❦

'My name is Devi,' the woman told Anil as they talked through the night, still holding each other on the bed. He had lost all desire for sex. He could not take this woman he had mistaken for his sister.

'Devi,' he began, choosing his words very carefully, as the plan itself began to form in his mind, 'I think we can help each other.'

She looked up at him. She was very beautiful, he realised, if you looked at the unscarred side of her face.

'You said you had met other girls in Bombay from our district?'

She nodded.

'A girl named Sunita, perhaps? She was a married woman but

193

there was a rumour that she was seen in our village, very poorly dressed and with just her bus fare. They said she had escaped from her mother-in-law in Bombay. I looked everywhere for her last time I visited my father but she had disappeared and he said the story was nonsense, she was a respectable married woman.'

'So you think she is in Bombay?'

'I think she must have come back here. There would be nowhere else to go.'

'Sunita, Sunita,' she said, very slowly. 'Would she be working like me?'

'It's possible.'

Anil sank onto the bed and Devi wrapped her arms around him. As they slept their dreams mingled. Dreams of bright skies and emerald birds with wings the colour of sapphire and fruit that tasted like sunshine and glittering fish drawn in nets from the ocean.

The next morning, she gave him an old shirt to cover himself and enough money to buy himself new clothes and a train ticket. He looked at the notes, folded and refolded due to who knows how many countings and recountings. He gave her his watch, an old English one with a leather band that William had passed on to him years ago. It didn't keep time well but Anil liked the swagger of a foreign-made timepiece on his wrist.

'I will be back in two weeks,' he told her. 'The monsoon is very late this year and we have no time to waste. Find Sunita for me and I will take you both to my mountains.'

'Anil's mountains,' she said and her smile lit the hut as if he had flicked a switch to illuminate the whole of Marine Drive.

'Devi has no reason to trust me,' he thought, as he picked his way along the beach. He turned around and saw her standing

194

outside the pathetic hovel, waving. It was an image still in his mind as he joined a long ticket queue at Victoria Terminus, side-stepping a huddled beggarwoman who sporadically heaved and shook as she coughed.

Chapter Twenty-nine

CHALAILI
JUNE, 1937

THE SOLIGANJ WEEKLY OBSERVER

Mr David Oakley, President of the Soliganj Business-men's League, has responded to recent remarks made by Mrs Rajat Banerjee, proprietress of Coronation Talkies, Chalaili. 'If Mrs Banerjee is so concerned about the status of businesswomen,' he told *The Soliganj Weekly Observer*, 'she should form a league for the ladies concerned.'

Thanks to Lydia's disregard for housekeeping budgets, Anil knew it would take very little time to save enough for his train fare from Chalaili to Bombay several times over. William had always required he keep an exact accounting of shopping expenses, drawn up in a ledger that would be signed each day. Anil continued to keep the ledger but now it was a work of enormous fiction because Lydia never looked at the figures. She just signed her name, Lydia Rushmore, and then peered at the connected letters as if she were wondering who that person was.

When he returned with Devi and Sunita, the housekeeping deception would have to stop. Anil disliked duping William but he would do anything to effect a reunion with his sister. Of course, it was possible she would not want to join him. As for Devi, the very idea of bringing a scarred prostitute to Chalaili was something that even Mrs Banerjee, the town's most unpredictable character, would scarcely contemplate.

He knew Lydia was the answer. She could be persuaded to employ the women, to teach them English, to take them on as special projects. William was the problem. Anil would need all the wiles at his disposal to get this idea past Rain Wallah.

Lydia was sitting on the front step in her usual position when Anil walked up to her. He was carrying a small cloth bag and was freshly scrubbed.

'Second part of holiday about to commence, Mem,' he announced.

Lydia looked up from her book.

'Does Sahib know?'

'Just overnight, Mem, please. Delicious cold dinner, no cooking, is waiting on dining table. Even serving from kitchen is not required.'

'Overnight? But, Anil, where are you going?'

'Bombay return,' he announced, waving his arm to and fro to indicate just how swift the passage could be.

'Anil, the truth, please.'

Her voice was slightly stern but Lydia found it difficult to get angry with Anil. He looked at the ground as he replied. 'This is the truth, Mem. But possible that my sister and my friend may come to Chalaili, too.'

Lydia knew that William would not countenance Bluebell

Cottage being used as a resettlement camp for Anil's relatives and friends. She could hear his voice. 'Next thing there will be hundreds of them, sleeping in the bloody hallways.'

'Anil, that is not a good plan.'

'It is the *only* plan,' he said, peeping up at Lydia.

She remained silent and he crept away down the ridge. Lydia was sure she could detect a certain jauntiness in his stride.

Chapter Thirty

CHALAILI
JUNE, 1937

THE SOLIGANJ WEEKLY OBSERVER
Mr K. Wallia, of Wallia's Pickles and Daily Needs, Chota
Chalaili Bazaar, announces the arrival of a shipment of
umbrellas with monsoon reinforcements.

Lydia had been toying with the notion of filling her empty hours by writing a romantic novel. That had always been her ambition in West Gamble and she had kept a series of notebooks about her neighbours and colleagues, inventing for them larger lives than they could have imagined including, if so deserved, terrible illnesses and operatic sorrows.

But Lydia was such a tedious Jane Austen kind of name, she thought, and then giggled as she considered a nom de plume.

'Yes,' she squealed, 'Eugenia Jambolana, of course.'

She remembered how funny she had thought the botanical name as she browsed in the library aboard the *Viceroy of India*.

It had Indian connections but was a conceit few would recognise and, if they did, so much the cosier.

The setting would be an Indian hill station and the characters her neighbours. The fact Lydia knew very little about the inhabitants of Chalaili mattered little. She had visited Charlotte Montague, even if under unusual circumstances, and knew she found her so-called friend Dorothy Creswell-Smythe to be insufferable. The Misses Craig of the Loch Fyne Tea Rooms and Mrs Banerjee of Coronation Talkies required no further embellishing to make them into first-class characters. And what fun to invent a seance, a party populated by faux-Apaches and a moonlight gymkhana with an overly refreshed postmaster coming adrift from his horse. Whatever I make up, thought Lydia, would be even better and funnier than the real thing.

Yes, Lydia felt she had a lively enough imagination to manufacture the lives and liaisons of Chalaili's finest. Besides, it would keep her mind off the abominable heat and the possibility of bumping into Simon Fraser-Gough.

She took creamy paper from the small desk William kept in a corner of the drawing room and a good pen from the top drawer. It would be easy enough to create fanciful names for The Crows and to describe the hill station's ethereal climate and vertical landscape. But she needed more inside information.

Lydia decided to press The Cheeky Man in the bazaar for more details. His name was a joke between Lydia and Anil. He was really The Chikki Man, purveyor of the most absolutely delicious toffee, made with cane sugar jaggery, coconut and other nutty flavours. The first time Anil had paused to encourage Lydia to buy some of the achingly sweet chikki, she had misheard the name as cheeky.

'Why is he called that?' she had asked Anil.

'Because he is chikki chap. Everyone knows him.'

It was some days before the nuance of his name became clear and still Lydia fancied he might pinch her bottom or wink salaciously. Anil had suggested he was 'doing night business' with Florence Gordon, the attractive Anglo-Indian assistant postmistress. Lydia had seen the woman in a cluttered cubicle behind the counter as she'd waited in line to post her letter to Evelyn. She was too embarrassed to admit she didn't understand the ambiguous term Anglo-Indian, whether it meant she was of mixed blood or just an Anglophile. The woman was petite with glossy brown hair. When she had stood and leaned forward across her messy desk, Lydia could tell she had the kind of bosom men would be tempted to leave home for.

No matter how flavoursome the wares of The Chikki Man, she couldn't imagine this well-groomed woman granting him her favours. Like all the bazaar traders, he was unkempt, his clothes a ragged pastiche of khaki cloth, shawls and pyjama-style pants. But he had once worked for a British family as a cook, according to Anil, and he spoke reasonable English. Lydia would cultivate him as a contact. He knew all the minutiae of the bazaar's goings-on and made frequent trips to Bombay to attend to jaggery supplies so he would be a source of wider knowledge on what was happening below on the plains.

She wrote him a note, never doubting that he could read, and pushed it into his hand as she purchased a slab of chikki. The Chikki Man took several steps backwards. The memsahib was shopping alone, which was unheard of, and she was passing him slips of paper. They exchanged looks and Lydia ambled off, chewing on her chikki, a very nice peanut version he had freshly made that hour.

Late that night, a pair of figures met at Twin Trees Point. The man handed a piece of paper to the woman, but not before grabbing her around the waist and kissing her deeply as his hands rose upwards to hold her pouting breasts. He jiggled them lightly and felt their contours, as if assessing weight and ripeness. A sudden gust of wind caught the pair like a lasso and they momentarily lost their balance, affording the man a chance to cup the woman's pleasantly rounded right buttock on the pretext of steadying her.

'That's enough,' she snapped. She was not displeased at the attention afforded her greatest assets but his odour of cigarettes and sugar was ever so slightly sick-making and she was anxious to read the piece of paper. He lit a match, and then another, repeatedly striking until she could decipher the handwritten note in full.

> *'Dear cheeky man,'* it began. Lydia hadn't waited to ask Anil to check the spelling. *'I would be very grateful if you would meet me on Friday next at The Metropole Hotel at 10 a.m. sharp. I write on behalf of the novelist Eugenia Jambolana who has an assignment that could interest someone of your talents and connections. Yours sincerely, Lydia Rushmore.'*

'Talents and connections,' swooned The Chikki Man, his chest swelling.

'This is outrageous,' spluttered Florence Gordon, but she was sensationally intrigued. After another lustful embrace with Vivek, for The Chikki Man had a name, after all, they parted and sped in opposite directions. Florence hastened back to her small cottage in the grounds of The Metropole Hotel, behind the gardening sheds and garages. She spent several hours flipping through piles of books stashed under her bed and consulting her precious London mail-order catalogues but could find no trace of the novels of Eugenia Jambolana.

Chapter Thirty-one

CHALAILI
JUNE, 1937

THE SOLIGANJ WEEKLY OBSERVER
The American divorcee Wallis Simpson has married the former King Edward VIII of England in a ceremony in France. The couple will be known as the Duke and Duchess of Windsor.

For weeks, Lydia lived on high alarm, not knowing if any photographs of her caught in disarray at The Chalaili Sanatorium for the Tubercular would suddenly appear. She cursed her stupidity in trusting Simon Fraser-Gough and was terrified of William's reaction if anything should come to light. She hadn't heard a word from Charlotte Montague. The monsoon was very late and the heat and utter dryness were causing her headaches.

Settling into her role as the novelist Eugenia Jambolana, Lydia still took a taxi to The Empire Club on Tuesday afternoons and raced up the front steps looking purposefully ahead, on course for the coolness of the library. On one occasion, she felt there was someone beside her and turned suddenly, handbag aloft, as if about to swat a pesky insect. It was Dorothy Creswell-Smythe, who merely gave Lydia a snooty look, wished her a good afternoon in her concertinaed voice, and marched on.

Lydia wondered what Dorothy Cresswell-Smythe knew . . . She was not entirely sure she could rely upon Charlotte Montague not to yap to her cronies at The Empire Club. A few drinks, the overwhelming urge to let slip such a palatable morsel of gossip . . .

'Blast,' said Lydia, weighing up the consequences, as she did dozens of times a day, and stomping her right foot.

The young sub-waiter Sachin brought Lydia's drinks to her usual library position and stood with the silver tray outstretched while she signed the chits. Lydia had asked his name and called him by it, which unsettled the boy. He was afraid of what might have happened to her at the hands of Simon Fraser-Gough who had paid him to spy on her. The memsahib looked unharmed but her eyes were glossy and flicked everywhere, as if fearful of intruders.

Sachin looked around the library, too, but it was almost always empty, save for Mrs Rushmore and, occasionally, those two mad old twins whom no one could possibly tell apart. They spoke not just Hindustani but the local dialect, Marathi, and tried to engage him in conversation about Mahatma Gandhi, which he feared was a dangerous topic to discuss with white women, even up in the Chalaili clouds.

Lydia was watching him, cracking ice between her teeth. He hurriedly took the glass-fronted bookcase key from the pocket of his jacket and opened the lock. Inside were bound volumes of club records and a copy of *Thacker's Indian Directory*.

Sachin didn't know what the book contained but it was regularly commandeered by Dorothy Creswell-Smythe and Charlotte

Montague so its words must be fascinating indeed. He handed it to Lydia, who gave him a puzzled smile, and then he scooted back to the bar.

She opened the book, published by Thacker, Spink & Co of Calcutta, and realised it was an annual containing listings of government departments and officials, addresses of post offices and telegraphic stations and myriad data on churches, missions, clubs and institutes.

The book was about five inches thick and unwieldy to hold and Lydia wondered why Sachin should think she'd find it of interest but then she found a more intriguing section: an alphabetical listing of Europeans residing in India and, she noted, a few prominent Indians. She looked for William's entry.

RUSHMORE, *William Ellis, Indian Forestry Service, Meteorological Officer First Class. Born Surrey, November 4, 1900. Stationed Chalaili.*

She sipped her drink. How boring, she thought. She turned back to the F listing.

FRASER-GOUGH, *Simon James, Indian Army Corps of Clerks, Staff Sergeant (Discharged). Born Calcutta, June 12, 1913. Married Miss Hilary Cook, April 20, 1935. 1 Daughter. Stationed Calcutta.*

Lydia gasped. He was married. He was a father. He was younger than herself.

꩜

Lydia was standing outside Coronation Talkies looking at the advertising bills for Mrs Banerjee's latest offerings.

'Bluebell! What a champion surprise.'

She froze.

Simon Fraser-Gough stopped beside Lydia and leaned around in front of her so his vinous nose was all but jutting at her forehead.

Lydia panicked and pushed against the double front doors of Coronation Talkies. They opened and she hurled herself in, but Simon Fraser-Gough followed in a flash.

'What's up, Bluebell?'

The foyer was dark and smelled of roses but Lydia surmised they were alone.

'I know all about your wife and daughter!'

'Dear old Hilary and little Molly?'

'You, sir, are a married man.'

'And you, Bluebell, are a married woman. Old Hils has gone back to England for a spell. Took little Molly, too, of course . . .'

'I'm not surprised she's gone. Found out about all your dirty tricks, I'll warrant. How could she hold up her head. You are a cad!'

'A cad? Whatever do you mean. Come on, Bluebell, be kind to this poor old tropical invalid.'

'Tropical invalid be damned. You are a cad of the highest order and were run out of Simla! Don't try to deny it . . .'

'Oh, that silly old misunderstanding.'

'Well, don't think you can try it again.'

'I don't think anything of the sort. I have put all that extortion business well behind me. Darned stressful, I can tell you . . .'

'Stressful! You remove my dress and perform who knows

what amusements upon my body and then take photographs for your nefarious purposes.'

'Heavens, Bluebell. No need for the school mistress's lecture, old girl. Firstly, you took off your dress, said you were awfully hot. Then you performed some kind of strange dance in your petticoat and collapsed on the bed. You asked me to call you Princess Something . . . Piddle Widdle, I think.'

'Liddie Diddie! It would have been Princess Liddie Diddie, if you must know . . .'

'Well, whatever it was, you fell asleep and I had to put your dress back on, which wasn't easy . . . You were like a limp doll. Then I went off to have my afternoon medicine and got caught up with that chee chee nurse, Valerie Collins . . .'

'Chee chee?'

'Eurasian, Bluebell, Anglo-Indian, call them what you will. It's that sing-song way they speak. You know, chee chee, chee chee. Some of the chaps call them flying fish. Neither fish nor fowl, you see. Anyway, you'd think she was white, you know, skin like bone china . . . damned shame, really.'

'Chee chee sounds very derogatory to me, Mr Fraser-Gough, but even so I really have no interest in the condition of Miss Collins's skin. I want to know about the photographs.'

'Photographs? Oh surely, you don't think . . . Look, I don't even own a camera. They confiscated it in Simla, which means some badmash of a desk wallah is using it now.'

'Why should I believe you?'

'Why not? There are no photographs, Bluebell. Surely the spies of old Queen Crow herself would have uncovered them by now.'

He even knows about those unfruitful investigations of Charlotte Montague's, thought Lydia.

'Then why did you lure me to your room?'

'I did not lure you, my dear. I invited you and you accepted. I thought you were very lonely and probably needed a kiss.'

'A kiss?'

She couldn't make out his features in the gloom of the foyer of Coronation Talkies but her imagination summoned his gingery face and over-nosy nose with mounting horror. They were standing very close to each other.

'Yes, please, Bluebell.'

Simon Fraser-Gough lunged at Lydia and would have pinned her against the nearest wall if the light had not suddenly snapped on. Mrs Banerjee had been observing the shadowy proceedings from behind the red imperial-crested velvet curtains leading into the theatre.

'Good afternoon,' she sang, with a swish of silk as she unclipped the door to the fishbowl ticket cubicle. 'Two tickets for this evening's talking picture presentation? May I suggest the privacy of the back row?'

Simon Fraser-Gough smoothed his buoyant hair and sauntered towards the now-seated Mrs Banerjee as Lydia flew through the half-opened front door of Coronation Talkies and on to the safe ground of The Strand.

Chapter Thirty-two

CHALAILI

JUNE, 1937

'In preparation for the annual rains, she must be
properly attired, including the wearing of waterproof
undergarments in a fabric such as light canvas.'
ETIQUETTE AND MANNERS FOR THE COLONIAL MEMSAHIB
BY HENRIETTA WEATHERBY, 1895

Mrs Banerjee's arrival at her new home was well timed.
Although the pre-monsoonal heat was intense and the
coolies struggled with their pushcarts along the path leading to Bungalow Number Seven, its only designation thus far, the rains were
conveniently delayed. Just a week thereafter and any kind of furniture-
carrying on the mud-clogged paths would have been nigh impossible.

Sham Lal's men were still hauling boxes and pieces of heavy
rosewood furniture through the front door when Anjali Gupta came
to visit, in her wake two of The Metropole Hotel's puffing waiters
bearing covered boxes of food. Anjali Gupta was breathy from the
exertion, too, and Mrs Banerjee sent Aruna to fetch cool water from

the pump in the courtyard at the rear of the bungalow. The two women sat companionably on the front step, Mrs Banerjee shifting with some effort when the men needed to pass. The sight of an intricately carved sandalwood bedhead passing high above their heads signalled to Anjali Gupta to mention the absent Mr Banerjee.

'We all look forward to meeting your husband.'

'It will be some time before he can get away . . . especially with the monsoon coming.'

'Ah, yes, the rain. Will you be all right up here, so alone?'

'I am not alone,' protested Mrs Banerjee, her arm sweeping along the ridge to the extended line of six bungalows. For the first time she noticed their gardens were as overgrown as her own.

'But surely you must have known they are empty,' cried Anjali Gupta. 'Families were evacuated to the lower ridge in 1932 when the monsoon washed away small buildings. A child was killed. Swept away. An English child.'

Mrs Banerjee stood up and walked to the front gate, hanging off the wire fence. Looking down, she could see the jutting rooftops of a lower row of bungalows. The ground beneath her ridge was shored up with an intricate assembly of bamboo poles and metal pipes and the odd exposed root of a massive deodar tree.

'Mr Rushmore, a famous expert on the monsoon lives down there, at the end.' Anjali Gupta stabbed her sun parasol in the direction of Bluebell Cottage standing a little removed from the other rooftops, like the leader in a flotilla of sailing ships.

'Ah, the Rushmores. If you remember, I invited them to the soiree the night Coronation Talkies opened . . .'

'Yes,' sighed Anjali Gupta and the two women stood together surveying the men carrying the last of Mrs Banerjee's substantial possessions.

Anjali Gupta would never have broached the subject of the ill-fated premiere party that had had to be called off, due to Mrs Banerjee's brief discomposure at Chalaili Hospital after the curtain rail collapsed on top of her. When she had arrived back at The Metropole Hotel in a taxi, several hours later, her left arm bandaged and resting in a splint, Mrs Banerjee discovered the Guptas sitting in the dining room, surrounded by the platters of finger food that had been destined for the party in the Maharani Suite. A couple of the permanently sleepy waiters had slid down the walls and were squatting in dishevelled piles.

'Come! Come!" Mrs Banerjee had cried. The waiters sprung up to attention and the Guptas rose, too, astonished at their prize guest's operatic entrance. 'Let's eat!'

Mrs Banerjee included the serving staff in the party and the wide-eyed men nervously helped themselves to the slightly soggy sandwiches and milky sweets displayed on the silver trays. The Guptas were too overcome to prevent this outlandish turn of events. Many of the waiters had been in the employ of The Metropole Hotel since the days when Ram Gupta's parents had run the hotel and Chalaili was a notable hill station. Before the monsoon rot set in, as he would lament to his wife.

The black-jacketed men were joined by the kitchen staff whom Mrs Banerjee rounded up by smashing through the swing doors with her one good arm to their smoky sanctum and hauling them out. One of the young cooks, suspecting he was to be dismissed, fell to the ground and attempted to kiss Picture Madam's ruby toenails, begging forgiveness for his inferior attempts at cooking her breakfast eggs.

'Nonsense, boy!' she flared, jabbing her open-toed blue shoe at his advancing lips with such force that she kicked him square in the nose.

212

With the staff assembled and the trays being handed from hand to hand, Mrs Banerjee accepted a sweet lime juice from Ram Gupta, took a decisive gulp and began an emotional speech. Much of what she said was indiscernible. She spoke a mixture of fast Hindustani and scattered English and blew her nose loudly throughout the proceedings. At every mention of the words Coronation Talkies, The Metropole Hotel staff, grown brave and sentimental at this momentous gathering with their employers and the Maharani Suite incumbent, burst into applause.

When Mrs Banerjee eventually departed upstairs to her suite, her vast bottom retreating like a battleship, the staff began cleaning up, keeping their eyes lowered, lest the Guptas should take the opportunity to berate them for their insubservience. But the hotel couple sat still, at once awed by Mrs Banerjee's grandeur and Bombay sophistication and struck, simultaneously, by the realisation that there was no way they could present her with the substantial bill for her premiere party.

'I will call this very exclusive residence Monsoon Cottage!' shrieked Mrs Banerjee, the volume of her voice bringing back Anjali Gupta from her reminiscences. The hotel owner's wife joined with Mrs Banerjee in a belly-shaking laugh. 'You are amazing, Picture Madam,' she said, with genuine admiration.

'Thank you, Anjali,' she said, using Mrs Gupta's given name for the first time.

Mrs Banerjee made a note to reserve two seats at Coronation Talkies within unpleasant closeness to the rowdy third-class section for the treacherous Mr Nightingale and his no doubt equally grasping wife. The Guptas, on the other hand, could expect VIP reception, any time they pleased.

Chapter Thirty-three

CHALAILI
JUNE, 1937

THE SOLIGANJ WEEKLY OBSERVER
The Ministry of Agriculture confirms that one-fifth of India is drought declared. 'If the rains do not come soon,' spokesman James Gill advised *The Soliganj Weekly Observer*, 'we will have a crisis on our hands.'

As she dressed for her meeting with Lydia Rushmore, as The Chikki Man's emissary, Florence Gordon was quite prepared for the Englishwoman to be clinically mad. In her opinion, most residents of Chalaili were ridiculously eccentric, a condition she attributed to the town's small size, its isolation, its lack of purpose.

Yes, that's it, she thought. Purpose. Chalaili has no *purpose*. It is just a place for sick people to recover and then move on. Those who stay have submitted to decay.

She shuddered at the realisation and inspected herself minutely in her full-length dressing mirror, as if she might have grown mould.

Despite her misgivings about the no-doubt-dotty Lydia, Florence Gordon dressed carefully in her cottage at the rear of The Metropole Hotel. It didn't take long to decide which ensemble to wear as she owned just two of what she would term 'going out' costumes.

She topped off her neat skirt and creamy silk blouse with a soft pink silk scarf and a jaunty beret. The mirror showed a slim woman in her late twenties, with olive skin, curly black hair and wide brown eyes. She turned sideways to admire her jutting bosom, holding in her already flat stomach to give her upper torso the appearance of a veranda awning.

Florence Gordon never wore Indian clothes and would have denied her native origins altogether were it not that her Bombay-born mother lived at Soliganj, dressed in widow's whites, visiting every second day the flower-festooned grave of her early-departed Scottish husband, Clive, a common clerk or box wallah for the Indian Railways.

Every so often Mrs Priyanka Gordon would arrive unheralded on the train from Soliganj and stomp her way to the post office where she'd berate Florence for her lack of letters and lapsed daughterly duties. 'You work in a post office and still you cannot send a letter!' was the habitual refrain and it always set the postal peons sniggering because privately they thought Florence Gordon far too uppity.

Florence Gordon led a quiet life, saving every last paisa for a fare to that faraway misty world called Great Britain where she was sure her half-share of English blood would earn her a suitable status in society. The Chikki Man was unwittingly helping her escape as the sums he regularly paid to be allowed to fondle her breasts in darkened circumstances were added to her savings tin.

In India, she felt scorned by both Indians and Britishers. Occasionally, a consumptive British officer on sick leave in Chalaili would hang around the post office waiting for mail and coughing like a seagull. Such men would always invite her to The Empire Club for dinner and a dance. There were few single white women in Chalaili and she knew the chaps went to some trouble with their evening dress, slyly anticipating the pleasure of her watermelon breasts. She's almost white, Florence Gordon imagined them saying to themselves, justifying the effort.

Lydia had been expecting The Chikki Man and was startled when the assistant postmistress swept into The Metropole Hotel dining room and sat down at her corner table set with a brass Reserved sign that Ram Gupta had unearthed and instructed one of his under-employed waiters to polish to a see-your-face shine.

'I am very well read,' Florence Gordon announced, removing her beret and shaking her curls with unnecessary coquettishness, 'and I have never heard of Eugenia Jambolana.'

Lydia felt herself blush. Florence Gordon regarded her with raised eyebrows as Anjali Gupta took orders for two Darjeeling teas.

'Are you English . . . exactly?' Lydia asked, aware her companion's exotic features did not quite complement her artificially clipped accent, quite unlike the lovely musical tones of Mrs Banerjee and Anjali Gupta.

'Scottish,' said Florence Gordon, confounding matters further.

'I see . . . Well, I am sorry, but I was mistaken about Eugenia Jambolana. She won't be visiting Chalaili after all and so won't require the services of The Cheeky Man or . . .'

'Cheeky man?'

Florence Gordon spluttered as she suppressed a hearty laugh.

'Are you all right? More tea?'

Unable to reply, Florence Gordon waved her hand at Lydia and tried to compose herself. She attempted to speak but out came a strangulated chortle.

'What part of Scotland?' Lydia was afraid the woman was about to choke but still felt it necessary to retain some decorum with a polite line of questioning.

Florence Gordon gasped, patted her hand against her pouting chest and finally replied, sitting straighter in her chair.

'Edinburgh, of course.'

'Of course.'

'I must go, Mrs Rushmore . . .'

'Call me Lydia . . . please do.'

There was a plea in her voice that Florence Gordon had not expected. She instantly realised how lonely the Englishwoman must be, newly arrived in this hideous backwater and married to that boring weather wallah. Florence Gordon had thought William Rushmore a prospect for herself at one time but he was so disparaging about all things British that she knew he would be no saviour.

'Perhaps we could go to a film one day?' said Lydia.

Florence Gordon hated films. The few she had seen on occasional trips to Bombay with her mother had been British or American and everything about them, their clothing, their good cheer, their fine houses, their blondeness, seemed to be mocking the smallness of her life and her questionable colour.

The pause made Lydia uncomfortable. 'I mean we could go to Mrs Banerjee's Coronation Talkies . . . not to Bombay or anywhere like that.'

'Perhaps,' Florence Gordon finally replied, looking down at her hands. Her nails were ragged and unpolished. Her rigorous economies made visits to the Lakshmi Hair and Beauty Studio a very rare treat.

'I must go,' she said, pulling on her cotton gloves and pushing back her chair.

Lydia watched the woman retreat. She had not explained her connection with the bazaar trader nor had she offered to contribute to the bill.

'Mrs Gupta,' said Lydia, as the hotel owner's wife came to remove the untouched tea cups and wipe the table, 'why is that woman so sad?'

'Florence Gordon, you mean?'

'Yes, the assistant postmistress.'

'Ha, she is not really the assistant postmistress. Just assistant to the postmaster. There is a difference.'

'What do you mean?'

'Mr Harold Gilbert is the postmaster but he has a condition that prevents him from attending the post office every day.'

'Condition?'

'Drinking condition, that is. Most days he is at The Empire Club. Under the billiard table, usually.'

'Oh, yes, William mentioned he favours the bottle. He's a neighbour of ours on the lower ridge . . .

'But this Florence Gordon . . . I am intrigued. Is she really from Edinburgh?'

'Edinburgh? Ha, she's from Soliganj, that one, and if you ask me those bosoms of hers are not permanent fixtures. You mark my words.'

Anjali Gupta flounced off, the whirl of her yellow dusting cloth seeming to hover in the air long after she had rushed through the door to the kitchen.

'Why is everyone in this place so complicated . . . and just plain crazy,' muttered Lydia as she gathered her bag to leave.

She walked down the front steps of the hotel and stood in The Strand, looking right, then left, then right again, like the movements of an oscillating fan.

'WHAT AM I DOING HERE?' she yelled. Anjali Gupta appeared on the top step and was about to ask Lydia if she was feeling alright when the British woman stomped off. The only other witnesses to her outburst were two monkeys loitering outside Grindlays Bank. They bared their teeth and let out screeches as unsettling as chalk dragged on a blackboard.

Anjali Gupta hurried inside. 'What are any of us doing here?' she asked her husband as he popped up from his table behind the front desk.

'Doing monthly accounts, actually . . . three days overdue,' he replied, descending from view.

Chapter Thirty-four

BOMBAY
JUNE, 1937

THE SOLIGANJ WEEKLY OBSERVER

The Twenty-first of June marks the fiftieth anniversary of the opening of Victoria Terminus (VT), Bombay, rightly recognised as one of the world's most famous railway stations. Designed by the able architect F. W. Stevens, VT is Gothic-Saracenic in style and has been likened by eminent visitors to a grand European cathedral. Mr S. Forshaw, President of the Soliganj Rail Appreciation Society, commented to *The Soliganj Weekly Observer* that we 'should feel honoured to be served by the Western main line, originating at VT'.

Anil arrived in Bombay in the late morning and sped to Juhu Beach. Fish-kites wheeled in unsteady circles and the sky was a grubby violet, full of impending rain. The monsoon was probably no more than a day away, and he imagined Rain Wallah getting all excited and bright-eyed about the weather business in store. Anil took a big breath of the ozone-heavy air and made his way over the rocks to the little gaggle of huts.

There was something different about the configuration of the ramshackle assortment. Some of the huts lower on the beach had been demolished. He realised in panic that Devi's had vanished.

As he approached, he saw her pimp, stirring a cooking pot over a small fire, lazily picking his nose and thoroughly examining the slimy excavations before flicking them on the sand. Anil walked up and asked where Devi had gone.

The man looked up and narrowed his eyes. 'What business is it of yours?'

'I am her, er, friend . . .'

'Friend?' The man spat on the sand, shifted his squatting position and resumed his stirring.

Anil walked to one side and sat on a rock. There would be other people there who knew her. She would have left a message for him. Creeping behind the man, he squeezed between two huts and pushed through the curtain hanging on the one farthest from view. A woman on the bed barely stirred. She looked up at him with glazed eyes and then held out her hand.

'Where is Devi?' he whispered, crouching down.

The woman waggled her fingers, indicating her hand was ready to receive money.

Anil could not afford to pay her for information. The money he had brought was not much more than the cost of three third-class tickets to Chalaili and he doubted she knew what he was talking about. He got up and walked back through the curtain while a stream of invective followed him.

He sat down on the sand, running the tawny grains through his fingers. A child of no more than nine or ten came and squatted next to him and passed him a piece of paper she took from the pocket of an old shirt she wore as a dress. Anil opened it and the girl moved closer. They looked at it together. There was a crude drawing of a train and two female figures, their stick shapes enhanced with breasts that looked like upturned cups.

'Did Devi give you this?'

The girl nodded and ran off, leaving a zigzag of footprints on the moist sand. Anil gave chase, waving the note.

He caught her and he leant towards her, breathing heavily. 'When did Devi go?'

'Not long ago,' the child replied, in a voice as tinkling as a bell. She began drawing with her bare toes in the sand.

'My sister and I used to make pictures in the sand,' said Anil, watching the marks take shape to form a tree and then a block house with sloping roof.

He looked at the shapes, the extra detail the girl had added in the form of a flower and a dog with a curling tail. There was a ribbon of smoke in the air above the roof. He was about to tell her she was a fine artist but she was gone, running off in the distance, her funny shirt dress flapping in the wind.

Black clouds were assembling on the horizon and the promise of rain saturated the air like a wet cloth. Anil couldn't believe the monsoon would choose this day, of all possible days, to unleash its fury. The city would be turned into a quagmire, rubbish would go rollicking along flooded gutters, shanty towns would collapse under the weight of turgid water. The hut dwellers on the beach were propping up their walls with bamboo poles, vainly pressing more patches of canvas on the roofs and lashing together summer-brown palm fronds.

As Anil made his way back to Victoria Terminus, he prayed

he would find the two women there. It had been exactly two weeks since he left and perhaps Devi had planned for their reunion to take place on the platforms. He imagined her clutching the hem of her blue and gold sari and asking officious railway employees for trains to the mountains. He realised he hadn't even told her Chalaili's name. Perhaps the officials, bristling in pressed uniforms and twirling their scoundrel-shifting lathi sticks, would throw her out of the station, discarded in the gutter like a piece of garbage.

The vision propelled him as he dashed across the city, imagining the force of the monsoon at his rear, big black clouds chasing him. He dodged traffic, flew across roads, skidded on the detritus of a dozen pavements before he saw the grand High Gothic cupolas and curlicues of Victoria Terminus.

The clock had crept to mid-afternoon and the scene was absolute chaos. Thousands of workers were surging on and off trains. A balloon seller was managing to impede many a passage with his bouncy construction of wares and Anil wondered why anyone would want to buy a balloon before getting on a train as it would bang-burst within seconds. But perhaps to buy one would be good luck. He could present it to Devi as if it were a precious jewel befitting someone with the name of a goddess. He stopped the seller, whose body was ever so slightly airborne, and chose a balloon in mango yellow. Then Anil realised he should buy a second one, in the hope Sunita would be with Devi, so he stopped the hovering man again and after some hesitation, chose one in lime green, the colour of the orchards in their village.

He stood uncertainly with the two waving balloons and was jostled in all directions so he sat down on a tin chair at a desk that stood oddly in the middle of the concourse. 'What are you

223

concerned about? The price of balloons?' jeered two schoolboys, sleek and assured in their smart blazers.

'What?' asked Anil, but the boys scampered off.

He closed his eyes to find a place of birds and butterflies, of green-green leaves and sharp sunlight, of a sister's happy smile. Concentrating every iota of energy in his body, he opened his lids, ready to move forward.

A tall Sikh gentleman stood in front of him, arms folded, moustache waxed tightly to perfection, eyebrows raised with amusement. 'Are you concerned that the people of Bombay are not getting sufficient sleep, particularly during daylight hours?'

'I beg your pardon . . .'

'Look at the sign!' belly-laughed the man.

Anil suspected the over-jovial Sikh chap was about to do a balloon grab-and-run. He'd had his share already of loose Bombay types so he held tightly to his presents for Devi and Sunita, stood up and walked to the other side of the desk. There was indeed a large cardboard sign, stuck on a metal pole he hadn't earlier noticed. It read, in ominous black lettering: CONCERNED CITIZENS' BUREAU. The Sikh walked off, shoulders shaking with merriment.

Anil checked the big announcement board for the platform for the afternoon departure of the Soliganj Limited Express and struck off in that direction, gold and green orbs dancing above him. Then he saw them. Sunita and Devi were crouched on the ground beside a wall decorated with an intricate carving. It was a carved shield broken into three layers: an elephant bearing a howdah, an engine billowing stone-frozen steam and the British coat of arms.

The ground was polka-dotted with the scarlet spittle of a million betel-nut chewers. Sunita was coughing and had almost shrouded herself with her cotton sari so that just her eyes were revealed. When she barked, the dirty ochre fabric rippled like a wave. Devi was alert, her eyes whipping across the faces of the packs of railway passengers. She had found a ticket-seller who gave her the platform numbers of trains to the mountains. She had hated his sly eyes but he was an old man and after he had sensed her desperation, he had told her to wait near the entrance for the Soliganj Limited Express.

She had been forced to drag Sunita to their perch. 'You are mad,' she croaked. 'Anil is far away.' People had stopped to stare at the scarred woman dragging the heaving bundle but there was little entertainment in the spectacle and they soon moved on. Once Devi was certain that Sunita was properly settled, she began her vigilance, leaping to her feet as any man of Anil's height and build approached.

It was the blue and mango-gold sari that Anil spotted first, just as he'd caught the shimmer of colour at the doorway to Devi's hut. He saw her before she noticed him and he saw, too, the defeated shape at her feet. He stopped and watched for a few seconds before charging forward. Devi had drawn her hair back, daring the world to look upon her disfigurement. Her eyes were as black and searching as a raven's. The woman at her feet lifted the tail of her sari from over her head and indicated she wanted water. Devi bent down and let her sip from a metal cup, wiping her lips dry with the firmness of her forefinger.

'Sorry I have kept you waiting, your highnesses,' said Anil, bending to one knee. Devi clapped her hands and commenced a skipping dance around the little tableau, grabbing both balloons from Anil's grasp and flying them like kites. Sunita looked up at her brother and stared and stared at him until her face trembled with tears.

Chapter Thirty-five

CHALAILI
JUNE, 1937

THE SOLIGANJ WEEKLY OBSERVER

Mr S. Forshaw, President of the Soliganj Rail Appreciation Society, has reported that a special departure of Soliganj citizens to Bombay on the twenty-first of June last was accomplished without a hitch. Passengers travelled aboard a festively decorated carriage and arrived at noon at Victoria Terminus to join fiftieth anniversary celebrations.

The humidity in Chalaili had been so high that moving one's hands in the air was like punching a damp sponge. As the expatriate population became slower and more enervated in their movements, as if their veins were silting up, William transformed into a firecracker of energy. Lydia no longer rose early to join him for soft-boiled eggs and strong tea before he pedalled off to work. She lay on their bed, her nightdress soaked in sweat, her wavy brown hair plastered to her head as if she'd just dunked it in one of Anil's earthenware water-cooling pots. She tried to read but the pages of her book stuck together and her clammy fingers left marks on the paper. Eugenia Jambolana was put away to a far corner of her mind until the heat subsided and she could concentrate on her writing.

Lydia watched the lizards scampering along the architraves of the bedroom ceiling, already determining their monsoonal hide-outs.

Anil had been due to return that afternoon from Bombay but he had not shown up. William told her he believed the trains would be delayed as the rains were beginning to hit the coast. He was shiny with excitement at the prospect of the monsoon.

William and Lydia took dinner at The Metropole Hotel dining room, their table positioned under a ceiling fan that swiped the air and redistributed the warmth rather than cooling the room.

Lydia looked around warily. That busty Florence Gordon could turn up at any time or even Simon Fraser-Gough. She was with William in public so seldomly. This could be the tubercular blackmailer's perfect opportunity to embarrass her . . .

She snapped back, realising William had said something to her.

'I told you so, Lydia,' he repeated, inferring Anil's disappearance was entirely her fault.

'I think Anil may have had family problems.'

She wiped her brow with a handkerchief, stalling a little before she spoke further.

'He is trying to help his sister.'

'His sister? She's married and lives in Bombay. I sent a present for the wedding . . .'

'And also a friend.'

'Christ.'

'Don't you mean "holy damnation"?'

Lydia expected William to explode but he put down his knife and fork and patted his lips on his serviette. She realised he was smiling.

'And don't *you* mean "galloping galoshes"?'

Lydia laughed so loudly that the Guptas exchanged glances as they sat at a nearby table and the sleeping waiters stirred from their perspiring dreams.

William and Lydia took a taxi to the junction of the lower and upper ridges and walked arm in arm to Bluebell Cottage past the row of neighbouring bungalows, their veranda screens already tied firmly against the expected rain.

Two glasses and a jug of mango juice had been left out. It was obvious Anil had returned.

Lydia didn't say a word as she poured William his nursery-style nightcap.

☾

The monsoon had broken in Bombay. William was up early and heard the early news on All India Radio. He hurried in to tell Lydia before he dressed for work. Lydia liked the clammy bed-bound mornings as they allowed her time to think. She tinkled the little brass bell by the bed, summoning Anil to bring her a cup of tea.

At first, Lydia had sipped pale Darjeeling, with neither milk nor sugar. But with patience and persuasion, Anil had converted her to chai. Bazaar tea, William dubbed it, dismissively, but Lydia found herself becoming addicted to its robustness and found a cup of chai negated the need for a large midday meal. Occasionally she thought of hunger and of the emaciated beggar woman with the snot-soaked baby on the Bombay waterfront and shuddered. Her sequestered life at Bluebell Cottage kept her at a safe remove from the poverty of India.

'Rain,' Lydia muttered, imagining that the days ahead would be silvery cold with showers, in the style of an English winter. Hot rain was a foreign concept and although William had tried to explain to her that she would find the monsoon very inconvenient, with its relentless soaking and steaminess, the ankle-turning ruts in the muddy roads, Lydia romanticised it in her mind, imagining bracing walks with her husband under a shared umbrella.

She rang the bell again and almost instantly Anil was at the door with the tea tray.

'Sorry, Mem,' he smiled as he approached her bed.

'Anil, did you bring your sister and your friend?'

He looked over both shoulders before replying.

'They are in a safe place, Mem.'

Before Lydia could ask more, he fled the room and she heard the rush of his sandals along the corridor.

That morning, Anil began rolling up the Kashmiri rugs in the front room, preparing to move them to an airtight cupboard. He would replace them with coir mats that would not suffer mould in the long wet days ahead. Lydia watched him from the bedroom door, drawing on one of William's cigarettes and holding an early gin. She smoked three times as much as she had at The Oaks, and had grown particularly fond of a drink or three in the slow, shadowy hours before William came pedalling along the ridge. She kept a traymobile freshly stocked so a gin with lime could be instantly thrust into William's hands when he emerged through the front door.

At first, William had found the ritual amusing, Lydia so eager to hand him a tumbler splashed with her favourite alcohol, a slice of lime afloat. Then he noticed that his wife's eyes were very glossy in the afternoons and he began to suspect she was several gins advanced by the time he arrived at Bluebell Cottage.

She drank deeply of the gin and tonic and then positioned herself across the doorway so Anil would have to push her aside to get through. He stood anxiously with a rolled carpet under each arm.

'Where is this safe place, Anil?'

'Kitchen, Mem,' he mumbled, cocking his head along the corridor.

Lydia moved to one side, allowing him to walk past, and she followed him down the hallway, swaying as she walked.

They entered together and there was a scampering, scuttling sound that Lydia would have picked as mice if she hadn't seen snatches of sari skirt disappear under the sink.

Anil told the women to come out and they crawled forward, kneeling in front of Lydia, not daring to look up.

'This is my sister, Sunita,' said Anil, tapping the ochre-coloured mound on the head.

'And this is my friend, Devi.'

Neither woman looked up but Lydia could tell by the way Sunita was breathing that she was unwell.

'Come and tell me the whole story, Anil,' she said, leading him back to the lounge room.

As they left the kitchen, the women did not move.

❧

Anil left no details out, not even his first visit to Devi's hut. He watched Lydia's face for signs of disapproval but her gaze never altered. They sat side by side in the front room like friends

230

enjoying a companionable chat. When she felt he had omitted anything, she pressed him for more information.

'How exactly did Devi find Sunita?'

'We are from neighbour villages. Even in a big city like Bombay, word spreads about those who have come from your place, especially when they are in the same . . .'

'The same profession?'

'My sister had no choice.'

'I am not judging anyone, Anil. What happened to her?'

'She got too sick, her pimp said the customers thought she would give them her coughing disease so he made her go begging. He wouldn't give her any medicine so she would cough worse and people would give more money.'

'So how did Devi find Sunita?'

'It wasn't hard. She had her name, her village, she guessed that she was a prostitute.'

'But why did you bring Devi here as well?'

'Because that night in her hut I thought she was my sister and then, even when I knew she wasn't, I had to give her something.'

'But what are we going to do?'

Anil was delighted that Lydia had included herself in this conundrum. 'They will work for free. I can share my food, already it is too much.'

Lydia wondered how she was going to tell William that two ex-prostitutes would be attending to his needs from now on, one of them very possibly with raging pneumonia.

'Leave it with me, Anil,' she said, but her voice was far from confident.

Chapter Thirty-six

CHALAILI
JUNE 1937

'I have no faith in the possibility of the existing [Government of India] Act to expand into an instrument of complete freedom . . . and the sooner it is replaced by something of Indian design the better.'

M. K. (MAHATMA) GANDHI

Devi and Sunita huddled together in the kitchen, covered in cotton sheets Lydia had brought out to them and left on the floor. The only view they had had of her so far was of pale legs encased in slithering sheaths that whispered when her calves rubbed together.

Sunita was the first to fall asleep, her stomach unaccustomedly full. Anil had smoothed her hair and kissed her forehead, promising that the memsahib would sort out everything by tomorrow. Devi watched the little performance and wished Anil would kiss her, too. She could remember few kindnesses in her life and Anil was like a visiting god, dispensing favours and organising adventures. Even the language he spoke in this house was from another world. He talked back and forth with the memsahib as if they were equals, never hesitating.

He retreated to his little room off the kitchen, leaving the door ajar. Devi watched him crawl into bed and she nestled down, stretching luxuriously in extra layers. Outside, the wind shook the bungalow and there were distant cracks of lightning and claps of thunder. Devi tied the ends of her burst ochre balloon into a bow and placed it down her choli blouse, next to her heart. No one had ever bought her a balloon.

She fell asleep dreaming of long pale beaches and white-topped waves that reared and bucked like horses.

☽

William did not come home that night. He tried to ring Blue-bell Cottage but the lines were down and it was too wet to send an office peon with a message. He presumed Lydia would realise he was on duty during the first hours of the monsoon's onslaught. Anil could advise her of this as he knew the annual pattern well.

Lydia started at every new blast of thunder and crack-pop of lightning but she was not overly worried about William's safety. He had warned her of his habits during the monsoon and she had picked up the phone to call him, so she knew the line was dead.

William sat in his office, head in hands, waiting for the fury of the monsoon to take hold. He had not thought through how a wife would cope with what was essentially a solitary existence on Chalaili Ridge. His neighbours were boorish snobs and they had ostracised him since the Petal Cameron incident.

☽

Lydia sat in the sitting room with her third or fourth glass of gin and tonic. She no longer kept count. 'Are you lonely, William?' she asked the gloomy room. 'Do you miss me when I am here and you are off with your infernal barometers and anemometers?' Although she didn't quite manage to pronounce anemometer, thanks to the workings of Beefeater London Distilled Dry Gin.

'DO YOU EVEN KNOW WHO I BLOODY WELL AM?' she yelled.

'Loneliness, William,' she continued, addressing the shadowy outline of the standard lamp, 'tell me what it is, please. Explain to me what loneliness is all about and how one has come to deserve it and how one should BLOODY WELL COPE WITH IT.'

Lydia hoarded little moments from her past and every so often she closed her eyes and brought them out and examined them as if they were precious stamps in an unremarkable collection. She closed her eyes tight and summoned The White Horse Inn, High Street, West Gamble, Surrey, England, 1913 or thereabouts.

Tap, tap on the lamp-lit front window, button-small Liddie Diddie nose pressed to the glass. Daddy is waiting for the little angel face to appear and he waves his pint and gulps it down and slaps the backs of his pub cohorts and she wishes she could go inside, to the clubby lounge with the gleaming horse brasses hung about and the smiling red-cheeked men with their jokes and secrets.

She knows Mummy would whip her senseless with a Mason Pearson Boar Bristle Hairbrush if she did.

Out comes Daddy, chuckling away. 'Is that my Princess Liddie Diddie?' he would ask without fail, as if it wasn't his daughter in front of him but perhaps his cunning wife disguised as a small girl with ribboned plaits.

Hand in hand, up the High Street, around the corner to Cherrybrook Lane, past the narrow terrace houses set right on the pavement, some with curtains not drawn, tables set for tea so close to the windows Daddy jokes that one night he'll just reach right in and steal his Princess Liddie Diddie a currant bun.

Out of Cherrybrook Lane and across the Common, leaf-heaped in autumn and frosty-white in winter but on this evening, the evening Lydia Rushmore is remembering as she sits at Bluebell Cottage, Chalaili, India, in the raging raining dark, it is high summer. The long twilight is soft and amber like honey and there are children bashing about on bicycles and throwing sticks to waggy-tailed dogs. The little girl wants to walk forever with her father across that enchanted place, to walk and walk and never turn left past the big beech tree into Bramble Close and reach the back door of The Oaks.

In the side lane of The Oaks, Daddy stops and reaches for the small silver flask in the inside pocket of his jacket. A fortifying gulp of gin. He wipes his mouth with the back of his hand and bends down to Princess Liddie Diddie height. He winks. She giggles. He holds the flask to her rosebud lips so she can pretend to take a sip of Daddy's special medicine. The slightest drop eases on to her tongue and she wills herself not to gag or pull a face. The liquid rages into her throat like a flame but she blinks back tears and looks up at Daddy. He nods and smiles. A smile that circles her like a soft, warm blanket.

'I love you, my Princess Liddie Diddie,' he says and swings her in the air and her skirt lifts and twirls and her plaits fly like maypole ribbons.

The door opens with a jerk. 'Go and get ready for tea this minute, Lydia,' says Mummy.

And then it is over and Lydia puts the memento back into its compartment, newly polished.

And then she reaches for her glass in the sitting room of Bluebell Cottage, Chalaili, India, thousands upon thousands of miles from West Gamble, Surrey, England, and it smashes to the floor. She tries to pick up the shards. She sucks at her cut thumb, the acrid taste of blood.

'Bleeding, William?' she yells. 'This isn't BLOOD . . . THIS IS YOUR WIFE HAEMORRHAGING WITH BLOODY LONELINESS.'

She stands, slightly rocky on her feet, and grabs the standard-lamp, shaking it. 'And Mr Important Cloud-Chasing William Rushmore, there is the question of A BABY AT MY AGE!' Now she is in a tussle with the lamp. 'YOU HEARD ME! I WANT A BABY TO LOVE ME!'

And then she falls back on the lounge as blood pools over her hand.

❧

William and Lydia had not discussed having children, but she suspected that as she had not fallen pregnant, it was a failing on her thirty-plus part. Perhaps if she entered into their love-making with more abandon, a child would be conceived. Lydia would look at the holidaying Indian ladies at the Lakshmi Hair and Beauty Studio in their swathes of brilliantly coloured silk and jangling bracelets and feel assaulted by the pungent musk of their perfume. With their bright enquiring eyes and heads bobbing in lively agreement as they talked among themselves, she imagined the ladies as a flock of exotic birds.

William noticed them, too. On the opening night at Corona-tion Talkies, he had blushed when one of the prettiest hooked her arm in his and paraded around the foyer, assisting him to sidestep the melee at the Sugar Floss Man's barrow. Later, in bed, Lydia caught a whiff on his skin of the jasmine that had been entwined in the temptress's hair . . .

Through the night, the rain continued to fall so heavily it was as if a battalion of drummers had taken up residence on Bluebell Cottage's roof. Lydia finally put all thoughts of babies and Indian sirens aside, gathered herself together and tied a scrap of material around her bleeding finger. She felt some relief that at least she wouldn't have to go out and face possible encounters with Simon Fraser-Gough and The Chikki Man's strange agent until the rain abated. She disliked Florence Gordon's frank stare and realised she had overstepped the boundaries by handing the vendor a personal letter, the contents easily open to misinterpretation.

In the morning, Lydia stood in her dressing gown and sur-veyed the rain-lashed valley from the sitting room window. Everything was a watery green, the distant hills faint blurs. The garden appeared more boisterous than usual, the sudden inunda-tion had already caused fresh growth. This was not the genteel rain of county England but a rebellious rampage of water that pelted and splashed and gusted and stormed. She wondered how Wil-liam would ever make it back up to Bluebell Cottage and prayed that Anil had enough food in the kitchen to provide for Sunita and Devi. Lydia feared for his sister and her sharp cough and shivered at the possibility of the poor girl's death.

Chapter Thirty-seven

CHALAILI
JUNE, 1937

'The fact remains that the doctors induce us to indulge,
and the result is that we have become deprived
of self-control and have become effeminate.'
M. K. (MAHATMA) GANDHI

Day two of the monsoon and venturing outside was still impossible. Lydia opened the tall door leading from the master bedroom to the veranda but breathing the soaked air was like inhaling bubbles. She gasped and slammed it shut. The phone was still dead and Anil was following her around the house begging her to do something for Sunita.

'She will die,' he said, accusingly, as if Lydia were somehow responsible for his sister's plight.

Lydia's eyes filled with tears. She had no nursing skills but with Devi's help, she carried Sunita to the double bed she shared with William, undressed her thin shaking body and wrapped her gently in a nightdress and soft velvet robe. Anil spooned her warm milk and the trio kept vigil by the bedside all day as the gunmetal sky turned to charcoal and the rain and wind whisked around Bluebell Cottage.

As Devi and Anil slept in their chairs, and Sunita lay vacant-eyed and shivering beneath a panoply of covers, Eugenia Jambolana floated to the sitting room and sat down at William's desk. She opened her spiral-bound journal and consulted her notes.

Lydia wrote through the shuddering night, page after page of feverish outpourings, her plot peopled by chisel-chinned adventurers and wan heroines, their various fortunes leading them to an Indian hill station stranded above the clouds, where the rain was thick and purple and the trees and flowers fantastically huge and high and of ravishing hues. There was a touch of pageantry in the way she described the weather and sharp satire in the treatment of The Crows. Conveniently, Eugenia knew them as The Ravens. Rather than the black swarm encountered by Lydia, Eugenia recognised their individualities and deftly described their ringing voices, as abrasive as auctioneers, and their clothes the colour of medicine.

In Lydia and William's bedroom, Anil dreamt of dry sunny skies and the thrum of waves on a long beach. At some point during the night he left his chair and climbed on the bed and lay beside his sister, on his side, his arm over her body. Devi saw his action but pretended to be asleep. She looked at Anil's profile and wanted to stroke his hair, taste his lips, but she checked such inappropriate longing. When she had first set out on the magic journey with Anil and Sunita, on not one but two trains, the second seemingly gasping for air as it trundled up the near-vertical track to Chalaili, she had imagined herself married to Anil, the devoted wife of this risk-taking adventurer.

But Devi knew she could not give him children. Her pimp had seen to that, offering her to a madman one night who had paid a handsome sum to thrust scissors into her so that her vagina became not a desired place of refuge but a gaping wound, bloodied and defiled.

During that long night of pain and humiliation, a little light that had glimmered inside, keeping alive her slender dreams, had died. She felt she was scarred right through, every crevice of her body, every inch of her childless womb, every iota of her never-still mind. Not until Anil had arrived and she had joined his thrown-together family had she felt safe. Just to know Anil was enough and she sunk into the wicker chair, ferociously hugging a cushion until she, too, fell into monsoon dreams.

꩜

It was just after dawn when Lydia stopped her frenetic scribblings and looked out the window. The rain had slowed but the sky was still low and steely. She had heard the squeak of Bluebell Cottage's gate and out of the soupy mist she saw William approach, an indistinct figure in a developing photo. He burst through the front door in a flurry of umbrella and dripping macintosh. Without realising Lydia was in the front parlour, he strode down the hall and turned into their bedroom.

'Good heavens!' he thundered as he encountered Anil and the two women. His servant and Devi leapt to attention and stood stiffly before him. Lydia followed William and was the first to notice Sunita was dead, all colour drained from her face and her eyes dark and distant. She touched William's elbow and he turned. 'Anil's sister has died,' she said.

Devi fell to a huddle and disappeared under her flowing sari pallu veil. Anil simply stood, his head bowed and slightly turned to one side as if he expected William might hit him.

William was so perplexed he had no idea where to start his questioning. Lydia was crying so internally she began to gulp. He walked towards the bed and pulled the lace coverlet over Sunita's head in a gesture so completely calm that Lydia would long remember it. Anil saw it, too, and lifted his eyes but William's face was hard and cold.

William returned to his office without saying a word to Lydia. She slept for hours on the lounge, curled in a ball. When she woke, a thin checked rug was arranged over her. She supposed Anil had placed it there and she kept it around her shoulders as she padded in stockinged feet to the kitchen.

'We must bury Sunita,' Anil announced as he stood warming chai in a small copper saucepan. Lydia looked aghast. She knew nothing of burials and the weather was against even the prospect of opening the front door, let alone organising a funeral.

'Was she Christian?' asked Lydia. She had read of Hindu cremation rites and wasn't sure she believed Anil had really been to a convent school.

'Please forgive me, Mem, but it is not the time to think of such things. We must dig a hole in the garden and put her there or we will all be sick.'

'We?' yelped Lydia. 'We must dig a hole . . .'

Anil caught the disbelief in her tone. 'All right, I will dig a hole . . . or . . . or . . . I will put her under a tree . . . . she must be covered, at least . . . please help Devi to dress her.'

Lydia and Devi entered the bedroom and stared at the shape

241

on the bed. It was like looking at someone playing hide-and-seek who had chosen a rather obvious place of concealment. The two women turned towards each other and they both shrugged, the actions independent but universal. Lydia wondered how she had ended up here in this room with a fire-scarred prostitute, abandoned by her husband, obeying orders from her servant.

Devi took the metal dish of water and handtowel from the bedside table, lifted the cover from Sunita's head, and damped down her face and hair. Her movements were slow and so fine her hands could have been anatomical illustrations. Lydia wondered at the care she took, the gentleness of her actions as if any sudden or too-hard movement could disturb the recumbent woman.

She looked at Lydia and pointed at the cover. Lydia nodded, understanding Devi wanted to know if she could lift Sunita in it. Anil appeared and Devi helped him carry off his sister, rolled and rolled again in the fabric like a bolt of carpet. Lydia stood still but heard the back door open and a fanfaronade of wind and rain issue forth. She presumed poor Sunita would be buried in the cover so she stripped the bed of its sheets and threw them into a corner. Then she hugged herself tight and began to whirl around the room, faster and faster, knocking over a lamp and bumping into the open door of the almirah until she felt drunk with dizziness and fell on to the bed.

William had warned her of monsoon sickness but the madness she felt went much, much deeper.

'WHY DIDN'T I TAKE SUNITA TO THE SANATORIUM?' she screamed.

She ran to the front door and raced into the immense rain. 'I HAVE FAILED EVERYONE!' she yelled.

Devi appeared by her side and drew her indoors, the two of them clinging and shivering.

'I have failed everyone, Devi,' she said, looking into her eyes. Lydia knew Devi couldn't understand but she continued speaking, teeth chattering.

'I am not the wife William needed, I have failed my friend Anil, I have duped The Chikki Man in the bazaar and that silly Florence . . . And who knows what that Simon Fraser-Gough is going to do next. I am GOING MAD.'

Anil arrived with towels.

'The sanatorium is only for the British, Mem Lydia,' he said, tears splashing his face. 'They would not have taken my sister.'

Chapter Thirty-eight

CHALAILI
JUNE, 1937

THE SOLIGANJ WEEKLY OBSERVER
Rainfall in Chalaili is reaching record volume this year.
Mr William Rushmore, District Meteorological Officer,
Indian Forestry Service, Sub-Branch Weather Warnings,
told *The Soliganj Weekly Observer* that precipitation could
approach the record levels of 1932 when 75 feet of rainfall was recorded in a one-month period.

Mrs Banerjee had named her Monsoon Cottage well.
It stood in such an exposed position that it was a
small miracle it did not blow clear off the ridge. When the mul-
titudinous force of the annual rains hit, she had just returned
from an evening at Coronation Talkies and Aruna was massaging
her feet with sandalwood oil as she partook of a little sesame-
flavoured ladoo and vigorously waved a fan patterned with cherry
blossoms that her father had acquired from Japan at the height
of his importing era. She was flushed so shiny with perspiration

it seemed she was lit from within by a secret source of heat and hydration.

The building began to shudder, the window shutters wobbled and a dreadful whining draft blew under the front door, down the hallway and out into the rear garden, like the breath of a dragon. Aruna was terrified but Mrs Banerjee felt faintly cheered by the prospect of confronting the peculiarly dreadful Campbell Nightingale in court if the house collapsed around her ears ruining the full inventory of Dhir family heirlooms (she had allowed her Mother to retain the silent Kelvinator). Such was her indomitable spirit that it never occurred to her she could be buried under monsoon-sluiced rubble or whipped into the air by a frantic gust and set sailing off the upper ridge, her Japanese yukata dressing gown, in a pushy yellow silk, swelling to a spinnaker.

'We will move to The Metropole Hotel,' announced Mrs Banerjee. 'Come, come,' she ordered Aruna as she bustled towards the phone, the swaying yukata a resplendent burst of gold that remained a momentary imprint of colour in the blackness as the electricity failed. Mrs Banerjee's hand was already on the phone as the lights went out, but her immaculate timing was wasted as the line was already dead.

By feeling their way along the walls and doorways, the two women found their respective boudoirs, Mrs Banerjee her comfortable room with its high single beds and Aruna her charpoy string cot in the alcove off the kitchen. Through the night the tempest continued, rain-plunged monkeys slipped all over the roof and clung to the eaves waving to and fro and howling to the heavens. Even such a scant toehold on the house provided the creatures with more safety than the surrounding bushes, which were rotating wildly as if engaged in a kind of frenzied folk dance. Those monkeys that tried to huddle on the veranda were washed away, arms flailing and tails whipping, in rivulets of muddy water.

'Ho, ho, that's your karma, you sugar bandits,' Mrs Banerjee called out as one especially large and bedraggled specimen hurled itself against the full-length window of her bedroom and went sliding down, its face wind-pressed against the pane.

'Love many, trust few, always paddle your own canoe,' Mrs Banerjee sang aloft in her high single bed but her usually jolly heart was not quite in it. She used to chirp that ditty in the playground at St Sophia Convent with Queenie Fat when the other girls would circle them and sing rhymes. Hateful flabby fleshy rhymes.

'Where are you, funny tubby Queenie Fat?' she asked herself. They had lost contact after graduation when the rich Bhatt family sent Queenie to England to be finished off, an expression that sounded to Premila like a sorry end at the hands of a paid assassin.

Mrs Banerjee was still reminiscing about raids on sweet shops with Queenie and shared scoops of nut-studded kulfi ice-cream when, just after midnight, Aruna appeared at the bedroom doorway with a candle, weeping with fear.

'Come, come, silly Miss Chowpatty,' she ordered and patted the adjoining bed. Aruna hopped between the unaccustomed covers and mistress and servant tried to sleep as the roof's tin sheetings raged and the monkey survivors performed their sodden acrobatics.

ஐ

Mr K. K. Rao had finished his duties for the evening and was doing a final tidy-up of his projectionist's booth when the first trickles of water insinuated their way under the double entrance doors of Coronation Talkies. He heard the gurgling-burbling but by the time he raced to the foyer, the trickles had turned to a stream. He careered up to the bathroom in his compact first-floor quarters and grabbed a handful of towels to press into the gap between door and floor. He suspected it would be a temporary measure.

The lights were still on but his experience of monsoons recently past told him that such newfangled inventions as electricity would be the first things to falter. He shot pell-mell to the storeroom at one side of the stage and grabbed anything and everything he could find. There was a great pile of material left over from Picture Madam's upholstering extravagances and he pressed the lot against the doors as if sandbagging a war-time bunker. Winds were howling and roaring but his battlements seemed secure. Taking a candle and matches from one of the desk drawers in the fishbowl office, he placed them within hand's reach and settled in for the night curled up on the double-cushioned cashier's chair. It seemed too dangerous to sleep upstairs because if the ground level flooded, he would be marooned as if aboard a raft.

As the water seeped through the barricade, but not too wetly, Mr K. K. Rao dozed off just as the lights failed in a shower of sparks. He dreamt he had opened his bedroom window and outside was a great foaming ocean into which he dived with the deftness of a kingfisher.

He swam and swam until his arms and legs ached and then he saw an island, amply curved with hills, and he made for it, his limbs leaden. He reached the shore and tried to climb but the formation was strangely soft and bouncing and he failed to get a grip. With every movement forward, he slipped back again until there was a sudden heave and the island sat up and it was

Mrs Banerjee with an enormous orange-and-white striped life-saver's ring around her waist.

She called down to Mr K. K. Rao to grab hold of the circular rubberiness so she could haul him along. 'Float, float,' she sang, but he couldn't get any purchase on the ring and he began to go under, his arms too feeble to continue swimming. Up he came, spluttering for breath. Banerjee Island began to move off with stately grace but with one wobbling arm she was casting him an unfurling length of sari in a pretty purple the colour of brinjal blossom. He hoped it was the full nine-yard measure as she was accelerating to a cracking pace. Mr K. K. Rao grabbed the rippling fabric and she hauled him along as he wriggled and swayed like a fish in a net.

He was enjoying his dream when he awoke with a shivery start. The lights had suddenly come back on and the massive chandelier in the foyer of Coronation Talkies was rocking wildly, throwing beads of coloured light in hectic patterns. He rose timidly from his seat and peeped over the counter and through the glass cubicle to see if a torrent had raced through, hopefully not with his employer in mid-sail.

His towelling-and-velvet dyke had held and the ruffian wind had dropped to a shuddering gust. Mr K. K. Rao walked upstairs, taking the candle and matches with him as a precaution. Tucked into his own bed, he prepared for his first coolly aerated sleep since the mercury had started its wretched ascent in early April. He was a fastidious man and he found it difficult to take his rest in a dignified manner with pre-monsoonal sweat trickling all over him, turning his armpits into swamps and giving rise to unpleasant infections between his toes.

The fresh climate in Chalaili was the chief reason he had accepted the job at Coronation Talkies, the offer having come to him via Mrs Banerjee's lawyer, an egregious customer who had handled various affairs for his mother, not long departed. In fact, his mother must have died around the same time as Mrs Banerjee's father as he had bumped into her in the legal fellow's Bombay office, although he could have sworn she was introduced by another name. He had been unable to take his eyes off her handsome bulk but felt ashamed of himself as she was young enough to be his daughter. His future employer had asked him in passing, as she shimmied into the law office's inner sanctum, if he thought she looked like Claudette Colbert and he had eagerly nodded but she had disappeared in a jubilant streak of red silk before he could say anything further.

'Mother, mother,' he sighed. In her steely opinion, no woman had ever been good enough for him to marry and as the only son (only child who had torn her womb to shreds, he reminded himself) he had to live with her and take charge of her affairs when his devil-may-care father got himself killed in some silly cycle accident. As sleep failed to descend, he recited aloud his mother's standard objections to all categories of brides-to-be:

Too Fat (like a two-times elephant)

Too Thin (mark my words, she'd snap in two during childbirth)

Too Tall (good for nothing but reaching top-top shelf)

Too Small (listen to me, she'll carry no sons in that close-to-the-ground womb)

Too Dark (what is she, some soot-woman witch)

. . . and even, astonishingly, given that most Indian mothers-in-law-to-be prize above all the presence of a high-class wheatish complexion . . .

Too Fair (white-as-ghost skin, good for finding in the night, that's all).

The bride-hunting rigmarole went on and on from the day after his nineteenth birthday (two weeks before his father was squashed by a runaway Raleigh) to her passing, six months hence. He was fifty years old, neat and dapper but unlikely to woo any maidens at this late stage. Like Mrs Banerjee, talking pictures consumed his life and, given that he had only minor experience as a senior trainee (no junior trainee in evidence, he reminded himself) at a Bombay theatre, he had been lucky to snare this position of chief projectionist (only projectionist, that is).

The slight drawback was that Picture Madam had been able to acquire just one projector and the foreign talkies came in three enormous cans, so there were always two small intervals one-third and two-thirds of the way through the film while he changed to the next spool.

Far too often, each hiatus would occur at some crucial stage, like a murderous gun blast or a romantic kiss, and there would be a chorus of booing and the occasional enraged outburst, 'What is this, some low-class, cheap-cheap fairground where ladies are left in the dark?'

Mr K. K. Rao found it hard to tell if the voice would be coming from the audience below or if it was his mother hissing in his unwed ear.

Miles away down on the plains at Soliganj, Patricia Nightingale couldn't sleep. Her husband was snoring and snuffling beside her as he had done during more than twenty years of up-and-down childless marriage. He always enjoyed the deep slumber of the blameless, although she knew such repose was far from warranted. The Nightingale bungalow rattled and whined as the rain smashed against doors, windows and bricks, and pools of water eddied and whirled on the cement-floored veranda. The peacock that usually strutted so imperiously around the garden was sheltering beside the front door, like a sodden blue rag. She wondered how Mrs Banerjee was coping in the condemned cottage her husband had rented her. Patricia Nightingale knew more than a little about her husband's nefarious dealings and realised the monthly outings to Coronation Talkies, with an overnight stay at The Metropole Hotel, were some kind of barter arrangement for the accommodation.

She was in awe of Mrs Banerjee. In such a short time, Picture Madam had all but taken over Chalaili and when Patricia Nightingale thought of the hill station it was in black and white, but touched up and tinted by a careful colourist and those patches of brightness were where Mrs Banerjee materialised.

Even the usually unobservant Campbell Nightingale noticed Picture Madam's screen-siren costumes and on their most recent visit to Coronation Talkies, he had been very taken with her red and green sari.

'You are a vision as wonderful as Christmas,' he had said, with a little bow.

Mrs Banerjee had laughed and laughed. 'My dear Mr Nightingale, it is only June,' was her retort, delivered with a particularly energetic whirl of bangles.

251

Patricia Nightingale sighed. Soliganj was so quiet it was barely conscious. It was all army and railways, swagger and soot. Her husband had been posted there as Housing Administrator, First Class, for three years and she longed for the upcountry bungalow they had left behind in the Nilgiri Hills with its backdrop of tea terraces and blue-mist mornings. She filled her time at Soliganj reading and sewing minutely detailed tapestries and performing the sort of polite clean-hands charity work that her fellow memsahibs engaged in, which mostly consisted of visiting nursing mothers in Soliganj Hospital and wheeling around a tea trolley, when a cuppa was the last thing the poor girls needed, some as young as fourteen or fifteen and with a lifetime of servitude in store.

Patricia Nightingale could tell just by looking in from the doors of the wards if a son or a daughter had arrived. Males were celebrated with the arrival of excited hordes of relatives and masses of marigolds and the best new season fruit while the mothers of daughters lay in their narrow cots and looked into space with dead eyes, even if their husbands were holding their hands and promising that the in-laws were thrilled to pieces, nonetheless, but too busy just now to visit . . .

She got out of bed and drifted down the hallway. The house was still airless after so many weeks of contained heat. As she opened the front door, the peacock fell through like a used mop and Patricia Nightingale stepped over him and danced into the rain, revelling in the feel of springy wet grass beneath her bare feet. 'Memsahib, memsahib, please, please,' called Tara, her maid, from the shallow protection of the veranda. She had woken at the sound of the swinging front door. But she was laughing, too, and raced on to the lawn. The two women held hands and danced around and around, their cotton nightclothes stuck revealingly to their bodies.

A figure appeared at the front door waving a kerosene lantern. 'Please explain what you are doing, Patricia!' yelled Campbell Nightingale, whose gaze was not so much directed at his wife as firmly fixed on Tara's near-nakedness. The maid ran off into the dove-grey gloom of the rainy dawn and his wife stood her sodden ground. 'I would have thought it was perfectly obvious that Tara and I were taking part in a Monsoon Supplication Ceremony,' she retorted and then she gathered her dripping nightgown and flounced past him, or as much as one is able to flounce in double-shirred poplin of the non-water-resistant variety.

૿

Ram Gupta allowed his table-waiting and kitchen staff to stay overnight at The Metropole Hotel. It was far too dangerous for the men and boys to make their way down to Chota Chalaili amid the surging torrents and muddy ditches. They squatted under the damask tablecloth flaps in the dining room as if camping out in the hills. Ram Gupta had to quickly enforce a no-cigarettes rule as most of them had lit up as they huddled in their snowy-white shelters and smoke came spilling out, propelled around the room by energetic winds and it appeared as if The Maharani Salon, for that was how Anjali Gupta had recently renamed the room for her own enigmatic reasons, was on fire.

Once all the cigarettes were extinguished and the male campers settled, Ram Gupta raced upstairs two at a time to check if his wife was in good spirits. Since she had decided to be bosom friends with Mrs Banerjee, she had become rather flighty and given to over-bossing him in public, but privately he liked her buoyant new moods, as she had previously displayed an advanced talent for sulking. Besides, a good cuff around the ear never hurt anyone, as long as she didn't administer it to him in front of the servants.

Anjali Gupta was sitting up in bed, her candle-illuminated face a ghostly mask of cold cream. 'I couldn't have taken much more of that murderous heat,' she sighed. 'Will you come to bed?' she asked her husband with what he took to be a wink, although it was a bit difficult to tell amid the weak spillage of light and the snow-woman face.

He hesitated just a second too long, adjusting his slippery-slide glasses, torn between the desire to join his pretty wife in their comfortable double bed and the need to return downstairs to ensure The Maharani Salon wasn't alight with two dozen camp-fires, not counting the cloth-covered sideboard.

'Suit yourself,' she tossed at him and blew out the candle. As he crept downstairs, he heard her cursing as her lathered face hit the pillow.

☙

Charlotte Montague had spent the afternoon squarely in front of an electric fan mopping her brow with fast-melting cubes of ice wrapped in handtowels. Her bunions had signalled days ago that the rains were due and this warning system was never wrong, as she had informed that daft William Rushmore on many an occasion, not that he ever listened to anything women said. Definitely a chap's chap, she had long ago surmised. The Petal Cameron Incident had provided enormous entertainment but no one really imagined he was about to rape the British Resident of Kashmir's wife amid the hydrangeas. He'd been hauled off muttering something about Dry Adiabatic Lapse Rate and that had made everything even jollier.

When the pompous Sir Ambrose and the Fallen Petal had

departed the club in a great rush, that shifty Campbell Nightingale had had everyone in stitches for once. 'I think he meant Dry Acrobatic Lapsed Rate!' he had yelled from the bar and the chaps had all fallen about. Even that appalling peacock-feathered Dorothy Creswell-Smythe had allowed herself a merry riposte. She'd stood up, clapped her hands for attention, and loudly announced, 'Didn't look at all cirrus to me!' Not everyone got the joke at first, which rather spoilt the effect as she had to spell out C-I-R-R-U-S, but that's what she should have expected, Charlotte Montague smiled, for having such a plum in her mouth.

Charlotte Montague remembered the way Petal Cameron's accent had changed after a few drinks. Her posh voice had disintegrated to a terrible flatness. It was a voice of hand-me-down clothes and cold potato dinners and Charlotte Montague had seen the angry look in Sir Ambrose's eyes as his wife's facade slipped clear away.

She thought of Lydia Rushmore and her predicament with that turnip-nosed adventurer Simon Fraser-Gough. Her espionage in Chota Chalaili bazaar had uncovered no photographs and the whole thing was too silly for words. Poor Lydia. It wasn't as if he were Mr Darcy or anyone with whom one would wish a permanent relationship.

Ah, Mr Dastardly, more likely, whooped Charlotte Montague, and hoisted up her chihuahua and waved it side to side with glee at her great wit. The little dog bared a set of miniature teeth and hissed at her, but Charlotte Montague was in far too gay a mood to notice.

As if by pre-arrangement, her bunions stopped throbbing at the precise moment the rains came. First there were big ploppy drops on the parched garden and then a patter that became heavier and heavier and louder and louder until all Charlotte Montague could see through the sitting-room window was a sheer stream of water lashing the glass as if the mali were on the roof with a wayward hose.

'Excellent,' she murmured to herself, reaching for a tiny brass bell to summon one of her brigade of servants to bring her a drink. Her husband, Edmond, was on banking business in Bombay and at this rate could well be unavoidably detained, which would certainly suit Charlotte Montague. She adored the idea of an enforced quarantine, with no demands on her brain or body, as long as the pantry held out.

Three decades away from 'home', two strapping sons dispatched to boarding school in Devon, and she loved dear old India with a passion. That's what she would tell anyone who cared to ask. Not the Other India, that is. Not the dirty, terrifying, overcrowded, undersanitised India that lay sprawling beneath Outpost Chalaili or, in previous postings with her banker husband, beyond the tweezered estates of Planet Grindlays Bank Bombay Bungalow or Planet Grindlays Bank Madras Mansion or Planet Grindlays Bank Calcutta Two-Storey Detachment.

What Charlotte Montague loved about the privileged and incestuous and stifling and dangerously rumour-ridden enclaves she inhabited was the respect she was easily able to muster among the younger impressionable wives. This was particularly so in Outpost Chalaili where so few people of importance were stationed that she retained her Queen Crow title with ease. Even Dorothy Creswell-Smythe had to defer to her, particularly since the arrival of Mrs Banerjee. Cranky old Dottie Smith, as Charlotte Montague privately referred to Dorothy Creswell-Smythe, had apparently been rude to Mrs Banerjee on the train from Bombay and the

Coronation Talkies proprietress had attempted to ban her from the opening night. Charlotte Montague had had to telephone Mrs Banerjee and ask her to reconsider, mentioning an exclusive tea invitation at the Grindlays Bank Bungalow, which she now realised, with a guilty start, she had not followed up.

As the lights failed and the monsoon chomped at the windows, Charlotte Montague already had a candle and kerosene lamp lit in the sitting room and a neat gin in a crystal glass beside her (bottle handy, reach down to the left and feel under the chair). She wore, like an invisible badge of honour, her triumph at surviving thirty Indian monsoons. In the old days on the plains before electricity and the introduction of blessed fans, she had slept during The Hot in the garden in a mosquito-netted four-poster with her shoes under the pillow, lest snakes and scorpions interfere with them during the night. On the final nights before the monsoon broke, the servants would lift the netting and wrap her in wet sheets, changed on the hour. Charlotte Montague loved mosquito netting; it felt like sleeping beneath a bride's petticoats.

When the monsoon monster's breath had settled and cooled, Charlotte Montague sometimes continued to sleep outdoors in her sturdy four-poster, one of the lowliest servants positioned over her with a big black umbrella. She would exist on a diet of the finest, drippiest Ratnagiri mangoes and watch her rain-nourished garden grow before her eyes.

'Ah, the plains,' she sighed, through the rosy gauze of remembrance.

Above the unholy orchestration of lamenting winds and boom-crash rain, Charlotte Montague could be heard singing mournful Celtic love songs in a respectable drawing-room soprano.

☙

Veronica O'Brien closed the glass front door of Lakshmi Hair and Beauty Studio and gave the painted goddess a goodnight kiss as she did every evening before returning to her cottage in the grounds of The Empire Club, positioned next to Dorothy Creswell-Smythe's identical abode.

She refused to embrace widowhood in the stoic manner of Dorothy Creswell-Smythe and had no interest in summoning Hugh O'Brien back from the grave, courtesy of candles, spooky music and one of those wobbling boards with dead-husband-raising properties that her neighbour had got made up in Chota Chalaili bazaar.

Veronica O'Brien had a lover. An Indian lover.

Tonight she was not going home. Blinky Singh was waiting for Veronica O'Brien at the rear entrance of The Metropole Hotel behind the wheel of his new car. She was closing Lakshmi Hair and Beauty Salon for a month during the wettest portion of the monsoon and Blinky was taking her to Bombay for a round of parties and various other activities that did not require spending time in the sloshing outdoors.

It was unusual that Blinky was driving himself but she supposed he didn't want his chauffeur to be privy to this extended assignation.

She hopped into his vehicle, which was long and low and she guessed was a sports model. He smiled and kissed her lightly on the cheek and she all but melted with excitement.

Blinky was not his real name. It was something that started with the same initial but had far too many letters. He'd picked up the Blinky tag in England while at university there. He was the son of a raja, he told her, but not the senior son and therefore plenty of money was thrown at him but there was none of the responsibility of being his father's heir.

He was ten years younger than Veronica O'Brien and he thrilled her to bits.

They set off slowly down the Chalaili Hills towards Soliganj. Water rushed against the wheels and the road all but turned into a river. Veronica O'Brien imagined the two of them setting sail across a vast ocean, never to return.

'Goodbye, Lakshmi,' she sang as Blinky patted her knee with one hand and steered gamely with the other.

Chapter Thirty-nine

CHALAILI
AUGUST, 1937

THE SOLIGANJ WEEKLY OBSERVER

Comment has been sought from Mr Ram Gupta, Proprietor of The Metropole Hotel, Chalaili, on how the unusually heavy rains have affected the hill station's touristic reputation. He informed *The Soliganj Weekly Observer* that there was nothing anyone could do about such an utterly unpredictable climate and tourists of all kinds would just have to take their chances.

Lydia gave Florence Gordon a gracious smile as she passed the letter across the post office counter. The rains had finally diminished to an occasional drizzle and she was enjoying the hearty freshness of the air.

'Air mail, please.'

'Of course, Mrs Rushmore . . . I mean, Lydia.'

Lydia was delighted that Florence Gordon appeared to be friendly after their awkward meeting weeks ago at The Metropole

Hotel. She weighed the thick letter and opened a big red-bound book with stamps of myriad denominations filed beneath leaves of tissue, like photographs in an album. As she flicked back and forth selecting the correct combinations, Lydia observed her bosoms. They were indeed large and upholstered, as if they had been carefully inflated.

When she raised her eyes, she realised Florence Gordon was glaring at her.

'Anything the matter, Lydia?'

'No, no, er . . .'

Lydia passed a handful of coins across the counter and Florence Gordon passed them back with a chit on which she'd written the price.

'Pay at the cash desk,' she said crisply, removing the stamped letter from the counter and popping it into the pigeonhole behind her marked Air Mail.

'Next customer, please.'

Lydia queued up again and handed over the chit and her money. She made no further eye contact.

☙

Florence Gordon locked up the post office at 5 p.m. sharp and supervised the sweeping wallah as he cleaned the floor and dusted the big wooden counter, fluttering his cloth over the weighing machine so it swung and jangled, even though she had told him a thousand times to hold it still while he wiped it.

When she was alone, she went into her little office and unlocked the top drawer. There was nestled Lydia's letter, addressed to a Mrs Thomas Moss, The Oaks, West Gamble, Surrey, England.

Her mother, thought Florence Gordon. Or maybe a sister.

The packet was overly thick as if it contained far more than obedient family correspondence.

Florence Gordon stared at Lydia's handwriting. It was confident, she thought, far more assured than its author. She tucked it into her handbag, turned off all the lights, double-checked the locks and set off at a brisk pace that suggested a robust journey. Her walk home to her cottage in the grounds of The Metropole Hotel took exactly two-and-a-half minutes as it did every working day, save for an extra full minute to accommodate some energetic umbrella-handling at the height of the monsoon.

The rains were almost at an end. Now there were light showers, the rich smell of soaked earth, leaves and flowers all polished up and the clatter-cry of crickets.

She was about to open her front door when she heard a voice calling her name. Coming up the path from her cottage on the opposite side of the hotel's rambling garden was Mary Christie, clutching a brown paper package.

'Damn,' Florence Gordon muttered to herself. She found the woman irritating. She was ten years older, also the issue of an Indian mother and British father, and every time Florence looked at the crepe-skinned widow she imagined she saw herself a decade hence, still marooned in this sodden hole, her bosom downwards deflated, her legs and hips thickened.

As far as Florence Gordon knew, there had never been any evidence of the unfortunately deceased Captain Archibald Christie. She privately wondered if Mary Christie had made up a husband to give herself a certain status and certainly not to deter unwanted admirers, of which surely there were none, not even frisky boys from the bazaar with their cooking smells and unimaginable fingernails.

'Your order has arrived,' called Mary Christie, her voice so high she was almost singing. The woman was a cheer-giver, always chirping away. 'On the train this afternoon . . . a nice big box from Bombay.'

'Come in,' said Florence Gordon. She hated the idea of wasting a drop of her precious gin on Mary Christie, of all people, but there was no escape.

The two women sat in Florence Gordon's sparsely furnished parlour. Mary Christie could see through to the bedroom from the sagging wicker couch and noticed the bed was unmade and clothes were flung about the floor. There was a discernible smell of coconut.

Mary Christie nursed an insipid gin flooded with tonic water.

'Any idea what's happened to Veronica O'Brien? Lakshmi Hair and Beauty Studio finally reopened today but there's a girl from Soliganj in charge. Her name's Poppy or something equally dilly . . .'

'No idea,' said Florence Gordon. She couldn't afford the services of Lakshmi Hair and Beauty Studio and had no interest in the whereabouts of Veronica O'Brien, especially as The Chikki Man had suggested to her more than once that she was free with her favours with Indian fellows and he wouldn't mind a piece himself.

'Oh well, I will try and strike up a conversation with this Poppy person. Aren't you going to open your order?'

Florence Gordon had no intention of disclosing the contents of her order from Princess Creations of Marine Drive, Bombay. She had an arrangement with the store that they would add her occasional package to the larger consignment from Colaba Trading that was sent every few weeks to Mary Christie's shop. And so

263

it was that Florence Gordon's foundation garments and novelty underwear made their illicit journey with the cigarettes, cigars, sweets, journals and assorted haberdashery items that Mary Christie ordered for her clientele.

Mary had surreptitiously opened one of the parcels, more than a year ago, and could still raise a giggle at the thought of the silken contents. She had had the devil's own job trying to re-arrange all the bits and bobs. The feathers, especially, were annoying characters.

Florence Gordon took a cigarette from a packet on the table beside her wicker chair. She allowed herself one a day, even though the contents of the packet usually were wilted when she finally progressed to the last few. She opened her box of Lady Brand Impregnated Safety Matches and lit up the cigarette, without offering one to Mary Christie.

'You'll have to excuse me, Mary dear,' said Florence Gordon, blowing an excellent smoke ring. 'I am so terribly tired. I'll open the parcel later on.'

'I thought we might eat together in the dining room . . .'

'Not tonight. I will have Anjali send a tray. Just a sandwich, I think. I have had a headache all day . . .'

Mary Christie gave her friend an enigmatic smile and downed the remainder of her drink in one fizzy gulp.

The two cottages occupied by the Anglo-Indian women had been built as grandly named 'Metropole bungalow suites' in Chalaili's heyday and they were smaller than any real residence, although undeniably luxurious by native housing standards. The Guptas charged peppercorn rentals and did little or no main-tenance to the forlorn buildings but pretty flowering vines and creepers hid most of the exterior imperfections. The hotel cleaners came in twice a week and Mary Christie kept a servant girl in an annexe at the rear who also mopped her shop. Neither of the two single women deigned to cook so meals were taken at the hotel or trays sent over or, occasionally, Mary Christie would be tempted by the spicy smells to share her servant's simple vegetarian meal of rice and chickpea dhal.

Florence refused any servants and loudly claimed to be allergic to Indian food as it upset her fragile stomach. When her mother visited from Soliganj, Mary's girl would be sent over to be on hand for any emergencies, particularly the need for Mrs Priyanka Gordon's feet to be massaged after the climb from Chalaili Station. Mary found it cosy to be accommodated so close to The Metropole Hotel and across the lawn from her friend, but Florence loathed the arrangement, as if the two Anglo-Indian women were a pair of forgotten bookends.

❧

Florence Gordon peeped through her window into the garden to ensure Mary Christie had crossed to her cottage and was not lurking nearby, ready to break through the savage bougainvillea vines and fly though her door. The older woman was fond of creeping about with a cricket bat, ever ready to wallop a monkey to kingdom come.

Mary Christie may have been curious about the latest lacy unmentionables from Princess Creations but Florence Gordon had more pressing concerns. She put the Bombay package aside and took out Lydia's plump letter. She fingered the superior quality of the parchment envelope as her kettle whistled its way to the boil.

Florence Gordon didn't have a proper kitchen, just an alcove to one side of the sitting room. It contained an enamel sink, a bench with a skirt of blue-and-white check curtains protecting the shelves below and a small gas burner on which she could heat a can of soup or prepare water for tea. She placed the back of the letter under the boiling kettle's cloud of steam and waited for the glue to soften. It took just a minute for the heat to do its work and the envelope flap to unfurl.

She pulled out the wad of folded sheets and settled into one of the two deep wicker chairs that matched her tipsy settee. Smoothing the paper, Florence Gordon read what appeared to be a covering note.

Bluebell Cottage
Chalaili, India

Dear Evelyn,

Please keep these pages in a convenient place. Read them
if you must, although I doubt they will make any sense
whatsoever. I had entertained the idea of writing a novel but
fear I have no talent in that direction. I have no safe place to
keep them here and will retrieve them from you one day, by
which time I am sure they will deliver me a good laugh or two.

Your loving sister,

Lydia

Florence Gordon put the page to one side and made herself more comfortable, positioning a faded floral cushion on her lap

to form a reading platform. She sat slightly at an angle, arms outstretched to make full use of the pool of honeyed light thrown by
her standard lamp. The next page contained just a heading and the
author's name.

THE CHALAILI CHRONICLES
by Eugenia Jambolana

Florence Gordon burst out laughing. So here was the real
identity of Eugenia Jambolana. What a perfectly ridiculous name
it was, like some sort of dance or exotic stew.

She reached for her tumbler of gin and tonic, fervently
wishing she had added more alcohol. The bottle was out of reach
and she was too ensconced in her pillowed seat to be bothered
moving.

Florence Gordon read slowly and thoroughly, devour-
ing every last detail of Lydia's overly emotional account of life
in an Indian hill station. She laughed out loud at the mention of
The Ravens and she instantly recognised the true identities of The
Empire Club ladies.

There was a strange story about a servant whose prostitute
sister had died in his master's bed but Florence Gordon glossed
over that episode because one thing she certainly did not care
about was Indian menials and their messy problems.

She lingered over a description of a Mr Charles Bird who
Florence Gordon knew in a trice to be that insufferable Mr Campbell Nightingale from Soliganj whose eyes always lingered too
long on her upper arrangements when he occasionally dropped
into Chalaili Post Office.

The strange little tale ended with a devilish account of the opening night of Coronation Talkies and a strangely sympathetic description of Mrs Banerjee, whose fictional name was Claudette. And then it was all over, abrupt and unsatisfying.

She knew that the newcomer Lydia did not have enough inside information to write a truly gossipy account of life in Chalaili but assistant-to-the-postmaster Florence Gordon most certainly did. What was more, she had access to a daily stream of letters to England. The missives, no doubt full of petty agitations and silly boasts, came flowing across the post office counter and their fate was in her hands, save for the few hours each week when that drunkard postmaster Harold Gilbert deigned to show his florid face and throw his weight about, bosom leering and rubber stamping and triplicate carbon copying.

Florence Gordon's steaming kettle was about to work overtime.

Mary Christie was annoyed that Florence Gordon always seemed so eager to get rid of her. She lay awake in her single bed, unable to sleep. Eventually she turned on her lamp and reached for a relaxing pill, as prescribed by Dr David Diaz of Soliganj.

Dr Diaz had been recommended to Mary Christie by Patricia Nightingale when she visited The Metropole Hotel Arcade shop one Tuesday morning after an evening at Coronation Talkies and an overnight stay. Dr Diaz was known to be very fashionable, which meant he freely administered his so-called relaxing pills to memsahibs gone batty with heat and solitude, the latter being a condition with which Mary Christie was well acquainted.

Mary Christie gulped down the pill and waited for its thickening effects, the weightiness of limbs and eyelids. She was worried about Florence Gordon, believing she had got herself mixed up with a Britisher, perhaps a married man. There was something so dangerous about Florence Gordon, that body, the defiance in her eyes.

Florence Gordon looks so Indian, thought Mary Christie, as the drug tricked her body into sleep. Florence Gordon may be beautiful but she could never pass for white . . .

Mary Christie knew that she was fair enough to pass. Oh, not as young and pretty and curvaceous as Florence Gordon but her skin was the colour of new wheat, her hair bronze, her eyes as hazel as a wild cat's.

She had fantasies about being introduced to London society. A lady from the imperial colonies. A survivor of monsoons and malaria, her English skin only slightly honeyed by the sun, her accent a really very fascinating mix of local influences. You know how it is . . . all those conversations with household subordinates, wobbling one's head to make oneself understood.

The bedside lamp was still on as Mary Christie fell asleep. Later, the nightmare would come, the one she feared, the one that all the relaxing pills at the fashionable Dr Diaz's benevolent disposal could not eradicate.

Mary Christie is accepted into Class A society in that far-away and over-dressed place called England. She marries a rich, handsome man with an upper-upper name and this gauzy hyphenated gentleman, who does not reveal himself in any detail in Mary Christie's dream, loves her dearly, his little colonial princess with the exotic past. She is the daughter of missionaries, conveniently dead. Tidy white corpses, as white as snowdrops.

Mary Christie is having the baby of her loving English husband and the nurses at the hospital are stroking her pale brow.

The hospital is in Surrey. She has heard about Surrey. It is where ladies who ride horses and grow roses live . . . So this hospital will be in Surrey, at a place called something with a High in it, for extra status.

The baby arrives and there is shocked silence.

Her husband's voice, far off.

'Is it . . . dead?' he asks.

'No, it is . . . we are sorry, how to put this, sir, but, well, it is black. He is black.'

'Black?'

'Dark brown, to be technical.'

Mary Christie tries to explain she has never been with any other man. Any brown, black or in-between man.

'It is me, dearest, I am not really white.'

'Not white?'

The skin the colour of new wheat, the bronze hair, the eyes as hazel as a wild cat's.

'My mother is an Indian!'

The husband lets out a cry and leaves.

A nurse, exaggeratedly blonde, takes the darkie baby from Mary Christie's arms.

And then she wakes up, in her little cottage at the rear of The Metropole Hotel. It is almost morning. The Liberty of London coverlet on her unshared bed is soaked with tears and perspiration.

Chapter Forty

CHALAILI
AUGUST, 1937

THE SOLIGANJ WEEKLY OBSERVER

The famed aviatrix Amelia Earhart must now be considered dead after being lost over the Pacific on July 2 in her attempt to make an around-the-world flight in as close proximity as practicable to the Equator. She was flying a Lockheed Electra in company with navigator Captain Fred Noonan and her last words broadcast by radio were, 'We are flying northeast.' Miss Earhart visited India recently, as reported in these very pages. Prominent Chalaili businesswoman Mrs Rajat Banerjee has informed *The Soliganj Weekly Observer* there will be a minute's silence before all screenings this week at her Coronation Talkies picture theatre to honour Miss Earhart.

William felt his world was shifting and quaking, bedevilled with shadows. Lydia's drinking was becoming a real problem. She has no self-restraint, he thought, as he sat on the edge of his desk and looked out his office window to the inviting greens of the Chalaili Hills. He longed to be out in the fields, collecting soil samples, testing their moisture levels, setting up his meteorological devices, alone with the clouds. Opening his mouth and catching raindrops on his tongue. A seven-year-old again.

The timetable of a married man did not suit him: the sitting at table for meals, the requirement to utter small niceties about society and the weather. Not that Lydia knew anything about the weather. What woman did?

William and Lydia did not exchange ideas. They traded information of telegraphic brevity.

William: Charlotte Montague has a new horse.

Lydia: Oh, is that so. What colour?

William: A bay, I think.

Lydia: Where does she keep it?

William: At the stables. You know, by the gymkhana grounds.

Lydia: I didn't know there were stables.

William: Remind me to take you there.

Lydia: I would like that.

William: Do you ride?

Lydia: No. More tea?

If British society during the era of colonial power in India had to be summed up with two words, mused William, there you would have it.

More tea.

Or in his wife's case: More gin.

A holiday home would do her good, thought William as he held the big desk with two hands and swung his lower legs to and fro like a child.

272

But what would her family think? She had been in India just a matter of months. His aunt and uncle would hardly approve, either.

William held his head in his hands. Even if Lydia were to go back to England and rally her emotional resources, it was a stopgap measure. The Brits would soon be out of India and there would be no polite colonial society in Chalaili to which Lydia could return. Of that, William had no doubt. His conversations with his chief office peon, Romesh, and the Indian members of the forestry service who drifted in and out of Chalaili on bivouacs assured him that independence for India was a necessary reality.

What he had never discussed with Lydia was that India would always be his home. He would never go back to live in England. Free of the mirror tricks of the bureaucracy of the Indian Civil Service, he would offer his services as a weather expert to someone, a hotelier perhaps, who might need advice on the best way to develop a botanic garden as a tourist attraction.

He imagined himself in partnership with Ram Gupta, turning the tentative rose-filled rear garden of The Metropole Hotel into something wild and lush and growing. A monsoon garden that tourists could visit in macintoshes, gathering further shelter from the conveniently shaped clusters of umbrella trees.

A trifle absurd, thought William, but he smiled delightedly at the image. That excitable Mrs Banerjee of Coronation Talkies could be prevailed upon to organise press coverage. She seemed to be quoted in *The Soliganj Weekly Observer* constantly on topics of talking pictures and the rise of the modern businesswoman. If the monsoon was late in arriving to quench the parched eagerness of Chalaili gardens, he imagined her on The Metropole Hotel's roof bossing about battalions of boys with black rubber hoses.

The Brits would go off in an almighty huff and leave India to the Indians but William had a clear idea of himself stepping out of a morning mist over the Western Ghats as if newly created, sent forth minted and ready for whatever life's next instalment might bring. Whenever this scenario presented itself to him, he was always alone as the snow-white haze parted. But on this day, seated on his desk, eyes closed, he saw a shadowy figure on the periphery of his fantasy. At first he thought it was his sad, beautiful mother but, no, the figure was too large. Then a startling gold cut through the cottony gauze and he realised it was Mrs Banerjee of Coronation Talkies, swirled about with a vapour trail of gods and goddesses and brandishing a gleaming sceptre. A silken sash was bound across her substantial bosom and upon it the words Mother India heaved and sighed in a very decorative cursive script.

William's heart was rocketing. He felt his own outline fade and falter from the ethereal vision as surely as British colonial rule in India would recede to oblivion. All in all, grumbled William, banging papers and books about his desk, it was a very unsettling apparition.

Chapter Forty-one

CHALAILI
SEPTEMBER, 1937

'One should never abandon one's husband for long
periods. If called away Home on matters of family
concern, keep the absence to a minimum lest one's
husband fall prey to the temptation of native vices.'

ETIQUETTE AND MANNERS FOR THE COLONIAL MEMSAHIB
BY HENRIETTA WEATHERBY, 1895

Very early one morning in September, the phone rang
in the front parlour at Bluebell Cottage. It was an unusual occurrence. William stirred and removed Lydia's arm from
across his chest. She shivered and mumbled something at him with
gin-hazy breath. He heard Anil padding along the hallway, slapping
the walls with his hand to feel his way.

'Hello, hello,' Anil shouted. 'Hello, hello,' he repeated, as
if he were calling from the veranda to someone on the far side of
Chalaili Valley. Anil had answered the phone several times since the
contraption had been installed and he viewed it suspiciously. He

was unable to advance the conversation beyond opening gambits and if the Rushmores were not at home to prevent it, he would simply hang up after several shouted Hellos and recommence his household duties, muttering to himself about the inconvenience of the silly talking machine. On this occasion, William pulled on his paisley printed dressing gown, turned on the lights and wrested the receiver from Anil, who was crouching in the dark, yelling at it with his arm completely outstretched.

Lydia heard the murmur of a conversation and deciding it was official weather business, stretched out in the double bed and prepared to doze off. William turned on the bedside light and lifted her gently in his arms. 'Anil is bringing tea,' he murmured. 'Your father is dead, my dear.'

Lydia looked at him without expression.

'Dennis Burnett,' said William.

He thinks I can't even remember my father's name, Lydia fumed. She sat up and reached for the cool, smooth comfort of the silver hip flask in the drawer of her bedside table. She felt the raised initials, their contours all but flattened by years of fingering. DWB: Dennis Walter Burnett. Lydia pulled the bedclothes over her head and clutched the flask to her chest. She squeezed shut her eyes until the tears came, stinging-hot and salty.

☽

'You must go home,' William announced at breakfast as they sat facing each other, waiting for Anil to produce his eggs and strips of buttered toast. 'Four minutes, Mem,' whispered Anil as he placed the boiled eggs in front of Lydia, as gently as if they were newborn babies. Lydia promptly burst into tears at his tenderness and held his arm. Anil shot William a helpless look and his master dismissed the servant with a brisk wave. The only way Anil could remove his white sleeve was to gingerly unhook Lydia's fingers. How bony they are, he noted, like the claws of a bird.

'Daddy's funeral will be over, dear, well before I arrive,' she reasoned, fixing William with tear-filled eyes. 'What good will it do? And, as a matter of fact, Bluebell Cottage *is* my home . . . our home.'

'You need a holiday. There has been too much . . . over-excitement.

'I have already called Bombay and booked your passage. You leave on the afternoon train, Lydia. The rains are well and truly over and there will be no delays. I have arranged for a government car to meet you at Victoria Terminus. You will overnight at the Seaview Hotel and then tomorrow the same car will take you to the docks. By an agreeable coincidence, there is a P&O ship departing for Southampton in the afternoon.'

Lydia raced to the bedroom and threw herself on the quilt and sobbed deeply. She felt as if all the anxieties and disappointments of her marriage to William were contained in that one sentence. 'You leave on the afternoon train, Lydia.'

How she longed to be held while her husband murmured, Stay, Liddie Diddie, my Princess Liddie Diddie.

Lydia wondered what William meant by 'over-excitement'. Did he know about Simon Fraser-Gough?

When she walked out of the bedroom, holding her small suitcase fastened with a sturdy leather strap, William was sitting in his wing-backed chair in the front parlour, positioned to over-look the valley through Bluebell Cottage's picture windows. Lydia always sat in the smaller chair, slightly back and to his right. Like a handmaiden.

In his hand he had a letter, which he crunched into a ball. She saw the veins stand up on his fist, blue-grey and ropey.

'Go for a little while,' he said, turning slightly to look at her. 'It really will do you good.'

His blue eyes were so cold that Lydia trembled as if she'd been thrown into a winter sea.

Chapter Forty-two

CHALAILI
OCTOBER, 1937

THE SOLIGANJ WEEKLY OBSERVER
Mrs Rajat Banerjee, proprietress of Coronation Talkies, Chalaili, has announced the formation of the Chalaili
Businesswomen's League. She has informed *The Soliganj
Weekly Observer* that gentlemen may apply for honorary
membership if sponsored by their wives, and can expect
access to events on Tuesday afternoons only.

William Rushmore's anxiously arranged marriage
eventually resulted in his Indian Forestry Service file
being reviewed, according to the arcane red tape that provided
employment for desk-bound thousands.

A triplicate form sent in April by William to Bombay
regional headquarters to announce his marriage surfaced on a
clerk's paper-shrouded desk just after Lydia's departure. No one
had realised he'd been residing at Bluebell Cottage since 1932 as
a single man but the innocuous form advanced his situation into

the clerical world's searching spotlight.

William's hands shook with rage as he read the memo.

'Bluebell Cottage should never have been occupied as single quarters. It has official status of family quarters. You are required to vacate forthwith and move to married childless quarters.'

'Married childless?' muttered William. He was glad Lydia was not around to read the memo. The phrase summed up so neatly the vacuum of their union.

William hated using the telephone, an instrument that so rarely worked, its very existence on his desk could better be considered a decoration. Reception was echoing and crackling with an irritating delay that caused him to repeat his sentences, just as the other person on the line was coming in with their next comment. But he overcame his repugnance to put through a call to Bombay and finally raised a desk jockey in the Forestry Service Sub-Branch Weather Warnings.

'No, it's not a mistake,' came the shouted reply to his interrogation about the status of Bluebell Cottage. 'We have a family with two children moving in next week. You and Mrs Rushmore may move to a smaller bungalow for one married childless couple only . . . ah, let me see. Yes, Bungalow Seven. Confirmation will follow in the internal mail.'

'Bungalow Seven is in the condemned line,' William shouted, standing so suddenly his chair was knocked sideways. But the connection was already dead.

'We are a childless married couple,' he roared at the mouldering walls, 'because my wife is always too drunk to have sexual intercourse with me and I am not man enough to force her!'

☙

Later that day, William rode his bicycle to the upper ridge and parked it under the purple shade of a banyan tree, a few yards from the first bungalow in the meandering row. The garden, he noted, had flourished magnificently during the long summer rains but the front fence, an unattractive mesh of interlocked wire, was leaning precariously forward. He was surprised to see a slim and pretty servant girl sweeping the front path.

'Bombay nit-wits,' muttered William. They must have moved a married childless couple into Bungalow Seven already, although he had not heard of any new arrivals. He paused to look at the view, deeper and less obstructed by treetops than that from the bungalows below. The surrounding vegetation was closer, denser, and he imagined living in a bungalow on the upper ridge would be like an internment in a cool green tunnel, a prospect he found delightful.

A rustle of silk and the chime of bangles caused him to turn and he saw Mrs Banerjee of Coronation Talkies standing by the gate. She gave him a quizzical look. 'Has Mr Nightingale sent you?' she asked, eyebrow arched.

William vaguely knew Campbell Nightingale, a minor administrative flunky from Soliganj. Unfortunately, he had been among the cluster of Empire Club members who had witnessed him in flagrante with the simpering Petal Cameron.

His eyes took in the spectre of Mrs Banerjee in a fine sari of a sensationally bright puce. A tipsy hand-painted sign on the gate announced Monsoon Cottage. 'Do you, er, live here?' he stammered.

'Of course I do. Come, come,' she announced, her bangles windmilling as she waved her arms. 'Miss Aruna Chowpatty, hurry, please, tea for two.'

☽

After proper introductions and a theatrical curtsey, Mrs Banerjee installed William Rushmore in the front parlour with its papered walls and over-assembly of furniture. None of the wallpaper patterns matched and the more faded strips were blotched with ancient patches of mildew. Aruna served tea and a plate of imported shortbread biscuits.

'Where is Mr Banerjee?' William asked, enjoying the buttery sensation as the biscuits dissolved in his mouth. He looked around the room as if his enquiry might cause the mysterious husband to appear, perhaps from behind the blue and yellow floral lounge or a standard lamp with gold-fringed shade.

'Dreadfully delayed, Mr Rushmore. More tea?'

'Yes, thank you. Now, Mrs Banerjee, this is a delicate matter, but I believe this house is British government property and I wonder how you come to be living here?'

'I pay my rent, sir, every month without fail.'

William made his deductions.

'To Mr Nightingale, I presume?'

She bobbed her head from side to side to indicate in the affirmative and sunk her teeth into a biscuit. 'I do not wish to make any trouble for Mr Nightingale. He gave me a very good rental, owing to the house's precarious position.'

William looked around the colourful room again and thought how much more agreeable it appeared than Bluebell Cottage's front parlour.

❧

The next time William called on Mrs Banerjee, a few days later, she was not at home.

'Metropole Hotel,' the serving girl told him and then shut

the door with such a thud the potted geraniums guarding the doorstep shrugged their cochineal-pink and white petals in surprise.

Good, thought William. Mrs Banerjee must have been contacted by that Nightingale chap. She will be making other housing arrangements while she stays at The Metropole Hotel.

He had left his bicycle at the office and he began to walk towards town, taking his time. He decided to wander through Chota Chalaili bazaar, thinking he might pick up a wooden carving or brass pot, something to add a fresh touch to his new home. Our home, that is, he corrected himself. Lydia had been gone for more than a month and quite often William forgot about her and realised, sheepishly, that it was something of a relief to have his wife out of the way and not to feel responsible for her lonely drinking. When she returned, of course, he would have to confront her about the small matter of the envelope from that tubercular cad, Simon hyphen-something. Lydia was not, after all, the mature self-controlled woman she had appeared to be while being assessed on his Aunt Sylvia and Uncle John's lounge.

William paused at one of the stalls set up by the hill-tribe traders who peddled their woven wares in the tangle of the bazaar, especially in winter when their knitted caps and sturdy shawls were much coveted. As he fingered a pair of scarlet woollen gloves, he was jostled by a passer-by and spun around. The man had lost his footing and was already bowing his head in apology. The small incident shifted William's attention away from his browsing and he noticed a familiar figure squatting at a little distance from him, cradling a cup of steaming tea, a Craven A dangling from his bottom lip. It was Anil.

Instead of causing a scene over the purloined cigarette and Anil's obvious shirking of his household duties, William suddenly felt very tired. Lydia had obviously caused this derelict behaviour, befriending his servant and indulging in who knew what familiarity in front of the bazaar traders. Anil saw his master staring and leapt to his feet, spilling the tea. William turned away and strode back up the hill towards The Strand, his blood racing.

At The Metropole Hotel, Anjali Gupta was sitting at a desk behind the front counter, intent upon copying entries from an enormous ledger to a smaller notebook. William was about to ring the little brass buzzer under the sign Attention Please when she looked up. 'Ah, William,' she said, with undue familiarity. William wondered if his wife was a regular habitué, possibly arm in arm with Anil for the afternoon tea service.

She looked at him expectantly. His cornflower blue eyes were narrowed.

'I have business with Mrs Banerjee,' he announced. The woman laughed, a shrill eruption that signalled she found his announcement to be hilarious. A mynah bird in a cage on the desk let out a cry that sounded to William like a wounded seal.

'You don't look like a chauffeur,' Anjali Gupta giggled, sidling from behind the desk and indicating he should follow her. She pronounced the word chauffeur as if it carried several French accents.

In the dining room, Mrs Banerjee sat at one of the tables, its usual starched white cloth folded to one side to accommodate her stash of books, pens and loose papers. She greeted William warmly. 'Tea, tea,' she called, clapping her hands to summon one of the somnolent waiters into action.

'Have you taken a room here?'

Mrs Banerjee looked at William in amazement. 'Of course not,' she retorted. 'Why would I move into a hotel when I am perfectly comfortable at Monsoon Cottage?'

The question hung in the air. William shifted in his seat and accepted a cup of tea.

'I am interviewing for a driver,' she said, tidying her papers. 'I have just purchased an automobile. Just now, my Bombay lawyer, a close family friend, is arranging for it to be driven up to Chalaili. It is a full-luxury ultra-modern Chrysler Air Flow Imperial. I take it you have heard of this latest model? Fully imported, I am informed, every screw and wheel and spring-sprung thing and, well, every last jing-bang inch of it.'

William did not answer but stared into his cup, wondering what his next move should be.

'Do you drive?' she asked.

This was too much for William. The woman, he muttered to himself, obviously was off her rocker. Next she would be offering him a job. He mumbled his excuses and fled. As he strode through the foyer, Anjali Gupta waved at him cheerily from behind the front desk as if they were old acquaintances. She blew a kiss at his departing back and wriggled her shapely hips. More than a little of Picture Madam's theatricality had rubbed off on the hotel owner's wife.

☙

Ram Gupta, unseen by his wife, stood along the hallway, suppressing a laugh. How beautiful she is, he thought, watching as Anjali Gupta caught some loose threads of hair and twirled them into her upswept coiffure. One or two white hairs stood out amid the black and he noticed how she squinted at the papers on the front desk. She was too vain for reading spectacles just yet.

They were both in their mid-forties. Just the two of us, he mused, stranded here in this no-status hill station that the

285

Britishers ignored and even the rich Indian tourists from Bombay eschewed in favour of its drier, less ladder-like neighbours.

Her parents dead, his mother and father retired to the south of India. Taking walks on a long beach each morning, rarely in need of umbrellas, constantly keeping in touch with him to make sure the family business was running smoothly.

'Where are the guests, Ram?' they asked over and over, like a stuck gramophone record.

Anjali Gupta was walking across the foyer.

'Don't let her ever hate me for keeping her here,' he whispered.

She spotted him skulking in the shadows.

'Come, come,' she called. 'There's work to be done. What are you doing loitering like some beggar.'

She didn't expect an answer and began to hum as she prepared to make a telephone call. Ram Gupta walked towards her and slipped behind the front counter with a little skip to his step.

Chapter Forty-three

CHALAILI
OCTOBER, 1937

THE SOLIGANJ WEEKLY OBSERVER

Mr P. K. Kumar of Kumar's Tea Emporium, Railway Road, Soliganj, has informed *The Soliganj Weekly Observer* that Autumnal Flush Darjeeling Tea is now available to his regular customers (waiting list applies to newcomers). 'This fine tea is gathered in the months of September and October after the monsoon has ended,' advised Mr P. K. Kumar. 'It has a smooth, medium body, but is not being sold in such grand supplies as usual this year, owing to the severity of the annual rains.'

William's plan to ignore the pen-pushers and simply stay put at Bluebell Cottage came adrift when a Mrs Samuel Carter arrived late one Friday afternoon. She was accompanied by two daughters, who looked to be in their early twenties and wore similar pink and mauve floral dresses. Like a pair of sweet peas, thought William. The little group seemed surprised to find the bungalow occupied. 'We had planned to move right in,' the woman told him as they pushed past William into the front parlour. 'My husband is the new Government Medical Officer at Chalaili Hospital and he will be joining us next week.'

They surveyed the surroundings with reasonable cheer and one of the girls, the far prettier, complimented William on the view, as if he had just finished painting it in time for their arrival. 'My name is Emma,' she said and he noticed that she blushed furiously as she spoke. Poor thing, he thought, her parents will be trying to marry her off as soon as possible.

Her twin mumbled her name. 'Elizabeth.' And then just stood, eyes down, with one hand on her mother's arm. 'One beautiful, one dutiful,' he thought, remembering a long-ago line of his Aunt Sylvia's. He wondered if that was why Lydia had not married earlier. Evelyn had beaten her to it and she had had to stay at The Oaks as unpaid servant to her parents.

William stood still. Anil hovered, waiting to be ordered to make tea. The three females were silent, too, the atmosphere thick enough to carve. Finally, the mother spoke. 'I presume all the furnishings are government issue?' Her voice was carefully modulated as if William may not grasp what she was saying.

'I, er, don't know,' William replied. He had no idea what might have been requisitioned and which items Lydia could have added to the mix. 'Private,' said Anil, rolling up a small Kashmiri rug, almost tripping up the twins, who were now standing shoulder to shoulder, their expressions amused.

'We are at The Metropole Hotel,' said Mrs Carter, preparing to leave. 'Our inventory will be here by next week but, if it suits you, we will move in tomorrow.'

It was a rhetorical question. Anil was already opening the front door and ushering them out.

☙

William instructed Anil to pack. 'We will leave by nine tomorrow morning.'

The personal effects fitted into William's battered steamer trunk and several cloth bundles. There were clothes, mostly, and a considerable number of books but nothing, William grimly realised, of any real value. Lydia had taken most of her small wardrobe with her and personal items of hers, such as a set of fine silver-backed brush and hand-mirror, Anil wrapped carefully in William's woollen dressing-gown. William passed to Anil a Kashmiri papier-mâché box decorated with a design of birds and flowers and a trio of carved wooden musicians, each about a foot tall and kneeling with individual instruments. They were painted in the fiery colours of the desert region of Rajasthan, complete with swirled turbans. He wasn't sure if they were really his, but he couldn't imagine any government inventory noting such decorations between the bath-tub and bed.

'Where to, Sahib?' asked Anil, loading up a pony cart he had ordered from the bazaar. William looked at him and the cooking pots he had loaded loosely in the cart. In the bulging bag slung over Anil's shoulder, he imagined he saw the outline of a candle-stick. Behind Anil stood Devi, the ghost-like waif who lived in the kitchen and whose presence William had never mentioned since the surreal night of Sunita's death. It was the first time William had seen her in daylight and although she pulled her sari pallu across her head and lower face, he noticed her terrible scars.

Without a word, he waved that his servant, Devi and the

289

coolie with the pony cart should follow him as he wheeled his bicycle. When their pathetic little procession reached the bottom of the ridge, he would decide whether to turn to the left to the upper line of bungalows or to the right into town.

☙

William was never to make that decision. As they approached the crossroads, Mrs Banerjee was alighting from her new car, the door held open for her by a young man in a peaked cap with splendid military braid. His ceremonial headgear didn't quite match the grubby knitted sweater and patched grey trousers he was wearing. Vehicles couldn't proceed past that intersection, due to the slenderness of the high and low ridge roads. William wondered where Picture Madam would be keeping her car, although he never doubted she would have devised some elaborate plan.

'You are moving?' she asked, somewhat unnecessarily given the mobile nature of their caravanserai. It was Anil who answered. 'Madam, we are homeless just now.'

'Never, never!' she exclaimed, clapping her hands so that her gold bangles rocked and resettled.

'Actually, Mrs Banerjee,' said William, 'you are occupying Bungalow Seven, which has been requisitioned for myself and Mrs Rushmore, who is presently overseas.'

'Mr Banerjee also is presently overseas.'

William began to feel panicked. Surely, he reasoned, this monumental woman couldn't be about to suggest a solution so unconventional it would cause his utter downfall. It was enough that she had recently appeared to him in a lurid vision, advancing like an Indian version of Boadicea.

'Please,' she gestured, sweeping her arm to indicate that the procession should accompany her. 'Let's have tea and talk about this sorry state of affairs.' Anil instantly began following her swaying bottom along the overgrown defile, ordering the coolie to stay put and guard the contents of the cart. William took off his canvas hat and wiped his brow. Mrs Banerjee and Anil were now walking side by side, chatting like old friends. She stopped to show him a rhododendron bush, plucking one of its rotund blooms in the process and poking it through her upswept hair.

William gripped his hat with both hands and took a deep breath. He knew he was entering dangerously uncharted territory. When he looked sideways at Devi, she peeped up at him with a raised eyebrow in a way that suggested she knew just what Mrs Banerjee was up to.

Chapter Forty-four

CHALAILI
NOVEMBER, 1937

THE SOLIGANJ WEEKLY OBSERVER
Yoga lessons are being offered to residents of Soliganj and
Chalaili. Ladies only should contact Mrs Ram Gupta of
The Metropole Hotel, telephone Chalaili 240.

William Rushmore's temporary habitation of Premila Banerjee's bungalow caused an eruption of gossip of a proportion never encountered in Chalaili. The Crows from The Empire Club called special crisis meetings but no amount of tut-tutting presented any solution. He was a married man. She was a married woman. Spouses were confirmed absent. Charlotte Montague wondered if William had got wind of Lydia's little dalliance at The Chalaili Sanatorium for the Tubercular and despatched her back to Surrey. She had refrained from apprising old Dottie Smith of the known details of Lydia Rushmore and Simon Fraser-Gough although this took much restraint after a few tongue-loosening beverages at the Creswell-Smythe woman's soirees, especially her

292

Apache costume party, not long into which everyone started gagging on stray feathers in the punch bowl.

Speculation was rife, too, about the actual existence of a Mr Banerjee but no one dared accost the picturesque Mrs Banerjee with such a proposition. She had become very influential in Chalaili during her brief incumbency and had even persuaded Anjali Gupta of The Metropole Hotel to offer yoga lessons in The Maharani Suite on Monday afternoons, not that any of the Memsahibs had dared attend, for who knows what shedding of undergarments such Indian gymnastics could entail.

Coronation Talkies was a successful business and even the notoriously snooty Dorothy Creswell-Smythe relished her weekly outings to view the likes of Mr Clark Gable and Mr Gary Cooper, although Mrs Banerjee afforded her a cool reception.

Mrs Banerjee's Bombay connections ensured that the films shown were the very latest releases. There was even talk that the titles were ahead of the offerings shown at the more salubrious hill stations, those flourishing outposts graced with the Vice-Regal imprimatur.

The British chaps turned a blind eye to the scandal. Mrs Banerjee was enormously fat but not lacking in physical allure. Privately, many wondered what it would be like to be adrift in her massive womanliness, hugged between her jelly-roll thighs in an almighty grip.

But knowing what a cold fish Rushmore was, they also found it impossible to imagine him so engaged, unless he'd found a way to measure Picture Madam's doubtless rollicking orgasms with one of his beloved weather devices.

After a few heated weeks, the gossip cooled. William Rushmore was an acknowledged bore and unlikely to be engaged in passion of any sort, announced Charlotte Montague to anyone who cared to listen during coiffure-curling sessions at the Lakshmi Hair and Beauty Studio. It was hardly any wonder, she declared, that Lydia should be taking her time to return.

Charlotte Montague happened to know separate bedrooms were being occupied at Monsoon Cottage. A reliable espionage network among assorted servants had ensured she was thoroughly apprised of the relevant facts.

Her sources were much less forthcoming on the subject of Veronica O'Brien, however. The proprietress of Lakshmi Hair and Beauty Studio had not returned from her monsoon holiday. Poppy Lee, the exotic-eyed hairdresser who had arrived from Bombay to take over in Veronica O'Brien's absence, claimed she knew nothing of the owner's whereabouts. She was employed by a friend of a friend from Bombay on a contract renewable on a monthly basis. She had moved into Veronica O'Brien's cottage in The Empire Club grounds and, according to her neighbour Dorothy Creswell-Smythe, was living it up in the wee hours, gramophone at full blare and silhouettes clearly seen against drawn blinds, dancing cheek to cheek, and much worse, anatomically speaking.

'There has been a rumour she ran away with the son of a minor raja,' confided Poppy Lee, as she tweaked Charlotte Montague's permanent wave in front of one of Lakshmi Hair and Beauty Studio's silver-edged mirrors.

Charlotte Montague looked fiercely at Poppy Lee. The girl, for that was all she was, twenty at the most, was mixed Indian and Chinese and it was not a happy recipe.

Really, thought Charlotte Montague, you cannot trust a hybrid tongue.

'I believe she has returned to England . . . in case of a war in

Europe,' snapped Charlotte Montague, who knew no such thing, but couldn't bear the idea of Veronica O'Brien holidaying in some palace with a raja. Indian princes were astronomically rich and, it had to be admitted, could be rather dashing and manly, even in pearled slippers.

Chapter Forty-five

THE SOLIGANJ WEEKLY OBSERVER
Interested parties are invited to attend the annual Anglo-
Indian Residents of Soliganj picnic in the grounds of the
Soliganj Public Library. Enquiries to Miss Constance
Rivers, Head Librarian, telephone Soliganj 118.

Florence Gordon lay in bed, her shoulders, legs and back
aching. She was beginning to wonder if it had been such
a brilliant idea to go into the publishing business with Vivek (who
she called The Cheeky Man at every available opportunity, just to
rile him). Now she was obliged to perform all sorts of unconventional sexual favours for him just so he would take the typed sheets
for her new gossip rag to Bombay and get them all set and printed
up. Via his vast network of jaggery contacts, Vivek appeared to
have unlimited resources, and he had assured her of the utmost
discretion, although she took that promise with a grain of sugar.

He was paying for all the costs involved, as he chose to

remind her every time they met, and last night he had insisted she perform a special sex act he referred to as the Himalayan Spinning Top. She had been forced to rotate upon his impressively durable penis while he slapped her bottom and screeched like a dying crow. All the while she had been terrified Mary Christie would come tripping through the garden with her cricket bat and candle lantern and witness the laughable scenario through Florence Gordon's not-quite-fitted curtains.

He had left just before dawn and Florence Gordon managed a few hours of uncomfortable rest before she got up, made tea and took the top copy off the small printed pile Vivek had left on her sitting-room table. It was a Sunday morning and she could take her time getting started for the day. She climbed into bed, fluffed up the pillows and wiped her reading glasses with a hanky before she began.

The Chalaili Bugle
VOLUME 1, EDITION 1
EDITED BY EUGENIA JAMBOLANA

INTRODUCTION
Welcome to *The Chalaili Bugle*

We all know Chalaili is a laughable blackwater (sic) in the middle of nowhere but it is surprising what goes upon (sic) behind closet (sic) doors. Was there ever such a colony of missed fits (sic)? The aim of this enterprise is to keep Chalaili residents up to dare (sic) with the secret lives of our friends and neighbours so we can all live together in harm money (sic).

Florence Gordon moaned and banged down her teacup. Six printing mistakes in the first paragraph. She knew Vivek couldn't read English. So much for his expert professional first-class buggering up typesetters. She took a deep breath and then found herself laughing. The mistakes were so funny they almost looked intentional. And she had to admit that the printing was good: deep black ink on pristine white paper, just one single-sided quarto sheet, closely set.

The Editor was sure there would be many more contributions for Edition II. Informants were invited to send submissions to a Bombay postal address (Vivek's third or fourth cousin; highly trustworthy; if proved otherwise, The Chikki Man had seen the last of the Himalayan Spinning Top).

ITEM ONE
True Or False?

There have been reported sightings of a particularly large Altocumulus Crowd (sic) that has caught the attention of our very own William Rushmore. The Cloud (Florence Gordon: 'Thank you, you nincompoops') changes colour several times a day but retains its rolls and rounded masses, which are speculated to be of special interest to Mr Rushmore after hours.

ITEM TWO
Believe It Or Not

A certain Chalaili resident of indeterminate colour is in possession of a cricket bat stolen in 1936 from the Soliganj Spurting (sic) and Recreational Club and not returned, despite an investigation into said disappearance. Said resident has put illegally obtained bat

298

to criminal use, involving slaying of indecent (sic) animals. '*Innocent* animals!' cried Florence Gordon, banging her free hand on her sugar-scented sheets.

ITEM THREE
Chums Are Fun

Thursday nights at Coronation Talkies are proving to be very successful with Bring A Friend For Free as the lure. Our informant notes, however, that not all Friends who are brought to the premises are Free to attend and there have been reports of undercover operatives in the back rows. No wonder Mrs Rajat Banerjee's special evenings have become known as Burns (sic) Are Fun. (Florence Gordon: 'Bums, bums, bums, you Bombay bird-brain idiots.')

ITEM FOUR
Sweet Success

The fame of Mr Vivek Chandra's excellent chikki has spread far and wide and readers of *The Chalaili Bugle* are invited to take advantage of discount price by presenting their copy at his Chikki Stall (Chota Chalaili, turn right past Mr K. Walia's Pickles and Daily Needs and stop before Radiance Suitings, Shirtings and General Underwearings). Please note this discount does not apply at competitor store Mr J. Mohan and Son (Deceased). Remember! Vivek Chandra's chikki leaves an inedible (sic) impression.

Florence Gordon laughed so hard at the final error that she almost fell out of bed. She had fought against the idea of a silly promotion for The Chikki Man's wares but he had refused to go ahead with the enterprise unless she agreed. She couldn't publish *The Chalaili Bugle* without him as all she had was a typewriter in the back room of Chalaili Post Office to tap out her notes after hours and secret access to the Britain-bound mail. There had not really been enough in the notes Lydia had posted to her sister, although she could thank her for Bums are Fun, a snippet no doubt gleaned by eavesdropping on the cawing Crows at The Empire Club.

The letters she had steamed open and then carefully resealed had so far been a bit disappointing. She could thank the bunion-suffering (short-listed snippet for Edition II) Charlotte Montague for 'colony of misfits' (letter to her sister, Catherine, two airmail sheets, double-sided, the thrifty cow). But most of the correspondence 'home' was silly bluster about bridge competitions and untrustworthy servants. What Florence Gordon wanted most of all was to embarrass the daylights out of the arrogant Britishers who treated her so rudely and always referred to her as Anglo-Indian or Eurasian, with elongated emphasis on the latter syllables, as if she were only half presentable. The thought of blackmail even crossed her mind now she had the power of the press at her disposal.

As she fingered her cooling teacup and flexed her strained thighs, Vivek's sugar-cooking boys already would have distributed the launch edition of *The Chalaili Bugle* under every doorway in the British parts of town with string-bound bundles dropped on the top steps of The Empire Club, The Metropole Hotel and Lakshmi Hair and Beauty Studio.

⌾

Mary Christie was the first to bang on Florence Gordon's door. She had just breakfasted at The Metropole Hotel and as she was about to leave, Anjali Gupta had handed her the launch edition of *The Chalaili Bugle*. 'This is very amusing,' laughed Anjali Gupta. 'I wonder who could be masquerading as Eugenia Jambolana?'

'Have you seen this treacherous codswallop?' demanded Mary Christie as she pushed past Florence Gordon into her sitting room.

Florence Gordon had carefully hidden all her copies as she had been expecting this intrusion. 'What is it?' she asked, eyes wide with innocence.

'Read it!'

Mary Christie slumped into one of the sitting room's old cane chairs with such vigour that it creaked and sighed.

'I'll need my specs,' said Florence Gordon, taking the copy from Mary Christie and sashaying into the bedroom, the cord of her imaginatively brief dressing-gown trailing behind.

'Not even decently dressed at this late hour,' grumbled Mary Christie to herself. She also noticed a number of bruises on her friend's calves and, as usual, a distinct scent of coconut mixed with sugar.

'Goodness me,' cackled Florence Gordon as she returned holding *The Chalaili Bugle*. 'I don't think William Rushmore is going to be too pleased.'

'William Rushmore be damned. What about the cricket bat?'

'Let me finish reading. Oh, yes, I see. Gosh, do you think that means you?'

'Of course it means me! Don't you remember I accidentally ended up with a cricket bat from the Deccan Cup last year. You were there . . .'

Mary Christie jumped up, the cane chair wobbled. 'It's you! It must be you! No one else knows about the cricket bat.'

'Well, obviously they do,' snapped Florence Gordon, searching though a mess of magazines for her cigarettes and matches. 'You'd be surprised what people know in this place.'

Mary Christie sat down again. She looked as if she were going to cry.

Florence Gordon patted her arm as she blew perfect rings of smoke, a trick she had learned from one of the convalescing soldiers who'd taken her to dine at The Empire Club. They'd had a lovely night out, even if his plasma bottle did keep getting in the way . . .'

'No one will read it. Don't be such a silly old stick . . .'

'That's not a good word to use.'

'Well, I'm hardly going to call you a silly old bat!'

The older woman managed a laugh as she wiped her snuffling nose. Good, thought Florence Gordon, she can bugger off now.

But Mary Christie sat back in the chair and started fiddling with the frilled edge of a cushion at her side. 'Florence, can I tell you a secret. I mean a real secret, something no one else in Chalaili knows or ever could know.'

Florence Gordon gathered her scanty dressing-gown around her and sat down on the settee. She wished she could make notes, like a proper news reporter.

'You are such a good friend, I feel I can tell you . . .'

'Go on, go on . . .'

'Well, Captain Archibald Christie wasn't really my husband.'

Florence Gordon had always thought as much and tried not to smirk.

'He was my father . . .'

'Your father?'

302

'Yes, he had a relationship with my mother and then he went back to England . . . He already had a wife and children. My mother killed herself . . .'

She began sobbing and sobbing. Florence Gordon flew to her little bathroom annexe to fetch a towel.

'No need for the water works. Come on, it was a long time ago . . .'

Mary Christie stopped howling long enough to look at Florence Gordon reproachfully. 'I am quite aware how old I am . . .'

'That's not at all what I meant . . . It's just that time heals these things.'

'I was brought up in a convent orphanage with all the other not-wanted Anglo-Indian children. Half-breeds, neither here-nor-theres, rotten thrown-away garbage . . .'

'Mary, dear, do not forget I am also Anglo-Indian . . .'

'But you have a mother! I've met her, Mrs Priyanka Gordon, emphasis on the GORDON, no shortage of airs and graces . . .'

Florence Gordon did not reply. The two women sat silently, neither looking at the other.

'You are the only person in Chalaili . . . and . . . and Soliganj combined who knows this,' said Mary Christie, finally, as she rose to leave. Eugenia Jambolana was pretty sure she could detect a threat in her tone.

Chapter Forty-six

West Gamble, Surrey
December, 1937

The Finchley Examiner

Snow fell yesterday in many parts of Surrey with record levels covering West Gamble and the upper and lower slopes of Box Hill. Such unseasonably early snow will no doubt herald a severe winter.

Lydia woke late and was temporarily confused about her whereabouts. There were footsteps outside the door and she prepared to call for Anil to enter with her bed tea. Rubbing her eyes and stretching, she realised with a start that she was in her niece's room at The Oaks. Anne had been displaced, sent back to share with Redmond, while Aunty Lydia took up temporary residence in what had been her spinster bedroom.

Lydia had been staying, at William's insistence, with his Aunt Sylvia and Uncle John for several weeks. She had been horribly ill with influenza but had been somewhat glad that her return to The Oaks was delayed.

There was a light tap at the door and Evelyn poked her head into the room, bringing with her a cold draught. 'You're awake at last,' she said, as if her sister were a naughty child. 'There's fresh tea in the pot downstairs. I'll be back in a few hours.' The sisters exchanged smiles and Evelyn bustled out. Lydia had been at The Oaks for less than twenty-four hours and there had been no time to discuss what would be done about Daddy's room. Carefully wrapping her woollen dressing-gown tightly around her, Lydia decided to enter the large bedroom at the front of the house, the one where she'd dressed for her wedding. She hoped there would be some sense of her father still in the room, perhaps a lingering vestige of his pipe or the macassar of his hair oil.

It was obvious from first glance that Evelyn and Tom had taken it over, probably days after Daddy's death. Her sister's slippers were discarded on the carpeted floor, by the end of the double bed. Lydia sank into a chair by the window and looked around. Her father's books had been replaced on the little shelf near the door by piles of magazines and paperbacks including, she recognised, many of those she'd left behind when she set off for India. She heard the family dog barking somewhere in the bowels of The Oaks and reluctantly left the room, lest Evelyn return early and accuse her of spying.

Lydia bathed and dressed before going downstairs. She had forgotten how cold England could be after so many muggy months in Chalaili. She passed the door of what had been Evelyn and Tom's room at the back of the upper storey, where her sister had slept in childhood, too. It must be empty, Lydia reasoned, so she opened the door, although it wouldn't fling wide, caught on a bulk of brown boxes. There were three distinct cardboard encampments, each labelled in Evelyn's sure hand: Mother, Father, Lydia. The sight made her feel numb, as if she had been despatched to an early grave.

Chapter Forty-seven

CHALAILI
DECEMBER, 1937

'There come to us moments in life when about some
things we need no proof from without.'
M. K. (MAHATMA) GANDHI

The brouhaha over Volume 1, Edition 1 (Collector's Item) of *The Chalaili Bugle* died down within days. William Rushmore seemed oblivious to the sarcastic slurs and there was no response from the unflappable Mrs Banerjee.

The Chikki Man reported morosely that business did not seem to be booming and he had even heard that several of The Crows had bustled up to the nearby stand of Mr J. Mohan and Son (Deceased) and offered him condolences on his bereavement. This somewhat puzzled the affable man as his son and first wife had died during a difficult birth, twenty-eight years earlier, and the single-sex womb of his harried second wife had forthwith produced six daughters. But he had bowed graciously and dispensed free jaggery sweets all round, which The Crows received but, as reliably reported by a Chikki Man operative, quickly handed to their servants as they walked away as Mr J. Mohan's hands had been all over them.

There were no letters to the top-secret post office box in Bombay. At first, Florence Gordon thought the mysteriously inefficient workings of the city's mail system might be to blame so she took to intercepting all outbound letters that passed through Chalaili Post Office but nothing turned up.

'I wish I could publish the truth about Mary Christie,' she murmured in bed as The Chikki Man lay by her side. She was trying to wean him off the exertions of the Himalayan Spinning Top by claiming it could damage his penis, although she feared that the rotten thing, always up at the click of a finger, was indestructible.

He appeared to be dozing off and she was really just thinking aloud.

'I feel sorry for her, really. Father shoots through, Mother commits suicide, brought up by nuns. No wonder she had to invent a husband with bad karma like that.' There was no response from her lover as she turned off the bedside light.

Chapter Forty-eight

CHALAILI
DECEMBER, 1937

THE SOLIGANJ WEEKLY OBSERVER
Play resumes today, eighth of December, at Brabourne
Stadium, Bombay, in the much-anticipated stoush
between the Cricket Club of India and Lord Tenny-
son's XI. At the close of play, as *The Soliganj Weekly Observer*
went to press, the tourists were 5 wickets for 300 runs,
with Jas Langridge on 129 and N. T. McCorkell on 2.
M. H. Mankad took two wickets as did S. N. Banerjee.
Opening batsman W. J. Edrich was despatched by Amar
Singh, caught K. R. Meherhomji, for a duck.

*D*evi had been right to raise an eyebrow about William's
move to Monsoon Cottage. Within minutes of arrival
at Mrs Banerjee's, she was despatched to Coronation Talkies to act
as servant to Mr K. K. Rao in his series of small rooms on the cinema building's upper floor.

Anil tried to protest but Mrs Banerjee was firm about the

new arrangement and pointed out she already had Aruna as her personal servant and she was not running a lodging house for the lower classes. William was unconcerned and Devi instantly acquiesced when Anil explained that Mrs Banerjee had mentioned a rate of pay that was much more than she had ever earned satisfying the dreadful needs of beach-prowling men.

'Mr K. K. Rao is a good man, highly trained in talking pictures,' she told Devi, who understood no English and regarded with amazement this in-charge Bombay madam who appeared to acknowledge no Indian language, except the occasional colourful explosion of Hindustani.

'He will not harm or abuse you or there will be hell to pay. Now, go, go!' she commanded and Devi took off, although she had no idea where she was headed. She sat under a tree at the end of the ridge until Mrs Banerjee's new driver, Vinod, appeared and drove her to Coronation Talkies. Devi had never been in a motor car and the experience was terrifying. She screamed the entire way, sliding around on the back seat as Vinod careered down the switchback tracks. By the time she arrived and Mr K. K. Rao opened the door, she fell down, kissing his smartly shod feet in extravagant gratitude that she had been delivered to him alive.

❧

Anil was not entirely happy about the move to Monsoon Cottage. When he had lived with William and Lydia, his had been the small room off the kitchen and he had decorated it with pictures torn from Memsahib's discarded English magazines. The last things he saw before he slipped into sleep were the abundant assets of a smiling blonde lady straining upwards and outwards as she decorated the top of a Christmas tree with a miniature winged version of herself.

His quarters had been cramped but proximity to the oven had ensured warmth in winter and in summer he had moved his string cot outside, wrapping himself in a mosquito net from Sahib's spare bedroom so anyone coming across him thus shrouded on a balmy night would have mistaken him for a slumbering ghost.

Aruna occupied a similar kitchen alcove at Monsoon Cottage and it would have been unseemly for Anil to be quartered anywhere in her immediate vicinity. Picture Madam's solution was to banish him to the garden shed, a damp hovel he was expected to share with Vinod the driver, the nephew of that puffed-up Bombay builder, Sham Lal. Vinod had been sauntering around Chota Chalaili bazaar for weeks, up to no good at all as far as Anil could deduce. The two men distrusted each other on sight. Vinod sported a drooping moustache and over-applications of hair oil and Anil suspected he had falsified his driving credentials because he hurled along Mrs Banerjee's full-luxury ultra-modern Chrysler Air Flow Imperial like an escaping gangster.

Mrs Banerjee knew nothing of this speculation. For such a successful businesswoman, she was given to emotional decisions and had hired Vinod on the strength that he arrived for his interview in the dining room of The Metropole Hotel wearing a near-new pair of traffic policeman's gloves. Anil surmised they were stolen and, as for the driving test Mrs Banerjee had organised, all Vinod had had to do was open and close doors and propel her to Coronation Talkies without actually causing loss of life on the way.

Happily for Anil, Vinod chose to sleep in the front seat of the full-luxury ultra-modern Chrysler Air Flow Imperial, parked at the intersection where the northbound road petered in the upper and lower ridges. He convinced his employer that this was for reasons of safety and security. Twice a day, he padded up the path and took his meals in the kitchen with Anil and Aruna.

Aruna barely spoke but Anil was delighted that she slapped more food on his plate than Vinod's, which he took to be a sign of her respect for his manliness. Vinod took his meals outside, squatting on his haunches in the garden, smoking and eating simultaneously and frequently breaking wind, sometimes so ferociously that Aruna would race outside and let fly a stream of such imaginative English expressions as 'monkey face palooka' and 'tub of mush'.

When Anil washed, using the cool sweet water from the garden pump, he stripped off to near-nakedness and Aruna would sing and chatter to herself as she mopped or swept, as if such activity would also keep her eyes gainfully occupied.

Everyone in Chota Chalaili, along the labyrinthine lanes and byways of the bazaar, knew that Vinod rented out the back seat of the full-luxury ultra-modern Chrysler Air Flow Imperial at fifteen-minute intervals for furtive lovers, and even for whole nights, Coronation Talkies closing time onwards, to shack-dwellers who viewed even a brief occupation of the capacious car as an exotic holiday.

Anil had seen the Romantics lined up awaiting their turns. The male Romantics, that is, while the female Romantics, with reputations to protect, would dash from the bushes at the last minutes, heads bowed and veiled, and launch themselves into the car's leathery depths.

Anil didn't know what was worse: the possibility of unmentionable stains on Mrs Banerjee's upholstery or the fact Vinod referred to the car as the CAFI, completely ignoring its full-luxury ultra-modern connections, as always insisted upon by its owner.

Anil challenged Vinod about his insouciance with the name,

explaining that words like luxury and modern were very important to Mrs Banerjee.

'Well, how about the FLUM CAFI?' laughed Vinod, narrow-
ing his eyes.

His rapid speech and inflected emphasis compressed the
initials to one word. Flumcafi.

By constant use, the word became accepted into the vernac-
ular of Chalaili's lower classes. Flumcafi was a bedroom, a holiday
destination, a retreat from the monsoon.

Anil groaned.

But he decided to keep quiet about Vinod's underhand dealings and Flumcafi abbreviations as Mrs Banerjee seemed very pleased
with him and he wouldn't put it past the seat-hiring scoundrel to
somehow turn the tables so it was Anil in the wrong.

More importantly, Anil's sights were set on moving into
Aruna's bed. He had not been with a woman since the aborted
night at Devi's shack but his virility was unlikely to be an issue,
judging by the amount of semen he squirted effortlessly into his
hand several times a week, some of it arcing skywards and landing
on the picture of the English Christmas tree, where it hung like
tinsel. Occasionally his masturbatory sessions were interrupted
when he imagined he heard scrapings and, terrified of an unscheduled appearance of Ghost Mother, he would turn painfully onto
his stomach and pretend to be asleep.

Meanwhile, Anil swept and polished Monsoon Cottage and
performed small shopping duties for William while Aruna cooked
and put herself in charge of going to the bazaar. This arrangement
meant that Anil was denied kitchen advice from Ghost Mother and
his chatty intercourse with the food stall owners. But often he followed Aruna at a discreet distance, enjoying the swing of her sari,

usually in serviceable cotton. Instead of a joyful pattern, Aruna wore single colours, usually saffron or tangerine, folds undulating like goldfish fins, as she walked swiftly down the hill.

Aside from the presence of his treasured English Christmas image and a Property of Indian Civil Service-stamped brass candlestick Anil had taken from Bluebell Cottage in a moment of anger at the move, his sleeping arrangements were dreadful. He decided to clean out the offending garden shed. Almost everything could be thrown out, he decided. There was enough old rubbish to constitute an archaeological dig. He moved decomposed newspapers and rusty pieces of garden equipment deeper into the garden, covering the mess with fallen branches and leaves. In the garden there was a little tricycle. Perhaps it had belonged to the dead child, the poor little thing hurried off the ridge by the 1932 monsoon. William, he remembered, had been called in to investigate, to wield his instruments and explain at an inquest how the terrible accident could have occurred.

Then Anil swept the earthen floor and moved his bedding away from the door where it had been hastily plonked when he moved in. During these rearrangements, he noticed a small tea-chest, the condition of the crating suggesting it was practically new. It must belong to Mrs Banerjee, he reasoned, containing little-used possessions she had no need of in the house. It would make an excellent table, especially during the wet months, when it was too soggy to sip his tea outside, leisurely drawing on a beedi or his dwindling supply of superior Craven A cigarettes that Lydia had left behind in the top drawer of her bedroom table and he had secreted in his bundles for the move from Bluebell Cottage.

But Anil's curiosity got the better of him. Mrs Banerjee was a woman of secrets, always cagey when William asked her questions

313

about Bombay. The chest could contain a few answers so looking around to make sure he was unobserved, Anil opened it, shook aside a few folds of cheap fabric forming a soft roof for the contents and there lay nestled a Bell & Howell projector, a spool of film already loaded. It was a miniature version of the model used at Coronation Talkies he had seen inside the projection room when Mrs Banerjee had grandly conducted an inspection for William.

She had included Anil, Vinod, Aruna and Devi, too, as if they were paying members of a small tour group.

Anil padded barefoot inside Monsoon Cottage. All was quiet. Vinod had collected Mrs Banerjee after breakfast and they had left on some kind of excursion, probably to the Lakshmi Hair and Beauty Studio where Picture Madam held court at least three times a week, always emerging with a high, hard coiffure that reminded Anil of a foreign lampshade.

Aruna was at the bazaar and would not return for a while, he guessed, as she was as prone to leisurely gossip sessions with friends as himself. William was at work and he had given up his habit of returning for hot lunch, a small gesture he had made during the time Lydia was at Bluebell Cottage. Anil realised that Lydia didn't know this was anything but William's usual bachelor routine and sometimes she had merely lain on their bed, complaining of a headache and leaving her husband to a solitary soup or omelette.

Anil hauled the projector inside and plugged its coiling lead into a socket in the dining room. Placing a few folded newspapers under it so as not to scratch the highly polished surface of Mrs Banerjee's dining room table, he returned to the shed and retrieved the length of fabric under which the projector had been coddled. It was off-white, as big as a sheet, and made a good makeshift screen when draped over the rail of the drawn curtains. Anil had no real idea how to make the machinery work but he had paid close attention to Mr K. K. Rao during his recent tour and so he began by pressing a switch on the side of the projector.

The machine cranked into life and the loaded spool began to roll, slowly and creakily. The black-and-white images thrown onto the crinkled screen were confusing at first. There were dozens of middle-aged women, their hair garlanded with flowers, their waving fingers flashing with gems. Some raised glasses to the camera, making such vivid eye contact with Anil that he was discomfited, as if they were really in the room with him. The toasting continued, several women started dancing, drawing into the frame of the camera's eye a succession of husbands, looking hot and uncomfortable in British-style business suits. There was no soundtrack, all the figures swirling silently like visitors bundled in on clouds from another universe.

Then he saw Mrs Banerjee. The crowd had parted to allow the cameraman full access to the seated bride, elevated on a flower-trimmed stage, looking demurely at the floor, weighed down with a monumental display of gold jewellery. Although her eyes were never raised, the identity of the bride was unmistakable. It was Mrs Banerjee's full figure, her arms stacked with bangles. An older, more anxious version of herself fussed about, pretending to shoo away the cameraman. Her mother, Anil decided.

The film went blank and then restarted. The same crowd of people, now looking very tired and a little drunk. Most were seated and the camera panned the entire room. It must be a palace, thought Anil, his eyes taking in chandeliers, tall columns wound with tinsel and marigolds, turbaned waiters standing stiffly with trays of glasses.

Food was being served on enormous platters and even via

315

the medium of monochromatic film, Anil could sense the glistening deliciousness of the chickens and ducks, roasted English-style, with legs pointing stiffly at the ceiling. There were close-up shots of trays of samosa and pakora, chunks of tandoori chicken and lamb in copper dishes with twin serving handles. A very modern wedding, he could tell, with no tethered goats or sacred fires or Aunties sitting on the floor.

Then the camera riveted away and began its journey up to the stage where Mrs Banerjee sat, head down. No thali thread was tied around her neck by an anxious groom, to declare the union completed. There was no groom. She sat alone. Her shoulders were heaving and Anil imagined he saw tears splashing down her cheeks. For an instant, Mrs Banerjee looked up and out, her expression one of damp, stubborn anger. Anil felt strangely dizzy. If the fury and wounded pride of this husbandless bride were unleashed, it would ignite the universe. He imagined Mrs Banerjee causing earthquakes and forest fires with just one determined glare.

Anil shivered as the camera's passage was abruptly halted by the advancing spectre of the bride's mother, her hand clamping the lens, rendering the performance over.

He sat silently, the camera still whirring as snowy film shot onto the cloth screen like a blizzard. Mrs Banerjee had been jilted. No handsome groom on a white horse, his face hidden under plump garlands, no nervous wedding night and blood-stained sheets to be displayed to stickybeaking relatives. He switched off the machine, returned it to the tea-chest, and tidied up the dining room. He should have felt a thrill of triumph that probably he was the only person in Chalaili to know the truth about Picture Madam. But he felt unutterably sad. Sad for Mrs Banerjee and for Lydia, too. Both women were alone in a sense, victims of their trusting natures. Life, he thought grimly, had betrayed them both.

What Anil did not know was that Vinod had already investigated the tea-chest. Not daring to fiddle with the projector, he had helped himself to a clipping from *The Bombay Chronicle* that had been folded underneath. He could not read English but he recognised Mrs Banerjee's photograph, alongside a separate image of a thin bespectacled young man. Vinod knew that for a few coins the professional letter-writer with a stand in Chota Chalaili bazaar would decipher it for him.

Chapter Forty-nine

FINCHLEY, SURREY
DECEMBER, 1937

THE FINCHLEY EXAMINER

Mrs William Rushmore of Chalaili, India, formerly
Miss Lydia Burnett of West Gamble, addressed pupils
at Finchley Primary School yesterday. The theme of Mrs
Rushmore's talk was life in an Indian hill station and
the patterns of the monsoon. During her presentation,
organised by Deputy Principal Mr John Rushmore, she
informed the assembled pupils that her husband is one
of India's leading experts on the topic of subcontinental rain. Mrs Rushmore mentioned she plans to write a
novel about India.

Lydia sat in Sylvia Rushmore's front parlour at Finchley, the one reserved to receive guests, where the
spinster schoolteacher from West Gamble had been introduced to
the blue-eyed weather man from Chalaili.

While Sylvia went to the kitchen to fetch sandwiches and

a home-baked sponge, Lydia looked at the framed photographs arrayed on top of the china cabinet. She had been too ill with influenza to pay any attention to her surroundings during her stay several weeks earlier at the Finchley house.

More than half the display was of William, Lydia noted, mostly as a serious-faced young child. She got up and moved across to look at them more closely, realising as she did that the mounted picture on the wall behind the cabinet was actually a map of India, and Chalaili was designated with a crude black cross. 'William made that mark there,' laughed Sylvia, as she put the afternoon tea refreshments on a small glass-topped table. 'I wish he'd done it more neatly.'

'I hadn't actually realised we were living so close to the coast,' said Lydia, accepting a cup of Earl Grey. It looked positively insipid compared with the milky muddiness served by Anil.

'Not much opportunity to travel around India yet, I expect,' said Sylvia brightly, dropping two sugar lumps in her Willow-Pattern cup.

'William must be like a son to you . . .' Lydia ventured, choosing her words carefully.

The older woman did not reply, merely arched her eyebrow over her raised cup.

'I mean, he doesn't have parents . . . I seem to know so little about him.'

'You must give him time to open up, my dear,' said Sylvia, briskly, but her matter-of-fact assurance was too late. Lydia had begun to cry, tears running down her cheeks and falling into her tea cup, held aloft like a small bucket.

'He doesn't love me, you see,' gulped Lydia, reaching in her skirt pocket for a handkerchief.

319

'Love doesn't always come into it,' said Sylvia, who was standing now, looking through the parlour's bay window to the winter-bare trees beyond.

'Whatever do you mean?' cried Lydia, amazed at her hostess's icy composure.

'Take William's parents, for example . . .' Sylvia began, then hesitated, aware she was entering delicate territory.

'William's parents?'

'They were killed in a rail accident. They were returning to Cornwall from London, not even sitting in the same carriage, funnily enough, as they had been to court to finalise their divorce. William's father, Ellis, and I were planning to be together. We were madly in love. John knew everything, of course, but we were all very civilised about it. Then he was gone and his wife, Diana, too. There was simply no choice. John and I had to stay together and raise William as our own. He was only seven at the time, he had no brothers or sisters, his grandparents were too old . . .'

Her voice drifted off. Lydia imagined the young boy, still in short trousers, being so cruelly orphaned and then coming to live in this pin-drop house, as full of silences as The Oaks. Not cosy, calm silences, but cold vacuums of regret and despair.

She wondered if he knew his Aunt Sylvia had been his father's lover. Did he sit on the landing and listen to the fights downstairs, the same beery slurs and bitter shouting that she and Evelyn had listened to, hugging each other, too terrified to move lest they make a noise. If Mother found them eavesdropping, their shortcomings would be included in her wild rantings.

'So,' Sylvia resumed, her hands trembling, 'John and I made an accommodation. We decided to stay together, for William's sake. He wanted to throw me out, raise the boy alone, but we had to put William's welfare first. It wasn't a happy house, though. William used to disappear for hours, rambling through the woods. He told me once he was only happy when he could look at clouds. He thought his parents were up there, you see, his mother spinning the clouds from white wool. She had been knitting him a cricket jumper on the train when she was killed. The needles and skeins of wool were in the personal effects delivered to us. I had to sign for them at the front door while William stood beside me. He kept the wool for years. He slept with it under his pillow.'

'And the rain?' Lydia was thinking aloud. She looked up at Sylvia, surprised the words had been formed. But there was no need to speak further. Both women knew the young boy had imagined his mother weeping from the sky as she worked away at her clouds, sometimes rendering them joyously puffed, but often streaked grey with grief.

Sylvia poured more tea, slowly and shakily. Lydia brushed away fresh tears, but this time she wasn't crying for herself.

Chapter Fifty

Chalaili
December, 1937

THE SOLIGANJ WEEKLY OBSERVER

The Eleventh of December marks the seventh anniversary of the awarding of the Nobel Prize in Physics to Sir Chandrasekhara Venkata Raman for his work on the scattering of light and for the discovery of the effect named after him. To commemorate this great honour bestowed on one of India's most eminent citizens, a bronze bust of Sir C.V. Raman has been unveiled outside Soliganj Public Library.

Florence Gordon finally had enough items for Volume I, Edition II of *The Chalaili Bugle*. It took several weeks of kettle-steaming and double-gumming but the Britain-bound mail eventually had yielded some promising items. Funnily enough, one of the snippets, about the peacock feathers favoured by Dorothy Creswell-Smythe, was tailor-written, just the right length and tone. She typed it all out and gave it to Vivek to take down to

Bombay. In his new bossy role as publisher, printer, distributor and Master of the Himalayan Spinning Top, he refused to be called The Chikki Man, even in their most intimately rotating moments.

And then began a chain of unfortunate events that heralded an end to the career of Florence Gordon, Assistant to the Postmaster, Chalaili Post Office, India.

Florence Gordon's mother took ill. Very ill, said the doctor who called her from Soliganj Hospital, not just attention-getting, worthless-daughter-who-never-visits-me sort of ill. Florence Gordon told the bibulous Harold Gilbert she needed three days leave and was walking to the station with her suitcase, looking exceedingly unhappy, when Mrs Banerjee's car pulled up outside Coronation Talkies.

Vinod opened the door and Picture Madam burst forth in a Christmas-cracker explosion of red and gold.

'Whatever is the matter, you look so sad,' she said, blocking Florence Gordon's path.

'My mother is dying.'

Florence Gordon looked at the ground. She didn't want to meet Mrs Banerjee's glittering eyes in case *The Chalaili Bugle*, Volume I, Edition I, Item 1, was mentioned.

'I'm taking the train to Soliganj,' she added.

'Nonsense!' exclaimed Mrs Banerjee, wresting away Florence Gordon's small case. 'Come, come! Vinod will drive you in my full-luxury ultra-modern Chrysler Air Flow Imperial. He is completely unoccupied this afternoon.'

Vinod scowled behind her back. As a matter of fact, he was thoroughly occupied, with reservations for three sets of Romantics in the back seat of the Flumcafi.

Mrs Banerjee ushered Florence Gordon onto the imported

leather upholstery. 'Train travel is very bad for the digestion, dear,' she added obliquely as Vinod took the wheel and the car went pelting off.

While Florence Gordon sat by her ailing mother's bedside, Vivek, The Chikki Man, was in Bombay attending to the final printing of the second edition. He couldn't really understand why Florence Gordon persisted with the silly little publication but he had enough spare money to indulge her hobby and would have spent twice that amount for the unrivalled access she was affording him to the bounce of her naked breasts.

Unfortunately, Vivek lost the second of the sheets that Florence had typed for him and there weren't enough words to fill the printed page, even including another promotion for his chikki stall, with mention of Mr J. Mohan and Son (Deceased) deleted. Following the style that Florence Gordon had introduced, Vivek began dictating to his printers:

ITEM FIVE
Secret Uncovered

It has come to our attention (Vivek was exceptionally pleased with this bit, copied from a report in a London newspaper one of his cohorts had read to him at the printing works) that a certain MC should not be using such a name as no army captain husband exists. She is an orphan, with father disappeared and mother dead by her own hand and we suspect secret money has been used to open a shop. (Vivek made up the last bit but he thought it added extra relish.)

When the edition was printed, delivered to Chalaili and circulated by Vivek's jaggery boys, Florence Gordon was still in Soliganj, by her mother's bed. Mary Christie hammered and hammered at her neighbour's bungalow door until her knuckles bled and then collapsed crying into the spiky bougainvillea, which is where Anjali Gupta found her, ominously pale and thorn-struck, having been alerted by the kitchen staff who'd witnessed the spectacle through the hotel's rear windows. Anjali took Mary into The Metropole Hotel and tried to calm her with warm sweet milk in the little office behind the front desk as she blubbered out the story.

'I just can't believe Florence would do such a thing,' said Anjali Gupta, who was also upset. She didn't quite know how to handle Mary Christie's distress so she left her shaking and heaving and put through a call to Mrs Banerjee.

Mrs Banerjee always had all the answers.

'Surely it's not possible!' cried Mrs Banerjee when she heard the news. 'Vinod drove her to Soliganj yesterday. She said her mother was dying . . .'

'That may be so,' Anjali Gupta replied, 'but she has committed a terrible deed. When she returns, I will ask her to vacate her bungalow immediately.'

'She won't be back,' pronounced Mrs Banerjee, who had a sixth sense about many things in life. 'I will send Vinod immediately to collect her things and take them to Soliganj. Tell Mary that no one cares about that scandal-vandal sheet!'

꩜

In many ways, Mrs Banerjee was right. Mary Christie was never challenged over the item, possibly for the rather sad reason that no one in Chalaili knew enough about her to have speculated on the existence (or otherwise) of the dashing Captain Archibald Christie.

When Vinod turned up at the hospital with her worldly goods, including an incriminating stash of Volume I Edition I of *The Chalaili Bugle* (with its spurious Collector's Item claim) uncovered in her bungalow, Florence Gordon was shocked to see him. She had not clapped eyes on the second edition and she almost fainted against the full-luxury ultra-modern Chrysler Air Flow Imperial when she read it.

'Sugar-eating, spinning top maniac!' she yelped.

Later, she would admit to herself part of the shock was that Vivek had managed to have the item about Mary Christie set without a single typographical error.

Mrs Priyanka Gordon died that afternoon.

'It's been just that sort of day,' Florence Gordon grumbled to the nurse as she gathered up her mother's hospital bundles.

Florence Gordon never returned to Chalaili. Harold Gilbert employed Elizabeth, the less attractive of the Carter twins, as his temporary assistant. He made his choice on the basis that she would be more diligent in her work and less flirtatious than her sister Emma, whose time was largely spent attending to the wounded constitutions of the (male) invalids at The Chalaili Sanatorium For The Tubercular and acquiring a taste for vodka and mango juice.

Within six months, Elizabeth Carter had her hair in a bun and was wearing (unwarranted) spectacles and running the post office. Her business model was Mrs Rajat Banerjee, Proprietress of Coronation Talkies, and her life ticked like clockwork with its triplicate forms and rubber stamps and a sandwich lunch Mondays to Fridays at The Metropole Hotel (except for one unforgettable afternoon when the Misses Craig took her for a gambol through Chota Chalaili).

If any customers cared to listen, and few did, Mary Christie would tell them Florence Gordon was working as a whore in

Soliganj, performing cheap tricks for shopkeepers. It was a fantasy of the older woman's but unerringly close to the truth. The Chikki Man left Soliganj several weeks after Florence's unscheduled exit and his competitor's stall flourished like never before, even after his wife had insisted on a new sign: MR J. MOHAN AND SIX DAUGHTERS (EXTANT).

☙

The one resident of Chalaili who was sorry to see the end of *The Chalaili Bugle*, and who wondered momentarily about setting up her own newsletter, was the Queen Crow herself, Charlotte Montague.

She sat in her fiercely gardened garden with the two editions on her knee. She took a pencil from her pocket and ringed two lines. *The Chalaili Bugle*, Volume I, Edition I, Collector's Item: 'Was there ever such a colony of missed fits?' *The Chalaili Bugle*, Volume I, Edition II: 'Still they linger here, like a failed scientific experiment.'

Failed scientific experiment! As if that busty Anglo-Indian postal clerk could ever have come up with such a thoroughly perfect phrase.

Courtesy of a misplaced notion of grandiosity and exclusivity, Charlotte Montague had considered the noxious outpourings of *The Chalaili Bugle* were directed at absolutely everyone except herself. And that is why she had sent letters to imaginary friends at non-existent English addresses, with no sender's details on the flap so they would not come winging back, undelivered. The correspondence was full of the most made-up mischief and ripe imaginings. She had realised from the outset, when snatches from one of her real letters home to her sister, Catherine, were quoted verbatim, that Florence Gordon must be the interceptor. It would never have been that gymkhana-going postmaster Harold Gilbert with his whisky-slurred breath. (Proof contained in another of her contributions: *The Chalaili Bugle*, Volume I, Edition II: 'Has the Postmaster General in Calcutta issued a secret edict decreeing that his postmasters flung near and far are required to work just one hour per day, with an hour off for lunch?')

The day had faded to dusk and peacocks were crying. 'Like babies being strangled' was one description of their cry in her letters to Catherine. Her sister had also been apprised of the fact that peacocks can defecate while they sleep, which Edmond Montague regularly declared was really quite a surprising talent. Charlotte Montague reread for the umpteenth time her favourite piece. *The Chalaili Bugle*, Volume I, Edition II: 'Is it true that Dorothy Creswell-Smythe is singularly responsible for the declining peacock populations of the Western Ghats? *The Bugle* has heard the Indian Forestry Service is to launch an Official Investigation into the Case of the Disappearing Vanes.'

Charlotte Montague shrieked with glee. What a pity *The Chalaili Bugle* had collapsed. That little piece of tattle really had been one of her best.

Chapter Fifty-one

BOMBAY
DECEMBER, 1937

THE BOMBAY ADVOCATE

Mr and Mrs P. S. Patel of Malabar Hill announce the marriage of their beautiful and beloved daughter, Kitty, to His Minor Highness, Lalji Desai, second son of the Raja of Randipur.

Leela Dhir had become a prisoner in her own home. That's how she would have described her predicament to anyone who would listen, but no one did. The weekly card-playing parties had stopped, at first slowing to an occasional trickle and then slamming to an unceremonious halt. Her brightly costumed friends, with their well-off husbands and chauffeured cars, refused to climb the stairs at Pink Fantasia, which, they muttered, was anything but pink, its cheaply painted walls blistered and pocked to reveal dirty grey cement.

The lift never worked, there were homeless families who had set up camp on the landings with their little stoves and cooking pots and filthy laundry hung over the iron banisters. Her one-time closest friends Sujata Patel and Bina Verghese dubbed the building Stink Fantasia and the name was adopted by the card circle whose members still despatched servants with invitations to Leela Dhir and then waited, smug smiles in place, for her polite refusals and updates from their menials on the building's latest travesty.

Pink Fantasia's watchman was paid a few paisa by the squatters to turn a blind eye and he spent the money on cheap arrack at a nearby stall and slept on the ground. At first, the furious residents would seek him out and drag him back by the legs to Pink Fantasia, slap him around the face and shove him onto his three-legged wooden stool by the double glass doors at the entrance. But he would simply doze off, with no concern about who knew how many unsuitables would swing their way past him into the cool shadows of the apartment block's vestibule.

Leela Dhir's only regular visitors were a pair of Alexandrine parakeets that swooped to her balcony at breakfast each morning and feasted their bright red beaks on the crumbs of bread and raisins she laid out for them as carefully as she had once supervised her weekly card soirees.

She had added her name to a petition that was to be presented to the owner's representative, a Mr J. P. P. Chatterjee, who had promised to meet with a sub-committee of Pink Fantasia residents. They wanted a lift that functioned, a watchman who actually watched, and the instant removal of, at last count, eight families, their actual numbers engorged with elderly and frankly over-smelly relatives, who were occupying the stairs and landings.

But Mr J. P. P. Chatterjee's promised visit did not materialise and several families simply refused to pay their rent and moved out. The premises remained empty but judging by the opera of plumbing noises that shook the building late at night and very early in the morning, their bathrooms were still in use. Leela Dhir lay in bed, imagining the filthy bodies of the squatters enjoying the luxury of warm running water. One morning, as she stood on her balcony after a sleepless night, she saw a line of young men, thin towels draped over their shoulders, filing into Pink Fantasia. The watchman, she deduced, was running the unoccupied apartments as communal bath-houses.

In a fearful fury, she rang Mr J. P. P. Chatterjee's number. She had tried it many times and there had never been an answer, just an echoing on the line as it rang and rang. She imagined an empty room, a telephone throbbing atop a desk piled with yellowing petitions from disgruntled apartment dwellers. She almost dropped the receiver in amazement when the telephone was answered. 'Yes, yes,' came a man's impatient voice.

'Mr J. P. P. Chatterjee? This is Mrs Dhir. Mrs Leela Dhir, bereaved widow of the first class importer-exporter tycoon Mr Shyam Dhir.' She spoke loudly and carefully, presuming she was addressing a complete birdbrain. 'I demand a meeting with the owner of Pink Fantasia. It cannot wait another day.'

'I see,' said the voice, as wearily as if several sub-committees of dissatisfied tenants were sitting on his shoulders. 'Please be at my office at 3 p.m. today and I will see what I can do.'

He gave the address and hung up with a polite exhortation that his caller should have a safe and happy journey to his office. 'Idiot,' muttered Leela Dhir, who did not care for Mr J. P. P. Chatterjee's obsequious tone. After hanging up, she realised she had no idea how she was going to make her way down the many flights of Pink Fantasia's over-populated stairs.

Leela Dhir bathed and dressed and shouted at her servant

to go and survey the stairs to see if she should take her wellington boots out of the Kelvinator and carry her good shoes, such was the state of puddled urine and even worse. The old servant refused, pleading that she was too ill to use the stairs.

The retainer had taken to conducting bazaar purchases via an intricate system of a wicker basket ferried up and down on a pulley made from dozens of Leela Dhir's stockings tied together. She would lower the basket over the balcony with money and madam's shopping list enclosed, held in a small package secured with a doubled elastic band. A kind young boy who had helped her up the stairs one day had been sub-contracted as her runner and for a percentage of goods (a potato, a handful of chillies, an onion, a serve of salt in a thumb's tear of paper and a few coins that madam would not miss), he did the shopping for her. He filled the basket when the mission was done and the servant hauled it up. It was a near-perfect solution to leading an apartment-bound exile without actually starving.

There had been only one mishap, on a windy day when the servant had been over-cautious as she raised the basket. A slim dark hand, adorned with a festival of cheap glass bangles, had shot from the balcony below, and helped itself to a newly slaughtered chicken. The servant had not been able to rant too loudly as Madam was taking her morning nap, as she always did when the servant was supposedly at the bazaar.

Her shopping boy had already disappeared so the servant had to venture out for another fowl, holding her sari pallu across her face to avoid the various stinky confrontations on the stairs. Upon her eventual return, as Leela Dhir was pacing the apartment, cursing the slovenliness of hired staff, the servant caught the unmistakable smell of chicken cooking as she hauled herself up the stairs, gasping between breaths like a freshly popped soda bottle.

332

At the prospect of an excursion to Mr J. P. P. Chatterjee's office, the servant took to her string cot in her tiny room off the kitchen and sat upon it, legs drawn up under her chin, as if riding a raft in a stormy sea.

'No, no,' she insisted, shaking her head from side to side.

Leela Dhir sighed loudly. There was no use. The woman was ancient and probably no longer right in the head. She struggled into the wellington boots her husband had given her years before, after he'd struck a deal with an important rubber factory in Madras, and tied a scarf around her nose and mouth in the style of a cowboy, as she had once observed on screen at Galaxy Talkies on a rare excursion with her too-loud daughter.

She allowed herself three hours to make it to Mr J. P. P. Chatterjee's office. She knew it would take at least half that time to get clear of Pink Fantasia.

Chapter Fifty-two

CHALAILI
DECEMBER, 1937

THE SOLIGANJ WEEKLY OBSERVER

Mrs Rajat Banerjee, proprietress of Coronation Talkies, Chalaili, has finally confirmed the rumour she is related to cricketer S. N. Banerjee. Mrs Banerjee commented that the Banerjee family is originally from Calcutta and is known to contain many famous sporting figures, including those associated by marriage. She would not be drawn on more exact details.

Monsoon Cottage was empty at three in the afternoon. William unlocked the front door and called for Anil or Aruna but there was no reply. He poured himself a straight gin from the traymobile in the over-stuffed front parlour and walked to his room, lying down on his double bed, propping his head with several extra pillows from a pile on the rattan chair in the corner. Mrs Banerjee occupied one of a pair of singles in her room across the hall. The beds were side by side, just inches apart, unusually high off the ground. William smiled at the thought of Mrs Banerjee huffing aboard as if mounting a horse.

The bedroom doors were exactly opposite, and William could see clearly into hers, the closest bed arranged with an assortment of cloth toys and dolls.

He had brought home papers to work on, pleading a head-ache, not that there was anyone to answer to. He had merely told the office peon he was sick, made a cursory attempt to tidy his desk and cycled off.

He needed time to think, to clear his head and allow the events of the past few weeks to settle in his mind. Here I am, he thought, a married man who has sent his wife back to England with barely a civilised farewell and now I am living with a married woman. An Indian married woman.

The bungalow was condemned, Mrs Banerjee was paying rent to that disgraceful Nightingale chap. The situation had been talked about for days at The Empire Club but it was of short-term interest, the consensus being that Nightingale was an eye-glazing bore, although obligingly useful in minor ways, especially when it came to acquiring extra government-issue household items.

The incompetents in Bombay had taken Bluebell Cottage away from William and he'd been too grand to consult Nightin-gale for a solution. If he made too much fuss with his bosses, all the sniggering over the Petal Cameron debacle would start again.

He heard a key in the front door, click-clack footsteps and the soft eddying of Mrs Banerjee's sari. Her attar of roses perfume preceded her down the hall and he looked up to see her turn into her bedroom. The lower half of her doorway was filled with the sway of sapphire blue silk. On top she wore a thick cardigan, but-toned tight as a tea-cosy.

'Hello there,' he ventured, and she swung around, performing a surprisingly graceful pirouette.

'Good, good,' she cried, clapping her hands. 'You are here!'

'I have a headache . . . and maybe a cold,' said William, hastily propping a file of papers over the glass of gin on his bedside table.

'Poor baby! I will fetch tea. Where is that lazy Aruna, that incompetent Anil . . .'

She closed his door and trotted off, calling for rascal servants. Through the half-open window, William heard raised voices in the garden. Anil must have been caught napping in his shed. He closed his eyes. After Anil has brought tea, he decided, he would write a letter to Lydia and then have an unaccustomed afternoon sleep.

But it was Mrs Banerjee who rustled in with the cup of tea. Noticing the jumble on his bedside table, she stood undecided for a second or two and then sat on the side of William's bed. She handed him the tea as he propped himself up on his elbow.

She had changed into some kind of vast petticoat and a floating dressing-gown, busily patterned with oriental blossoms and exotic long-tailed birds. Her hair, usually caught up in elaborate confections and decorated with flowers or even sharpened pencils, poked through like the combs of a Japanese geisha, was swinging free. It reached to her waist and was unusually shiny.

William was reminded of the blue-black tresses of the prostitutes he'd visited in Bombay, when he first arrived in India. He had been unbearably lonely and hadn't particularly wanted their favours, just for them to hold him and talk of small things. Even now, if he tried, he could summon the scent of coconut and jasmine in their hair and their murmuring voices, slender hands making feathery strokes along his arms and across his chest.

But this was not the time to think of prostitutes, with Mrs Banerjee on his bed. She was babbling on about the upcoming program at Coronation Talkies, her eyes sparkling, her always animated hands waving about. William had not been this close to her before and he realised with a start that she was much younger than he had imagined. He had thought of her as around forty but she was probably only in her early thirties. Her skin was smooth and the colour of milk coffee, her teeth very white and straight, and when she smiled, a pair of dimples appeared, as if added for emphasis, either side of her broad grin.

'Sleep, sleep,' she trilled, when she saw William had finished his tea. She stood up and bent over to take his empty cup. In that movement, William was afforded a deep view inside her petticoat. Hugely rounded and floating free, like two lightly held party balloons, he glimpsed the awesome spectacle of Mrs Banerjee's naked breasts.

William did not write his letter to Lydia that afternoon. He lay on his bed after Mrs Banerjee's fragrant departure and reached for his notebook.

'Cumulonimbus mammatus,' he wrote. In brackets, Downward Bulging Clouds. And he laughed at his inventive wit.

When William had finished with his bosom joke, he wondered what his next move should be. Mrs Banerjee was turning out to be quite a sexpot. It was possible that his wife would not return. He had not done enough to make her part of his life in Chalaili and she was afflicted with neediness, that particular failing of women. Lydia was intelligent but her endless pepping-up with gin made her unpredictable.

Surely she must have realised that the marriage had been a convenience for both parties. Why else would she have wed him so hastily if not for the respectability that a husband provided. At this very minute, amid the suffocating confines of West Gamble and Finchley, she was probably entertaining her friends and family with exaggerated stories about life in India.

☞

At Bluebell Cottage, the telephone rang three times that evening, its insistent burbling causing Dr. Samuel Carter to repeatedly push back his dining chair and stride to the hallway where the heavy black instrument sat on a small table. 'Who is it, dear?' his wife called, as he barked into the telephone. Thousands of miles away, Lydia shouted, too, her successive wails of 'William, is that you?' bouncing into space and then echoing back. The two voices did not connect. When Lydia tried again the next evening and the next, there was no reply, the Carters and their protesting twin daughters having taken off on a family holiday to a beachside hotel in Bombay, a retinue of harried servants in their wash.

Chapter Fifty-three

CHALAILI
DECEMBER, 1937

Anjali Gupta shocked her husband by advising her intention to take a job. Two jobs, to be precise. She intended to help out Poppy Lee at the Lakshmi Hair and Beauty Studio and to enter the employ of Mrs Banerjee as an usherette at Coronation Talkies. She had to admit to herself that her private yoga lessons had not been a great success as only Mrs Banerjee had shown up and she was barely capable of sitting on the floor, let alone manoeuvring herself into the furled goddess position.

'Are you insane, madam?' spluttered Ram Gupta as they sat at breakfast in The Metropole Hotel's dining room.

Their little scene was witnessed by the hotel's only guests, Campbell and Patricia Nightingale. It was a Tuesday morning and the Nightingales had arrived in Chalaili the previous evening for their monthly visit to Coronation Talkies. It had been an enjoyable occasion. Mrs Banerjee was showing *Mr Deeds Goes to Town* with that debonair Gary Cooper, and Patricia Nightingale was pleased to note there were many of Chalaili's top circle in the audience, including Charlotte Montague, the uncrowned queen of local society. Mrs Banerjee had shown the Nightingales to inferior seats at the front but she had insisted they move and only just in time, too, before Charlotte Montague and her entourage arrived.

'Just Saturday mornings and early afternoons at Lakshmi Hair and Beauty Studio, Ram, and Saturday nights at Coronation Talkies, showing seats and assisting in the office.'

'I can understand Mrs Banerjee needing help but . . . surely you don't want to be hanging around a hair salon, Anjali. Won't Veronica O'Brien be back in Chalaili soon?'

'I had a telephone call from her last night.'

'Oh, I see. She is where?'

'The French Riviera, overlooking the sea, with Blinky Singh.'

'Blinky bloody Singh? You mean that wastrel son of the old Raja of Kandathala? You have got to be joking!'

'Keep your voice down . . .'

Anjali Gupta looked over her shoulder but, fortunately, the

340

Nightingales were scolding the waiter that the tea was cold, and cups and saucers were being clattered about the table.

'Veronica O'Brien said she was having the jolliest time imaginable and may never return,' Anjali Gupta continued, her voice steady as she cracked the head of her boiled egg with rather more force than was necessary. Ram Gupta pushed his sliding glasses up his nose and watched his wife's spoon dispense with the skerricks of shell. She had bashed the egg in a way that suggested she wished it were his skull.

'That may be so . . . but Blinky Singh is a man about town and she shouldn't count on anything permanent.'

'She didn't mention anything permanent. Not all women want everything to be permanent, you know. Sometimes there do not need to be strings attached. Strings can be like, well, like being hung by the neck, you know.'

'Anjali, my sweetest one, what are you trying to say? It's just that I need you here.'

Ram Gupta was whispering, aware the Nightingales had fallen silent at their nearby table.

'You can manage perfectly well. It's not as if we have many guests . . . not a single occupant of the Maharani Suite since Premila left.'

'Premila?'

'Mrs Banerjee, you banana brain.'

Ram Gupta laughed. He loved his wife to pieces and he had to admit this new take-command manner suited her immensely. It reminded him of Mrs Banerjee, the emphatic way she was stating her case, waving her bangled arms for extra effect. He had never before noticed Anjali wearing such an array of bangles.

☽

341

Ram Gupta looked out of The Metropole Hotel dining-room window and across The Strand towards the blue-green of the hills.

The little boy, still-born, lying on a table and covered with a striped towel, its edges a tangle of escaping threads. Anjali Gupta, perfectly still, face seemingly frozen, not even one tear escaped from her pain-dulled eyes.

Her husband puts a hand on her forehead, lifts sweat-plastered strands and runs his fingers through her pillow-flattened hair.

'I will always love you . . . you are my world,' he tells her. 'There will be more babies . . . other babies.'

'No,' she whispers, closing her eyes, turning away from him. 'The doctor says no more.'

'It doesn't matter, Anjali . . . we have each other. Please don't turn away from me . . .'

☙

'Have you been listening to me?'

Ram Gupta returned from his reverie. His wife had finished her egg and was calling for more tea. They had never spoken of babies since that day. 'Dead Baby Day' she had written in her journal, the book she kept under their bed. He had found it one morning while retrieving a kicked-aside shoe. He had flipped page after page to find some mention of her love for him.

'How lucky I am to have such a good husband,' she had written. Just the once. But it was enough for him.

'Well, well, my darling wife. Picture Madam and Hotel Madam . . . quite a pair, I am thinking. You have my permission for both part-time positions, but Saturdays only, and no ridiculous uniform in some dancing-girl colour.'

342

'I do not need your *permission*,' his wife informed him, standing up to leave the table. She pronounced the word permission as if it contained three times the number of letters. As she strode off, Patricia Nightingale shot her a conspiratorial smile.

Chapter Fifty-four

BOMBAY

DECEMBER, 1937

'There are moments in your life when you must act . . .

A little voice within us tells us,

"You are on the right track . . ."'

M. K. (MAHATMA) GANDHI

*L*eela Dhir finally made it to Mr J. P. P. Chatter-jee's office. She was pleased her arrival was at the appointed pip of three o'clock, but that's the only pleasure she derived from her excursion.

As she had feared, the stairwell and landings of Pink Fantasia were in an horrific state. There were bodies huddled under blankets, half-naked children running around, even a family taken up residence in the broken-down lift, its doors wedged open by two bamboo poles. She paused to look at the lift dwellers and was struck by the cosiness of their abode. An oil lamp lit the vignette as a mother suckled a baby and stirred a cooking pot over a smoky fire. Several sari lengths, in bright block prints of red and green, had been draped across the ceiling and hung from the walls. There was an emaciated trail of marigolds around a broomstick holding aloft the sari tent. The cavern looked like a transplanted Christmas tableau and when the woman raised her head and smiled, she had the face of a madonna.

The world is upside down, gone mad, Leela Dhir decided, tentatively placing her wellington boots on each step until she finally made the bottom. Straightening herself, she began to exit the building, surprised to see the watchman on his stool, seemingly awake. He opened the door and before she could speak her mind to him, she slipped on a squashed cauliflower leaf and found herself propelled on to the pavement, like a circus performer from a cannon.

Leela Dhir walked several blocks and found she was relishing the exercise after what felt like months of convalescence. She caught a reflection of herself in a shop window and noticed she was much fatter. 'I'll be the size of Premila soon,' she said out loud, adjusting her sari. The thought of Premila quickened her step. How dare that daughter of mine imprison me in such a ghastly fashion while she gads about with her infernal talking pictures.

Mr J. P. P. Chatterjee's office was on the top floor of a narrow building on Marine Drive opposite the swathe of the Bombay waterfront and not far from Leela Dhir's old home. She knew the precinct well so having confirmed the Chatterjee name on the building's board of tenants, she sat on a wooden bench overlooking Chowpatty Beach and bought a slice of watermelon from a vendor. She daintily spat out the seeds one by one, enjoying the fruit's succulent pinkness. For the first time that day, she let herself relax.

Up and up Leela Dhir climbed until she reached a door with a printed sign, Mr J. P. P. Chatterjee Representing De Souza Investments. She paused to change into her proper shoes, then realised she had left them on the bench at the beach.

She sighed with frustration, then squared her shoulders and knocked lightly. A male voice told her to enter. She pushed the door into a single sunny room where a man sat at a desk. He did not stand up to greet her, but motioned she should sit in the chair opposite him. 'Now, Mrs Dhir,' he began, with no formal introductions, 'I believe you wish to vacate Pink Fantasia.'

'Vacate? I said nothing about vacating. I want the owner to fix everything in the building. The lift, the squatters, the lazy beast who passes himself off as the watchman, the family cooking in the lift, causing fire hazards. I would not be in the least surprised if Pink Fantasia were burning down as we sit here . . .'

'Cooking in the lift? Come now, Mrs Dhir. Look, the building is to be pulled down within a few months, so there is no point. The owner has been made a very handsome offer by a hotel company and work will begin . . .'

'Pulled down! How can you countenance such a thing without consulting the permanent tenants of each apartment? This is outrageous.'

'Permanent tenants?' Mr J. P. P. Chatterjee looked genuinely puzzled. 'But each apartment has a short lease. Or did, I should say . . . my records show you are the last one.'

Leela Dhir banged Mr J. P. P. Chatterjee's desk. 'Do not treat me like a fool! My daughter, Mrs Rajat Banerjee, a very powerful businesswoman in picture theatre circles, took a lifetime lease on the apartment for me when my husband died.'

'Yes, yes, I see your daughter's signature here,' he said,

smoothing out a wad of papers. 'She paid in advance for a lease of two years. Obviously we will owe her some money for the balance as you have been at Pink Fantasia for, er, less than a year, I believe.'

'Show me that,' Leela Dhir shrieked, grabbing the papers. But she could see little without her glasses, which were by the side of her bed, back in her doomed boudoir at Pink Fantasia.

'Who is the owner?' she challenged, again banging the desk.

'Her name is Miss Dolly de Souza.'

'And what does she do, this Miss Dolly de Souza?'

'She is an investor, Mrs Dhir. She has been buying real estate in the city for some time, having come into bequests from, um, gentlemen admirers.'

Leela Dhir slumped in the chair. She could not imagine a world of gentleman admirers and real estate deals. She was unsure where to vent her fury, at this pipsqueak of a man or to reserve it for her treacherous daughter.

'You have not heard the end of this,' she declared as she departed. Mr J. P. P. Chatterjee looked up from his papers as she harumphed out the door, and noticed she was wearing wellington boots, spattered with greasy vegetable scraps.

Leela Dhir delayed her journey home by looking in shop windows and ambling through a grassy park, twilight shadows softening its rubbishy edges. A policeman in khaki uniform strolled towards her, swinging his lathi, which he would soon use to shove vagrants from the benches. He bowed slightly as she passed and twisted the sharp corner of his handsomely groomed moustache. On another occasion, she may have been flattered, but the day had been one of awful betrayals.

She tried not to cry. Who knows what battles were in front of her but, for now, she had to accomplish the ascent to the fourth floor of Pink Fantasia, past the nativity vision of the woman in the lift. Soon that little family would be homeless, too.

Chapter Fifty-five

CHALAILI
JANUARY, 1938

Mrs Banerjee announced that she would show Anil
the ropes of picture-house management. In reality,
it was more like strings — sweeping, snapping the seats up so
patrons could easily walk between the serried aisles; and standing at interval in front of the audience with a tray of ice-creams.
Mrs Banerjee made him stand for the full fifteen-minute interval, even if there were just three or four people in the audience.
She presided over the till in the fishbowl office in the foyer,

gathering in the coins and notes with her ruby-ornamented fingers.

Anil was thrilled at even such a minor entree to the glittering world of the cinema. Every time he looked at Mrs Banerjee's merry face, he thought of the shocking wedding film and he was full of admiration for her kindness and bustle. Most women would have melted away with shame, even British women with those stiff upper lips William spoke about, although Anil found the lips of the talking pictures memsahibs to be anything but stiff. Claudette Colbert, in particular, had a mouth as luscious as a sticky plum. Oh yes, Anil had observed the opposite of stiff upper lips, that was for sure.

Anil wanted Mrs Banerjee to be happy and he hoped one day Mr Clark Gable would arrive in Chalaili and stroke his moustache in front of Mrs Banerjee. The nearness of that moustache would make Mrs Banerjee very happy, of that he was convinced.

Anil wished Lydia could be happy, too. She had been kind to him and indulgent, wanting him to be her friend, not knowing or caring about the gulf that lay between the British and the natives, as he had heard his race called in the bellowing tones of All India Radio on William's crackling set. But Lydia was gone and maybe she would never come back. Anil decided to devote himself to Premila, as he privately thought of Picture Madam.

On Saturday evenings, Anjali Gupta was not a mere usherette or office assistant, as she had suggested to her husband, but was completely in charge of the till, a duty she performed with precision, given her experience at The Metropole Hotel's front desk. Anjali Gupta's undisputed capabilities left Mrs Banerjee free to enjoy the pictures with William. Anil doubted it was a good idea for his master to be seen sitting next to her, but different rules about such mixing seemed to apply when the woman involved was a successful entrepreneur and President of a businesswomen's league, even with a lowly membership of two, counting herself and Anjali Gupta.

He was sure Mrs Banerjee hadn't broached the topic of Mr Banerjee with William. Anil knew little of the world of Bombay lawyers but he realised Mrs Banerjee must have found a way of acquiring a married name, despite her red-faced wedding day, and that some unsuspecting legal wallah would have felt the full force of her enraged presence.

So William went to Coronation Talkies every Saturday night, walking to the end of the ridge with Mrs Banerjee, then transferring to her car, Vinod waiting with the door open. A smirking fellow, thought William, but Mrs Banerjee would hear nothing said against him, although she wondered why the back seat so often smelt of coconut oil and talcum powder.

It was several weeks after the regular excursions commenced that Mrs Banerjee put her hand on William's arm on the final passage home, to 'steady herself' in new shoes. Anil followed later, being left to sweep and close up, although Anjali Gupta made sure the till was cleared before she left, whisking the money off to the safe at The Metropole Hotel.

William did not notice at first how closely Mrs Banerjee walked beside him, how the one straight gin she poured for him in the parlour would stretch to hours of convivial drinking and chatting. He realised after a few weeks that he preferred his new life in Mrs Banerjee's house on the rarefied upper ridge to the hushed existence he'd had with Lydia at Bluebell Cottage. He rarely thought about his wife but when he did, he imagined Lydia and Mrs Banerjee as friends. There was this shadowy idea of

Lydia reading a book on Mrs Banerjee's window seat with its bro-cade cushions and over-stuffed bolster twinkling with little shards of mirror in the Rajasthani style. He knew it was from Rajasthan because Mrs Banerjee had told him so at breakfast. She had leaned over the cushions and plumped them up, hitting them square centre with her strong hands. As she bent forward, the scooped neckline of her dressing-gown heaved and billowed.

Chapter Fifty-six

CHALAILI
JANUARY, 1938

THE SOLIGANJ WEEKLY OBSERVER
M. K. (Mahatma) Gandhi has given an interview to press at Victoria Terminus, Bombay, before departing for Segaon. Unfortunately, our reporter was unable to make the press gathering and pose a question on behalf of Soliganj citizens due to construction works on the Soliganj–Bombay line that have resulted in lengthy delays for travellers over the past weeks.

Lydia's letter began, '*Dear William, I trust you are well and that Anil is keeping Bluebell Cottage to your satisfaction. Everything is fine here and I go each morning to Finchley Primary School where I am helping out the teaching staff and in the afternoons I visit the library or take a walk. You will be surprised to learn that West Gamble Infants' School has closed, due to lack of funding. I have even given a talk about India to pupils at Finchley Primary School, as arranged by your*

Uncle John, who has been very kind to me and has driven me every-
where I need to go. I am staying with Evelyn, Tom and the children,
as you know, and they send their very best regards.
With affection, Lydia.'

William had not known about Lydia's residential arrangements. The letter had come to him by chance when he bumped into
the postman as he walked over to Chalaili Hospital to consult Dr
Samuel Carter about a persistent cough. The postman confirmed
to William that he knew he had moved from Bluebell Cottage to
Mrs Banerjee's house, even if Lydia did not. He wondered how
many of her letters had not been delivered to him, perhaps due
to intervention by an over-bangled hand. William knew he should
raise the matter with Mrs Banerjee, although it was possible there
were forgotten letters and who knew what other foreign items
lurking in the recesses of her large black handbag

He wrote back to Lydia immediately, explaining he was not
at all well. He dismissed this as a small white lie as he was indeed
coughing as he wrote. He placed the letter on a silver tray on the
hall table at Monsoon Cottage for Anil to post. That evening, when
he struggled into dinner, the letter was gone and he thought no
more about it. Mrs Banerjee had personally cooked him two lightly
boiled eggs and had trimmed three slices of buttered toast into
perfectly aligned soldiers. Later she brought him a cup of cocoa in
bed but he pretended to be asleep. As she turned to straighten the
curtains, he watched her through fluttering slits. Her unleashed
hair fell to her waist in a satiny wave and beneath her nightgown,
he imagined the Banerjee breasts swaying like giant mangoes ready
to drop.

It was Mrs Banerjee's birthday and William wondered if there would be a telegram from Mr Banerjee or even a surprise appearance. She never mentioned him and there were no photographs around Monsoon Cottage. She seemed happily enthroned in her single bed with her furry toys. He wondered why she didn't inhabit a more spacious double bed. He sometimes glimpsed the folds of flesh around her waist and hips when she wore her tightest sari blouses. He knew that Indian culture prized such girdles of excess fat as symbols of prosperity and wealth. He, too, found her weight attractive. It suited her racy laugh and excessive jewellery, her bountifulness as she trilled for him to 'Open! Open!' and in she'd pop a caramel. Fully imported caramel, as she would be sure to emphasise.

Mrs Banerjee didn't drink alcohol and in that William found a small failing. He had enjoyed sipping gin with Lydia at Bluebell Cottage, at least in the first few months or so before he realised she had an over-fondness for it. He took his straight but knew just the right ratio of tonic water to add to Lydia's and when she took the glass he would make a joke about the quinine in the tonic keeping malaria at bay. And she would smile, although she had heard the line dozens of times.

On her birthday, Mrs Banerjee was unusually quiet and William realised he should have bought her a present. He crept into the garden to find Anil, who was sleeping in his shed, dreaming of a fleshy composite of Claudette Colbert and Aruna Chowpatty, as Mrs Banerjee was still wont to loudly call her confused servant when shouting over a misdemeanour. William sent him into town to buy chocolates from Mary Christie's little shop in The Metropole Hotel's arcade. Anil also brought back a red rose that he had stolen from Anjali Gupta's garden. Mrs Banerjee knew at once the source of the rose and William soared in her estimation. He was a man who stole flowers for a lady and then there were the chocolates . . . her favourite soft centres, two layers, no expense spared. 'Tonight,' she told William, 'you will be my guest for a special evening at Coronation Talkies.'

Anil was surprised when Mrs Banerjee said he could have the night off. 'A holiday for my birthday,' she told him. 'Won't there still be many people wanting to see a talking picture?' he asked. 'No, there will *not* because Coronation Talkies is closing tonight.'

Vinod dropped off William and Mrs Banerjee at Coronation Talkies and she told her driver he could have the rest of the evening off as she would be returning to Monsoon Cottage with Mr Rushmore by taxi. Vinod was delighted as he could squeeze in several extra Flumcafi bookings. There certainly was no shortage of Romantics in Chota Chalaili bazaar, any time of year.

She jangled her hoop of keys like a hospital matron and expertly opened the side door. Switching on just one dim light, Mrs Banerjee showed William to a seat in the front row of the First Class section.

'What film is it?' he asked.

'You will see.'

William was aware the theatre was empty but merely presumed they were early and the audience would drift in later. He fancied he heard the distant roar of an energetic wind and made himself comfortable, low in the seat, as the screen flickered to life. He shut his eyes for a little while but he didn't nod off. He was aware of movement in front of him and looked up at the stage. There, in front of the screen, spilling out of the contours of the celluloid Claudette Colbert and dressed in the ballooning pants of a harem dancer, stood Mrs Banerjee. With a bow and a skip, she began gyrating from side to side, turning and twirling, her mane of hair caught in an enormous tail that swung like a metronome.

As he sat open-mouthed, she spun around and placed the forefinger of her right hand against her lips indicating William should be quiet. It had not occurred to her that he would be rendered utterly speechless.

She tripped to the edge of the stage and with some effort wheeled across the boards a hefty apparatus that looked like a giant fan. 'Good God,' William muttered. It was George Windsor's retired wind machine, abandoned after his fateful last appearance at what had been The Elphinstone.

'Now, now,' she yelled. William slipped further into his seat and anxiously looked around for signs of onlookers to this performance.

Someone just offstage flicked a switch and the machine whirred to life, cranking itself up slowly with a grinding sound that became louder and busier until the propellers began to spin like those of an aeroplane. Mrs Banerjee had imagined the effect of the wind would be to give her a pleasingly ruffled appearance as she performed her dance, lifting her veils like kites and creating an irresistible symphony of colour and movement.

The machine continued determinedly, creating such a bluster that even Picture Madam in all her stoutness could not keep upright. She went flailing backwards off the opposite side of the stage and then the machine conked out. William could hear voices backstage, Mrs Banerjee's high and agitated as she tore strips off her collaborator. William hoped it was Anil, rather than the beaky-faced projectionist, Mr K.K. Rao. William knew it was nigh impossible to shock Anil.

After a few moments, she reappeared, took a bow and resumed her dance, as if the hiatus had been as inconsequential as a sneeze. Just as William was about to stand up and suggest she stop, Mrs Banerjee leapt from the stage, skipped up the aisle and landed on the floor in front of him with extraordinary lightness. William remembered a photograph he'd seen of a circus elephant performing a ballet twirl on its hind legs and how he'd been mesmerised by its daintiness. He fell back in his seat as she tore aside her heavily brocaded harem-girl brassiere and unleashed her stupendous breasts into his upturned face.

ᴗ⟩⟩

That evening, Mrs Banerjee moved from her virginal cot into the double in William's bedroom.

He found the new sleeping arrangements rather uncomfortable as she took up more than half the bed. But he found her presence comforting, too, as if some great maternal life force was protecting him. Mrs Banerjee was his mother and Aunt Sylvia rolled into one, with the added benefit of twenty-four hour invitations to explore her bouncing breasts and accommodating vagina, even if he did have to devise sideways manoeuvres to gain access to the latter.

When William penetrated her, she shuddered and moaned in a way that he found comical at first. The bed heaved and creaked, she held her breasts aloft to him as if offering a pair of melons for his delectation. Sometimes, with the same unlikely elegance she had displayed in her seduction dance on stage at Coronation Talkies, she knelt below him and pushed his legs apart. Her fingers oiled with a creamy lotion, she rubbed his penis up and down with the pump action of a piston.

On those occasions, William ejaculated into her hands, squealing like a twelve-year-old. In years of masturbation, from his boyhood bed to lonely bachelor nights at Bluebell Cottage, he had never achieved the intensity of feeling that Premila's stroking was capable of arousing in him. 'Good, good,' she would declare after his climax, as if he were an obedient child. He lay helpless on the sweaty sheets while she sailed off in her oriental dressing-gown, returning with a warm soapy flannel to wipe his retired member.

Given William's passive attitude towards the female sex, he realised the new residential situation suited him well, even if Mrs Banerjee's sexual appetite was as unflagging as her sweet tooth.

Chapter Fifty-seven

CHALAILI
FEBRUARY, 1938

THE SOLIGANJ WEEKLY OBSERVER

Mrs Rajat Banerjee, Proprietress of Coronation Talkies,
The Strand, Chalaili, has announced a Marx Brothers
Film Festival will be held at her cinema during the last
two weeks of February. *A Day at the Races* (1935) will
inaugurate the festival. Mrs Banerjee told *The Soliganj
Weekly Observer* that she plans many such themed film
festivals in 1938, with Mr Clark Gable among the stars to
be featured.

Mrs Banerjee found herself bored when William was off
with his tedious weather balloons and rain devices.
All his talk these days was of a submission he had put to the Agri-
cultural and Horticultural Society of India to annexe a stretch of
parkland near Chalaili's wilting lake and construct a glass house.
'It will be a miniature replica of the glass pavilion at the Lal Bagh
Botanic Gardens in Bangalore,' he explained to her. 'And that in

itself is a replica of the Crystal Palace built for the 1851 World Fair in London.'

He was already planning the estate and kept an alphabetical list of his intended plantings: apple, banana, flamboyante, guava, mango, monkey puzzle tree, papaya, peach, pomegranate, quince, sour lime, tamarind and walnut.

'It's a perfect spot, Premila. The *cedrus deodara* and *eugenia jambolana* will provide excellent shade . . .'

'Eugenia Jambolana!' she roared. 'That was the name that houri witch postal woman used in *The Chalaili Bugle* . . .'

'Really?' said William, who had paid no attention to the scandal sheet.

'Did you have anything to do with her?'

'Of course not,' he protested.

'Then how would some lowly clerical creature who possesses no Botanic Gardens brain but a PERFECT SET OF STAND-UP BOSOMS know about *eugenia jambolana*?'

William looked at her in exasperation.

'See, you have no answer, do you!'

'Premila, please . . .'

'And don't think I don't know about your secret visits to the Lakshmi Hair and Beauty Studio to look at those half-and-half bosoms of Poppy Lee!'

'Premila, you sent me there! You told me Poppy Lee had diversified the business and was giving men's haircuts. You even made the appointment . . .'

'Yes, well, maybe so, but how was I to know you would rub against her bosoms.'

'Premila!'

'Don't think I haven't seen her, leaning against the male

customers. That's why she has di-ver-si-fied, William, as you so grandly put it. It's so she can tempt the men into who knows what hanky-panky. Huh, it's a wonder that Florence Gordon hasn't reappeared. The pair of them could set up night business in The Metropole Hotel's back garden. Those two would do it behind a bush . . .'

Premila swept up her sari pallu and retreated, loudly shouting for Anil to bring tea and aspirins.

Chapter Fifty-eight

CHALAILI
FEBRUARY, 1938

Coronation Talkies was running smoothly with the capable Mr K. K. Rao in charge of all things mechanical and Anil acting as factotum and cleaning up each morning, although never quite as thoroughly as the proprietress would wish. The picture theatre needed a little something to recreate the excitement of its opening. Not its premiere, exactly, with over-sugared monkeys and collapsing curtains, but an initiative to stir things up.

Picture Madam sat in her bedroom on a wooden stool in front of a low dressing table with three hinged mirrors. The configuration afforded her a trio of images, including her handsome profile, albeit with a succession of chins. The looking glass was tarnished in various spots and her reflected face was mottled, as if she had contracted an unpleasant skin disease or had stood too long in the rain.

But the result of the triplicate reflections on the patchy surface conspired to make her rather more elongated than was her natural condition.

'Perhaps I am not so fat after all,' she murmured, arching her eyebrows.

That morning she had languished under the covers with her bed tea while William was dressing. She was sorry about her outburst over Anglo-Indian bosoms. He had stood sideways to her doing up his buttons and the sight of his bare legs and slightly protruding member beneath his flapping white shirt caused a sudden stirring. She threw back the eiderdown and lifted her nightdress around her waist.

'Float my boat,' she trilled at him.

'What boat?'

He raced to the door and pressed his back against it. 'The servants . . .' he muttered. 'Whatever are you doing?'

'Look, look,' she whispered, arching her back and opening and closing her legs in great scissoring movements.

'Really, Premila, put your, your . . . boat away.'

'Your ego is absolutely colossal!' she pronounced with a corny American accent, imitating Claudette Colbert in her very favourite film.

'Please, let's not be Peter and Ellie in that infernal movie . . . please, not again,' said William, hastily grabbing his trousers, shoes and socks. He would finish dressing in the hallway.

'Boat is just a figure of speech, idiot!' she shrieked as William retreated.

Mrs Banerjee spent the morning in bed, forlorn and, in her mind, cruelly abandoned. She was feeling slightly nauseous and feverish. Grabbing her jar of cold cream from the bedside table, she slathered it all over her forehead, cheeks and neck and commenced her facial exercises. She opened her eyes wide, yawned extravagantly while clenching her chin and then turned her head from side to side a full dozen times, with cheeks puffed. Then, ignoring her unsettled stomach, she got out of bed and began her exercise regime with a skipping rope. Everything in the room shook and wobbled as she turned the rope faster and faster. Bottles fell off the dressing table and a bedside lamp clattered to the floor but still she jumped and jumped.

'That's better,' she said as she puffed back onto the bed. Her regime had had to be suspended while she was resident in the Maharani Suite at The Metropole Hotel as the Guptas, bless their silly souls, thought she might come crashing through the ceiling and land in the dining room.

The combination of healthy exertion and the super-vertical image in the mirror had conspired to lift her spirits no end. She pulled out the bottom drawer of the dressing table and removed a carefully rolled film poster, a precious memento from her days working at Galaxy Talkies in Bombay. She unrolled it and studied the alluring form of Fearless Nadia dressed in cape, mask, high leather boots and Wild West costume and brandishing a whip. Fearless Nadia, who was actually Mary Evans, a circus performer from Australia, had shot to fame as the lead actress in *Hunterwali*, a Wadia Movietone talkie that had been a box-office success in 1936. Her follow-up had been even more of a smash. *Hurricane Hansa* was its title, starring, among others, Master Mohammed and Minoo the Mystic.

Mrs Banerjee decided she would insist Mr K. K. Rao contact Wadia Movietone instantly and procure a copy of *Hurricane Hansa* and there would be a special screening at Coronation Talkies. The sound would be in Hindustani so the Britishers in Chalaili would need translation but that's where Mrs Banerjee intended to participate. She would appear in costume and translate the film from the side of the stage, perhaps with the odd crack of a whip for added effect.

'Fearless Premila!' she laughed to herself.

She called Anjali Gupta to tell her of the plan but her friend was not so sure it was likely to succeed. The vision of Picture Madam in riding breeches and boots was difficult to imagine but, predictably, she was not to be deterred. Anil was dispatched to the bazaar to fetch fabric merchants and to arrange for a boot salesman to call at Monsoon Cottage with a full range of his most outstanding wares.

Fearless Nadia rode an equally fearless horse, Punjab Ka Beta, and was always rearing off cliffs, jumping walls of fire and leaping across the roofs of moving train carriages. She smashed scoundrel men in the jaw and was a saviour of the oppressed. Mrs Banerjee decided a horse would not be absolutely necessary for her appearance as Fearless Premila.

☙

Anjali Gupta arrived in the middle of the afternoon to assist her friend in selecting the makings of her costume. 'Sit, sit,' Mrs Banerjee boomed as she grabbed the pot from the tray Aruna had brought to the front room of Monsoon Cottage. Picture Madam did not so much serve tea as administer it, forcing a cup upon Anjali Gupta and tipping several shortbread biscuits into its saucer.

'Everything is arranged. Mr K.K. Rao has ordered the film . . .'

'Is there a . . . a . . . script?' asked Anjali Gupta, stumbling over the unfamiliar word as a shortbread dissolved in her mouth.

'A script?'

'Yes, I believe it is the written words from the film.'

'I know what it is, my dear, dear woman. But why would I need such a thing?'

'But, Premila, you have to translate it and read the English words when Fearless Nadia speaks in Hindustani . . .'

'Not necessary. I will improvise. I suppose you know what improvisation is?'

Before Anjali Gupta could reply, Aruna led in two bazaar traders from the hallway. They had arrived via the back door, the one routinely used by servants, although Anil and Aruna always wandered in and out of the front entrance, frequently bumping into William and Mrs Banerjee in this house where rules had flown out the window and roosted who knew where.

The two women put down their teacups as the men opened big loosely tied bundles and spread before them bolts of light woollen fabrics and a dozen or more pairs of leather riding boots. Mrs Banerjee took her time feeling the weight and softness of the wool and consulted Anjali Gupta about the best colours for a full riding costume. Her friend was of little help as she had never ridden a horse and she also suspected Mrs Banerjee had no experience whatsoever in such matters.

'Perhaps dark blue, Premila?'

Mrs Banerjee's face tightened. 'Dark blue has never done me any favours,' she glowered.

'Well, grey is very flattering . . .'

367

'Nonsense, nonsense, brown is better or black, even . . .
I suppose yellow is not worn commonly on horseback?'

The traders nodded, eyes wide, and continued to sit on
their haunches as Mrs Banerjee sailed out of the room on a seemingly urgent mission. She returned within a minute with a roll of
paper and instructing Anjali Gupta to hold one end, she unfurled a
poster of Fearless Nadia in *Hunterwali*.

'Look, look,' she commanded the men, whose eyes were
now as wide as Picture Madam's precious Royal Doulton saucers,
part of a dinner setting that had been a Banerjee wedding gift from
one of her father's influential London connections.

The men looked. They looked at the poster and they looked
at Mrs Banerjee and they looked at Anjali Gupta and they looked at
each other.

Mrs Banerjee stabbed the poster with a scarlet-polished fin-
gernail and then pointed energetically at herself. Bang, bang, in
her bosom.

The men continued to look as if they had just been requested
to custom-make a pair of trousers to fit the Taj Mahal.

At last one of them stood and took off the tailor's tape measure that had been slung around his neck.

'You may go now, Anjali, my dear,' the lady of the house
commanded, ushering her out the front door. She did not want
even her closest friend to be privy to the exact measurement of
the Banerjee hips.

☙

William got wind of Mrs Banerjee's plans several days later when he
bumped into Mr K. K. Rao taking an afternoon constitutional along
The Strand. In fact, he had nearly run over the projectionist with

his bicycle so it seemed polite to stop and apologise and engage in the sort of light conversation that William loathed.

'Will you be attending the special *Hurricane Hansa* performance?' Mr K. K. Rao asked him.

'Hurricane who?'

'*Hurricane Hansa*, starring Fearless Nadia and Mrs Banerjee.'

'I don't know anything about it,' William confessed. Since the morning he had declined to float Mrs Banerjee's boat, things between them had been somewhat strained.

'Mrs Banerjee is dressing up as the famous actress Fearless Nadia and performing on stage while the film *Hurricane Hansa* is screening. Hopefully, there will be no additional hurricane with the wind machine . . .'

'It was YOU,' gasped William, realising it was the projectionist, not Anil, who had been Mrs Banerjee's accomplice the night of the seduction scenario at Coronation Talkies.

'It is of no importance,' Mr K. K. Rao shrugged.

'This Fearless Nadia woman, is she . . . does she . . .'

William faltered as he tried to find a discreet way of asking if she was fully clothed for her role.

'Yes, Mr Rushmore?'

'She's not a loose woman . . . by any chance? You know, a dancer of a certain kind?'

Mr K. K. Rao shook with mirth and, quickly recovering, tried to convert his laughs into coughs.

'She is a horsewoman. Very agile and brave. I believe she uses a whip.'

William moaned, mounted his bike and cycled as if driven by storm clouds up the hill to Monsoon Cottage. He was terrified Mrs Banerjee might appear in public in her lingerie, not that her unmentionables could really be covered by such an insubstantial word. He thought of the silly Petal Cameron's wispy panties and Lydia's sensible white cotton knickers of the kind he imagined girls wore when they played tennis. Why were women all so confoundedly different and unpredictable . . . and as for Premila, she really was in a class of her own.

☙

Mrs Banerjee was sitting on the front veranda, spilling out of a narrow rattan chair. She acknowledged William's arrival with a weary wave of her handkerchief.

'We must talk, Premila.'

'Talk? Now you want to talk? Now, after you have used me like a toy.'

William was confused. She was the one always demanding sex.

To his horror, she began crying uncontrollably, rocking backward and forward in the chair.

'Come inside,' he urged, opening the door.

She began moving, dragging the chair with her. William saw that she was wedged tight.

'Aruna! Aruna!' he yelled down the hallway, turning away, not wanting to witness Mrs Banerjee's humiliation.

He heard Aruna running and, without looking at Mrs Banerjee, he announced he would talk to her inside, when she was fully composed.

Mrs Banerjee waddled into the front room and stood by the window seat. Across the rear of her roaring red sari was patterned the imprint of the chair.

'What is all this about Fearless Nadia?' William asked.

'It is useless, useless,' she sighed. 'I am exercising and clenching my chin and rotating my head at least a full dozen times every morning and still I am so fat that the monkey-face palookas in the bazaar say they cannot make me a pair of riding breeches because no horse could carry me and they cannot be so cruel to an animal and the fact is . . . Well, the fact is you prefer midget Anglo-Indian postal clerks with perfect breasts and half-oriental hairdressers . . .'

William tried to intercept to protest his innocence with Florence Gordon and Poppy Lee.

'Well, the fact is, William dear, I had no intention of riding a horse. Very often Fearless Nadia is strolling ladylike beside Punjab Ka Beta and not galloping on the roofs of railway carriages.'

William was completely lost. She seemed delirious and he wished she drank alcohol so he could pour her a stiff gin and calm her down.

'I was going to stand by the side of the stage and explain what Fearless Nadia was doing and that was all. No giddy-up acting . . .'

William gulped down his second straight gin and stared at Mrs Banerjee. He had never seen her so despondent. In fact he had never seen her look serious. She made every moment they spent together a riot of colour and laughter and warmth. Well, except for the other morning when she presented him with her boat.

'My mother always told me I expect too much from life.'

William knew this was a maternal warning, not a compliment of any kind.

He had an inspired idea.

'Premila, dear . . .' he began.

'Yes,' she murmured, looking at him with glistening eyes.

'Why do you want to be Fearless Nadia when you are already Claudette Colbert to me?'

371

'I am?' she squealed, clapping her hands.

'Will you let me be your Clark Gable?'

'You are already, William. Why just this morning I was thinking how a moustache would suit you, thin but not too thin . . .'

'No, no, I mean we could REALLY be Peter Warne and Ellie Andrews in *It Happened One Night*. You already know all the lines and you could teach me my part . . .'

'Yes, yes,' she cried, tears dried and all thoughts of riding breeches and rearing stallions forgotten.

'Aruna can erect the Wall of Jericho from one of my old saris . . . let me call her.'

'Spick and span,' Aruna announced when she had hung a sari length the colour of tamarind on a makeshift clothesline across the bedroom. Her voice was cheery enough but in her heart she did not feel happy about Mrs Bannerjee's cavortings with a married man and even burying her head in her pillow at night couldn't drown out the seismic moans her mistress made in bed. Anil, on the other hand, was unwilling to miss a single gasp or groan and could be found in the bushes by the side veranda outside the double bedroom most nights waiting for the next volcanic eruption from within.

William knew there was no turning back. As they lay in bed after dinner, William uncomfortably compressed to one side, Ellie fed Peter his lines as she massaged him with so much coconut oil he had to hold the side of the bed to keep from sliding off.

As he gripped the bedhead, Premila hoisted herself up and sat astride him. 'Go on,' she urged.

William gasped and in a fair imitation of an American accent dutifully took his cue.

It was going to be a very long night.

Chapter Fifty-nine

CHALAILI
MARCH, 1938

THE SOLIGANJ WEEKLY OBSERVER
The twelfth of March marks the eighth anniversary of the
departure of M. K. (Mahatma) Gandhi from Ahmedabad
on foot at the head of a band of civil resistance volunteers
on a 100-mile journey to Dandi that has become known
as The Salt March.

The vividly costumed Bombay holidaymakers pressed their
faces against the front windows of the Loch Fyne Tea
Rooms. 'A Little Piece of Scotland In The Indian Hills' read a sign on
a far wall, painted a heathery mauve and with framed paintings of
tungsten-coloured lakes and morose-looking stags on rocky pedestals.

They tried the doorknob, wobbling it every whichway but it
wouldn't yield.

'Hardly ever open. Nutty as fruitcakes,' called out Harold
Gilbert as he strode past on his way to one of his rare spurts of
industry at the Chalaili Post Office.

The trippers cursed the decision to visit this dilapidated hill station. They had already strolled to the treeless Twin Trees Point, and been all but lifted off by a whoosh of wind for their trouble. Rapscallion monkeys had followed their passage back to The Strand, baring the full extent of their dirty piano-key dental work. The Metropole Hotel would be serving lunch (Indian and Continental; Reservations Preferred) in its near-empty Maharani Salon from noon to 2 p.m. sharp but that gave the tourists almost half an hour to occupy.

The bazaar held little charm, being exactly like every other bazaar, and the one local attraction, the reputedly delicious chikki, was today, of all days, unavailable. One chikki stand was permanently closed and the other shut for sign-painting. The word SIX was being altered to SEVEN and the proprietor informed the little party that he really wasn't in the mood for sweet-making.

They were huddled under the tartan canopy of the Loch Fyne Tea Rooms in a breeze that could have come rollicking off the Scottish moors when a small foreign woman appeared and asked them, in flawless Hindustani, if they would move aside so she could open the door.

They stood to one side as one (or other) of the Misses Craig battled with a large key. 'Can we get refreshments here?' asked the Mother of the group hopefully. It had been her idea to visit Chalaili and her voice was cracking with desperation.

'Hot cup of chai? Certainly, follow me.'

The group followed the impish white-haired woman through the Loch Fyne gloaming as if she were a tour leader. Without pausing to usher them to a table, she opened a pair of double doors, wide enough for a bus to motor through. Beyond lay a cavernous room where the second Miss Craig was all but buried in printed flyers.

'If you help us fold these, you can have as much tea and Scottish shortbread as you like!' chirped the tour-leader twin.

After rubbing their eyes to ensure they weren't seeing double, the perplexed holidaymakers agreed, stripped off coats and gloves and scarves, and began folding propaganda for the Indian Independence movement. A grainy photograph of Mahatma Gandhi peered out of the topmost crease.

'But you are British . . .' the Father of the Bombayites protested.

'We are Indian!' the Misses Craig replied as one.

'We may have Scottish blood but we were born here,' explained Heather (or was it Margaret) as her carbon-copy sister made chai in a big metal saucepan. 'Parcelled off to boarding school in Glasgow for a while, but who could stand that climate!' The guests nodded in agreement. They had just seen the grey lochs and windswept crags of the front room's paintings.

'We want India to have her Independence,' she continued. 'The British have done their bit and now they can shove off. It'll all be over in ten years, mark my words.'

The Bombayites gave each other amused looks and accepted the steaming tea served in little glasses. It was fine bazaar tea, better even than the chai stands at Victoria Terminus and the esplanade at Chowpatty Beach.

'Premium leaves from the Chalaili Hills,' smiled the tea-making twin as she passed around a big tin of biscuits with a bagpiper on its hinged lid. Behind her hung a framed copy of the Sunday edition of *The Bombay Advocate*, July 11, 1937, its headline blaring: OUR OBJECTIVE REMAINS INDEPENDENCE.

The chai loosened tongues, encouraged conviviality. The travellers forgot their bookings on the afternoon train and talked well into the early evening, debating politics and lamenting the corruption endemic to the civil service. They were astonished at the knowledge of the Misses Craig and their vast network of contacts. The sisters dropped high-up names as casually as if flicking flecks of dandruff.

'But why do you hide behind this tea room that never opens?' quizzed the Mother, emboldened by the fact the day had turned into such a curious success.

'It's all a front,' winked Margaret (or was it Heather).

And with that oblique statement, she picked up the telephone, and holding it away from her ear as it let out the noise of a fleet of honking geese, dialled a three-digit Chalaili number. In rapid Hindustani, she ordered their dinner from the daughtered-up Mr J. Mohan, who was the only shopkeeper in the bazaar with a telephone. She hoped he was not in such a bleak mood that he would deliberately neglect to send a servant around the stalls to gather the required food.

But the dishes arrived within half an hour, borne in metal tiffin carriers by a procession of boys who threaded their way through the ghostly Loch Fyne Tea Rooms' tables and laid out the feast on a cleared space of the back room's work table.

Included in the order were several unlabelled bottles.

In the unlikely event that anyone had looked through the windows of The Loch Fyne Tea Rooms next morning, they would have observed a family sleeping on chairs, slumped across tables with arms folded and, on the floor, the Father covered in a blanket of Mahatma Gandhi posters, his unperturbed face radiating the most exquisite calm.

Chapter Sixty

CHALAILI
MARCH, 1938

THE SOLIGANJ WEEKLY OBSERVER
World news in brief: Austria has been proclaimed as a
Federal State of the German Reich on the same footing
as Bavaria, Saxony and Wurttemberberg. German leader
Herr Adolf Hitler has incorporated the Austrian Army
into the German Army and placed it under his command.
'I have decided to place . . . the aid of the Reich at the
disposal of the millions of Germans in Austria,' the leader
said.

*M*rs Banerjee had noticed a surliness about her servant,
who she still thought of as Miss Aruna Chowpatty,
always using the full appellation when her dusting or cooking skills
were found wanting.

Mrs Banerjee suspected Aruna's sulky looks indicated disapproval at her mistress's live-in liaison with William Rushmore. Aruna
had no opportunity to have sex, or not that Mrs Banerjee knew of.

Even servants, she realised, must have a need for it. Judging by the exploding population of India, the whole jing-bang country was mating day and night.

Perhaps Aruna was jealous, too, thought Mrs Banerjee. It had to be admitted her couplings with William did occasionally reach a volume that even a clasped hand over a mouth could not quell. Mrs Banerjee's mouth, that was.

Her joy at engaging in sexual intercourse with William was unparalleled. Mrs Banerjee did not care that he was white. That he was boring. That his front teeth reminded her of a rabbit. That he was married to some stick-woman from England.

She felt wanted, needed, desired. She encouraged William to slap her bolsters of flesh, to hoist and squeeze her breasts, to prise apart her thighs as if opening a pair of monumental doors.

He didn't care that she was not slim. That she was not possessed of a perky bosom. That she was not white. That she was married and therefore not free to be engaging in such salaciousness, or so he thought.

'Aruna, Aruna,' she muttered as she lay alone on her bed. Of course the girl knew there was no Mr Banerjee. Or not a Mr Banerjee that belonged to this Mrs Banerjee. Aruna had been one of her mother's servants during the fuss-muss nuptials. Would Aruna tell William?

Mrs Banerjee smoothed her hair and clothes and summoned Aruna to the front parlour of Monsoon Cottage. She dismissed her on a holiday, announcing that Monsoon Cottage had a surfeit of servants and Aruna could take her time returning from her faraway village. The girl's eyes narrowed dangerously but she didn't say a word.

Anil wasted no time in packing his few clothes and Indian

378

Civil Service-stamped brass candlestick and moving into Aruna's kitchen quarters. He was puzzled at the girl's displacement, although she had told him she had had enough of her employer's night noises and wanted to return to her village with the large stash of money she had saved while in Picture Madam's employ. She was due to leave on the afternoon train.

Anil panicked. Perhaps Aruna would not return. He raced to town, thieved another rose from Anjali Gupta's garden and went down on his knee to Aruna. It was a slightly comic gesture, not performed quite as smoothly as he had observed on the screen at Coronation Talkies. Aruna had only seen one-third of a foreign picture, on the opening night of Coronation Talkies and, presuming he was attending to his sandal, she walked away.

Anil caught her and announced his intentions. Aruna coolly informed him she would give his offer some consideration and Anil was delighted, having learnt from his education in talking pictures that this almost certainly meant a yes. But before Aruna went off on her enforced holiday, she had a last act to perform. She was fond of Mrs Banerjee but this affair with a married Englishman was just too disgusting. She decided she would have to expose her. Aruna waited outside William's office at lunchtime, a small figure under a large black umbrella. As William emerged and prepared to open his own brolly against a gusty spring shower, Aruna thrust a packet of letters in his hand. Their umbrellas momentarily locked in a conspiratorial embrace and William noticed her eyes were flushed with tears.

William read the letters from Lydia when he arrived at Monsoon Cottage. Mrs Banerjee was holding court at the Lakshmi Hair and Beauty Studio and Anil was singing film tunes as he chopped vegetables in the kitchen. William was quite alone in the front parlour with the bay window and the brocaded seat, hovering above which he often glimpsed the Banerjee breasts as their owner plumped the cushions.

The letters were sweet with the attar of roses favoured by Mrs Banerjee and had been folded and refolded with contrary creases. There were seven, each dated a few days apart, and progressively warmer in tone. Lydia wrote that she had come to regret their separation and felt she had not tried hard enough to be a loving wife. She was intending to give up the consumption of alcohol in daylight hours. There was a picture of her with Evelyn, in front of a stone church, girlish in their smiles and with curls tossed back. He had just finished reading the seventh letter when he heard Premila click the gate and tip-tap in her tottery high heels up the front path. In that final missive, Lydia had expressed concern at his ill health and indicated she was preparing to depart for India.

His one letter to her, mentioning his bad cold, had indeed been posted, probably thanks to Aruna.

William waited for Premila to pat her freshly styled hair and enter the front room. He had put Lydia's letters in the pocket of his jacket, which was still a little damp from the rain shower. 'Come, come,' sang Premila, 'take that off at once. You will catch a chill.' William jerked away from her but she merely raised an eyebrow and opened her colossal black handbag. 'There's a letter for you, William. English stamps.'

William could not be sure if Mrs Banerjee had read Lydia's letter. The gum on the envelope seemed firm. Lydia had posted it at Southampton, with a first-class airmail sticker, the day she sailed for Bombay. But the mail from Bombay to the mountains was twice as slow as any international passage and the letter indicated Lydia would be in India by the end of the week, just three days away.

'I must move to The Metropole Hotel,' William told Mrs Banerjee at dinner. 'My wife will be here this week.'

'Utter nonsense,' she chirped, heartily buttering her bread. 'I will move back to the other bedroom. Wall of Jericho is erected. No trumpets necessary. When she goes, it will be business as usual. If Mr Banerjee comes home, same conditions apply.'

William had grave doubts about the existence of Mr Banerjee and was even more certain Lydia intended to stay in Chalaili. 'On Thursday, I will go to Bombay for a few days to see my mother,' Mrs Banerjee continued. 'When I return, if the situation has deteriorated, you can both move to The Metropole Hotel. That is that.'

William had no idea what she meant by the situation deteriorating but he knew he had to move to The Metropole Hotel. That night he developed a terrible headache and was unable to sexually satisfy Mrs Banerjee, which displeased her as she was feeling particularly perky with her new permanent wave.

Chapter Sixty-one

CHALAILI
MARCH, 1938

THE SOLIGANJ WEEKLY OBSERVER

While Herr Hitler was undertaking a conqueror's parade through the streets of the Austrian capital on the fourteenth of March, British Prime Minister Neville Chamberlain made a foreign policy statement to a crowded House of Commons yesterday. He stated that Germany's actions would force an acceleration of Britain's rearmament program in which defence requirements must take priority over men and material. But Mr Chamberlain also reiterated that Peace must continue to be Britain's aim.

*A*side from his full-luxury ultra-modern Chrysler Air Flow Imperial back-seat hirings, Vinod had organised another supplementary business to fill the long hours when Mrs Banerjee did not require his services as a driver and the Romantics were occupied in the non-romantic business of earning a small living in Chota Chalaili bazaar.

His other underhand enterprise was a transfer service between Chalaili Station and the town proper, using Mrs Banerjee's car. There were two trains from Bombay via Soliganj each day, arriving at 10.30 a.m. and 4.30 p.m., and the morning schedule, in particular, suited him immensely, as Mrs Banerjee liked to arrive at Lakshmi Hair and Beauty Studio at 10 a.m. dot-sharp several times a week to mingle with the ladies and discuss the latest talking pictures. During the afternoons she often napped or took tea with Anjali Gupta at The Metropole Hotel. There were not many customers for his luxury Flumcafi connections but just a few fares each week kept Vinod's pockets nice and plump. Any stranger to Chalaili took one look at the alpine ascent up The Strand and headed with relief to a taxi or to his Flumcafi back seat, willing to pay almost anything to be borne aloft into town.

He realised he was in danger of being found out by his employer but he had been emboldened by his possession of the newspaper clipping from her tea-chest. He had decided against taking it to the professional letter writer in the bazaar who could read it for him. Such a consultation would draw a crowd and once Mrs Banerjee's secret was known, his bargaining power would be useless. Vinod surmised the press article contained a shocking revelation. The bridal finery she was wearing in the picture suggested she had been abandoned on her wedding day, probably by the man whose picture appeared separately, although he looked on the shy and scrawny side, and was unlikely to be to Mrs Banerjee's taste.

The morning train chugged to a stop and a few passengers got off. Vinod spotted two women, one middle-aged and wearing a widow's white sari, the edges trimmed in what he instantly noticed was an inappropriately festive gold. With her was an old

383

bent servant, carrying a cloth bag and a bamboo bird cage, her feet clad in wellington boots several sizes too large. They stood uncertainly and then the widow shooed off her servant to find transport.

'Go, go!' she cried, twirling her gold bangles in a way that Vinod found oddly familiar.

He hurried down the platform and introduced himself to the woman in charge. The red bindi spot on her forehead shone like a brake light, declaring danger.

'May I know your destination, madam?' he enquired. 'My motor vehicle is at your service.'

'Come, come,' said the woman, prodding the servant, and the two followed Vinod as he engaged a coolie to carry their small amount of luggage. He would pay the fellow an anna or two but add much more to the women's transport bill.

When all were comfortably seated in the car, the two women side by side on the back seat, Vinod asked again for their destination.

'I am here to visit my daughter, Mrs Rajat Banerjee, a talking picture theatre proprietress. Do you know her?'

Vinod spun around. 'Well, er, yes, everyone knows of her,' he stammered.

'Hurry, hurry,' said Leela Dhir, looking out the window to form her first impressions of the hill station of Chalaili. The two parakeets sat glumly in their cage. They had not eaten so much as a raisin since breakfast.

☙

William was in a lather. With Lydia arriving amid signals of reignited passion and a new sobriety, and Mrs Banerjee acting so unconcerned, he realised he would never understand the other sex. He knew he was slightly in love with Mrs Banerjee, but not in a deep, enduring sense. He felt safe with her, she looked after him, spoilt him rotten and made his life fun. A small part of him wondered if he might have a maternal fixation for her, but it was too painful to think of his own mother.

He wondered if he could resume a life with Lydia. They were too alike . . . lonely, unhappy, willing to make compromises because that was the easy way. They were peacemakers, products of childhoods devoid of fun. He could not be responsible for her sadness.

It was unimaginable that the two women would fight over him, when he would have preferred to be alone.

There was no one he could talk to about his dilemma. Since he had moved to Monsoon Cottage, many of the Chalaili expatriates had simply ignored him, although he noticed a few of The Empire Club chaps spoke to him more encouragingly than usual, their voices iced with envy.

Mrs Banerjee, however, was something of a star, always surrounded by an adoring circle of men and women, who loved her animated discussions of films and the gaiety she managed to inject into every minute of life.

Premila knew how to live, thought William. He and Lydia did not.

William sat on the top step of Monsoon Cottage's veranda and held his head.

'Tea, sahib.'

Anil placed a cup and saucer on the step and patted William on the shoulder. It was a gesture that would have been unthinkable before Mrs Banerjee came along to revise social standards with her hugs and pats, regardless of class or caste. Blast, thought William, my servant is the only real friend I have.

☽

Vinod drove slowly, backwards. The gear lever on the Flumcafi was stuck in the reverse position. His two passengers did not comment when he reversed up the hill to The Strand proper and, luckily, the few pedestrians about that afternoon were using the handrails and did not get in his way.

There was no time to take the Flumcafi down to a mechanic in Chota Chalaili bazaar and no way he could take his passengers to Monsoon Cottage, where they might discover the famous picture theatre proprietress sharing her bedroom with a married Englishman. Coronation Talkies would not be open at this hour so he decided to drive the women all over Chalaili on a sightseeing mission. It would just be like being on the wrong side of a railway compartment, he decided. Railway passengers rode back-to-front all the time.

Luckily, they both fell asleep so he kept on propelling Mrs Banerjee's car slowly backwards until finally the widow awoke and demanded to know where they were.

'We are arriving just now at The Metropole Hotel,' Vinod replied, backing into the porte-cochere. He would pretend he had an errand and run inside to check if Mrs Banerjee was there.

The front desk was unoccupied. Anjali Gupta had taken to practising yoga at all hours and applying face-whitening packs. Currently, she was performing a particularly tricky manoeuvre on the bedroom floor. Her husband was running all over the hotel, attending to dozens of small crises, wondering when his wife was planning to unweave herself and get back to work, fairer-skinned or otherwise.

386

Vinod pressed the bell several times before Ram Gupta came skidding into the foyer.

'Where is Mrs Banerjee?'

Vinod's face glistened with perspiration.

'Lakshmi and Beauty Hair Studio for a special appointment, I have heard, with many ladies signing up for private yoga lessons with my good wife, no males allowed. . . .'

Before Ram Gupta could finish speaking, Vinod pushed open the double glass doors leading from the foyer to the shopping arcade and catapulted through. The salon was full of susserating silk saris and heady perfume. He spotted his employer under a drying dome, flicking through a magazine.

'Young man . . .' Poppy Lee began, trying to halt him. But she was not quick enough. He dropped to his knees in front of Mrs Banerjee and began to wail.

Poppy Lee quickly removed the dryer so Mrs Banerjee could hear what he was saying.

'What is it, you fool, an accident, I suppose! Always I am telling you, not too fast . . .'

'No, no, Madam,' Vinod murmured, suddenly aware he had an entranced audience waiting for his next words. 'It is your mother.'

'My mother? What about my mother?'

'Outside, Madam.'

Mrs Banerjee's face faded from an over-heated red to the chalky white of her favourite Regal Rani talc.

☙

Vinod was sitting in the gutter outside The Metropole Hotel, wondering what discussions were going on between Mrs Banerjee and her mother, when Anil came running towards him.

'Where on earth have you been, you idiot? Memsahib Lydia arrives on the afternoon train and you must pick her up, no delays. Sahib says most important that you bring her here to The Metropole Hotel.'

'But . . .'

'But . . . nothing! None of your funny business. She is two days early. She telephoned Sahib's weather office from Bombay to confirm she has bought her ticket on the Soliganj Express . . .'

'What about Monsoon Cottage?'

'Too dangerous to take her there. I must find Mrs Banerjee . . .'

'She is inside,' said Vinod, pointing to the hotel. 'With her mother.'

'Her mother?' yelped Anil. 'Her mother is in Bombay.'

Vinod sighed deeply, imagining secrets exploding in all directions, smashing like hail drops over Chalaili. He had a feeling he should have put his blackmail plan into action weeks ago.

Chapter Sixty-two

CHALAILI

APRIL, 1938

'Forgiveness is the quality of the brave,
not of the cowardly.'

M. K. (MAHATMA) GANDHI

Leela Dhir sat opposite her daughter and the two exchanged unyielding looks. Anjali Gupta had arranged the women in the bamboo-furnished lounge annexe of The Maharani Suite and then retreated, leaving Leela Dhir's servant to sleep in a corner, the old woman clearly exhausted from such an involved excursion. On the low wooden tea table between mother and daughter sat the caged parakeets, their heads turning from side to side like tennis umpires.

'I didn't know you were fond of birds?' enquired the daughter, opening proceedings.

'They are my only friends.'

The mother reached with a theatrical gesture for a folded handkerchief down her cleavage. The daughter noticed she had gained quite a lot of weight since she had last seen her.

'Mummy . . .'

'Listen to me, Miss Premila Dhir or Mrs Rajat Banerjee or whatever else you call yourself! You are a disgraceful liar! You told me you had negotiated a permanent lease for my apartment. All the time it was just rented from one day to the next. Rented! Leela Dhir living in a rented apartment like some common . . .'

'I had no choice,' the daughter interrupted, bursting into tears.

The mother clapped her hands for the servant to pour tea but there was no shifting the old woman, who had turned one of the wellington boots into a pillow.

'But, Mummy, it was Miss Dolly de Souza's fault.'

'You mean that real estate madam?'

The daughter's eyes widened as she wondered how much Leela Dhir might actually know. The mother picked up the china teapot, her hand shaking.

'Yes, Mummy. Real estate madam and Daddy's mistress.' The daughter burst into a fresh typhoon of tears.

The mother dropped her cup and saucer. The pieces fell to the polished floorboards and broke. The birds screeched. Cheap bazaar china, she thought. Fine bone china would bounce. She was trying to gather her thoughts before continuing this otherworldly conversation.

☙

Leela Dhir's daughter, the womb-bursting daughter of whom she has been simultaneously ashamed and afraid, stands by The Maharani Suite windows, silent and statue-still. She closes her eyes. It is a late Friday evening in the sophisticated Dhir residence at Chowpatty

Beach, Bombay. The teenage Premila is on her way to the kitchen to chat to the servants, to fill her lonely ravenous tummy with soft mango kulfi, made fresh that day by the yellow-eyed cook from Kerala. 'The taste of the sun, Missy,' he would say, spooning it into Premila's waiting mouth, obediently opened like a baby.

But before she reaches the sweet, happy kitchen, Premila hears a scuffling sound coming from the little box room near the back entrance. It is where non-perishable rubbish is stored for collection and the soiled washing is gathered before being handed over to the dhobi wallah. She creeps up and pushes open the door just enough to see her mother on hands and knees.

Leela Dhir, top-circle party-giver and queen of snobs, is holding a pair of white underpants. Men's underpants. Her husband's underpants. Premila watches her mother tug at the garment and turn it inside out, baring the side with loose threads and stitching and the remnants of the day's events. She presses the cotton to her face, forces the crotch of the pants into a ball, sniffs and sniffs and sniffs the bunched material, her nose working like a bloodhound.

She is after the scent of her husband's semen, the mingling of a woman's fluids, the undeniable stench of recent sex . . . ammonia and fishiness and sour salt-sweat. Premila watches her mother lower the underpants and cradle them against her breast and cry and cry until the creased, crunchy cotton is sodden. She has washed away the evidence with her tears.

☙

In The Maharani Suite, the mother is glowering at her daydreaming daughter.

'Well, Premila?'

'Mummy, he left her a lot of money. Secret import-export money. Enough to buy entire buildings.'

'And how do you know all this?'

The daughter turned away from her mother. Chalaili was not busy at this time of day. She could see Vinod through the window, sitting in the gutter beside her car, uncharacteristically idle, a nimbus of cigarette smoke circling his head like an undeserved halo. Mr K. K. Rao was taking a leisurely afternoon walk along The Strand, tapping his way with a furled umbrella. In his wake strolled Devi, clearly devoted to the kind man, her veil flowing freely, her shoulders squared, her scarred face on view for all to see. Premila seldom saw Devi outdoors. The girl cleaned Coronation Talkies quietly and efficiently, occasionally taking a nap across several seats when her back ached from mopping and sweeping. If Anil or Mr K. K. Rao came across the sleeping girl, they tiptoed around her and it was not unknown for Devi to wake and find a man's jacket across her shoulders, shielding her from the old picture theatre's worrisome draughts.

Several ladies were walking away from the hotel, having emerged from the Lakshmi Hair and Beauty Studio, patting their lacquered coiffures and mock-kissing cheeks as they parted ways. A gang of langur monkeys was sitting on a railing between Coronation Talkies and the Post Office with arms crossed, like a row of old duffers on a park bench. The humiliation over the sugar-floss fiasco seemed centuries ago.

Even if the truth meant an end to this cosy life in Chalaili, Premila knew she was too tired for more lies.

'Mummy,' she began, sitting down again and straightening the folds of her yellow sari. Yellow, the colour her mother found so unfavourable for two-legged elephants, she noted, with a slight fizz of triumph.

'Miss Dolly de Souza made an appointment to see me . . .'

'What are you talking about? Since when did young girls from good families have such appointments . . .'

'Listen! She telephoned the house one day, after the wedding. You were lying down.'

The mother nodded. She acknowledged she had done a lot of lying down after her daughter's wedding, usually with a face pack of lentil flour mixed with water and milk to lighten her skin.

'Daddy had just died, she had read about our misfortunes in the newspaper . . .'

'Your own marital misfortunes!'

'Yes, yes. Anyway, she asked me to meet her . . . It was at the suggestion of Daddy's lawyer.'

'Your father's lawyer? What fantasy is this?'

The daughter rushed on, not wanting to be subjected to extended interrogation on the subject of Mr Sameep Shirodkar.

'Where?'

'In the lobby of the Taj Hotel, where we would take tea.'

'What? So . . . so . . . like some rumpty-tumpty chorus girl, you went wriggling your hips around the Taj Hotel . . .'

'Please, don't interrupt, Mummy! I met Miss Dolly de Souza there and she explained that she had just purchased Pink Fantasia and she could make an apartment available at a very reasonable rental, because the building was due to be sold within a few years.'

'So, all along you knew your mother was being incarcerated in a condemned building by some chance-met scoundrel woman. Premila, from the day you were born there has been wickedness in your veins . . .'

'I thought she was trying to help us, Mummy. There wasn't enough money from Daddy's estate for your apartment and for . . . for . . . my talking picture theatre.'

'Pictures, always pictures,' the mother wailed. 'And now you tell me this ridiculous story, like one of your talking picture tales . . . What does she look like, this devil woman?'

'She's Anglo-Indian, very fair.'

The daughter moved forward, anticipating a fainting attack at this disclosure. To Leela Dhir, being part-Indian was even worse than being all foreign.

But the mother simply sat still, the wind in her substantial sails deflated.

'Anyway, I found out later that everyone in the building had some connection to Miss Dolly de Souza. There were gentlemen she was blackmailing, an elderly relative who was taking too long to die off and hand over jewellery to her. She put everyone in there at special prices and then waited for the building to disintegrate . . .'

'You knew this and you did nothing?'

'I had paid two years ahead and you never complained. I just thought the matter would resolve itself.'

'And two years later, when your mother had not conveniently passed away?'

'By then, I thought I would have enough money to move you here and make you very comfortable. Gita, as well.'

'Gita? Who do you mean by Gita?'

The servant stirred slightly but it may have been Anjali Gupta tapping at the door with fresh tea that disturbed her, rather than the unaccustomed mention of her name.

Chapter Sixty-three

CHALAILI
APRIL, 1938

THE SOLIGANJ WEEKLY OBSERVER
M. K. (Mahatma) Gandhi has initiated discussions with Lord Brabourne, Governor of Bengal, regarding the release of political prisoners. He has called for a suspension of agitation while negotiations continue.

Ram Gupta sat in what he referred to as his office but was really no more than an alcove adjacent to the front desk with a diagonal view to the foyer and double entrance doors. He was poring over his hotel's monthly accounts, making various notations with a fiercely sharpened pencil, which he also used to make satisfying investigations in his ears when he was absolutely certain his wife was not looking.

Mrs Banerjee had paid two weeks in advance for her mother to stay in The Maharani Suite and had mentioned that she herself might be joining her, depending upon what she referred to as 'prevailing circumstances' at Monsoon Cottage. The money would be helpful, given that The Metropole Hotel had just one or two other guests.

'Mrs Banerjee is not her usual self today,' he observed to his wife as she dusted the keys hanging on a numbered board behind the front desk, their wooden tags banging together as she whipped them with her cleaning cloth.

'I've told you to call her Premila, like everyone else does.'

'She hasn't personally invited me to call her anything but Mrs Banerjee,' Ram Gupta retorted. He immediately regretted his pompous reply. Anjali Gupta's eyes were flashing dangerously.

'I don't think she wants to be reminded of the Banerjee connection just now,' she said, her face softening as she sat in the chair on the other side of his paper-strewn desk. From her pocket she brought out an old newspaper clipping, folded as small as a calling card.

'Vinod, that no-good fellow she insists on keeping as her driver, gave me this just now. He says we must put it in the safe, in case it falls into the wrong hands. Does he think I can't read?'

She handed her husband the rectangle of paper, and he smoothed it open. The surface was so greasy that passages of newsprint instantly became imprinted on his hand. Ram Gupta's glasses shot down his nose, were recovered, shot again, and the see-sawing continued until he finished reading the report under the towering headline: SOCIETY WEDDING ENDS IN JEERS.

'Poor, poor Premila,' he sighed. That was the appropriate way to address her after all. Her groom, Rajat Banerjee, eldest son of the Malabar Hill by way of Calcutta Banerjees, had failed to show at the wedding. The newspaper reported that unconfirmed sources suggested he was last seen at the Bombay docks, boarding a ship for Shanghai. The jilted bride's father, an import-export tycoon, was demanding the return of the dowry.

'But she took his name, Anjali, why would she . . . ?'

'Oh, for pity's sake, don't you understand anything?'

Anjali Gupta hurried out in tears, leaving her husband to contemplate this extraordinary news as he attempted to rub *The Bombay Advocate* newsprint from his right thumb.

Chapter Sixty-four

CHALAILI

APRIL, 1938

'It is difficult but not impossible to conduct
strictly honest business.'

M. K. (MAHATMA) GANDHI

William sent Romesh, his chief peon, to summon Anil to his office. William's orders were clear and concise. Anil was to return to Monsoon Cottage and remove all trace of his master's belongings from the double bedroom.

William would go to Monsoon Cottage shortly and pack a suitcase to move to The Metropole Hotel.

The other twin-bedded room must appear as if it was William's bachelor quarters. Anil was also to inspect every room in the bungalow to ensure Mrs Banerjee hadn't sprinkled incriminating evidence around.

William was convinced Lydia would insist on visiting the bungalow and it had better appear as if he had been installed in the guest bedroom.

'Evidence? Like what . . . what . . . what?'

Anil was babbling with anxiety.

'How should I know?' Lipstick marks or . . . or . . .'

'Yes, lipstick marks, lipstick marks,' Anil confirmed, as if ticking off an inventory.

'Yes, that's it, lipstick marks or that infernal rose perfume of hers . . . it could be anywhere, even my underwear.'

'Your underwear?'

Anil was so impressed by such a prospect, he broke into a huge grin.

'That's enough of your damned cheek. Just go, would you, there's no time to waste.'

✡

William sat at his desk and replayed in his mind the phone conversation he'd had that morning with Lydia. She had called him from Bombay upon arrival at the docks. He thought of her asking to use the telephone in the shipping manager's office. She would have been nervous, unaware of the protocols, and would have offered too much money.

He regretted his outpouring to her but felt cleansed, too, at the confession about Sylvia. Everything seemed so much clearer. How he had been unable to resist Mrs Banerjee's boisterous advances, had done her bidding in bed. He was a fool where women were concerned, always the little boy waiting for them to lead the way. Lydia was different, so aloof and uncertain.

The only way to save his marriage would be to confess about his affair with Mrs Banerjee. He would take Lydia away from Chalaili. It would be easy enough to arrange a transfer and Lydia might even forgive him completely, now that she knew the truth about his childhood. He had that matter of Simon Fraser-Gough up his sleeve, too. He knew his wife hadn't really done anything scandalous, but just the same . . .

He shut his eyes and went over the words he'd exchanged with his wife.

'I telephoned Bluebell Cottage and was told by a Mrs Carter that you no longer live there. What's been going on?'

Lydia's voice was small and weak.

'I took a room in Mrs Banerjee's bungalow as there was no other government accommodation. I was thrown out of Bluebell Cottage as it was meant to be for families, not couples . . . you know, childless couples.'

'I am aware we have no children, William. Where is Mrs Banerjee's bungalow?'

'On the upper ridge, it's actually Bungalow Seven. Mrs Banerjee decided to call it Monsoon Cottage.'

He tried to lighten his voice, as if he thought the name to be a good joke.

'But all the houses up there are government property, William. How could she be living on the upper ridge?'

'Mrs Banerjee is very well connected. Everyone says so.'

'I have missed the view of Chalaili Valley,' Lydia said, almost to herself. 'Everything in West Gamble is so small and ordered. People live such miniature lives . . .'

Her voice trailed off and then returned, louder and bolder.

'I know about your mother, William, and now I understand everything.'

'What about my mother?'

'I had a long talk with your Aunt Sylvia and . . .'

'She told you what a lonely little boy I was and how I am

unable to relate to women. Is that it?'

'Well, not quite . . .'

'And did she tell you how she made me dance with her in that front room at Finchley every evening after dinner? How Uncle John would be sent to the pub and she'd turn on the gramophone and I would have to waltz with her, while she pressed herself against me and murmured my father's name. Is that what she told you?'

'No!' Lydia protested. Everything was going horribly wrong. She had not meant to upset William, just to reassure him that she understood his loneliness.

'No, I didn't think so,' William continued, his voice bitter. 'No more than she would have told you how she crept into bed beside me at night and took my hands and ran them over her . . .'

'That's enough!' cried Lydia, her voice trembling. 'What on earth has got into you, talking like this . . .'

'I was only a boy, Lydia, a boy . . .'

As his voice trailed off, the line went dead.

Lydia tried again and again but the Bombay operator couldn't connect her to the temperamental Chalaili exchange.

☙

Anil sped around Monsoon Cottage, making sure all William's personal possessions were in the second bedroom. He even took his pipe and box of Golden Parrot Safety Matches away from an ashtray in the front parlour and placed them beside one of the single beds, so it would appear William was not given to idle evenings with Mrs Banerjee, lighting up and setting sail suggestive rings of smoke.

He found it hard to believe Lydia would be fooled but there

was nothing more he could do. Anil decided to check the garden shed, to ensure the projector and its secret cargo were safe in the tea-chest. If Lydia went snooping out there and found the film of the aborted wedding, then it would be even more difficult for William to explain his residential arrangements.

As he returned, he yelped with alarm. Mrs Banerjee was standing in the kitchen, looking pale and unwell. Vinod must have dropped her off at the junction of the upper and lower ridges.

Anil was about to advise her why he had moved William's clothes and personal effects but she anticipated his explanation and raised her hand.

'It's fine, Anil. I was here myself to do the same. Everything must be ready for Mrs Rushmore's arrival.'

The unlikely pair left Monsoon Cottage together, walking along the ridge to where Mrs Banerjee had told Vinod to wait with the full-luxury ultra-modern Chrysler Air Flow Imperial. Anil noticed there was no assault of attar of roses.

'Why do you have no beautiful smell today?'

'I am not well enough for perfume, Anil,' she replied, and ushered him into the back seat of the car as if he were a dignitary and she a humble handmaiden.

She sat beside him and gripped the seat. 'Vinod is spending the day driving backwards, Anil. It is a temporary thing but I suggest you close your eyes until we are stationary again at Coronation Talkies. I must check on Mr K. K. Rao and Devi. Everything feels so topsy-turvy.'

Anil gulped. There were days when Mrs Banerjee was absolutely bonkers.

Chapter Sixty-five

CHALAILI
APRIL, 1938

'To call woman the weaker sex is a libel; it is man's
injustice to woman . . . without her, man could not be.'
M. K. (MAHATMA) GANDHI

After Vinod had handed Anjali Gupta the precious piece
of paper, he combed his hair and nervously smoked
two English cigarettes in quick succession, although he realised
he might not be able to afford such luxuries much longer. Then
he drove Mrs Banerjee to Monsoon Cottage, waited for her, took
her to Coronation Talkies and proceeded with Anil to Chalaili
Station. It was turning into a ridiculously busy day with no possibility of extra earnings, and all the reversing in the Flumcafi was
making him feel decidedly unwell.

Anil waited on the platform, holding a red rose. He had felt
too upset to plunder The Metropole Hotel's unguarded garden so
he had asked Anjali Gupta if he could have one. She was running
through the foyer, in tears, and told him to do whatever he liked,

she had no use for roses just now. Anil knew she was Mrs Baner-jee's closest friend so it was natural she would be worried about the imminent arrival of William's wife.

Anil didn't know what to feel. He loved his easy life at Monsoon Cottage and the eccentric benevolence of Mrs Banerjee, who never made him feel like a mere servant, even when she was at her bossiest. He couldn't imagine returning to the timid silences of life with William and Lydia.

Lydia stepped off the train and Anil wanted to cry. She looked very small and thin, her face pale and anxious. Lydia spotted Anil and waved. She wanted to hug him as she handed over her suitcase. She stopped herself in time and asked Anil how he was, where was William, all the questions coming out in a rush. Anil bobbed his head and presented the rose, evading her interrogations.

'Let's walk all the way up to Monsoon Cottage. I'd like to stretch my legs,' she said.

Anil froze. Monsoon Cottage? Hadn't William told her he would be at The Metropole Hotel? How much did she really know? He wanted to wring the neck of William for putting him in this galloping galoshes situation.

At that moment, Vinod appeared at the station entrance and snatched Lydia's bag from Anil. The back door on the passenger side of the full-luxury ultra-modern Chrysler Air Flow Imperial was already open.

'Please, Madam,' he insisted, all but shoving her inside. He closed the door and the two men stood to one side in animated conversation.

Lydia had no notion what was going on. Anil was behaving very strangely and the oddly luxurious car smelt strongly of talcum powder and hair oil. Just when she was about to get out and demand to be taken to see William, the men hopped into the front seats.

Anil stared straight ahead. Vinod turned and introduced himself.

'Madam, we will go to The Metropole Hotel.'

'Whose car is this?'

'It is the Flumcafi,' Vinod replied.

'The Flumcafi?'

Lydia presumed it was just another Indian word she didn't know.

'Flumcafi, Flumcafi,' she repeated, with a giggle.

The two men looked at each other.

Lydia surmised that William had taken a room at The Metropole Hotel while their new residential arrangements were being sorted out. She closed her eyes.

The car jolted backwards. She opened her eyes. Vinod had his left arm across the back of the driver's seat and was peering through the rear window as he reversed up the lower incline of The Strand.

'We are going backwards,' she said.

'Correct,' said Anil, who was also facing her, keeping watch for unexpected pedestrians.

Lydia didn't open her eyes again until the Flumcafi was reversed into the porte-cochere of The Metropole Hotel. She adjusted the belt on her light woollen dress and squared her shoulders as she climbed the front steps.

❧

Leela Dhir observed the arrival of the Englishwoman through The Maharani Suite windows. Premila was pacing up and down outside Coronation Talkies, her head lowered.

405

Good heavens, she thought, that automobile is being driven backwards. It looked exactly like the one she had hired at Chalaili Station.

'Don't tell me . . .' she exclaimed. The servant, still asleep on the floor, shifted slightly.

Leela Dhir wrapped her favourite shawl tightly around her.

Her daughter had rushed off amid wailings and waving of hands but despite the revelations of her husband's mistress and nefarious business dealings, she felt strangely calm. Premila was awash with guilt and Leela Dhir knew this was an excellent state of affairs. While her daughter was so tormented, she could demand almost anything she liked. Firstly, Premila could organise for her mother's possessions to be removed from Pink Fantasia and be deposited somewhere more suitable. Leela Dhir was beginning to think that even though Chalaili was a socially disgraceful backwater, it would be a satisfactory choice for now. Premila's bungalow would surely be large enough to accommodate her.

Her eyes came into focus on the sign above Coronation Talkies. A man on a ladder was clicking big black letters, one by one, into a grooved line. Leela Dhir waited until he had finished, her grip on The Maharani Suite's curtains tightening so hard, her fingers ached. '*One Hundred Men and a Girl*' it announced.

'Prem-i-la!' she hissed.

'Starring . . .'

The letters continued to plip-plop into place.

Leela Dhir gulped. 'Please, please,' she whispered, terrified her daughter might have turned her strange talents to acting.

She relaxed her fingers.

D-e-a-n-n-a D-u-r-b-i-n.

It didn't sound like the sort of name her daughter would

406

invent for herself, although Durbin sounded perilously like some kind of nightclub dancer's hat.

Leela Dhir lay down on the over-sized bed and closed her eyes. She thought of the Ruby Revolver lipstick on her husband's shirt, his too-smooth excuses about late appointments. Rather than anger, she felt enormous weariness, as if rising from the bed would require the service of a team of bullocks to haul her up.

Leela Dhir tried to reprise the discussion she had just had with Premila. It seemed likely that no one in Chalaili knew the truth about her lack of marital status. Even that oily-boy driver who'd brought her from the station, quite possibly, she now real-ised, in the reverse gear position, referred to her as Mrs Banerjee and judging by the way the hotel owner's wife bowed and bustled, Premila commanded more than a little respect, despite screen-ing talking pictures with suggestive titles, surely only made to appeal to the sexed-up lower classes and those Anglo-Indian rail-way clerks with their knees always showing.

She opened her eyes and looked at the ceiling. The paint was peeling in patches and the chandelier needed a thorough dusting. Oh, my complicated daughter, she thought, exiled to this mouldy hill station, all because of that despicable Banerjee family with their pretensions and ridiculous demands over money. Shyam had had to threaten court action to get back the dowry, there had been newspaper reporters at the gate, the yellow-eyed cook from Kerala had chased them away with a wooden chapatti roller. She allowed herself a little giggle at that memory.

And all the time that scrawny son of theirs, that Rajat char-acter, had been a homosexual. The last anyone had heard of him he was living in Shanghai and selling its wealthy residents Kashmiri double-knot silk carpets. As if that didn't say it all.

Leela Dhir thought again of her husband, his straight back and molten eyes, and wondered if he had ever loved her. She was the one who came to the marriage with money, the Punjabi doctor's daughter with the fine education and social connections who'd been carried off to Bombay by her ambitious husband. Her family had paid for Premila's costly convent schooling while Shyam Dhir was off importing and exporting and, as now was revealed, impaling Miss Dolly de Souza.

She had been too proud to seek their assistance when she was widowed. Her father was dead now and her mother thought Leela Dhir lived in a modern apartment in the style of Bombay's famous Taj Mahal Hotel, entertaining her social circle who all arrived in a modern mechanical lift, in one luxurious whoosh to the fourth floor. Leela Dhir's mother said she was unable to visit Bombay and use a modern mechanical lift, a situation that suited her daughter down to the ground, as it were.

Leela Dhir began to cry but some of those tears were shed with relief that she was no longer trapped at Pink Fantasia. She wiped her eyes and patted her cheeks. She would have to try and be a model mother, lest her daughter despatch her back to Bombay.

Chapter Sixty-six

CHALAILI
APRIL, 1938

'Mootsuddy: A native accountant. Hindustani: *mutasaddi*.'
HOBSON-JOBSON: A GLOSSARY OF COLLOQUIAL
ANGLO-INDIAN WORDS AND PHRASES BY
COL. HENRY YULE AND A. C. BURNELL, 1903

*V*inod collected Mrs Banerjee from outside Coronation Talkies. She slipped down into the back seat of the full-luxury ultra-modern Chrysler Air Flow Imperial and directed him to drive around and around. But very, very slowly, due to the gears being inconveniently stuck in such a contrary position.

She was not quite ready to return to Monsoon Cottage. The unscheduled appearance of her mother in Chalaili was an almighty shock. If the residents found out about the disgrace of her called-off wedding and the intricate web of lies she had spun, she would have to leave. She realised, with a little tug, how much she loved the hill station and how she had had such a sensational effect on the place that even her affair with the enigmatic William Rushmore had become strangely acceptable in society's eyes.

Chalaili was such a self-contained globule, she mused. Like a talking picture, with no intrusion from reality.

Down on the plains, Mrs Banerjee knew changes were rapidly taking place. The anti-British movement was in full fling. *Hindustan Zindabad! Mahatma Gandhi Ji Kai!* The cries were not audible at Chalaili where the hill-tribe locals were not the least bit interested and the indomitable Brits feigned a similar lack of concern.

Mrs Banerjee did sense a modicum of unease among the memsahibs who feared their days of unlimited servants and inflated status could be close to an end.

She put her head in her hands. So much had happened. The Misses Craig had been hurried out of town one chilly dawn by the Superintendent of Police from Soliganj and his gangster-goons. The doughty Scottish lassies had plastered posters of Mahatma Gandhi all over Grindlays Bank and the Chalaili Post Office one night and would have done their worst to Coronation Talkies if Mr K. K. Rao hadn't woken from one of his vibrant sea-salty dreams and chased them off.

She thought of that poor silly Florence Gordon and her ill-fated gossip sheet, and all because her blood was mixed up and she didn't know how to fit in. Mrs Banerjee allowed herself a little chuckle at the memory of *The Chalaili Bugle*. There had been some speculation after the first edition that *she* was Eugenia Jambolana, although she would hardly have published a description of herself as an Altocumulus Cloud.

Florence Gordon just wanted to break free and Mrs Banerjee knew how that felt. No one in Chalaili seemed completely content, except perhaps that flibbertigibbet Poppy Lee at Lakshmi

Hair and Beauty Studio who, it was rumoured, had taken up where the Soliganj-despatched Florence Gordon had left off, vis-a-vis the giving of favours to tubercular fellows and the more moneyed of bazaar traders. Poppy Lee seemed happy alright, always with too big a smile on her face.

Where was Veronica O'Brien, she wondered. Anjali Gupta absolutely insisted the pretty Irishwoman was in France, drinking champagne and looking at sunsets over the ocean, with the son of a fantastically wealthy raja. That would never have happened, mused Mrs Banerjee, if her railway wallah husband hadn't got himself killed on some rackety old train track somewhere. Mrs Banerjee only half-believed Anjali Gupta's tale. Was it possible Veronica O'Brien could have run off with that Simon Fraser-Gough chap who had been so intent on kissing Lydia Rushmore in the foyer of Coronation Talkies?

Mrs Banerjee thought about Simon Fraser-Gough and his unsatisfactory nose and decided it was unlikely, after all. Charlotte Montague had told her weeks ago, as they sat side by side under Lakshmi Hair and Beauty Studio's drying domes, that Simon Fraser-Gough was a blackmailer and she had written a note to William about him, lest he get the wrong idea about poor Lydia.

But my life here is happy, she mused, and it's not fair that my past should be uncovered and flaunted about for all to laugh and pass judgement. I will have to make that very clear to my mother, she decided. Mrs Banerjee had not intended to cause Leela Dhir such misery, despite the hurtful references to baby elephants and the colour yellow. How the devil was she to know Pink Fantasia would be such a prison?

Mrs Banerjee closed her eyes as Vinod drove backwards down The Strand. She allowed her mind to stalk the past, a painful excursion she had not taken since she left Bombay. After the failed wedding, she had stayed in her bedroom for weeks, refusing to receive the many visitors who called at the Dhir residence, everyone wanting to see the jilted bride, as if she may have shrivelled up like a salted snail.

Then her father died. When the news came of his heart attack, she had wondered if he had expired on top of Miss Dolly de Souza, but it was confirmed to have taken place at his importing-exporting office, in very respectable conditions, witnesses in attendance.

Mother and daughter were united in their grief and Premila couldn't help but be a bit pleased at the deflection of attention away from her own plight. But she had adored her charming father, as wicked as he was, and the thought of spending her life caring for her overwrought mother was more than she could bear. It was during the period of mourning that she decided she would use whatever money was due to her to purchase a picture theatre. She realised it would have to be far from the tittle-tattle world of Bombay.

Premila had left her mother keening and banging pillows with grief to attend the reading of her father's will and to organise the settlement of his estate with the family lawyer, Mr Sameep Shirodkar. There were just the two of them in his large, wood-panelled office in a grand colonial building near Victoria Terminus and the lawyer spoke very softly, in the well-modulated tones of one used to an audience.

'Dear Miss Dhir,' he began, elbows on desk, hands templed, 'your father has made two separate arrangements, the first for Mrs Shyam Dhir and yourself, and the second is a charitable bequest.'

'Charity?' questioned Premila. She was not aware that her father had had any benevolent streak.

'Yes, Miss Dhir, that is correct. It is, in fact, a very large bequest, but there is also ample money for Mrs Shyam Dhir and yourself to lead comfortable lives, although it may be necessary for you to sell the family home and buy something a little more, er, modest . . .'

'Which charity, exactly?' enquired Premila, eyebrows arched.

'Let me see, so many papers on my desk.'

Sameep Shirodkar had expected to be dealing with a sobbing widow who would not dare challenge him, not this keen-eyed maiden. The press had mentioned her age as mid-twenties, but he realised the Dhirs had subtracted a few years from the truth to assist the marriage process. He looked at the relevant papers. Ah, she was thirty-two.

Premila could see he was stalling, having smugly believed the jilted Dhir girl, as she had overheard the clerk announce her, would be so grief-stricken she would not demand to know any details of her father's affairs. He continued to shuffle files, knocking over a small brass bell that fell to the carpeted floor with a soft clink near Premila's feet.

He walked around the desk and reached down to retrieve it and as he did, she leant forward, so their eyes met at an awkward angle. He gasped with pain as Premila stood on his outstretched hand.

'Would the charity happen to be known as Miss Dolly de Souza?'

Sameep Shirodkar rose clumsily from the floor, rubbed his hand and walked back behind his chair. He remained standing, arms crossed in courtroom pose, and surveyed Premila, who was now regarding him with eyes slanted, nose imperiously aloft, as she had seen her mother do so often, usually with great effect.

413

'How much do you know?' he asked, his voice now rougher and more searching.

'I know, Mr Sameep Shirodkar, that Miss Dolly de Souza was my father's mistress and I believe you know that, too, you, you mootsuddy!'

He sat down and rearranged the papers in front of him, his hands slightly trembling. He was unaware of the Dhir girl's devotion to her copy of *Hobson-Jobson Glossary of Colloquial Anglo-Indian Words and Phrases* in her long unproductive hours in the Galaxy Talkies rear office. The term mootsuddy clearly was offensive and he wished he knew the meaning.

'You'll find it somewhere between moorpunky and moplah,' snapped Premila.

'Pardon?'

'Mootsuddy, you fool. Native accountant.'

Sameep Shirodkar concluded the girl was mad. Perhaps the shame of her wedding day had affected her brain.

'Whenever the mootsuddies cease to yield you proper obedience, you must give them a severe flogging . . .'

'Very well, what do you want me to do, Miss Dhir?'

'I would prefer that my mother did not find out about my father's infidelity but unless you do as I request, I will have no option but to tell her and, as you know, she is an influential woman. Your part in all this subterfuge would not go unnoticed . . .'

'That sounds like blackmail to me, Miss Dhir.'

'Which is a greater crime than manipulating a will?'

Premila stood and shook her right arm at the lawyer, its quota of bangles whirling like rotors. 'I want you to do two things instantly. The first is to effect whatever is necessary to change my name and then have your flunkies find me a picture theatre in good condition for sale and, if it is suitable, I will purchase it. It must be outside Bombay.'

'Change your name to what?'

'To Mrs Rajat Banerjee.'

'But everyone knows that Banerjee back-to-front fairy boy failed to show . . .'

'Everyone does NOT know. Only in Bombay do the very top people know any such thing.'

Premila was to have several more meetings with Sameep Shirodkar, who she persisted in calling Mr Mootsuddy and even, on one particularly inflamed occasion, Mootsuddy Fancy Pants. He began to grow ever more fearful of her eventful arrivals and the possible permutations of mootsuddy.

Miss Dolly de Souza was also a demanding woman who had energetically bestowed her favours upon him on several occasions and he feared she was not above creating a scandal if things did not go to her advantage. The two women were formidable opponents, each in her own semi-hysterical way.

A four-storey apartment block, Pink Fantasia, was purchased by De Souza Investments, a company Sameep Shirodkar assisted his client to form. Another of her lovers, a harried chap recently relocated from Calcutta named J. P. P. Chatterjee, was put in charge of day-to-day running, although he also worked as a sales manager at one of Bombay's top hotels and was forced to spend his time racing between his elegant tourist establishment and the small office that served as headquarters for De Souza Investments. Like Sameep Shirodkar, he had a wife and family.

On the surface, Pink Fantasia was a functioning apartment block in a most reasonable location, and Sameep Shirodkar was able to persuade the jilted Dhir girl to take out a two-year lease for an apartment for her mother. She was told that the building would be pulled down after that time to make way for a luxury hotel. Although Sameep Shirodkar was not sure of the complete picture, he had gleaned from one brief meeting with the forever-alarmed Mr J. P. P. Chatterjee that Dolly de Souza had installed other residents who were connected to her in the building. He imagined an intricate web of deceit and revenge as terrified men begged their families to move to Pink Fantasia and then watched the building crumble around them. He suspected the collapse would take not much more than one year.

Dolly de Souza was due to make a mountain of money but the jilted Dhir girl was a winner, too. She had her mother out of the way, cash in hand, a new identity and her own theatre at a hill station that, Sameep Shirodkar noted with relief, was some distance from Bombay. The theatre had been available at cut rate as Chalaili was known as one of the wettest places in India, something that the jilted Dhir girl, for all her flashy convent education and command of Anglo-Indian colloquialisms, did not appear to realise.

Mrs Banerjee was surprised that her mother offered little resistance at the sale of the family house. It had been a white elephant, so large and old-fashioned, she told her daughter, and she boasted to her friends of modern conveniences and sea views in such a way that suggested her move to Pink Fantasia was tantamount to instalment at a hilltop palace, where Leela Dhir would reign like a maharani, her head only just below the clouds.

The new Mrs Rajat Banerjee was delighted that Mr Shirodkar's representatives had found her a picture theatre, even if it was in a nondescript hill station that British society largely overlooked. Only in her dark moments, when sleep would not come, did she contemplate what her future would be like. She was grossly fat, a married woman in name only. Still a virgin, she had thrown away any chance of romantic happiness. Unless, unless, she murmured as she appraised the acreage of her naked body upon her rumpled bed, I can enjoy men the way Dolly de Souza does. She stroked her unclaimed bosoms, pulling their extended nipples, and patted the undulations around her stomach. There will be those who will want all this, she decided. From her experience so far, men were utter nincompoops.

Chapter Sixty-seven

CHALAILI
APRIL, 1938

'The unity we desire will last only if we cultivate
a yielding and charitable disposition towards one another.'
M. K. (MAHATMA) GANDHI

Vinod returned Mrs Banerjee to the intersection of the higher and lower ridges. After day-dreaming out the window, she sang at opening night pitch through the final moments of their drive around Chalaili in the Flumcafi, as if summoning strength and purpose.

She stomped along the ridge leading to Monsoon Cottage. It had been raining most of the day and the slick ground was littered with dislodged branches and rocks impeding her way.

'An obstacle course, as usual,' she cried aloud, jabbing the metal point of her furled umbrella at oozy mounds of leaves.

'My life has been one jing-bang obstacle course,' she continued, her voice abating as she suddenly stood absolutely still, a position utterly foreign to her.

If anyone had approached Mrs Banerjee at that moment, they would have mistaken her unmoving bulk for that of a civic statue. She stood astride the rain-sodden path, brown-black eyes fixed upon the blocky outline of Monsoon Cottage. From her vantage point to one side, she could see the lights were on in the living room and in the double bedroom, oblongs of honey-yellow glowing feebly out of the moody greyness of late afternoon.

'Jing-bang, jing-bang,' she repeated. It had been Queenie Bhatt's favourite expression. The thought of her childhood friend made Mrs Banerjee relax her fortified position, sweep up her muddy sari skirts and press on. 'I loved you, Queenie,' she murmured. 'You and Daddy and . . . and . . . William . . .'

Her voice faltered as she reached the gate to Monsoon Cottage. William would be packing his clothes to move to The Metropole Hotel, to be reunited with that desiccated wife of his. What happened in the next few minutes would set the future course for Mrs Banerjee and she was seized by a determination so fierce it had colour . . . a menacing red aura that crackled around her contours.

'Come, come, tea for two?' she trilled, bursting with a bang and a thump through Monsoon Cottage's front door. She startled William who was coming out of the bedroom they shared, in either hand a small suitcase secured with tan leather straps.

'I don't have time . . .' William's voice trailed off at the sight of Mrs Banerjee's face. Her makeup was not of its customary freshness, but streaked and shifted. Her vermilion lipstick had dribbled clownishly from the corners of her bottom lip. She appeared to be radiating steam, like a wet blanket left to dry in the sun.

'Here, Premila,' he said, handing her a handkerchief.

She took it absently and patted her brow. William walked past her, down the hallway to the front door, swung it open and deposited his cases on the veranda. Then he turned to Mrs Banerjee and removed his khaki bush hat, twirling it in his hands.

'Time for goodbyes, my dear friend,' he said, looking downwards, apparently fascinated by his shoelaces. 'I have left a few things, in case Lydia wants to . . . well, anyway, I will send for them very soon.'

'Don't take your cases . . . You can tell Lydia everything and come straight back to Monsoon Cottage. To your home . . .'

He looked up at her and sighed. 'Premila, please. You know I can't do that. Lydia is my wife and I must do the honourable thing . . .'

'Men are leaving their wives every day, William, even honourable gentlemen like you. Besides, what about her kissing that cad in the foyer of Coronation Talkies . . . that Fraser-Gough fellow with the big hooter and ginger hair. Frightful looking, if you ask me . . .'

'Kissing? There was no kissing . . .'

'I know a kiss when I see one, William. Pucker up, out comes the tongue . . .'

'Oh, really, Premila! Simon Fraser-Gough is probably in prison by now. He tried to blackmail me. There was a photo . . . anyway, Charlotte Montague took me into her confidence and I am convinced nothing happened. I didn't tell Lydia . . . she would have been quite unhinged by it all.'

'Oh, yes, poor, poor Lydia.'

'Premila, stop it. She is my WIFE.'

Mrs Banerjee made a move towards William and he backed away. It was a slight retreat on his part but it was all Mrs Banerjee needed to soar into action.

'You cannot leave us,' she announced, clasping her hands together as if about to launch into an aria.

'Us? But Premila, dear, I will have to take Anil as well . . . I can arrange another servant for you.'

'I am perfectly able to organise servants of any shape or size or description, William. But I am not referring to Anil. I am talking about our baby. B-A-B-Y. Yours and mine. Here, here.'

Mrs Banerjee patted her stomach and peered down at it as if expecting the almost-baby to suddenly uncurl, reach out through quivering flesh and premium-quality tissue-fine Benares silk and shake its father's hand.

'Baby?'

William dropped his hat.

'Yes, baby, William. It is what eventuates when a man and a woman . . . a healthy woman such as myself with first-class child-bearing potential . . . have jiggery-pokery sex all day and all night.'

'All day and all night!' William spluttered. 'Premila, why do you always have to exaggerate everything. . . .'

Mrs Banerjee was crying.

'I need some fresh air.' She whimpered and pushed past him, down the veranda steps and into the small front garden of Monsoon Cottage.

She turned back and William was standing on the veranda as if atop a stage. She dropped with a thud to her knees and looked up at him from the lawn like a supplicant, head tilted.

William looked over Mrs Banerjee toward the dusk-shadowed valley. He didn't know how to calm her. He tried to summon a vision of his mother.

'Mother!' he yelled with a terrible boom that seemed to ricochet off the far hills and whip back to the faintly illuminated tableau.

'Yes, Mother,' confirmed Mrs Banerjee from her uncomfortable kneeling position. 'Ladies who give birth are mothers . . .'

William ignored her and continued to look out at the darkening sky. He was not a man who inhabited the past, and definitely not the most painful corners and slammed-shut cupboards of childhood memory.

He shut his eyes tight-tight.

His mother would know what to do but her serene face would not come to him. It had been too long since he dared venture into such dangerous mother-summoning territory. Anil had told him once about his Ghost Mother and her unheralded kitchen appearances and help with recipes and household advice and William had laughed uproariously and then felt ashamed when he saw Anil's crestfallen face.

He had not known how to comfort Anil either when Sunita had died in the bedroom of Bluebell Cottage. And when Lydia's father had gone and she needed her husband's love and protection, he had just sent her away. The only honourable thing he had done was not to raise the blackmail note with her but that was really, if he admitted it, because he wanted her out of Chalaili.

William looked down at Mrs Banerjee and realised what a preposterously sad sight she was, an enormous complex bundle plonked in the middle of the grass.

'Are you sure Mr Banerjee is not the father?'

'Quite sure . . . Mr Banerjee has never availed himself of . . . of. . . .'

She lifted her hands and made a sweeping outline of her body.

'Of all this.'

William thought of his first sexual encounter with Mrs

Banerjee and the comical way she had screamed and yelled. It had not occurred to him she was a virgin. It always seemed she was acting out some over-dramatic scenario from one of her talking pictures.

Perhaps she was acting now. It would be a clever trick to convince him to stay. William knew she loved the status of being an Englishman's mistress. He wasn't such a fool that he didn't realise everyone in Chalaili suspected his relationship with her was more than that of a lodger.

'Why not, Premila? Is he a homosexual?'

'Yes!' she cried.

That was enough for William. Obviously she was making it all up. He turned and picked up his bags, strode down the steps, edged around Mrs Banerjee and opened Monsoon Cottage's tipsy wire gate.

'It's time you learned to have a more realistic relationship with the truth, Premila.'

Mrs Banerjee hauled herself up at surprising speed and ran towards him, through the gate, slipping momentarily on the rain-rinsed lawn. William thought of the night at Coronation Talkies when she had performed her astonishingly dainty harem dance and unhooked her enormous beaded harness that defied the very word brassiere. Now she had that same burning glint in her eye.

'William,' she said, smiling at him with her gruesome upside-down lipstick line. 'There is no Mr Banerjee, as such. Well, he does exist somewhere, but we were never married. He jilted me. I am single. I can prove it. A film was made of the doomed wedding. The baby is yours and Lydia must be told about it and that I love you, William. That we love each other. When she hears

423

about my condition, she will understand that you must divorce her barren womb and marry me.'

'Marry you!' William's retort was a mixture of disbelief and anger. His face went the bruised-blue of a thundery sky. 'I could never marry you, Premila!'

'Why not?'

Mrs Banerjee's tone was dangerously challenging. She held her stomach and pursed her red-ruined lips.

'Wipe off that infernal lipstick, Premila,' he said in a low voice and turned to leave.

'Tell me why NOT, Mister Oh-So-Important Rain Wallah and Maharaja of the Monsoon. Oh yes, I know all the names they call you . . . Why NOT! Is it because you don't care about me and our baby . . .'

'I do care about you, Premila. I always will. But I don't believe there is a baby. It is a trick. How could there be a film? You would have told me before now . . . This is just your talking picture madness . . . Real life is simply not like this.'

'It is NOT a trick. Come inside, there is not just a film. I have doctor's reports and everything . . . Mary Christie is ordering me special wool from England. Lovely palest green and yellow, so knitting can be done in advance. Personally, I would like a son, daughters being known to be such troubles to their mothers . . .'

She prattled on and on, by now standing so close to William he could smell the caramel sweetness of her breath.

He closed his eyes and wondered if he was going to cry.

'I cannot marry you, Premila, because you are . . . you are . . .'

'Too fat?' demanded Mrs Banerjee.

She saw the yellow-eyed sugary-smelling cook from Kerala

waving a spoon at her, bringing it closer and closer to her little-girl mouth.

'Here comes rice pudding, missy, melt-in-the-mouth and all your favourite ingredients. Oh so nutty-butty, cashews, almonds, pistachios . . . Open wide. And open again, missy, do not be lonely, you are welcome in this kitchen any time, most welcome. Mother, Father need not know . . . open wide, be ready inside.'

Miss Premila Dhir, primary-school student and convenient justification for the sums that spidered down and around the columns of the cook's housekeeping ledger . . . But Madam Dhir, of course I must spend so much . . . Missy is demanding sweets day and night . . . What would you have me do?

'Too FAT?' Mrs Banerjee repeated, with a quaking roar.

'No!' William cried. Two sets of eyes snapped open.

'That's not it, Premila, don't be so silly.'

'It's because you are . . . you are, please understand why I must say this, Premila, you are a . . . a . . . native.'

'A native?'

Mrs Banerjee was so shocked she lunged forward and beat William's chest with her fists, moaning in disbelief.

'Premila, I am sorry. I am really, truly sorry. It's just how it is. You are a native and I am, well, I am English.'

The word was an absolution. William imbued E-n-g-l-i-s-h with so much weighty duty and circumstance that the burden of its implications caused him to fall backwards over the slippery ridge, his arms flailing and grasping at wind-hurried clouds as he was engulfed by the deep green boundlessness of Chalaili Valley. His screams evaporated to a whine. The whine and high creak of a tree branch in a storm. His khaki hat followed him, spinning in the air.

It was not just Englishness that effected William's exit. Mrs

425

Banerjee chose the moment just before his capitulation to enter into a swooning trance and press her body against his.

Mrs Banerjee regained her balance and looked into the nothingness beyond. She retreated to the wire-mesh fence, holding it for support. She heard the full-luxury ultra-modern Chrysler Air Flow Imperial pull to a stop at the intersection of the upper and lower ridges. The engine was switched off. There was the slam of a door.

'Vinod!'

She had forgotten she had told him to return in half-an-hour and reverse William down to The Metropole Hotel for his meeting with Lydia.

Mrs Banerjee picked up the suitcases by her feet and, whirling around and around like a discus thrower to ensure maximum velocity and distance, hurled them one after the other over the ridge.

Then she smoothed her hair, straightened her draperies and marched inside Monsoon Cottage, flexing her fingers to calm their trembling.

Mrs Banerjee was in the double bedroom, observing her streaked face in the dressing-table mirror, when Vinod knocked lightly on the front door and, without waiting for a reply, sauntered down the hall.

She was about to berate him for bursting in, when she saw the reflection of his amiable face. Now was not the time for lecturing servants on polite entrances. Vinod and Anil would be needed as her allies in the complicated days ahead.

'Oh, it's you, Vinod,' she said, as if greeting a friend casually encountered. She hoped he wouldn't notice the shakiness of her voice.

'Yes, come to collect Sahib Rushmore, as personally ordered by yourself, for Metropole Hotel transfer service.'

'He decided to walk instead,' Mrs Banerjee replied, wiping at her eyes and lips and cheeks with cold cream, the vigorous actions disguising her quivering mouth.

'Walk? What about his suitcases?' Vinod looked around the room.

'One in each hand. He would not be stopped.'

'But I didn't pass him on the way . . .'

'Vinod, dear, do not forget you are driving backwards today and it's possible to miss many things. Alternatively, he could have gone to that musty old weather office of his. Please, please, I cannot be held responsible for his exact whereabouts.'

Chapter Sixty-eight

CHALAILI
APRIL, 1938

THE SOLIGANJ WEEKLY OBSERVER

Mr K. Wallia of Wallia's Pickles and Daily Needs, Chota
Chalaili bazaar, has announced the arrival of double-
reinforced mountain model Hero Cycles, ideal for the
peculiar conditions of the Chalaili Hills.

*L*ydia waited in The Maharani Salon dining room of
The Metropole Hotel for William to arrive.

She felt giddy-headed and apprehensive. Their telephone call
that morning had not gone well and she stared out the window at
The Strand rehearsing the conversation she would have with William when he arrived.

An old man walked past, holding tightly to the hand of a little boy. A grandfather and grandson, she thought. The man said
something and pointed but the lad, instead of following the direction of the gesturing arm, turned his head upwards and peered at
the whiskery old face and beamed a smile so broad it almost split

his face. The old man cupped the child's face in gnarled hands and leant down and planted a kiss on a small tilted nose.

And then they went off, still hand in hand, the best of friends, the teacher and the pupil, the past and the future. The old man walked slowly so the lad could keep up with him and the boy walked slowly so his grandfather wouldn't be left behind. Lydia saw the complicit ruse in the way they kept perfect time, as if marching.

Was that the way she had walked with Daddy, Lydia wondered, when they ambled home from The White Horse Inn. Would a stranger, passing by or following along, have detected the completeness of their little world and nodded knowingly at the way they fitted together, like comfortable shoes.

Did the boy have a harridan mother at home, ready to roar at him for being late, then to turn to the old man (her father, perhaps) and berate him for slowness and carelessness. She would break the spell between them as idly as pulling at a loose thread.

'Mothers,' sighed Lydia aloud.

William's relationship with his mother must have been so complicated. When had Diana Rushmore realised her husband was in love with his brother's wife? Had there been stiff little parties and covert looks that lingered too long? Did Ellis Rushmore dress more finely than usual when his brother John and the silky Sylvia visited for tea? Were there arm-in-arm turns in the garden and a woman's face uplifted with a melting smile . . . Did a little boy notice his mother's tear-stained eyes?

Anjali Gupta brought Lydia the gin and tonic she had requested and looked past the Englishwoman and through the window.

'No sign of William yet?'

Lydia shook her head and swirled the ice cubes in her glass, dislodging three pips from the roughly cut slice of lemon.

She looked up at Anjali Gupta.

'I was just practising what to say to William,' she confided. 'We have to talk about a lot of things.'

'My mother always said not to be disappointed if a discussion did not go the way it was planned.' Anjali Gupta drew out a chair and joined Lydia at the table. 'She said to remember that the other person will not have learned the lines you have prepared for them.'

Lydia didn't have time to absorb the wisdom of this advice. Vinod swaggered into The Maharani Salon and loudly cleared his throat.

'Yes?' snapped Anjali Gupta, who had been meaning to have a word with Mrs Banerjee about the way her servants wandered around the hotel as if they were paying guests.

'Has Sahib Rushmore arrived yet? Apparently, he is walking.'

'Walking? Why would he be walking with suitcases and all to carry?'

'Mrs Banerjee told me just now . . .'

At the mention of her bosom friend's name, Anjali Gupta sneaked a look at Lydia but she was resolutely examining the pips floating in her drink.

'Well, don't just stand there. Go and find him and help him with his luggage. I have a room waiting and Memsahib Lydia is tired . . .'

'Yes, so very tired,' confirmed Lydia, standing up. 'May I check into the room, or must we wait for William?'

'Come now, I will take you upstairs. I am sure William can't be far away. Go, Vinod, you first-class dawdler . . .'

꩜

Vinod drove backwards along The Strand and down to William's office. His bicycle was there, leaning against the side of the creaky old vine-covered building, but William was not at his desk, nor to be found in the dark corridors.

Vinod resumed his seat and reversed up to The Metropole Hotel, where Anjali Gupta was standing behind the front desk, writing notes in the ledger.

'No sign of him,' Vinod announced.

'The Empire Club? Lakshmi Hair and Beauty Studio? Church, even . . .'

Anjali Gupta knew it was absurd to think of William under one of Poppy Lee's hair-dryers, although there was a scant chance he could be there, conspiring with Mrs Banerjee, who she hadn't seen all afternoon.

'You go to the club and the church, please, Vinod.' The latter seemed unlikely, too, unless he was asking for forgiveness for his recent transgressions in the Banerjee boudoir.

Vinod sped off and Anjali Gupta walked the short distance along the arcade to the Lakshmi Hair and Beauty Studio but it was in darkness, a padlock on the door. She looked at her watch: after six and darkness fast approaching.

Mary Christie was closing up, too, and the two women, turning away from the facing doors, almost collided.

'Hello, Anjali, how are you?

'Very fine, thank you, but in something of a hurry . . .'

'Have you seen Mrs Banerjee today? Her order for knitting materials has arrived . . . the loveliest palest lemon and spring green angora wool you can imagine . . .'

Anjali Gupta called over her shoulder as she ran off. 'No, not since this morning.'

431

Mary Christie watched Anjali Gupta's retreating figure until she disappeared into the hotel's foyer. The double glass doors swished back and forth after she had swept though.

Lydia lay down on the double bed, rearranging the two pillows so her head was at an angle. She had never been in a guestroom at The Metropole Hotel and was surprised at the shabbiness. It smelt musty and the uncurtained window was streaky. Anjali Gupta kept the downstairs area so clean and fresh but Lydia knew there were few guests and like everyone else in Chalaili, the hotelier's wife was no doubt prone to grim periods of inertia.

'Monsoon Cottage,' said Lydia, addressing the ceiling. She felt uneasy about her husband's move from Bluebell Cottage. 'Secrets, more secrets,' she murmured, turning on her right side and closing her eyes.

Lydia fell asleep for several hours and awoke in darkness to a soft but insistent tapping on the door.

'William? William!' she called out and the door opened slowly, a hand crept around the door jamb and flicked on the light.

She rubbed her eyes. It was Anjali Gupta, followed by Anil and Vinod. The three entered the room and stood side by side, like an official deputation. It bothered Lydia that two male servants should be standing over her bed but Anjali Gupta was in charge and apparently she saw nothing untoward about the arrangement.

'Yes?' said Lydia, straightening her hair and sitting up.

It was Anil who replied. 'Sahib William is not here?'

'Clearly not,' Lydia laughed. 'Unless you think he is under the bed!'

'Under the bed,' repeated Vinod, dropping to one knee.

'Get up, you silly fool.'

Anjali Gupta pulled at his collar.

'Lydia,' she said, sitting beside her on the faded leaf-patterned coverlet. 'William seems to have disappeared . . .'

Lydia looked at her blankly and then at the two men. No one was smiling or looking sly-eyed, as if attempting to conceal a joke.

'He left, er, Mrs Banerjee's residence . . . Well, he left there, and he has not been seen since.'

'Perhaps he went to his office or . . . or . . . The Empire Club. You know, for a drink.'

'No, Vinod has checked most thoroughly. He is very reliable, as you know.'

Lydia did not know anything about the extent of Vinod's reliability, especially after her experience of his back-to-front chauffeuring, but it didn't seem the time to contradict Anjali Gupta.

'Anil has checked Chota Chalaili and the station . . .'

'The station?'

Lydia gulped.

'To book a train ticket for tomorrow morning's service,' announced Vinod, self-importantly.

'Memsahib Lydia knows what stations are for,' said Anil, administering Vinod a sharp elbow to his ribs.

Anjali Gupta was still seated by Lydia, patting her right arm. 'He seems to have left Chalaili.'

'But how, why . . .'

Anjali Gupta felt she could answer the first element of Lydia's question. He must have taken his bicycle. Vinod had seen it parked by his office but during a later search, supervised by Ram Gupta, there was no sign of it.

As for why . . . Perhaps he had run off with Mrs Banerjee,

although there would be no fitting Picture Madam on a Hero Cycle, even William's relatively new double-reinforced mountain model.

'Anil, tell me again, how was Mrs Banerjee when you saw her earlier this evening?'

'Perfectly well . . . getting ready for night business.'

Anjali Gupta winced.

'Yes, I picked her up at Monsoon Cottage and dropped her at Coronation Talkies,' added Vinod with a grin. He was basking in the knowledge that Anjali Gupta found him reliable.

'She wasn't planning to go somewhere . . . Bombay, perhaps?'

'Bombay?' chorused Vinod, Anil and Lydia as all three looked at Anjali Gupta in surprise.

'Silly me,' Anjali Gupta replied. 'But . . . but that is where William must have gone, urgently called by his superiors there. Weather business and all that.'

'He would never go anywhere without telling me,' said Anil, shaking his head.

'Urgent mission down the Chalaili Hills requires the services of the Flumcafi, not a bicycle,' said Vinod, who very much hoped every-one would forget about William's Hero Cycle. It was almost new and Vinod anticipated he could sell it for an excellent price down at Soli-ganj if only he could escape unseen down the Chalaili Hills.

Anjali Gupta was pleased Mrs Banerjee was not in the room to be assaulted by Vinod's airy use of the Flumcafi abbreviation.

They all nodded, even Lydia, at the fanciful thought that William would take a bicycle trip to Bombay.

'He must have had a local errand,' whispered Lydia.

'Yes, yes, local errand,' the other three repeated, gratefully, holding on to the words. But their voices were small and unsteady.

Chapter Sixty-nine

CHALAILI
APRIL, 1938

'Confession of error is like a broom that sweeps away
dirt and leaves the surface cleaner than before.'
M. K. (MAHATMA) GANDHI

Two weeks after William's disappearance, Lydia moved into Monsoon Cottage. Mrs Banerjee had given her an open invitation knowing, thanks to Anjali Gupta's inside information, that the Englishwoman's passage to England was booked one clear month before the baby was due. It didn't occur to Mrs Banerjee that the baby could be early. She knew enough of life's hurdles to believe there would be no premature release from the watermelon-shaped bundle she was carrying.

But it was Anil who helped Lydia make up her mind to accept Mrs Banerjee's invitation. He arrived at The Metropole Hotel one morning, holding a red rose, as she was having breakfast. Ram and Anjali Gupta witnessed him handing Lydia the flower and exchanged amused looks, by now well used to Anil's regular pillaging of their garden.

'Please, Memsahib Lydia, we need you there. Mrs Banerjee is very tired and lonely.'

'Lo-ne-ly?'

Lydia attenuated the syllables, tossing them into the echoing cavern of The Maharani Salon. The word hung shivering in the air, like the reverberation of a crashed cymbal.

'Lonely, lonely, lonely.' She peered searchingly at the ceiling to see where the word might land. Anil turned to Anjali Gupta with appealing eyes. The hotelier's wife looked away and busied herself with straightening an already straightened tablecloth.

Lydia stood and walked into the hallway, across the little foyer and out to the front steps. She breathed deeply. The air in Chalaili was always charged with pine, like a hospital.

Lydia had known instinctively that Mrs Banerjee was pregnant. Her large girth had disguised her condition well but after William vanished, all vanity had gone to the wind, including the enslavement of foundation garments.

'Who is the father, Anil?' asked Lydia, turning to face him as he stood uncertainly by her side, twisting the rescued rose she had tossed aside as she left The Maharani Salon.

'Anil not father!' he exclaimed. 'Mr Banerjee, husband of Mrs Banerjee, is father of course.'

Lydia realised he had misunderstood her question and she gave a little laugh. Anil laughed, too, and they looked at each other for what seemed to Lydia like an eternity.

'Baby, baby,' said Lydia.

'Baby, baby,' repeated Anil, unsure how much Lydia had guessed.

'Perhaps one day you will have a baby, Anil.'

'Yes, my betrothed bride is in her village.'

'Really, Anil, I had no idea. Are you marrying Devi? Does she live at Monsoon Cottage, too?'

'Devi?'

Anil looked away. Lydia knew nothing of the events of the past six months. If was as if Chalaili existed in a great bubble untouched by the outside world, unknowable by those who attempted to look in.

'I am betrothed to Aruna, Mrs Banerjee's former servant.'

Lydia remembered Aruna, the attractive girl who followed her mistress everywhere, casually repeating Picture Madam's decorative English expressions.

'Bamboozle,' Aruna had said to Lydia one day in the Chalaili Post Office queue as if it were a standard greeting.

'Bamboozle,' Lydia had replied and she smiled as she remembered Florence Gordon's raised eyebrows and shut-purse lips.

'Where is Devi?'

'She works at Coronation Talkies as assistant to Mr K. K. Rao.'

Lydia sighed. Mrs Banerjee always organised everything so perfectly, while she had been incapable of even getting poor coughing Sunita to a doctor.

'I will move to Monsoon Cottage tomorrow, Anil, but there is one condition.'

Anil felt uncomfortable at the mention of that word condition. It was how Mrs Banerjee described her pregnancy.

'Mrs Banerjee must agree to a memorial service for Sunita in the garden of Monsoon Cottage . . .'

'No, please,' Anil interrupted. 'Sunita is safe in the garden of Bluebell Cottage.'

'Sunita is alone, Anil. Alone, alone, alone, alone . . . She must not be left alone. None of us must be alone. Do you understand?'

Lydia's eyes were wild and bright and Anil knew he must not argue. If Lydia didn't agree to live at Monsoon Cottage, his services could be terminated by Mrs Banerjee's mother, still ensconced at The Metropole Hotel. She definitely had her eye on the second bedroom for herself, and his cosy kitchen alcove, which still smelled stirringly of Aruna's sandalwood soap, for her declining servant and those ugly caged birds.

⁂

Mrs Banerjee listened to Anil as he spoke of Lydia's proposed memorial service for Sunita and wanted to know all the details of where she came from and how she managed to die at Bluebell Cottage.

'William Rushmore let her live there in the kitchen . . . with pneumonia, coughing and spitting?'

It was a rhetorical question. She held both arms of her chair and rose with difficulty, making her way to the window seat in Monsoon Cottage's sitting room. The embracing view, with its cloud-colliding mountains, never failed to lift her spirits but today she saw something foreign amid the greenness. She sent Anil off to fetch tea, not wanting to share the spectre of William Rushmore sitting calmly on a passing cumulus, regarding her with a most sceptical expression.

Despite her role in his accidental demise, Mrs Banerjee felt little emotion about William. Deep in her heart she had doubted he would have married her or acted as a proper father to the forthcoming baby.

She had merely planned to persuade him to get Lydia out

438

of the way, make her feel horribly unwanted so she would flee back to that cold, huddled England with her stick legs and orderly bosom.

The most Mrs Banerjee had been expecting was a continuing relationship with William, the promise of sex and comfort and companionship. Now she had discovered he was a man who allowed a fatally ill prostitute to die in his house, and not before she had foisted her germs on to the kitchen utensils.

'Why didn't William take Sunita to the hospital?' she screamed at Anil as he delivered the tea tray.

'It was the time of the monsoon . . . he was measuring rain.'

'Rain! Rain! Rain!' Mrs Banerjee shouted, banging the bowed glass of the picture window. 'Look, there's your precious Rain Wallah!'

She grabbed Anil's arm and forced him to look out. He saw nothing but blue-green valley and blue-grey sky and one lazily drifting cloud.

'I can't see anything,' Anil protested, trying to wriggle free from Mrs Banerjee's grip.

'Look, on the cloud. He's . . . he's . . . oh bugger, he's raising his hat at me.'

Mrs Banerjee let her arms droop by her sides.

'No one ever knew that man.'

'I knew him,' protested Anil, who had had enough of women's unfathomable theatrics for one day. 'His mother lived on a cloud . . . he told me so one morning when he was having a cup of tea on the front steps and she passed by.'

At this revelation, Mrs Banerjee fell back onto the window seat.

'Did she haunt him? When he looked at clouds, was she always there . . . by any chance?'

'Oh yes,' replied Anil, who was enjoying his employer's discomposure. 'She was knitting clouds all day long.'

'Something strong to drink, please . . . a potion of some sort,' managed Mrs Banerjee, in a tiny voice.

Anil took pity on his employer and prepared her a pregnancy special, as personally demonstrated to him in the kitchen at The Metropole Hotel by Anjali Gupta, who seemed well versed in baby matters for such a childless woman. He warmed a saucepan of milk and added saffron, jaggery and ground almonds, stirring slowly, slowly.

'Potatoes with ginger to soothe . . . beans with garlic to cleanse . . . carrots with ghee for strength . . .'

Ghost Mother had arrived in a puff of turmeric-coloured smoke.

'Okra with . . .'

'Mother, please,' interrupted Anil. 'I would rather know about William Rushmore. Is he with you . . . up there in the clouds? With his own mother, I am thinking.'

Mrs Banerjee was advancing heavily down the hallway complaining of her thirst. Ghost Mother disappeared, leaving nothing but a few bright yellow spots on the kitchen's earthen floor.

❧

Anil used his byzantine network of contacts in the wandering lanes of Chota Chalaili to organise for the unmarked grave to be dug up and Sunita's body moved in the back of a pony cart. He stood with Mrs Banerjee, Lydia, Devi and Vinod as his sister was properly laid in Monsoon Cottage's garden. Mrs Banerjee had ordered a small marble stone that read simply: Here lies Sunita, beloved sister of Anil and friend to many.

Anil had not been around when Mrs Banerjee phoned through the order and she had not known Sunita's family name or date of birth. None of the little gathering seemed to mind the slightness of the gravestone's inscription and everyone cried, including Vinod, who was so overcome he declined afternoon refreshments and catapulted to the Flumcafi, tapping his wristwatch.

Mr K. K. Rao was very sceptical of a Christian burial for a Hindu and said he would like to attend, to see if the soul protested. But Mrs Banerjee informed him that the various religions of her servants and their first-blood relatives and the journeys of their souls were none of his business and ordered him to stand outside The Metropole Hotel in case Leela Dhir emerged.

'Take her to tea . . . or something.'

All she needed was her mother to come wandering over to Monsoon Cottage and discover a prostitute's grave amid the mango trees. Every time Leela Dhir arrived in the full-luxury ultra-modern Chrysler Air Flow Imperial, for she refused to walk anywhere in this staircase of a town, she monopolised Lydia. She banged on about Bombay high life and the latest imported refrigerators and sharing hairdressers with the Vicereine of India. She would admire Lydia's brooches and initialled handkerchiefs and lipsticks until the Englishwoman would be fainting with boredom. Frequently Lydia just gave the things to Leela Dhir and all but bustled her out the front door and over the ridge.

'No, no, please not over the ridge,' pleaded Mrs Banerjee to her reflection in her three-way bedroom mirror.

The Carter family at Bluebell Cottage had been horrified at the disclosure of a low-caste corpse amid the luxuriant plantings

441

of the former Rushmore garden. Mrs Carter had every last crevice of the kitchen scrubbed with carbolic soap, up and down and in and out, and reported all details of the sorry affair to the unflappable Crows at The Empire Club.

The pearl-complexioned Emma Carter wept and wept at the news and required revival by her current beau, a handsome subaltern in the last stages of recovery at The Chalaili Sanatorium for the Tubercular. They toasted the mysterious Sunita with Calcutta Cups, a mix of Guinness and tonic water that Emma found disgusting to swallow, but she loved the jolly after-effects. They spoke of Sunita as if she were a dew-fresh garden sprite, imbuing her with a meaningfulness she had not enjoyed during life.

Emma's tightly bunned sister, Elizabeth, merely raised an eyebrow at it all and carried on with her gummings and stampings at Chalaili Post Office, which she called the CPO with a grandeur that suggested it was a prominent mail exchange and not a musty two-room building responsible for one delivery per week. She bossed about the clerical staff with such force that they occasionally longed for the return of the pneumatic Florence Gordon.

Elizabeth Carter was referred to behind her back as Post Madam, but not so discreetly that she wasn't aware of the name, and it thrilled her to share a status, by association, with her heroine, Picture Madam.

✑

The day after Sunita's service, Mrs Banerjee despatched Anil to William's office and had him pack up his papers and files into cardboard boxes. Vinod drove Anil with the cargo to the intersection of the upper and lower ridges and the two servants ferried the boxes to the garden shed. Then Vinod disappeared in the Flumcafi.

Unbeknown to Mrs Banerjee, he'd had a tip-off that there was an unusually high number of passengers due to arrive on the morning train from Soliganj.

She walked out to the garden to supervise Anil and saw her tea-chest. Anil noticed her looking at it and turned his head away.

'How long have you known, Anil?'

'A long time,' he replied in an almost inaudible whisper.

'Did you tell anyone?'

'No, never.'

'Why not?' she asked, settling herself onto the chest. Anil stood closer to her, afraid she would crash through.

'Because you are a good woman, Mrs Banerjee. Everyone thinks so. You make people feel special.'

His eyes were unable to meet hers but if they had, he would have seen tears.

Minutes passed before she spoke.

'The Guptas know,' she told him. 'That no-good Vinod gave them evidence.'

'Vinod is not a bad man,' said Anil, surprised with himself that he should defend the car-renting hustler. Vinod had told him about the newspaper cutting and how he had given it to Anjali Gupta for safe-keeping.

'He could have tried to blackmail you or just told everyone, to make fun. But he didn't want to hurt you. We all admire you, Mrs Banerjee. You make our lives so much . . .'

Anil struggled for the right word. Mrs Banerjee looked at the ground, her slightly trembling shoulders indicating she was crying.

'So much bigger . . .'

'Thank you, my dear Anil,' she sniffled. 'Anyway, my untrustworthy mother is here now and soon I will have no more secrets. But, please, do not tell Lydia of this. That is all I ask.'

She stood up and left the shed. She knew she could depend on Anil.

He watched her walk towards Monsoon Cottage, the flailing hem of her deep blue sari stirring the dust.

☙

Lydia soon found that she liked sharing Monsoon Cottage with the unstoppable Mrs Banerjee. The bungalow rang with laughter and majestic commands, which Anil attended to without any sign of complaint. The women went to Coronation Talkies for each new film and it was Lydia who suggested uniforms for Anil, Vinod and even Anjali Gupta on Saturdays.

Mrs Banerjee designed long-sleeved silk shirts with entwined C.T. stitching on the top right-hand pocket. Western-style shirts, completely modern, in a very announcing yellow. Anjali Gupta wore hers over her sari and frequently got caught up in drifts of fabric escaping through the cuffs. Ram Gupta thought it wise to make no comment.

After returning from Coronation Talkies, the women talked well into the night at Monsoon Cottage, Lydia with a double gin and Mrs Banerjee with cocoa or a pregnancy special drink.

Lydia often spluttered at Mrs Banerjee's talking picture post-mortems.

'You squashed cabbage leaf!' she yelled at Anil one evening when he spilled drops of cocoa in her saucer. The women had been to see *Pygmalion* and Mrs Banerjee had made notes of Professor Henry Higgins' most colourful turns of phrase.

Mrs Banerjee collected phrases, Lydia discovered, and showed them off, like a collector of coins or things of value might display their prize pieces.

'You're pixilated, Lydia,' she declared. It was a favourite word of Mrs Banerjee's, from *Mr Deeds Goes to Town*, and she had not had much occasion to use it.

'Pixilated, pixilated, pickshilated, pickshilated' repeated Lydia. The word became damnably difficult to pronounce as the evening wore on.

Mr K.K. Rao was practically running the picture theatre although he sometimes opened late, for no proper reason, other than he was occupied with visits to Leela Dhir, still installed, but at a heavily discounted tariff, in The Maharani Suite. Coronation Talkies was just making enough money to keep going and Anjali Gupta refused to be paid for her Saturday evening services, referring to her employment as her private escape.

On warm mornings, Anil brought them tea trays to the veranda and laughed with them at their little jokes. He turned away when Mrs Banerjee patted her mammoth stomach, hinting at a lavish night out in Bombay and a friendly reunion with the elusive Mr Banerjee. He wished Aruna would return from her village so he could ask her what he should do. He wasn't looking forward to the arrival of this two-colour baby.

It was so strangely convivial that Mrs Banerjee began to fear Lydia would delay her departure to England. Mrs Banerjee had to be careful not to be too opposed to the notion of William's return, a possibility still entertained by Lydia.

Lydia was aghast, however, that Mrs Banerjee had had William's office stripped.

'But when . . . if . . . he comes back?'

'Thieves will take everything from his unoccupied office, dear lady. It is for security purposes only.'

At first, the police had been involved in the search. Two senior officers spent a week at The Metropole Hotel, questioning everyone of interest to their investigations, conducting their interviews at a prime windowside table in The Maharani Salon as Ram Gupta's waiters elbowed each other aside, arguing who would serve the next round of tea.

Mrs Banerjee had been one of the first of William's acquaintances to be summoned. She was his landlady and the last person to see him.

She replied briskly to the men's questions, wiping her brow with a rose-scented handkerchief and sighing heavily.

'What were the last words Mr Rushmore said to you before he, er, left your bungalow, Mrs Banerjee?'

'Aah, let me see . . . I believe he shouted goodbye.'

'Shouted?'

'It was windy and wet . . . possibly you are not familiar with the climate in Chalaili?'

There was a stiff silence during which the officers closely examined their freshly delivered slices of a very good cherry-speckled cake.

Mrs Banerjee rose and approached their side of the table, depositing a pile of complimentary tickets on the white cloth.

'I do hope you will avail yourselves of my picture theatre during your visit to Chalaili? I am showing *A Day at the Races*, a comedy starring the Marx Brothers, although personally I do not think they are blood relatives, so many different hair styles . . .'

'Yes, yes, most kind, most kind,' the more senior man replied, spraying particles of fruit cake.

❧

Each morning during her stay at Monsoon Cottage, Lydia tried to call George Windsor, William's superior, at the Bureau of Meteorology in Bombay. His secretary hesitated and obfuscated, citing meetings, field trips and visiting VIPs.

Lydia felt completely defeated. William, she decided, had simply run away, unable to deal with her knowledge of his childhood. She scanned the far side of Chalaili Valley, half expecting to see smoke rising from the isolated forestry service *dak* bungalow.

'William!' she screamed one morning, pressed against Monsoon Cottage's front fence, shaking her fist at the sky.

Anil raced out, expecting to see William walking along the ridge. Lydia stood pale and still, white knuckles gripping the wire mesh. Mrs Banerjee appeared on the top step and looked up at the clouds.

'Don't you ever sleep? And why don't you jolly well take off that stupid hat.'

Lydia stared at Mrs Banerjee's retreating back.

'I will return to England, Anil.'

Lydia's voice was small and cold. Anil looked behind her and saw Mrs Banerjee closing the curtains with a determined swish. Since William had disappeared, she had developed an aversion to looking out of windows.

'Maybe you will see William in England?'

Lydia looked at Anil curiously.

'Do you really think he went to England?'

Anil shifted his feet and looked at the clouds.

447

'I think he is with his mother. In the sky. The English sky.'

Lydia looked up, too. 'You don't believe he ran away from me. You think he's dead, don't you?'

'Yes,' replied Anil, and turned away.

Chapter Seventy

CHALAILI
JUNE, 1938

THE SOLIGANJ WEEKLY OBSERVER
A drinks reception will be held in The Maharani Salon
of The Metropole Hotel, The Strand, Chalaili, at 4 p.m.
on the nineteenth of June, to farewell Mrs William
Rushmore who leaves for England next week, after the
unfortunate disappearance of her husband. Friends and
colleagues of Mr Rushmore welcome.

Lydia refused to leave Chalaili without a memorial service for William. There were protestations
from all quarters, save Mrs Banerjee at Monsoon Cottage, where
things were uncharacteristically silent, that he was not officially dead, merely missing. But Lydia would not be deterred.
A small drinks reception in William's honour was organised at
The Metropole Hotel, even though Anjali Gupta insisted that the
notice in *The Soliganj Weekly Observer* should indicate it was a farewell for Lydia.

Most of his associates from The Empire Club were in attendance and a sprinkling of Indian Forestry Service officers from other stations in the Western Ghats stood in unaccustomed suits and polished black shoes.

'Jungle Wallahs,' murmured Mary Christie to the bunned and bespectacled Elizabeth Carter as the older woman manoeuvred herself around the tanned lean men during the service, making luminous eye contact. She whimpered with disappointment when none of them stayed more than a socially acceptable half-hour.

George Windsor had made his way up from Bombay and delivered a meandering speech, all to do with William's contribution to the advancement of society's knowledge of the treacherous patterns of the monsoon, which made tears slosh down Lydia's cheeks as she thought of his cloud-knitting and rain-crying mother. She decided to forgive George Windsor for his telephone avoidance tactics.

'Who was he, really?' Lydia asked Mrs Banerjee and Anjali Gupta as they stood beside her, clutching their drinks.

Both women looked at the ground and the moment was rescued by Anil.

'He hated roses, Mem,' he said to Lydia and she smiled a little. The flower had been handed to her earlier, thoughtfully she supposed, by Dorothy Creswell-Smythe.

Mrs Banerjee, with none of her gaiety in evidence, was like a perished balloon.

The Crows were a gaggle of black, from toe to towering hat. Dorothy Creswell-Smythe refrained from a peacock feather adornment just in case that common postal clerk Florence Gordon had read about William's memorial service and decided to march up from Soliganj and show her treacherous face. Of course this omission in the matter of headgear was obvious to Charlotte Montague whose lips quivered with victorious mirth.

'*Two* grieving widows . . . but only one of them pregnant,' laughed Charlotte Montague to her husband, who muttered back that her sharp tongue could mow a lawn. He had to admit to himself, however, that he was as intrigued as the rest of the gathering by the sight of Mrs Rushmore and the ballooning Mrs Banerjee side by side.

Mrs Banerjee held Lydia by the arm, as if she were in danger of floating off. In turn, Anjali Gupta held on to Mrs Banerjee, so the two smaller women looked like bookends, shouldering a huge load.

Charlotte Montague looked keenly at Lydia. You have not *requested* enough of life, she thought. You settled for far too little. Charlotte Montague wondered if she should tell Lydia about her note to William about Simon Fraser-Gough and their subsequent telephone conversation, polite but slightly strained. It could have gone so wrong if William had not believed Lydia's innocence. But he did. Simply, fully.

She had been right to meddle. Just this once.

Charlotte Montague moved towards Lydia and stood by her side.

'Hello, dear.'

'Hello, Charlotte. I have been meaning to call on you . . .'

'No explanations necessary. I just wanted to tell you one thing.'

Lydia looked at her expectantly.

'William loved you. That's all.'

'But . . .'

Charlotte Montague was already leaving, her husband in her wake.

Lydia was about to follow but she felt Mrs Banerjee's grip tighten on her arm.

'I must sit down, Lydia. The baby . . .'

Vinod and Devi stood to one side with a shabby woman in a massive cardigan. She was wearing wellington boots and had handed a cage containing two bright green birds to Mr K. K. Rao, who took it without comment.

Ram Gupta kept apologising profusely to Lydia and Mrs Banerjee that his premises were so humble, so unworthy . . . He addressed both women equally, as if each had been widowed. It would be some weeks before the bruise on his leg completely disappeared, where his wife had delivered a surreptitious but effective kick with her yoga-toned right foot.

Leela Dhir sat in a corner chair, dressed in a fresh white sari, her strong grey locks elaborately coiffed, courtesy of a morning session at the Lakshmi Hair and Beauty Studio. Noticing Mr K. K. Rao carrying her precious birds, she signalled him over. 'Come, come,' she chirped.

As the waiters circulated with aerated drinks, vegetable samosa and sandwiches, Mrs Banerjee noticed that Mr K. K. Rao was still engaged in conversation with her mother, who appeared wildly animated, her eyes as large as ink wells as she regaled the projectionist with stories of Bombay society. Mrs Banerjee was pretty certain the words Pink Fantasia and Kelvinator were being mentioned.

Lydia had sunk into a chair, clutching an untouched drink. Anjali Gupta sat beside her for long intervals, holding her free hand. Gita was clumping about in the wellington boots, taking sandwiches three at a time from the tray. 'Don't you have other footwear?' demanded Mrs Banerjee of her mother's servant. 'Where are your sandals?'

'In the lift at Pink Fantasia,' she replied, sprinkling moist particles of curried egg, taking full advantage of her unexpected elevation from semi-imprisoned menial to hotel guest.

'The lift?'

'Your mother made me give them to a young woman who was living in the lift with her baby. She said she was the madonna herself.'

Mrs Banerjee began to feel queasy but she didn't know if it was the realisation her mother might be going mad or another bout of morning sickness. She felt she was being watched. She rushed to the windows of The Maharani Salon and hastily drew the velvet curtains. There was a murmuring among the guests at the sudden dimness.

Mrs Banerjee didn't care two hoots about their frank stares. She was in no mood for a heavenly intervention by William Rushmore with his infernal cocked eyebrows.

⁙

That night, Lydia telephoned the Rushmores in Finchley, Surrey, to tell them of William's disappearance. Her passage was booked on one of the last passenger liners from Bombay to Southampton. War in Europe loomed and already many ships were being converted to troop carriers.

There was no point delaying the terrible news any longer.

John took the receiver after Sylvia had been told. She had gasped, a strangled cry turning into an otherworldly scream.

'I had better attend to her, dear,' he told Lydia.

'We are so very sorry,' he added. 'If you would care to stay with us, then . . . I . . . we . . . would like that very much. It is what William would want . . . would have wanted, too.'

His voice choked and drifted off and Sylvia's wails could be heard echoing along the hallways of the silent cottage in Finchley, Surrey, ricocheting around unwelcoming rooms. Lydia imagined Sylvia's screams as things of substance, hard and glittering, cutting through the walls, shattering the windows, cracking the chimney, bursting over the village of Finchley like black thunder.

Chapter Seventy-one

CHALAILI
SEPTEMBER, 1938

*M*rs Rajat Banerjee, nee Premila Dhir, experienced her
first contractions in the front row of the First Class
section of Coronation Talkies, with Claudette Colbert and Clark
Gable on the screen and her mother by her side.

As her wails went up, the Nightingales stayed put with their
box of assorted chocolates, debating the merits of hazelnut whirls
versus strawberry creams. Anita and Sonny, visitors from Soliganj
on an illicit date, broke free of their arousing tangle and scooted
through different doors. Leela Dhir caught Sonny and demanded
he race to The Metropole Hotel and fetch Anjali Gupta.

Within twenty minutes, the expectant mother and Official

Banerjee Well-Wishers arrived at Chalaili Hospital after a sardine-squash journey in the full-luxury ultra-modern Chrysler Air Flow Imperial, driven at breakneck speed by Vinod, who had had to eject a Romantic Couple well before such an exit was decently warranted.

Mrs Banerjee was seated uncomfortably on a heat-of-the-moment-discarded sandal on the back seat. Anil had catapulted himself into the car at the last minute, landing on his employer's shelf-like excuse for a lap. She could scarce tell which pain was worse, the sharp birthing contractions or Anil's right elbow in her stomach.

'And if you call this automobile the Flumcafi one more time, I will kill you, no jing-bang trouble at all,' screamed Mrs Banerjee, who decided there was never likely to be a better time to let fly at her servants and to hell with non-sequiturs.

Vinod ducked, expecting his employer to throw something at him. Which she would have, gladly, if she could have moved.

He wondered if she knew about the Romantics as well. He sighed with relief when she shifted her fury to Anil.

'Get off my stomach, you number one idiot among idiots!'

Anil tried to move but he was wedged. Leela Dhir took up most of the other side of the back seat. He was trying to lift himself up when the car stopped and Vinod hopped out. The doors on the full-luxury ultra-modern Chrysler Air Flow Imperial opened towards the centre of the vehicle. Suicide doors, they called them, according to Sameep Shirodkar, who had purchased the vehicle in Bombay on Mrs Banerjee's behalf and according to her luxury-loving wishes.

At the best of times, Mrs Banerjee's exit from the back seat was ungainly. She shoved Anil and he tipped out on to the ground.

Her mother climbed over her yelling for first-class doctors. Vinod stood to attention and saluted, behaving like the chauffeur he had never been.

Mrs Banerjee let out a tormented yell that could be heard from one sorry end of Chalaili to the other.

☙

It was this odd gathering that greeted the hospital admissions staff, including a young male visitor from Soliganj wearing a shawl the colour of a spring sky. Anil and Leela Dhir supported Mrs Banerjee, all holding hands and lurching as if slightly tipsy.

The child was born as the dawn sneaked in, pale and fuzzy as a peach, over the high hills and dipping valleys of Chalaili. Anjali Gupta, Anil and Vinod waited outside the delivery room, seated together on a hard bench. Leela Dhir slept in a high-backed chair, a white hospital blanket she had imperiously commanded wrapped tightly around her.

'Ladies, ladies,' called the nurse. 'Come and see the baby boy.'

She rudely told the men they could wait their turn as they attempted to rush in front of Anjali Gupta. Leela Dhir snoozed on, snoring lightly.

Mr K. K. Rao had appeared in a great rush from the direction of The Metropole Hotel and stood by Leela Dhir's chair, his grey hair an alarming new black, as if he had suffered a reversal of shock.

Anjali Gupta leant over the crib by the hospital bed as Mrs Banerjee fixed her with a determined glare.

'Look, Premila, he has blue eyes,' she murmured, gazing at the baby's crinkled little face.

'Rajat Banerjee is Anglo-Indian. All mixed up, Scottish, too . . .'

Mrs Banerjee's eyes never left her best friend's face.

'This is how you treat me, lying there with my grandson beside you and strangers gathered around you but, oh no, do you wake your mother . . .' Leela Dhir had arrived in an eruption of streaming wool.

'I am not exactly a stranger, Mrs Dhir,' Anjali Gupta corrected her.

'Not you, dear lady,' boomed Leela Dhir as she attempted to unravel her arms from the blanket to gesticulate at the nurse.

'I mean this never-before-seen woman . . . who is she?'

'It's the nurse, Mother, which is why she is wearing a nurse's uniform.'

'Yes, yes, very well . . . now where is my grandson?'

Leela Dhir bustle-hopped towards the crib and as she did so, Premila twisted herself to one side and caught her mother's arm. As she unravelled from the coarse blanket, Leela Dhir's clothing became flecked with white woollen fluff.

'Please, Mummy . . .'

Anjali Gupta walked away to look out the window, her eyes filled with tears. She feared for her friend. Her over-active mother could hardly be trusted not to reveal every last detail of the Banerjee wedding disgrace.

Leela Dhir looked into her daughter's face, heavy with fear and still slightly swollen with pain.

'Please don't tell anyone about Rajat Banerjee, Mummy . . .' she murmured.

Leela Dhir unpeeled Mrs Banerjee's fingers one by one and gave her a wink. She looked into the crib.

'The baby's eyes are blue!'

Mrs Banerjee shut her eyes as tightly as she could. She saw a Leela Dhir-shaped space in the hospital ward where her Mother had been standing before she champagne-popped into the atmosphere and buzzed about the room and flew out the window and shouted 'Blue! Blue! Blue!' all over Chalaili like a town crier.

Mrs Banerjee opened one eye very slowly and peeped out. Leela Dhir was holding her grandson with a beatific smile on her face.

'Mummy, I was telling Anjali Gupta that Rajat Banerjee's family has English blood, Scottish even . . .'

'Oh, yes,' Leela Dhir airily replied. 'That Banerjee crowd is more mixed-up than you could imagine.

'Now, Anjali, would you be a dear and get that bone-lazy Vinod to drive to your hotel and fetch my servant. Tell her to bring me a coat. I am not properly dressed for a hospital engagement.'

She looked down at the sleeve of her cardigan and flicked off several little mounds of white wool.

She waited until Anjali Gupta had gone.

'Now, Premila, are you sure you want to persist with this silly lie . . .'

'What else can I do . . . Anyway, who did you *think* was the father . . .'

'I suppose I knew,' replied her mother in an uncharacteristically small voice. 'I had heard a little gossip . . . I just wanted a grandchild and now, a boy, a healthy boy, it is a miracle . . . Premila, are you happy?'

Premila had never been asked by her Mother if she was happy or unhappy or hot or cold or thirsty or, most definitely, hungry.

'Yes, happy, happy, happy. I am going to call him Clark Gable Banerjee.'

Another Leela Dhir-shaped space occurred, this time because she really *had* spun into the air, out the door and down the corridor to find the person in charge and demand to know what rights Grandmothers had in the matter of choosing their First Born Grandson's name. Catching up to her hurried Mr K. K. Rao, inky hair dye on his collar, his shirt not changed since his early evening appointment at Lakshmi Hair and Beauty Studio. A private closed-door appointment, curtains drawn, the eyes of the goddess Lakshmi averted. His titivations and plans to woo Leela Dhir were a little secret between himself and Poppy Lee, or so he hoped.

☙

When Anjali Gupta returned to the ward, trailed by a yawning Gita holding Leela Dhir's overcoat, Mrs Banerjee was resting.

Leela Dhir had returned from her furious circuits of the corridors of Chalaili Hospital and was asleep in a chair by the crib. Anil was curled up on the floor.

The nurse came in, swinging the door shut. 'Baby Banerjee's father is where?' she demanded, searchingly, as if the missing parent could be concealed, perhaps under the draped folds of ice-white sheets. She was newly arrived in Chalaili and did not recognise Mrs Banerjee or know of the salacious gossip.

Anil shot to his feet and gabbled his innocence in the matter of parenthood.

'Forms must be filled out,' said the nurse, ignoring his protestations.

'I will do,' responded Mrs Banerjee, snappily. 'Anil, tell Vinod to drive back to The Metropole Hotel and fetch Campbell Nightingale. He and his wife stayed there last night after the pictures. Quick, before he returns to Soliganj. Tell him it is urgent

460

that he contacts my lawyer in Bombay . . . I have already spoken to them both about what must be done.'

How fortuitous to have given birth early on a Tuesday, thought Mrs Banerjee. She was looking forward to her little blackmail plan involving Campbell Nightingale and the birth certificate.

'Your signature is not enough. Two responsible adults must be signing . . .'

'Here,' commanded Leela Dhir, grabbing the overcoat from Gita and taking from its right-hand pocket a fine Watermans fountain pen plated in silver, monogrammed, a long-ago anniversary present from Shyam, she realised, with a small shiver.

'We are both responsible. Come, come, show me where I should put my name.'

Epilogue

THE FINCHLEY EXAMINER

Television has been introduced to India. The first telecast took place on September 15 in New Delhi. It is too early to predict whether the advent of television will affect India's thriving cinema industry, mostly based in Bombay and known colloquially as Bollywood.

Lydia sat at a wooden table in the garden, her work papers arranged in tidy piles. It was a late summer morning and the air was warm and buzzy with bees. She looked up as she heard the click of the front gate and saw the postman hand John Rushmore a square bulky parcel.

'More pages from my publisher?' she called out. The postman gave her a wave. Lydia was quite the celebrity in Finchley. He often arrived with a visitor or two who wanted the bestselling authoress's autograph, books clutched and pressed open, ready to be signed. She always obliged. The postman knew she had an addict's hunger for attention and the village residents were perpetually amused by her Indian blouses and waistcoats, flamboyant flared skirts and cascading earrings and bangles.

'Parcel from India,' John replied. He set aside his gardening gloves and handed Lydia a form to be signed. The postman took it back, folded it into a pocket at the side of his satchel and cycled off, whistling merrily.

Lydia looked at the parcel. It was postmarked Bombay and the return address in its top left-hand corner indicated it was from the Bureau of Meteorology. She gasped and John leant down to put an arm around her shoulders.

'What is it, dearest?'

'W . . . William . . .'

Her hands were trembling.

'John, give me a minute alone, my love. Would you make a cup of tea?'

John strode off through the side door of the vine-covered house and into the kitchen, from where he had a clear view of Lydia through the mullioned window. She was staring at the brown paper-wrapped parcel, running a finger over its lattice of string. The sun caught her honeyed hair and dozens of little shards of mirror twinkled like diamonds amid the embroidery of her Rajasthani waistcoat.

'Have you any idea how much I love you?' he murmured, knowing she could not hear him. He had asked her to marry him and she had laughed and said there was no point as she was already Mrs Rushmore. And then she laughed again and he had tried to smile, his body aching.

Could William be alive after all this time, he wondered. The thought stabbed at him. After Sylvia's death, he and Lydia had drifted together as if it were the most natural progression possible.

He found her beautiful beyond measure: serene and funny and slightly muddle-headed. The substantial difference in their ages seemed to mean nothing to Lydia. She slept curled into his back like a wee animal attached to its parent.

Lydia had volunteered for treatment to arrest her drinking. Her sister Evelyn reported to him, with a smugness he found unattractive, that Lydia had had to be poured off the P&O liner when she arrived back from India. She was still wearing her solar topi, according to Evelyn. A terrible gaffe, apparently, as one was meant to take off one's colonial headgear when one reached the Suez Canal, or some such rubbish. John knew nothing of the protocols of shipboard life and doubted he ever would.

Evelyn also reported Lydia had been dressed like a gypsy in layers of fabric that looked like cut-up bedspreads. That was undoubtedly true as she had arrived to stay with John and Sylvia, after a brief recuperation period at The Oaks, in some kind of multi-hued Indian garment that she called her coat of many colours.

For several weeks, it was quite the talking point in Finchley.

John arranged the cups and saucers and decanted milk into the little jug.

Lydia was still staring at the parcel resting in her lap.

She had an appetite for sex that occasionally embarrassed John.

'I am making up for lost time,' she would giggle, guiding him into her again and again. She burned pungent Indian incense by their bed and dabbed sandalwood oil on her pulse and temples. John sometimes felt nauseous amid the smoke and ligneous smells but if he complained, Lydia would waggle her finger at him, growl and bite her bangles as if she were in exquisite pain.

He had asked what she meant by lost time.

'Wasn't William a proper husband to you? In bed, I mean . . .'

'He tried to be. It wasn't his fault. I was a different person then . . . I was drinking like a ghastly fish. It just didn't quite work. Then there was Simon Fraser-Gough and, well, it was all such a silly misunderstanding.'

The kettle had boiled, its thin whistle jolting John out of his reverie. He looked out the window again and saw Lydia still staring at the parcel. He added a pair of scissors to the tea tray. They would open it together.

John cut the knot and Lydia peeled away the paper wrapper to reveal a metal box. It was William's. There were his engraved initials: WER. She recalled how he had shown it to her shortly after her arrival at Bluebell Cottage, sifting through the contents and carefully explaining their importance.

'My mother's knitting wool.'

Lydia remembered how his voice had dropped when she fingered the skein, yellowed and brittle.

'My parents.' A photo of Ellis and Diana Rushmore on their wedding day. Stiff and posed, unsmiling, staring at the camera with a kind of fear, as if expecting the apparatus could explode at any moment.

Various government documents, a newspaper clipping about the English boy who had been swept away in the 1932 rains. The article quoted William Rushmore, a world authority on the subcontinental monsoon.

An envelope addressed to William Rushmore Esquire, care

of The Empire Club. No stamps. It had been crumpled up and then smoothed out.

Lydia didn't recognise the handwriting. The flap on the reverse was tucked in and she pulled it open. A piece of paper with The Empire Club insignia and just two words. 'As discussed.'

Two photographs. Small and square. Slightly fuzzy. Lydia wiped her reading glasses with a hanky and peered at them.

She gasped. They were of her, on a bed, petticoat in disarray, arms lolling, one small white breast exposed, like an iced cupcake.

'Gosh, Liddie,' said John, leaning over her shoulder. He started to laugh.

'I can understand why William kept those under lock and key. You don't look awfully well, though. In fact you look dead.'

John took the photographs from her and turned them over.

'No date. But there's a studio stamp.'

'Studio?'

'Well, whoever developed the film, I suppose. Vincent Collins's Photographic Requirements, Bombay.'

Lydia closed her eyes.

'Collins, Collins . . .'

She dredged a name from that long-ago fiasco at The Chalaili Sanatorium for the Tubercular.

'Yes, yes, Valerie Collins!'

She was the Anglo-Indian nurse that Simon Fraser-Gough had mentioned. The chee-chee one. The flying fish. Lydia had even asked Charlotte Montague if she knew of the girl but the older woman had no information, not being one to concern herself with the whereabouts of the serving classes.

So that was how Simon Fraser-Gough had escaped detection when he needed the film developed. Handed it to Valerie Collins to despatch to Vincent . . . a brother, perhaps. Charlotte Montague had never thought to send her servant spies beyond Chota Chalaili bazaar to find the photographs.

But Charlotte Montague must have sensed that as long as Simon Fraser-Gough was hanging around, it wouldn't be the end of the matter. Yes, yes, thought Lydia. Charlotte Montague spoke to William about the incident and that's why she told me at his memorial service that he loved me.

'There is a letter as well.'

Lydia looked up at John. He handed her the single folded sheet that had become caught in the discarded wrapping.

'Would you read it for me, please?'

John smoothed the page. It was typewritten and carried an official insignia.

Bombay, India
10th of July, 1959

Dear Mrs Rushmore,

We hope this letter finds you at the last known address for your husband, William Ellis Rushmore, Meteorologist and Indian Forestry Service Officer, First Class.

We enclose herewith a metal box recovered by one of our field officers from the northern side of Chalaili Valley on 1st of July last. The box was locked and we took the liberty of forcing it open to ascertain the identity of the owner.

Our files show that your husband was reported missing in 1938

467

and we regret to advise you that following this discovery of
his personal possessions, we must presume he has perished
in Chalaili Valley.

This regrettable situation will mean a review of the pension
that is paid by the British Government to your London bank
each quarter. A lump sum will be due to you as his sole heir
and we urge you to contact the relevant authorities forthwith.

Kindly acknowledge receipt of this item by return mail so that
we may close our files on the matter of W. E. Rushmore.

Yours sincerely

Dr. Hanwat Singh
Regional Director
Bureau of Meteorology
Bombay, India

'Perished?' questioned Lydia. 'It sounds so . . . so . . .
lonely . . . and final.'

'Liddie, it has been twenty-one years. You can't have thought
he was alive all this time.'

'Sylvia always believed so . . . Just before she died, she
begged and begged me to go back to India and find him.'

John stiffened at the mention of his late wife. Even fifteen
years after her passing, she had the ability to creep up on him, like
a draught.

'There is one more set of proofs of my novel to read and
then I will go to India. I have to bury the box there.'

468

'Liddie, bury the box here, in Finchley. This was William's home.'

'No, India was his home. You just don't understand . . . Besides I can do some research for my next book. I always feel such a fool writing about India when I haven't even been there since the British left . . .'

'Nonsense, Liddie. You are a publishing sensation. All your readers adore you. *A Hill Station Romance* by Eugenia Jambolana has been reprinted five times . . .'

'Please let me go, John.'

Her hazel eyes implored him to say yes.

'Can't I go with you, Liddie . . . I haven't travelled much and since my retirement it isn't as if I don't have the time. Only the roses would miss me . . .'

They looked at the espaliered roses with their fluffy heads bobbing in a light breeze.

'William hated roses, you know.'

'That's because Sylvia told him his mother was carrying roses aboard the train . . . They found them with the body. Well, never mind, all that is past history.'

John looked at the collection of his nephew's possessions. Was this all he owned of value?

'Liddie, was he wearing the Rushmore family signet ring when he disappeared, do you think?'

'I doubt it. It was too big. He said his father had fatter fingers. He always meant to get it adjusted. He usually kept it in the bedside drawer.'

'Oh, well, maybe he took it with him in the box. And the person who found it stole it before handing it in. Those sort of things happen in India, don't they?'

The missing ring made Lydia feel uneasy. Had Anil taken it to a jeweller to be resized? Had the servant handed Mrs Banerjee a small jewellery box during Lydia's last weeks at Monsoon Cottage. Lydia recalled a whispered conversation about the exorbitant cost of repairing jewellery items and a discrepancy with the change. But perhaps that was another piece of jewellery. Lydia fiddled with her bangles and tried to remember more. Well, it wasn't as if Mrs Banerjee was short of gold ornaments to be making their imperfect passages around the tinkers of Chota Chalaili.

'An airline ticket for one, then?'

Lydia looked at John. His eyes were watery.

'I'm afraid so . . . please understand.'

He got up and started to walk inside.

'I will ring Evelyn and tell her. Your sister will want to know what you're up to.'

'Of course she will,' Lydia called out.

She screwed the wrapping into a hard crunchy ball. 'And there's no way she's going with me, the interfering cow,' she added to herself.

'India is mine, all mine,' Lydia said aloud, to the roses and the bees, as she rearranged her papers and began pencilling corrections to the opening chapter of *A Passion For Clouds* by Eugenia Jambolana.

CHALAILI
OCTOBER, 1959

*L*ydia boarded the Soliganj Express at Bombay's Victoria Terminus. She was astonished at the number of passengers. She had had to bribe the ticket seller to secure a first-class seat. There was no longer a ladies coupé and the carriages were full of Indian families chatting loudly and happily, passing around delectable-smelling snacks and sugar bananas torn from candelabra-like bunches.

She wondered why so many people were headed to the Western Ghats. Could Soliganj, or even little Chalaili, have become holiday destinations, she wondered, although she found the prospect unlikely.

There was an exodus of passengers at Soliganj but some rearranged their bundles and changed to the Chalaili toy train. Lydia remembered Soliganj as a dusty railway cantonment, much complained about by Patricia Nightingale. She asked the conductor why the trains were so busy.

'Big, big film star is visiting Soliganj today. Chalaili passengers are buying first-class silk direct from factory or visiting big, big film star's birthplace.'

Before Lydia could question him further he hurried off to clip more tickets.

Lydia slept through the toy train's unsteady ascent, clutching her handbag. She dreamt of William. He was sitting on a cumulus surrounded by his papers and weather-measuring paraphernalia. His khaki bush hat was flipped at an angle and he looked young and happy. He was wearing a cream cricket vest, the waist band unfinished, the strands of wool merging into the white puffiness of the cloud. His cornflower eyes were so electric they pierced her dream and she jolted awake with a grunt.

Lydia alighted on Chalaili Station and breathed the health-making air. She saw the familiar Burmese pagoda spire on the stationmaster's office, the town's embrasure of deeply forested hills and pots of geraniums lined up in soldierly rows along the platform. Everything seemed so cheery and alpine after the seething madness of Bombay.

Then she saw the sign. A huge hoarding hung over an archway at the town end of the platform. Home of the Banerjee Silks, it announced, in shattering yellow paintwork. There was a drawing of an Indian maiden in an equally declaring yellow sari, winking and beckoning with suggestive red-tipped fingers. Her hourglass figure was over-heavy in the upper regions, with breasts popping out of a sari blouse. They looked as if they'd been inflated with a bicycle pump.

Lydia presumed it was meant to be Mrs Banerjee.

Lydia passed under the archway and was confronted with several larger-than-life cardboard cut-outs of a stern-faced woman with agitated eyes. The figures were being worn on the backs of a pack of small boys, held in place by leather straps around their waists. The woman's image also appeared in a row of immense posters plastered on to the facades of buildings so it felt to Lydia that Chalaili was being guarded by an army of Amazons. Vote for Me said the message under the woman's photograph.

A van crawled past, roof-mounted megaphone blurting. Several young men sat side-saddle on its tinsel-decorated bonnet, tossing out hard sweets in twists of saffron-coloured paper. The announcements were in a mixture of Hindustani and English and the word Queenie was a much-repeated component of the message.

Lydia stood uncertainly at the bottom end of The Strand clutching her suitcase. She could scarcely recognise Chalaili. Far from the atrophied, fungus-ridden outpost she had imagined it would still be, the town was ablaze with activity.

The government building where William's office had been located was no longer festooned with ivy but painted eye-stinging white, its windows bordered in bright yellow. A wooden notice above the porte-cochere announced Banerjee House in black-bold lettering. In smaller script, Lydia read that the finest sari silks in all India were manufactured in Chalaili.

She heard the solid clicking of machinery and the bang-clang of looms but the tinny sounds could not obliterate the clear laughter of women, rising like a tide. Lydia smiled to herself at the unstoppable enterprise of Mrs Banerjee and was pleased her old acquaintance was doing so well.

In the British days, thought Lydia, there would have been porters running to take my bag and guide me to The Metropole Hotel. But no one paid her the slightest attention, not even the auto-rickshaw drivers who buzzed about in their green-and-yellow three-wheelers like swarms of angry dragonflies.

She started her climb towards The Strand proper.

Lydia gasped. The neon sign hoisted over Coronation Talkies was stupendous, each lollipop-coloured tube the size of a child. Even though it was late morning, the sign was illuminated and the letters blinked and winked, although Lydia instantly noticed that several weren't working and she imagined Mrs Banerjee boxing the ears of some poor lighting wallah until the sign was fully functioning again.

The name of the film appeared to be *Spat Tales*. Lydia hadn't heard of it.

She looked more closely and attempted to fill in the blanks. *Separate Tables*.

On the wall, a hand-painted poster of David Niven, looking much more like Clark Gable than was strictly credible. Coming Next Week: *Gigi*.

Leslie Caron looked oddly Indian in her painted depiction. Lydia stared at it for a full minute before realising she was a ringer for Claudette Colbert.

Lydia chortled. Mrs Banerjee was still in good form.

The Metropole Hotel stood opposite, looking particularly spruce with terracotta-tubbed pelargoniums on the steps and front porch and lustrous silk curtains drawn across the street-facing windows.

Lydia walked into the foyer and put down her bag beside the front desk. The rusty bird cage on one corner of the counter had its door held open by a pencil stuck through the wire, as if at any moment the occupant would return from an afternoon's outing.

She tapped the brass bell anchored to the counter and called out, 'Hello!'

'Coming, coming,' came the reply, echoing along the timber-floored corridor. It was a male voice and she heard hurried foot-steps before a man wearing a neat dark business suit burst into view.

'Ram Gupta?'

Sunlight was coursing from the porch through the open door and beaming on to the man's face. She couldn't quite make out his features.

'Galloping galoshes!'

He dropped a handful of keys and they fell to the floor with a terrifying clatter.

☙

Anil installed Lydia in The Maharani Salon and ordered tea. He snapped at the waiters with a goodly dollop of the trademark Banerjee bossiness.

Just as they were finally settled and Anil had stopped flapping his starched linen napkin at imaginary flies, a woman walked in with a girl who appeared to be in her late teens.

Lydia raised an eyebrow at Anil and he coughed.

'You remember Aruna?'

'Why, yes, Aruna Chowpatty, Mrs Banerjee's maid . . . did you . . . are you . . . ?'

'Married? Yes, yes. Please come, Aruna. You remember Mrs Rushmore?'

Aruna scowled at the Chowpatty reference and did not reply. She pushed forward the girl who was wearing a royal blue pleated skirt and crisp white blouse buttoned to the collar, very similar to Lydia's demure outfit. Lydia was pleased she had decided against packing her mock-Indian costumes, with their tiny bells, mirrors and flounces.

'Your daughter of course?'

Lydia directed the question to Aruna but it was the tall, poised girl who answered her.

'Very pleased to meet you, Mrs Rushmore. My name is Sunita Varma.'

'Ah, Sunita.'

Lydia did her best to warmly greet Sunita but the name struck her with the cold deep thump of memory.

'Could you open the curtains, please, Anil . . . or Aruna . . . or Sunita?'

No one moved.

'Curtains must remain closed during daylight hours. Mrs Banerjee's orders,' said Anil, finally.

'Mrs Banerjee? Does she run the hotel as well as . . . well, it's just that I noticed Coronation Talkies is still in business and I passed by the silk factory, which was humming . . .'

'Anjali Gupta and Mrs Banerjee own the hotel. Ram Gupta died more than ten years ago. Very sad. His heart.'

Anil tapped the left side of his chest.

'Oh dear, I see, poor Anjali.'

Lydia stared into her teacup. Anjali Gupta had worn her husband's steadfast love wrapped around her, like a warm shawl. She must have been devastated by his death.

She looked up at Anil. 'So, you work here now?'

'I am the manager.'

Lydia instantly regretted her clumsy question. She should have realised that Anil's suit denoted an elevated status. Now he was one of the jing-bang higher-ups, as she recalled Mrs Banerjee had referred to anyone in command.

Lydia sipped her tea and looked around. The room was spotless, there were fresh flowers in cut-glass vases on every table. On the walls were dozens of film images from the 1930s and 1940s. In pride of place, framed in gold, was a poster for *It Happened One Night*. Clark Gable appeared to be kneeling and was smiling up at Claudette Colbert, his pencil-narrow moustache tilted at the ends with a waxiness that matched his perfectly arched eyebrows. Claudette had one hand across her chin as if holding in place the lower fold of her glistening lips.

Her eyes were enormously brown, her hair combed forward and artfully manoeuvred into kiss-curls.

'Do you have vacancies?'

Lydia almost giggled at her request, remembering The Metropole Hotel's occupancy levels in the old days were so dismal that an entire clan could have turned up unannounced and been instantly accommodated.

'Yes, yes, a room is possible, even at short notice,' replied Aruna, finding her voice at last. She stepped forward with a slow twirl-swirl of sari in a coquettish pink.

Lydia couldn't remember the servant Mrs Banerjee always referred to as Aruna Chowpatty speaking much English, but she obviously did so now. The pushy colour of her sari had Mrs Banerjee's signature written all over it.

'Sunita, check if room number six is made up.'

'Certainly, mother.'

The girl strode off.

'Your daughter works here as well?'

Anil and Aruna both cleared their throats before he replied.

'Sunita is studying to be a doctor. It is holidays just now. Mrs Banerjee insisted on her education in Bombay . . . no expense to be spared. She is an honours student.'

'Oh, I see, that's wonderful.'

Lydia thought of the other Sunita, shivering and coughing in the kitchen of Bluebell Cottage, denied medical attention while she, the memsahib, ginned up in the sitting room.

'And . . . Devi? You know, the girl . . .'

'Of course we know who Devi is.'

Aruna's reply was crisp.

'She is the manageress of Coronation Talkies.'

477

'Chalaili headquarters,' added Anil, suggesting there were Coronation Talkies picture theatres being spawned the length and breadth of India, which did not surprise Lydia one jot.

'I always wondered about her scars . . .'

Lydia had used Devi as a character in her second Eugenia Jambolana novel, *The Disappearance at Twin Trees Point*. She had researched bride burnings and her fictional heroine had been set alight by a grasping mother-in-law disappointed by the ten-cow dowry.

Devi had been saved at the last moment by a passing British soldier named Peregrine Potter. Lydia shivered at the absurdity of the plot when viewed from the reality of 1950s India. Bride burnings, yes. British saviours, no.

'She still has the scars, although Mrs Banerjee has suggested surgery by a top Bombay doctor, London-trained, all costs to be met by her good self . . .'

'Yes, but . . . I presumed it was a dowry burning. I never thought to ask, really . . .'

'Her hut burned down.'

It was Aruna who spoke and Lydia noticed she gave Anil a dark look.

'If you remember, she was a common and possibly unsuccessful prostitute on Juhu Beach. There was a fire when she first started working there. She's never had a husband to burn her up . . . at least not one of her own.'

'Please, Aruna, how many more times must I tell you there has never been anything between Devi and myself . . . She is like my sister.'

Lydia was feeling slightly feverish. She hoped the flim-flam novels of Eugenia Jambolana with their gaudy plots would never make their way to the Western Ghats.

The defiantly drawn gold curtains were casting a liverish glow upon The Maharani Salon's uncomfortable assembly.

'Anyway, I will just stay a few days because William's belongings . . .'

'William?' Anil and Aruna chorused the name and exchanged panicked looks.

'Yes, William's personal effects have been found. . . .'

Lydia hesitated, wondering if she should take out the metal box from her large handbag and show Anil and Aruna the contents.

'Anil, do you remember his signet ring? Was he wearing it the day he disappeared?'

Anil shook his head from side to side, avoiding eye contact with Lydia.

A well-timed interruption.

Three figures followed Sunita into The Maharani Salon. They were instantly bathed in yellow.

Anil began the introductions with two foreign women, the taller wearing Western dress. She peered at Lydia with unravelled eyes.

'You remember Mary Christie?'

'Why, of course, the little shop . . .'

'My husband was Captain Archibald Christie of the First Bengal . . .'

The smaller Englishwoman looked as if she wouldn't harm an ant but she gave Mary Christie a swift kick to her left ankle as a signal to stop what Lydia deduced could be a lengthy speech.

She was dressed in a sari the colour of ripe pomegranate, the shiny material hanging oddly on her stooped white shoulders.

'I am Patricia Nightingale.'

She curtseyed to Lydia, pale aquamarine eyes averted.

'My disgraced husband hung himself,' she added, to no one in particular.

The man standing behind Mary Christie and Patricia Nightingale came forward.

'Remember me?' he asked Lydia. 'I am Vinod . . . you know, the driver.'

'Oh, yes, of course.' Lydia smiled at him. At least he didn't appear to be as unhinged as the women. Patricia Nightingale looked like an escapee from a madhouse.

'How is the driving business these days?'

'Very well, thank you. I run a fleet of tourist buses. Offices in Bombay, Soliganj and Chalaili.'

'That must keep you busy?'

'I have a business partner in Soliganj. Florence Gordon . . . from the post office. You remember her?'

Mary Christie screamed at him.

'Do not mention the name of that Eugenia Jambolana witch from hell itself!'

Lydia swallowed hard. Eugenia Jambolana? What were they talking about . . . *She* was Eugenia Jambolana, acclaimed authoress of Raj romances.

'Eugenia Jambolana is known to you?'

She was asking Mary Christie but the woman was already fleeing the room.

'It was a spiteful newsletter. A scandal-vandal sheet, according to Mrs Banerjee. She probably didn't consider it worthy of mention to you when you returned to be with William. Well, not be with him, actually.'

It was a long speech for Anil. His English was much

improved, thought Lydia. She couldn't quite fathom the Eugenia Jambolana connection but she knew her books were so fraudulent she must never let her publisher distribute them in India. There had been talk of a Bombay release.

Lydia felt faint. Eugenia Jambolana romanticised a Raj-era world of twittering memsahibs and dashing adventurers. India had changed so much it was almost unrecognisable to her. About to go to press was another of her dewy fabrications in which faithful servants saved wasp-waisted English beauties from rogue tigers and the fearful grip of malaria.

'Where is Mrs Banerjee? I need to speak to her urgently.'

Feet were shuffled and covert glances traded. No one replied.

'With her family? I presume the baby was born after I left Chalaili?'

'I have seen no baby,' Aruna announced, folding her arms across her bosom. This was true as she had returned to Chalaili when Mrs Banerjee's son was three years old.

'Oh dear, well is she with Mr Banerjee, perhaps?'

'Mr Banerjee?'

The refrain was tumultuous.

It was Anil who spoke above the outcry.

'The Mr Banerjee to whom you refer . . . you mean her husband?'

'Yes, who else?'

'Well, actually *that* Mr Banerjee is not connected with Mrs Banerjee just now. She is in Soliganj today. Anjali Gupta, also. They are preparing for the opening of Coronation Talkies Sub Branch Soliganj this evening.'

'Then I will go and find them. Mrs Banerjee will know what to do concerning William's belongings.'

'No, no, not a good idea. You are tired,' insisted Anil, wringing his hands.

'Let her go!' shrieked poor Patricia Nightingale. 'Put an end to all the madness and lies.'

Lydia drew back her chair and looked at her watch. There was ample time to catch the afternoon train down to Soliganj. She handed her suitcase to Vinod, not knowing who else to give it to. Lydia was relieved when he took it with a gracious smile.

The group parted as she left The Maharani Salon and no one followed her except Sunita.

'The Englishwomen are a bit cuckoo. Mrs Banerjee lets them live here without paying but she makes them stay out of sight when the tourists come. She has to be particularly watchful of the Nightingale creature, who takes off her clothes when it rains and dances down The Strand.'

Lydia tried not to giggle as she and Sunita passed the first room along the corridor from the front foyer. The door was open and Lydia looked in. A very old white-haired woman was enthroned in a grand leather armchair. Her feet were being massaged by an elderly dapper man who sat on a low tapestry-covered stool. By his side stood an empty birdcage and in a far corner, slender sticks of incense were burning, plumes of smoke encircling a pair of wellington boots. His hair was the colour of licorice.

The woman waved at Lydia as she passed by and bobbed her head in greeting.

'That's Mrs Banerjee's mother. She used to be a leading Bombay socialite, apparently. She nags everyone all day long and Mr K. K. Rao is the only one who can handle her.'

The thought of the former Coronation Talkies projectionist handling Leela Dhir caused Lydia to splutter. So poor Mrs

Banerjee had not been able to escape her mother after all.

The train was pulling in as Lydia purchased a ticket. She was almost submerged by a torrent of women who pushed their way down the platform and into the carriages. Lydia finally found a seat amid a rustling ocean of gold, ruby red and tropical orange. She realised they were the workers from Banerjee Silks, each costumed in what Mrs Banerjee must have decreed as their uniform. Some of them had their hair oiled and braided, each rung caught with a sprig of jasmine. Nose studs, earrings and bangles glittered furiously in the afternoon sunlight and she heard the words Clark Gable and Banerjee mentioned over and over.

Lydia decided Mrs Banerjee must be showing *It Happened One Night* at her new cinema. At least some things stay the same, she thought, as she sat squashed on a hard bench seat, feeling as dowdy as a sparrow. The women swayed and clapped their hands before breaking into a catchy song.

'It is from his latest hit film. Everyone is singing it, in Bombay and all over India.'

The man who had spoken gestured his hand in an arc as if to indicate the sweep of the song's success. He was a middle-aged, corpulent Indian in a silk suit so shiny it could have been used to semaphore messages. He had a jolly hockey-sticks English accent.

'So, dear lady, you are a fan as well?'

'A fan? Yes, I suppose I am a fan . . .'

Lydia felt too fizzy-headed to complete her reply. She had no idea what was going on but knew that Mrs Banerjee would explain everything. Then she remembered Anjali Gupta would be at the opening, too, and she felt reassured that she would look after her, as Mrs Banerjee would no doubt be at her most voluble and pronounced during the proceedings.

The man handed her a calling card.

'Occasionally I need British ladies to play extras. You know, to take tea with lemon and shout at servants and so forth.'

Lydia looked at The Shiny Man's card, embossed in gold: Mr B. B. (Bunty) Kapoor, Shiva Motion Pictures, Bombay.

As the passengers hurried off at Soliganj she saw The Shiny Man handing our more of his cards to the prettiest of the excited Banerjee workers.

Lydia allowed herself to be carried along by the crowd. She remembered the opening of Coronation Talkies at Chalaili more than two decades earlier. She could see the sugar floss-chewing monkeys and Charlotte Montague's wheel-sized hat and Anil with his upturned tiger-taming chair. She shut her eyes. There was Mrs Banerjee, near-buried under the collapsing stage curtains but with her knees and, more importantly, her spirit refusing to buckle.

The crowd continued its billowing, hands were raised above heads to coil and clap to music blaring splutter-hiss from a tannoy. Lydia's feet barely touched the ground as bodies were pressed, prodded and then swiftly funnelled into a narrow alleyway, soon to pop out like uncorked genies into a large cement-paved square, its buildings decked with ribbons and garlands of marigolds.

Lydia saw another Coronation Talkies neon sign, this one twice the size of its Chalaili counterpart. All its letters, she noted, were in full flashing order.

The sign loomed atop an ochre-painted building, as big as a town hall. In front of Coronation Talkies Sub Branch Soliganj stood a high stage with a skirt of golden silk, its corner posts and front edge garlanded with coloured Christmas tree lights.

Dozens of women were handing out election pamphlets, their identical buttercup sashes printed with the message, Let

Queenie Go In To Bhatt For You. On the stage was another of the Amazonian cut-outs, but much fatter and older. It moved forward and Lydia gulped.

It was the real Queenie Bhatt, local member of parliament and candidate for chief minister of state. She commanded absolute dominion over the stage, her canoe-like shoes bordered by the stage's twinkling trails of merry red and green reindeers and early Christmas angels.

Queenie Bhatt lifted her hands and the cheering subsided. She spoke in Hindustani, pausing here and there for obvious effect. The people cheered during these momentous intervals and then she shooshed them as she spoke again, her voice surprisingly high and light.

Lydia looked around but couldn't see Mrs Banerjee. She was wedged tight by the crowd, poked by impassioned elbows and even, she suspected with a shudder, the odd sly penis.

The weight on her arm told her William's metal box was still in her handbag but she couldn't be sure of holding on to it for much longer. She closed her eyes to count to ten and pray for strength.

'Thank you, Queenie, dear.'

An entire orchestra erupted from Mrs Banerjee's mouth as the microphone pinged and squealed and trumpeted. Lydia opened her eyes. A ripple of anticipation was moving across the silken crowd, their happy faces etched against the mulberry sheen of encroaching dusk. Lydia looked up.

Mrs Banerjee's occupation of the stage made Queenie Bhatt look like a frail length of ribbon. Picture Madam threw a shadow over the front rows of the audience. Her hair was completely grey and swept up into a confection adorned with bobbing red flowers. Her sari was the colour of a summer sunset, its wide brocaded border studded with what Lydia took at first to be shells but which she soon realised were pearls of irregular shape and size, glistening like multiple rows of teeth. Mrs Banerjee's arms and wrists wore their signature armoury of gold.

'A round of applause, please, for our most favoured candidate for chief minister of our prosperous and beloved state, Madam Queenie Bhatt!'

With everyone's arms wedged so tightly, applause was muted. But delirious roars went up as Mrs Banerjee waved the waddling Queenie to one side and the sackcloth cover on a massive easel-mounted poster suddenly began to fall away, revealing a hand-painted image for the Coronation Talkies Sub Branch Soliganj premiere film.

'Idiot buffoons!' screeched Mrs Banerjee at several young men who were struggling to replace the covering.

Lydia shook with joy to see Mrs Banerjee in such champion form.

The crowd was becoming restless but Mrs Banerjee continued her speech, first in English and then in Hindustani. In a performing voice she thanked a lavish assortment of Soliganj petty officials who could be seen standing to one side of the stage, each overfed stomach as puffed as a pouter pigeon.

The first signs of impatient heckling started and a mantra went up.

'Clark Gable, Clark Gable,' the crowd shouted.

'Now, now, without further ado, let me introduce the most famous money-making star in all India. The one you have been waiting for. The toast of Bombay, the leading man of a hundred sure-fire successes. The beloved child of Chalaili and, yes, Soliganj also, one could say . . .'

A woman sprang to her side as Mrs Banerjee rocked on her